A SPY'S
DEVOTION

A SPY'S DEVOTION

Book One in the Regency Spies of London Series

MELANIE DICKERSON

Waterfall
PRESS

Published by Waterfall Press, Grand Haven, MI

www.brilliancepublishing.com

Amazon, the Amazon logo, and Waterfall Press are trademarks of Amazon.com, Inc., or its affiliates.

ISBN-13: 9781503950511
ISBN-10: 1503950514

Cover design by Mike Heath | Magnus Creative

Printed in the United States of America

CHAPTER ONE

April 1811. London, England.

Mr. Nicholas Langdon wasn't supposed to be here.

Miss Julia Grey blinked, but he was still standing across the room from where she sat at the pianoforte.

It was the first party of the Season, and several of her aunt and uncle's guests surrounded him. And in spite of the recent wounds he'd sustained fighting in the Peninsula, he looked as handsome and whole as he had the last time she'd seen him, a year and a half ago.

Just then, Miss Phoebe Wilhern, Julia's cousin, turned and saw him—and gasped loudly enough to be heard by everyone in the room. Phoebe's face turned pink, and the hand she lifted to cover her over-joyed smile never quite reached her mouth.

Julia stood to go to Phoebe, to admonish her not to make her feelings so obvious. Julia had spent the last year and a half trying to help Phoebe forget her infatuation with the faraway army officer and think of other things besides her obsession with Mr. Langdon.

Melanie Dickerson

"Do sing for us, Miss Grey." Mrs. Caldwell hovered by Julia's elbow, smiling. "We all know you play exceeding well, but we insist on hearing your heavenly voice."

Julia hesitated, but she wanted to draw attention away from Phoebe. She chose some music while her cousin was still staring at Mr. Langdon, her mouth hanging open, her eyes wide. Phoebe was never very good at hiding her feelings, and her infatuation with Mr. Langdon showed all over her face. Thankfully, he was talking with Mr. Hugh Edgerton and didn't seem to notice her.

Julia began playing and singing, staring at the sheet music to make sure she didn't forget the notes. When she glanced up again, Phoebe was standing in front of Mr. Langdon and talking to him.

When Julia finished the song, polite applause erupted.

"Won't you play my favorite song?" an elderly guest entreated, leaning on his walking stick and plucking the song he wanted from amongst the sheets of music. "You played it so well several months ago, as I recall."

She longed to go to Phoebe and urge her not to expose herself to gossip. Instead, she said, "Of course."

Mr. Langdon looked as though his shoulder wound had healed. He'd also suffered a leg wound. Would he have a limp?

He nodded politely to Phoebe and walked away. No limp, but Phoebe gazed forlornly at his perfectly straight, retreating back.

Phoebe had been Julia's constant companion since Julia was six years old and Phoebe was four. And although Phoebe was impulsive, she did listen to Julia's admonitions—usually. If Julia told her a man had an insincere countenance and a bad reputation, Phoebe refrained from flirting with him. If Julia advised her to take a shawl because the air was chilly, Phoebe would comply. Then, in the middle of their walk, Phoebe would invariably exclaim, "Julia, if you had not reminded me to bring a shawl, I would have been miserably cold," and spontaneously embrace her.

A few days before, Julia had confided in Phoebe about Mr. Richard Barrington, who she had thought might ask her to marry him, but he had suddenly shifted his preference to a girl with an inheritance of ten thousand pounds. With a fierce look, Phoebe said, "I can't imagine any man *not* falling in love with you, Julia. Mr. Barrington must be an utter fool."

Julia's heart had swelled with love for the affectionate girl.

And now, feeling she had little choice, Julia played the old gentleman's requested song and hoped her cousin wouldn't do anything too impulsive or indiscreet.

***

Nicholas Langdon surveyed the room where the dancing would take place. Young ladies in gauzy dresses of pale pink, blue, yellow, and white floated about like butterflies. It was a lovely sight to one who had been isolated from his home country, across the sea with only his fellow officers and soldiers in the Peninsula for almost a year, followed by months of convalescing here in London.

And he could not help noticing Miss Grey seated at the pianoforte, playing and singing with the voice of an angel.

As he dwelt on Miss Grey's sweet, demure expression, her dark curls that caressed her cheeks, and the brightness of her eyes, Edgerton approached him with a glass of brandy in each hand.

"You've been gone too long, Nicholas." Edgerton handed him one of the glasses. "You've forgotten that Miss Grey has no dowry, and you've only your officer's pay."

Nicholas cut a warning glance at his old school chum.

"Now, don't look at me like that. I saw you staring at her." Edgerton gave him his customary snide grin.

He'd forgotten how much he disliked Edgerton's caustic opinions.

"Miss Grey is only after the wealthiest husband she can catch," Edgerton continued. "See her smiling at Dinklage? He's a whey-faced imbecile, but he has fifteen thousand a year."

She wasn't exactly smiling at Mr. Daniel Dinklage. She only acknowledged him with a nod, since Dinklage had been staring at her.

"Thank you for the warning, Edgerton, but I hardly need it." Nicholas was well enough acquainted with mercenary young ladies that he wasn't likely to attach himself to one too soon. He'd had his heart crushed and his ego bruised two years ago and didn't intend to go through that again.

"Her cousin is the one you should be thinking of." Edgerton nodded slightly to his right, bringing Nicholas's attention to Miss Wilhern, who was staring at him with eyes as big as teacups.

"I won't be here long enough to think of anyone. I'm to sail back to the Peninsula in a week to rejoin my regiment."

Miss Wilhern seemed to regain her composure and dipped a slight curtsy. Now he had to acknowledge her, so he bowed in her direction. She started toward him.

"*She* has a dowry of twenty thousand," Edgerton said softly. "And since you have only a week to enjoy such flirtations, I shall leave you to it." Edgerton's smug face turned away as he headed in the opposite direction.

Nicholas greeted Miss Wilhern, careful not to express peculiar regard, lest she think he was singling her out. He remembered her as a girl who used to make calf eyes at him and try to talk with him at every opportunity before he went off to war.

Miss Wilhern inquired after the shoulder and leg wounds he had sustained in his last battle and then expressed her heartfelt thanks for his courage and valiant service, on behalf of herself and every man and woman in England. She immediately followed that with her sincere gratitude to God for saving him and bringing him back, whole and well enough to venture out tonight.

He had to admit, her enthusiasm was gratifying. Perhaps Edgerton was right: he should be more interested in Miss Wilhern than Miss Grey. A girl with twenty thousand pounds and an obvious infatuation with him was, by definition, attractive.

He asked her to dance the first dance and then excused himself to find something a little less robust to drink. He didn't want to be stumbling about the dance floor because he'd drunk too much.

Edgerton was pouring himself another glass of brandy. Several other men were standing nearby, talking and drinking, including the host, Mr. Robert Wilhern.

A deafening sound exploded behind him. Nicholas spun around. A servant was bending to pick up a heavy glass decanter he had dropped on the floor.

The memory of being shot flashed through his mind, the sudden sharp pain of a bullet tearing through his shoulder. At the same time, his horse had reared, causing Nicholas to fall to the ground and break his leg.

His heart was pounding inside his chest, while everyone else was ignoring the incident; indeed, they had already completely forgotten it.

He concentrated on slowing his breathing as he thrust away the vivid memory, stuffing it into the corner of his mind. He tried to focus on the party and its guests. After being in a war, battling for his life, and seeing death all around him, such a gathering as this was almost surreal, the standing about doing nothing, dressed in fine clothing, striving to appear wealthy, fashionable, and important.

"You are fortunate in Miss Wilhern's attentions."

Edgerton had not seemed to notice his brief moments of panic, but the man's voice was too loud, and Nicholas noticed Miss Wilhern's father cutting his eyes at him—to gauge Nicholas's reaction to Edgerton's statement, no doubt. Nicholas took a sip of his weaker port wine rather than replying. He was about to excuse himself and go back to the music room when Edgerton asked him, "What will you be about this next week, while you are furloughed and unfettered? You could come to the club with me tomorrow."

Edgerton would be at the gaming tables, no doubt. What was the appeal of betting thousands of pounds on the roll of the dice or the suit of a card?

"I've a task, a favor for a fellow soldier, to carry out tomorrow."

Edgerton raised his brows. "Oh?"

"A soldier who was in the battlefield infirmary with me. Before he died, he gave me something and asked me to deliver it to a relative here in London."

"How interesting." And Edgerton truly looked as if he meant it. "What was your brave friend's name, if I may ask?"

"Richard Beechum."

Edgerton stood strangely still, his mouth going slack as his eye twitched.

"You knew him?"

Edgerton shifted his feet and shook his head slightly. "Me? No. Not I."

His reaction seemed a bit odd, and so did the look on Wilhern's face as he glanced their way, his eyes narrowed, his jaw clenching.

"So." Edgerton cleared his throat. "This Beechum had a token for his sister, perhaps? A special watch fob to give to his father?"

"No, it was a diary. He asked me to take it to someone I've never heard of. But of course, in dying for his country, he deserves to have this small favor done for him."

"Oh yes, of course! Of course. You're a good man, Nicholas. None better. You will do the thing. It will get done. We'd better get to dancing. I hear the music starting."

They both moved toward the larger room where the dancing would commence.

***

If Julia knew Phoebe, she would soon want her to switch to a livelier tune, something she and the guests could dance to.

Sure enough, when Julia sang the last note, Phoebe caught her eye and winked. Phoebe spread the word that they were about to begin a reel. While several guests paired up to dance, Julia found some appropriate music. Happily for Phoebe, Mr. Langdon had asked her to dance; they were standing up together at the head of the line.

Julia felt a flutter of excitement for Phoebe, who looked triumphant in her pale-blue dress ornamented with ribbon and lace.

Mr. Langdon's snow-white neckcloth stood out against his dark hair, and he was fashionably dressed in dark-gray breeches and waistcoat, black Hessian boots, and a black double-breasted frock coat.

Julia's mind raced as fast as her fingers. Would Mr. Langdon break his own rule and dance with Phoebe more than once? Or would Phoebe get the first dance with him, only to watch him dance with every other girl in the room for the rest of the night?

Even though Mr. Langdon was of above-average height, he moved gracefully. He was nothing like his older brother, whose countenance was less serious, almost careless. His brother, Jonathan, was also stouter and more pale complexioned, a perfect contrast to Mr. Langdon's dark hair and skin, brown eyes, and crow-black brows. Their grandmother was from Spain, and her heritage had made its presence known in the younger son. Mr. Langdon was handsome, Julia had to admit, and though he appeared somewhat reserved, he had expressive brown eyes.

Phoebe certainly wasn't the first girl whose heart had been captured by him—nor was she likely to be the last.

Julia watched how he interacted with Phoebe. He did not look overly friendly as he danced with her, although he engaged in conversation with her and appeared attentive as they waited their turn in the round.

He had not been as fortunate as one might have assumed in his choice of wife, however. Two years ago, his fiancée had thrown him over for a wealthier, older man. A betrayal like that would make some men bitter, and, at the very least, cautious.

When the dance ended, Mr. Langdon gave Phoebe a quick nod and then turned and seemed to be asking Julia's friend, Miss Felicity Mayson, to dance.

When the next dance was over, he asked another young lady. Phoebe, meanwhile, also danced with other partners. She stared too much at Mr. Langdon, but Julia was proud of her for not trying to flirt with him. Indeed, she had little chance to, as he danced every dance.

Julia remained busy playing for the lively crowd. Everyone looked to be having a good time, even Phoebe.

Everyone, that is, except Miss Sarah Peck, who sat in the same position all night, near Julia and the pianoforte. Julia took a moment here and there to speak to Sarah, but she had no time for real conversation. No one else said a word to her, as though her station as a governess made her invisible.

Julia had paused to choose some new music when Mr. Langdon suddenly approached Sarah with Julia's aunt, Mrs. Wilhern, by his side. Her aunt introduced them, and Mr. Langdon asked Sarah to dance.

Julia was so gratified at his kindness, her breath hitched in her throat. Perhaps Mr. Langdon was more worthy of Phoebe's high regard than Julia had thought.

Sarah smiled for the first time since the party had begun as Mr. Langdon gave her his full attention for the duration of the dance.

Sarah came back to her chair with color in her cheeks. Julia couldn't remember the last time anyone had asked the young governess to dance.

But perhaps his actions had been calculated to charm. Some men's only obvious purpose in life was to make conquests of silly young females, although Mr. Langdon didn't seem to be that type.

Julia had heard nothing but praise from Phoebe's lips since she'd first met him two years before. His fiancée had jilted him for the older Mr. Tromberg, which resulted not only in making Mr. Langdon eligible again, but also making him the object of romantic sympathy—just the sort to make young girls' hearts flutter. He'd had his pick of dance partners that Season.

Then, during Julia and Phoebe's second Season, Julia had heard just as many lamentations from Phoebe, for Mr. Langdon had been sent away to the Peninsula to fight with General Wellington. Now that he was back, Phoebe was no doubt hoping to gain his attentions, and affections, before he must return to his duties as a lieutenant in the Peninsula campaign, fighting Napoleon.

Julia's hands hovered over the piano keys to start the next dance tune. "Excuse me, Miss Grey."

Mr. Langdon stood at her side with a young lady. "May I introduce someone to you? Miss Grey, this is my younger sister, Leorah Langdon. She would be delighted to play if you would do me the honor of dancing with me."

Realizing her mouth was hanging open, Julia closed it and addressed his sister. "I am much obliged to you." She stood and gave Miss Langdon her place at the instrument while quickly donning her gloves.

Turning to Mr. Langdon, she placed her gloved hand in his and allowed him to lead her toward the dance.

Was he also trying to make a conquest of *her*? But in the small crowd, perhaps he was afraid of running out of partners and did not want to break his rule of never dancing with the same young lady twice in one night.

Julia was fond of dancing, but rather than focus on enjoying a dance with an agreeable partner, she should be thinking how she might direct Mr. Langdon's interest toward Phoebe. She might never have a better opportunity, and Phoebe would never forgive her if she did not take every possible occasion to help her win Mr. Langdon.

As they lined up facing each other, she tried to think of something complimentary to say about Phoebe. But once she looked upon his countenance, it was impossible to look away. His warm brown eyes had a thoughtful tilt, his thick dark hair slanting over his forehead like a blackbird's wing, his side whiskers reaching almost to his jawline . . . the combined effect made her heart beat strangely.

Had she truly once thought his blond, fair-skinned brother more handsome?

The dance began, and she seemed to understand Phoebe's infatuation. There was something about his bearing, the expression of his countenance. Of course, he must know Phoebe and many other girls fancied themselves in love with him. Well, *she* wouldn't be one of his conquests. Overly handsome army officers had never been to her taste, and she loved her cousin too well to ever fall for the man on whom Phoebe had pinned her hopes.

As they danced, every girl in the room was looking at him as though her dearest wish were to be an army officer's wife. They were looking at Julia as well. She wore her white muslin gown with the square neckline, but as was her wont, she wore little ornamentation, only a small amber cross around her neck and her pearl earrings. Her hair, which she had curled herself, was completely unadorned. She hoped she didn't look too plain.

Instead of worrying about her appearance, she turned her thoughts to how to influence Mr. Langdon to think favorably of Phoebe.

Julia rather liked matchmaking, and she always enjoyed pleasing Phoebe. And if Mr. Langdon were to ask Phoebe to dance a second time tonight, the girl would be in raptures.

"You are smiling. Are you enjoying the dance so much?" Mr. Langdon quirked an eyebrow at her.

"I enjoy dancing very much, thank you."

"I should think you were ready to get away from the pianoforte for a bit."

"Indeed. You are very kind." His words seemed to suggest he was fishing for a compliment, but when she looked him in the eye . . . What was it that was so unnerving about his eyes that made him seem as if he cared?

She certainly could not allow herself to be silly about this man. She thought a moment and then said, "I am no great dancer. Not like my cousin Phoebe, who is such a spirited girl. She dearly loves a ball."

The look in his eye changed. Had she said something wrong?

At that moment, in the natural course of the dance, they were forced to change partners. When they came back together again, Mr. Langdon said, "You play and sing exceptionally well, Miss Grey. And I don't say that lightly, as my mother is something of a connoisseur. But I remembered this about you from the several occasions when we attended the same parties two Seasons ago."

"Thank you." She was surprised he remembered. "Are you pleased to be home? I am sure your family was very glad to see you." She blushed, remembering he had come home due to the grave nature of his wounds. "I should say, once they were sure of your complete recovery."

"Yes, of course."

"You are quite recovered, then?"

He smiled down at her. "Yes, thank you. My broken leg healed quite nicely, don't you think?"

"Nicely enough to allow you to dance." She almost smiled back at him but then remembered that Phoebe might be watching. And she didn't want Phoebe to suspect what Julia was thinking at that moment, which was how graceful a dancer, how charming a conversationalist, and how handsome he was.

"Do you enjoy playing and singing as much as you enjoy dancing?" he asked.

Was he only trying to make polite conversation? Or was he thinking that her aunt and uncle had forced her to play so that their daughter could dance? At a ball, they would engage a small orchestra to play, but at a smaller party such as this one, Julia usually ended up at the pianoforte. It wasn't as if she had no choice. But she knew Phoebe wanted her to, and she would do almost anything for her cousin. Some people no doubt characterized Julia as the Wilherns' "poor relation," but she owed so much to Phoebe's parents. The Wilherns had taken her in when her own parents had died, leaving her very little inheritance. How could she refuse such a small act of service?

"I do enjoy playing, and I would rather play than sing."

"And would you rather play than dance?" She must have looked uncomfortable, because he said, "Forgive my impertinent questioning. I've been amongst men, some of them quite rough, for too long. You are equally graceful at playing and singing and dancing."

Of course, it was the polite thing to say, but he did say it most charmingly.

"Your sister plays well," Julia said. "She is very gracious to take my place at the pianoforte."

"Leorah does play well and is gracious but still not quite grown up at heart, I'm afraid. She's only three years younger than I. Tell me, Miss Grey, would you believe that my elegant little sister used to put toads and lizards in her pockets, walk through muddy creek beds in her bare feet, and defeat her brothers in archery competitions?"

Julia couldn't help laughing, but then she immediately felt guilty, hoping Phoebe hadn't seen her merriment under the gaze of Mr. Langdon's overly cheerful face.

His smile was too appealing for anyone's good.

"You shouldn't tell such tales. Your sister would not like it."

"On the contrary, she loves to tell those stories even more than I. She regaled the entire company of guests at my parents' last dinner party with how she wrestled a poor defenseless rabbit from the jaws of a fox when she was ten."

Their turn came and they obeyed the rules of the dance, taking each other's hand and whirling to the music. When they had another chance to speak, she said, "Your sister reminds me of my cousin Phoebe. Even now she enjoys a good tromp through the woods on the family's country estate. She would go fishing with the groomsmen if my uncle would allow it."

They switched partners for a few moments, Julia congratulating herself on again turning the conversation to Phoebe. When she faced Mr. Langdon, he had a strange look on his face.

"When you dance with me, I want to hear about you, not your cousin."

Blushing as if she'd been caught doing something wrong, Julia tried to think of what to say. Should she give him a good set down? He was rude to tell her what she could or could not speak of. But she sensed that he had caught on to her scheme of trying to manipulate him into an attraction for Phoebe.

How annoying to be so transparent.

"So when a lady dances with you, she must stick to the subject you choose?"

"No." He leaned his head nearer hers and said softly, "But you should know that I find you *quite* as interesting as your cousin Miss Wilhern."

The dance ended. The other participants applauded politely as Julia stared up at him.

"Thank you for the dance, Miss Grey. I hope to have the pleasure again . . . soon." With that, he bowed politely and turned away.

Julia was staring at his retreating back, just as Phoebe had earlier in the evening. She turned and made her way toward the refreshments.

She stood in a corner, drinking her lemonade and fanning herself. How strange that she should have been caught in Mr. Langdon's spell. What kind of loving cousin would blush as she remembered the handsome face of the man her cousin admired leaning over her?

She was mostly hidden behind one of her aunt's potted plants, a large rubber tree, as she stood against the wall, forcing her thoughts back in order.

Taking another sip of her lemonade, she recognized her uncle's voice very nearby.

"Langdon has the diary? You are sure? We shall have to retrieve it—tomorrow."

Julia peeked around the plant's large leaves. Her uncle was talking to Mr. Edgerton. They stood with their backs to her. She should reveal her presence, as it would be very rude to continue eavesdropping on their conversation, but a small frisson of fear stopped her—the harsh tone of her uncle's voice did not fit with the occasion, as well as the fact that they were speaking of Mr. Langdon.

"How do you propose—" Mr. Edgerton began a question that was interrupted by her uncle.

"You must go first thing in the morning. If you fail, I'll send a man—two men." Her uncle lowered his voice even more. "We will talk no more tonight, not till after the guests have gone."

As her uncle and Mr. Edgerton moved away, Julia let out the breath she'd been holding.

Their conversation was so strange. Something about getting a diary from Mr. Langdon. But what could her uncle want with a diary?

CHAPTER TWO

Nicholas sat in the sitting room facing east. This was his favorite room in the morning, as he liked to see the sun slanting in the windows. The rest of the family was still abed, and he had sent his valet, Smith, to ferret out the whereabouts of one Garrison Greenfield, the man to whom Beechum had bade him take the small leather diary. His only direction, besides the name Garrison Greenfield, was the Horse Guards in Whitehall. He must have meant the War Office. Whatever the case, Smith would find him.

Nicholas sat reading the newspaper, still catching up on all the political news since he had been away, when Foster announced that Hugh Edgerton was calling. *So early in the morning?*

"Show him in."

Edgerton greeted him with a weak smile. His eyes were red and puffy.

"Must be something important to bring you out so early." Nicholas nearly chuckled at the way Edgerton winced and shielded his eyes from the bright sunlight.

"Important?" Edgerton stood still a moment. "Not at all. What makes you say that? I wanted to call, as I know you may be off again soon."

Edgerton proceeded to talk of the war, and he asked Nicholas several questions about his time in the Peninsula, about General Wellington, and what Nicholas thought the future position of the British army would be. It was beginning to strike Nicholas as very strange conversation, not at all what Edgerton usually talked of.

Edgerton wandered over to the small desk against the wall. "Have you caught up on your correspondence since you've been convalescing?" He leaned over the desk, and though Edgerton's body was blocking his view, Nicholas believed he heard Edgerton open and close the desk drawer.

"Do you need something?" Nicholas walked toward him.

"No." Edgerton straightened and took out his snuffbox, carefully taking a pinch of the brown powder. "I thought I saw some cigars in your desk, but I was mistaken."

Soon afterward, Edgerton cordially bid Nicholas a good day and left, expressing a wish to meet him again before Nicholas sailed.

While Nicholas was still puzzling over why Edgerton had called on him so uncharacteristically early and then left so abruptly, Smith arrived back from his errand.

"Did you locate Greenfield?"

"No, sir. And there is something odd about it."

"Odd?"

"When I inquired about him at the War Office, a clerk told me to wait, and he went and fetched another man with a colonel's uniform, who asked me why I was looking for Garrison Greenfield. I told him my master had something to give him. He asked, 'Who is your master?' 'The William Langdons of Lincolnshire and Mayfair,' said I. 'What would the Langdons of Lincolnshire want with Garrison Greenfield?' he asked. I said, 'I already told you, and if you cannot tell me where to find him, I shall be on my way.' The man looked hard at me. I thought it best that I come and tell you what he said before I inquired any further."

"Thank you, Smith. You did well. I shall investigate myself."

Very odd. Nicholas tried to think who he knew at the War Office. His father would know someone. He'd go ask him and then send a letter today, requesting a meeting. And later . . . he should look and see what was in that diary.

Going upstairs, he remembered his brother had left the day before. Jonathan had told him that his wife, Isabella, planned to make some changes to the nursery and some of the other rooms at the Abbey before their first baby came.

The family estate, Glyncove Abbey in Lincolnshire, was where Nicholas, Jonathan, and their sister, Leorah, had grown up. But it was more his sister-in-law's home now than his own. But that was as it should be. Jonathan was the eldest son and rightful heir.

Nicholas went into his father's study to find him staring out the window.

"Ah, Nicholas. I suppose you will be going back with the next ship heading to the Peninsula, eh?"

He cringed inside, but army life was his fate, unless he were to sell his commission. He had thought to make the church his profession, but his father had pressured him since he was a small boy to become an army officer. A clergyman, he said, had no chance of making his fortune. He had joined the army more to please his father than anything else. Over the many days and weeks of his convalescence, he'd had plenty of time to ponder what a foolish reason that had been.

"Yes, Father. I leave in a week. But at present, I need to ask you— who do you know at the War Office?"

"The War Office?" His father's voice boomed, seeming to fill the entire room. He stroked his chin. "McDowell, of the Westmoreland McDowells, a second son who is in the Foreign Office. Then there's the Griffiths' third or fourth son, but he's little more than a clerk in the Home Office, I understand. Why do you ask?"

Nicholas cringed inwardly at the way his father qualified men as to their birth order. Just the way he said the words "second son" showed that he held them in lesser esteem, while "third or fourth son" carried even more of a stigma. Nicholas had always known that, in his father's eyes, he was lesser than his brother, Jonathan. And the making of Nicholas's military career was his father's pet task, much like altering the nursery and children's rooms at Glyncove Abbey was Isabella's.

"I was only curious." For some reason, he didn't want to tell his father about the diary.

"Not thinking of transferring to the War Office, are you? There's no glory in that, and you could hardly make your fortune there." His father picked up his pipe and began stuffing it with tobacco. "Little enough chance to make your fortune in the army, even in wartime, but at the War Office? No chance at all. Speaking of which"—he paused to puff on his pipe as he lit it—"is it time for me to pay for your advancement to captain's rank?"

"Not yet, Father." He frowned, but his father would never notice, nor would he notice the wry tone of Nicholas's voice. "I need more experience."

"More experience?" his father bellowed. "You've had nearly a year's worth of fighting and been wounded besides. Another year, my boy, and then it will be high time you were made a captain, at least. Perhaps even a major."

"I appreciate your interest, Father, in furthering my military career." This elicited a grunt from his father.

He was eager to leave before his father began to outline plans and strategies for Nicholas's future as a great army officer. Besides, he had the information he needed.

He headed back to write a letter to Philip McDowell, with whom he had a friendly acquaintance. In his short letter, he requested to meet with him as soon as possible.

After making sure his letter would be sent by the two-penny post and arrive later that day, he went to his trunk and found the diary. He undid the metal clasp over the brown leather cover and opened the book. He carefully flipped the pages. Most of them were blank. But when he came to some writing, he paused to read it. There was some unimportant talk of Beechum taking the post chaise for a visit to his grandmother as well as a description of a bird's nest he had found. Nicholas skipped a few pages until he came to one that made no sense. The passage was filled with what looked like words, but instead of words, the letters and numbers and symbols seemed to be strung together randomly. He studied it more closely, but there was no sense to be made of it. He turned the page and found more of the same, just gibberish at best, undecipherable code at worst.

Code. Perhaps this diary was written in some sort of code.

He leaned closer and searched through the entire book. He could not make out a single word of the rest of it. He used his fingers to probe the inside of the covers, looking for a hidden pocket where something had been concealed, but there was nothing. All the information Nicholas had was that the diary had belonged to Richard Beechum, now dead, and the name Garrison Greenfield.

If what was written inside the diary was sensitive information, perhaps it was best if he made a copy of it. On the other hand . . . perhaps it was safer not to. If it were to get into the wrong hands, it could be dangerous. Still, better to have two copies than one. Nicholas grabbed a stack of parchment and dipped his pen in ink and began copying the first page of the diary.

It was dull work. After half an hour, he was tempted to stop. But it wasn't as dull and tedious as lying still in bed for months with a broken leg and a bullet to the shoulder. After enduring the pain of travel with serious injuries, and then the inactivity of convalescence, he could certainly persevere through the task, as the diary could prove to be an important message pertinent to the safety of his fellow Englishmen fighting in a foreign field for crown and country.

***

Julia sat in front of the looking glass preparing her hair, as they were all invited to Mr. and Mrs. Smallwood's for a dinner party. She was thinking of her dance with Mr. Langdon. True to form, he had danced all night but never with the same girl twice.

Julia couldn't seem to stop thinking about him. But she would never allow herself to develop an affection for the man her cousin wished to marry. And she still blushed to think he had seen through her scheme of trying to influence him.

As if Phoebe needed any help getting a husband, with her twenty thousand pounds. Phoebe's reckless infatuation with Mr. Langdon and Julia's loyalty to Phoebe had caused her to do something she wouldn't normally do. But from now on, Julia would be strictly sensible—and stay away from Mr. Langdon.

She could hear Phoebe in her dressing room across the hall, doling out instructions to the lady's maid, Molly, who was dressing Phoebe's hair for the party.

Julia pinned the last strand of her own brown hair in place. Her hair was easy to curl, and it was much too thick to need false locks to make it look tall and full. Still, her coiffure was rather plain. She could ask Molly for help with some ribbon, pearls, or other ornaments, but she dismissed the thought, not wanting to displease Aunt Wilhern, who could become extremely vexed if Molly was helping Julia when *she* needed her.

"Can't you make it higher, Molly?" Phoebe's voice carried through her open doorway.

"I'm trying, miss," Molly's patient voice answered.

"See how flat it is? I look like I just came in out of the rain."

Phoebe could occasionally be petulant with the servants and her parents, but with Julia she was invariably affectionate and warm. Julia admired her cousin's ability to make conversation without being intimidated by even the most formidable military officer or dowager. Phoebe's verbosity and easy banter made her a favorite with many. She did perhaps go a bit too far at times with her talkativeness and drew a muttered "Impertinent girl" occasionally, which Phoebe never seemed to hear.

A knock came at Julia's open door. Sarah Peck stood at the threshold.

"Come in, Sarah." Julia had long since stopped calling her former governess by her surname. She was too near Julia's own age to take offense, and Sarah had become Julia and Phoebe's companion since they no longer needed a governess. Julia and Sarah were of similar natures, and Sarah was also an orphan, brought up to educate others.

Sarah stepped in and shut the door behind her. Her pretty face bore a sad, drawn look and an almost wild glint in her green eyes. Her reddish-blond hair was pulled back away from her face.

"What is it?"

"I am departing tomorrow, to go to my new situation."

"What? You are leaving?" Julia had thought the Wilherns would keep Sarah on as a companion for Julia and Phoebe, at least a while longer.

Sarah nodded. "A situation in Sussex Mrs. Wilhern found for me, with four boys and two girls." A tear slipped down Sarah's cheek.

Julia stood and placed her hand on her friend's shoulder. "Oh, Sarah."

Sarah sniffed and fumbled to reach her handkerchief. She dabbed at her eyes and blew her nose.

Julia tried to think of some words of comfort. "I shall miss you terribly, and I know Phoebe will too. Please do write to us. We will write too, if you wish it."

Sarah nodded. "Yes, I thank you for that." She looked Julia in the eye, grabbing her forearm and leaning close. Her voice strained and insistent, even strident, she said, "Julia, you must marry."

Julia was taken aback by her sudden entreaty, as well as by the intensity in Sarah's red-rimmed eyes.

"I will do my best, Sarah, but you know we always promised each other never to marry unless there was a strong attachment."

"Who was that man I saw mooning over you two nights ago?"

Julia blinked, trying to think whom she meant.

"I saw a young gentleman staring at you all night. He did not ask you to dance, but you gave him no encouragement at all. I believe his name is Dinklage."

"Daniel Dinklage? He couldn't be interested in me. Everyone knows his mother intends him to marry well. He might be interested in Phoebe—she has twenty thousand pounds, but I have no—"

"Listen to me." Sarah tightened her grip on Julia's arm. "He isn't interested in Phoebe. He's interested in you. His eyes drank you in every moment of the evening. You should secure his affections, and as soon as possible."

Secure his affections? "I hardly know the man."

"Julia, do you want to become like me?" Her voice lowered to a rough whisper. "A governess? Torn away from the family you have come to love, every few years sent to live with new strangers, with no real ties to anyone?" Tears swam in her eyes, and her chin trembled. She gave Julia's arm a little shake. "Make as advantageous a match as is in your power."

"Sarah!" Julia blinked, hardly able to believe her friend's mercenary plea.

"Marry any gentleman rather than become a governess. To be a governess is a living death, like being in the grave and yet alive. It is always looking at love, observing it, but never able to touch it." She covered her mouth as a quiet sob escaped her.

"Oh, Sarah." Julia groped for the right words. "God will never forsake you. You must believe that. Something good will come to you. You are a commendable, faithful, handsome young woman. You never know what your future may hold." Julia grasped Sarah's trembling hand.

"No, you know it isn't likely . . . that I shall ever have a family of my own, that anyone would ever want to marry . . . a governess." Sarah was crying in earnest now, her head down and face covered with her handkerchief.

Sarah looked up, her face red and blotchy. "You must marry, Julia. Promise me."

Julia didn't know what to say. She wanted so much to ease her friend's distress. But with such a tiny inheritance, Julia knew her prospects were not promising. Still, she had never believed she was in much danger of being forced to earn her own way. She was part of the family. She had always imagined that, if no one ever sought her hand, Phoebe would invite her to live with her whenever she married. After all, Phoebe had often asserted that she couldn't do without her.

"Promise me," Sarah demanded. "If a gentleman shows interest in you, you will not discourage him. You will do what you can to ensure his attachment to you. And if he is not unworthy, you will accept him."

"Of course, if I am able to love him. But, dear Sarah, please don't worry about me. And please don't cry."

"I must finish packing." Sarah wiped her face and clutched her handkerchief tightly as she raised and lowered her fist to emphasize her words. "Don't forget Mr. Dinklage, Julia. You must encourage his attention tomorrow night at the ball. Promise me you will."

She'd hardly given Mr. Dinklage a second thought. He was painfully shy and not very handsome. However, he would inherit a fine estate in Derbyshire when he came of age.

"I will try, Sarah. Now don't think of me. All will be well."

Sarah, with one last backward glance, left the room.

As everyone knew, Julia would receive only 230 pounds upon her marriage. With such a small dowry, Julia was well aware, if anyone married her, it would be for love alone.

At least she'd never had to be on her guard against fortune hunters.

But Mr. Dinklage . . . he was not abhorrent. He was barely taller than herself, and with his hazel eyes and receding brown hair, he wasn't particularly handsome. But that shouldn't matter. If a person was kind, respectable, and sensible, they tended to look the handsomer for it.

Did Mr. Dinklage have those qualities of kindness, respectability, and good sense? He was gentleman-like enough, as far as she had noticed, but was he sensible? The fact that Sarah had caught him "mooning" over Julia, a girl with very little dowry, did not bode well for him being sensible, she was sorry to say.

A heaviness came over her as she thought of poor Sarah, so distraught, leaving them to go live with strangers. Truly, being a governess was almost worse than being a scullery maid. At least a house servant could commiserate with her fellow servants, could have friends. A governess, brought up in polite society with the benefits of education, having lived a life of leisure, must live amongst a family not her own, unable to mix with either the family or the servants, as she is beneath the family's station but above the servants'. She is alone, and there is little chance her situation would change.

She understood Sarah's urgent pleas for her to encourage the attentions of Mr. Dinklage. But it felt wrong, low and common, to try and secure a gentleman's affections when *she* felt no real affection for *him*. But perhaps when she got to know Mr. Dinklage better, her fondness for him would be forthcoming. And besides, she had promised Sarah she would at least try.

She would not see Mr. Dinklage tonight at the Smallwoods' dinner party, but she felt certain he would be invited to the ball tomorrow night at the Caldwells'.

It should be an interesting ball.

***

Nicholas headed toward Whitehall and the War Office. He brushed his hand over his coat and the inside pocket where he had tucked away the mysterious diary. It was a fine April morning, and he decided to walk instead of riding. The air was crisp and light, and after his meeting with McDowell at the War Office, he could go see his old school chum, John Wilson, who had started a charity mission near Bishopsgate Street. There was no better man than Wilson.

A little boy darted out from a side alley. "Sir, won't you let me show you these elegant dueling pistols my father asked me to sell for 'im? Ain't another pair like 'em in all of London."

The boy appeared to be about eight years old, with dirty brown hair that had been cut unevenly. His cheeks were chapped, and his eyes were red. His ragged clothes hung on his bony frame, and his bare toes were black with filth from the street. He motioned with his hand and his head for Nicholas to follow him back into the alley from which he had come.

"I've no interest in dueling pistols," Nicholas told him. "But when was the last time anyone fed you?" He began calculating how much money he had on his person. His own father would disapprove of giving money to beggars, but how could Nicholas turn away from such obvious need? He dug into his pocket and brought out several coins.

"Come. I'll show you the pistols." The little boy continued to motion him toward the alley.

While Nicholas looked down at the coins he planned to give the boy, a blur alerted him to something coming toward his face. Before he had time to react, a thudding blow connected with his forehead. His vision went black, the vague sound of coins spilling from his hand and clattering onto the street ringing in his ears.

CHAPTER THREE

Rough hands grabbed him by the arms. Nicholas blinked away the darkness. Two tall men with dark handkerchiefs over the lower half of their faces were dragging him toward the alley.

His vision was still blurry. Nicholas kept his eyes mostly closed, calculating what he could do to inflict the most pain on them and escape.

His attackers obviously thought he was unconscious. The first man held a block of wood in one hand, which appeared to be the weapon he had used to hit Nicholas in the head. Nicholas couldn't see the other one, as he was dragging Nicholas backward down the alley, holding him under the arms.

Using the element of surprise, he kicked the block of wood out of the hand of the first man and then kicked him, hard, in the groin.

Nicholas jumped to his feet and landed a blow to the other man's nose. That man drew a knife. Holding his nose with one hand, he slashed at Nicholas with the other.

Nicholas anticipated the move and sidestepped just in time to escape a stab to the midsection. But in jumping out of the way, he stepped on the first man, who was lying on the ground, moaning.

The downed man grabbed Nicholas's ankle, throwing him off balance. As the second man lunged at him again with the knife, Nicholas fell flat on his back in the alley, banging his head.

Two gray-green eyes loomed over him as the second man held the knife to Nicholas's throat.

Nicholas reached up and yanked the handkerchief off the man's face, revealing snarling lips and even, white teeth.

The man's eyes widened, and he fumbled to pull the handkerchief back up over his nose and mouth.

Nicholas seized the hand that held the knife and twisted the man's wrist as hard as he could, at the same time throwing his opponent to the ground and then rolling over on top of him. The knife fell from his loosened grip as the man cried out in pain. Nicholas pinned his foe's wrists to the ground.

Shuffling footsteps were coming toward him. A boot slammed into his ribs and then shoved him onto his back.

The first man, breathing hard and with sweat pouring down his forehead, stood over Nicholas. Before Nicholas could move out of the way, the second man brought his foot down on Nicholas's wounded left shoulder, digging in with his heel.

Nicholas cried out. The pain sent his vision spinning and growing black as the man continued to press into the very spot where the bullet had penetrated his shoulder.

Nicholas's cry of pain turned into a roar of anger. He grabbed the man's foot and pushed up with all his might. But as he raised his good shoulder off the ground, the second man squatted beside him and slammed him back down. He reached inside Nicholas's coat, into his breast pocket. Then the two of them ran away.

The attack was over as suddenly as it had begun.

Nicholas lay on his back in the alley, breathless with pain. He felt inside his breast pocket with his right hand.

The diary was gone.

Nicholas's head pounded, and his shoulder felt as if he'd been shot all over again, but his arms and legs still worked. He clenched his fists, staring down the alley the men had run down. There was no sign of them. No doubt they were long gone.

Nicholas must get out of the filthy alleyway. He raised his shoulders off the ground, but the sharp pain in his shoulder caused him to gasp. He ignored the pain and sat up.

"Sir, are you hurt?" A man hurried toward him. "I saw the whole thing from my apothecary shop across the street. Those filthy beggars. Who should think such foul fellows could be lurking around this part of London?"

Nicholas accepted the stranger's offer to help him get to his feet. The pain in his shoulder was intense, like a fiery poker stabbing him. Had all the mending in his shoulder been undone? He suspected if he looked inside his coat he'd see the wound open and bleeding again.

It was as if the miscreants had known of his shoulder wound and had purposely attacked him there. But how could they have known? And how did they know about the diary? Stealing the diary was obviously the object of their attack. They hadn't demanded money, and they could have killed him if they'd wanted to.

"If you can make it across the street to my shop, you can rest yourself there awhile." The man fetched Nicholas's hat and handed it to him.

Nicholas took a few steps. "I am very grateful for your help. I think I am well enough now, and I have an appointment that I must keep. But thank you for your kind offer." Nicholas looked him in the eye. "May I have your name?"

"Adam Brewer, apothecary. That is my shop there"—he pointed across the street—"where my son is my apprentice."

"Nicholas Langdon."

"Imagine, a gentleman being attacked in the streets of London. What is this country coming to, I ask you? A crying shame, it is. If my son were here, he'd help you look for the brigands, but I sent him on an errand not ten minutes ago."

Nicholas smiled at the man's good-natured fussing. "It would be fruitless to try to catch my assailants now. I must see to my business. Good day, Mr. Brewer. And thank you again."

"Most readily, most readily. I shall keep a sharp eye out for those blighters, you can be sure!"

Nicholas went on his way, but his stomach sank at the thought of having to tell McDowell at the War Office that he had lost the diary. If only Beechum had told him how important the book was. But the only thing he had said was, "Give this to Garrison Greenfield at the Horse Guards . . . Whitehall, London." Those were his last words. After he'd handed Nicholas the diary, he had slipped into unconsciousness and died a few hours later.

When Nicholas reached the War Office, his shoulder still burned ferociously and his head throbbed. But he forced himself to concentrate on his task. This had now become a more serious matter than he had imagined.

He was taken to McDowell's office, where the young man, near Nicholas's age, stood and greeted him. Philip McDowell had always been an amiable, but not overly talkative, gentleman. He had sharp blue eyes, which Nicholas remembered, and a trim, reddish-brown beard, which was new.

"Thank you for seeing me," Nicholas began, "but I am sorry to say, I have bad news." He swallowed and took a breath. "I was attacked on the way here. I was bringing you a diary given to me by Richard Beechum just after I was wounded in the Peninsula. Two men stole the diary out of my coat pocket." He quickly added, "But I copied the entire diary, and the copy is at my father's house in Mayfair."

Both men had remained standing, and now McDowell stared hard at Nicholas. "This is serious indeed. Did you see your assailants' faces?"

"I saw one man's face, but he was not familiar to me. They wore handkerchiefs over their faces. Both had brown hair, and one of them had green eyes."

"If they weren't after your money and only stole the diary, they must have known already of the diary's existence."

"Exactly," Nicholas agreed. "I am afraid I mentioned the diary to a friend at a party I attended two nights ago."

"Whose party? What friend?" McDowell seemed to lean toward him, his expression intense.

"At the time, I was completely unaware the diary contained anything out of the ordinary or was anything other than a man's war diary. Beechum, the man who gave me the book, was a stranger to me. We met in the infirmary, as we had both just been wounded. His injuries were more serious than mine, and he asked me to take the diary to a man named Garrison Greenfield. I assumed he was a relative or friend. Beechum was barely able to talk, so I did not question him further. Then he died."

"I understand." McDowell nodded for him to go on.

"I have been convalescing at home for the past two months, and my first entry back in society was two nights ago at a small party at Mr. Robert Wilhern's home in Grosvenor Square. I mentioned to Mr. Hugh Edgerton that I had an errand, to deliver a diary that was given to me by Lieutenant Richard Beechum to a Mr. Garrison Greenfield. Had I any inkling that the diary contained sensitive or important information, I certainly never would have mentioned it, even to an old school chum like Edgerton." Nicholas felt his face grow warm as he realized what a blunder he had made . . . a potentially serious blunder.

"Hugh Edgerton, you said?" McDowell grabbed a sheet of paper and quickly wrote the name down. "Is he involved with anything underhanded or suspicious that you know of?"

"No."

"Who else heard you speak of the diary? Did you say exactly where you planned to take the diary?"

Nicholas thought back to the party. "I did not say where I planned to take it. I only mentioned the name Garrison Greenfield. I asked Edgerton if he knew him, since I thought he reacted oddly when I said the name. At the time, I thought little of it. As for who else might have heard, I believe Mr. Wilhern heard me." He thought some more, trying to see in his mind's eye the men who had been standing around him. "There were some others who had possibly been close enough to hear but weren't part of the conversation. Mr. Anthony Youngblood, Mr. Geoffrey Thigpen, and Mr. Daniel Dinklage. Other than those three, plus Wilhern and Edgerton, I don't believe anyone else could have heard me mention the diary. However, it's impossible to say for certain. People were milling about. It was a party."

McDowell was occupied in writing down the names.

"I did not know the diary was of any significance. The thought that I may have compromised any national secrets or anyone's safety . . . I am heartily sorry."

"You could not have known, and it is most fortunate that you made a copy of what was in the diary. That will save us much conjecturing about what secrets may have fallen into the hands of enemy spies." He tapped the paper on which he had been writing. "Wait here. I believe my superior will want to speak to you."

Nicholas sat, horrified at what he had possibly revealed to England's enemies.

He felt his side, suspecting one of his ribs may have been cracked in the scuffle. His headache was severe, but there was little to no bleeding from the blows to his head. He opened his coat and saw a blood stain on his white shirt over his old bullet wound, where the thief had ground his heel in.

Anyone who knew Nicholas would have heard of his wounds received in battle and would have known of his shoulder wound and his broken leg, now healed. But they had also known of the diary. Who could it have been? Mr. Edgerton? Mr. Wilhern? Or one of the other gentlemen at the party?

Who of his acquaintance would betray their country?

A serious-looking gray-haired man entered the room. Nicholas stood quickly, which made him dizzy, but he managed to focus his eyes after a moment.

McDowell made the introductions. "Langdon, this is Colonel Thomas Stockton of the Foreign Office. Colonel, this is Lieutenant Nicholas Langdon."

The colonel asked Nicholas to start from the beginning and tell him everything about the diary and what had happened. Nicholas went through the whole story again, adding more details this time of Mr. Beechum, the night of the party at the Wilherns', and getting attacked in the street. Colonel Stockton listened mostly in silence, his penetrating eyes trained on Nicholas.

When Nicholas was finished, and after a few grunts, Colonel Stockton said, "I will require your services, Lieutenant Langdon, as an officer and a member of your social circle, to help us discover who stole the diary. It will require utmost discretion, as I'm sure you understand. This is a matter of great national importance."

"Sir, I am eager to help in every way possible. My only problem is that I am supposed to be on my way back to my regiment in the Peninsula within the week."

"We can write to your commanding officer and have your return delayed." He waved his hand as if it were a simple process. "McDowell will look into the other men who might have overheard you speak of the diary. And if you could give us a list of every man in attendance at the party, that would also be appreciated. But I want you, Lieutenant Langdon, to personally investigate Mr. Edgerton and Mr. Wilhern. Find out whether they have family connections to France, any sort of motive for spying for the French, or any problems with debt that might make them willing to spy for our enemies for monetary gain.

"In the meantime, I ask that you go home and retrieve the copy you made of the diary. The sooner we have that, the sooner our expert decoders can go to work on deciphering it."

"Of course."

"I am placing my complete faith in you, Lieutenant. I need not emphasize how necessary are your loyalty and discretion."

"Sir, you may depend on it. I consider my highest loyalty, next to God, to be to my king and my country. I shall be as discreet as the grave, you have my word as a gentleman."

The colonel nodded, looking satisfied.

"But, sir, if I may ask . . ."

"Yes?"

"Who is Garrison Greenfield, and why was my servant not allowed to see him?"

"We wondered why your servant was looking for him and were planning to send someone to question your father about it. Mr. Greenfield was one of our men. In fact, he has been our most trusted agent, integral in discovering what was happening across enemy lines. He has been missing for months and presumed captured, or dead."

Nicholas absorbed this information in silence.

"Now, I will send two of our men with you to fetch the copy you made of the diary."

As Nicholas was escorted home in the company of two guards, his head was spinning more than ever. He had to find who had attacked him and why they had stolen the diary. He couldn't bear to think that by allowing the diary to be stolen, he might have caused some secret of great national importance to be leaked to the enemy.

CHAPTER FOUR

Julia rode beside Phoebe and opposite Mr. and Mrs. Wilhern in their new carriage. The streets of London were crowded, as usual, as they made their way slowly to Mrs. Caldwells' ball. Julia was only half listening to what Phoebe was saying as she prayed silently for her nerves to settle.

". . . Nicholas Langdon, as a name, is rather plain. I would prefer him to have a more romantic-sounding name—something like Drake Westmoreland or Cameron Beauchamp or Nathaniel Torrington. What do you think, Julia?"

"His name hardly matters, Phoebe. Besides, 'Nicholas Langdon' is a perfectly respectable name."

"I suppose you are right. I shall be very proud to be Mrs. Nicholas Langdon." She let out a long, dramatic sigh.

It was positively astonishing that Phoebe could be so indiscreet about the object of her affections, after Julia had taken such pains to warn her not to display her feelings so openly. But at least Phoebe was honest. Julia often didn't tell even Phoebe, the person she was closer to than anyone else, what she was thinking and feeling.

Finally, they arrived. Julia looked around, but she saw neither Mr. Daniel Dinklage nor anyone else of her acquaintance. Perhaps it was God's way of keeping her from flirting with Mr. Dinklage.

Julia was almost sorry that the hostess would have no need of her to play the pianoforte, as Mrs. Caldwell had hired a small orchestra for the ball. Julia played to calm her own emotions, whether sadness, contentment, joy, or frustration. Letting her fingers draw music from the ivory keys eased any gloomy feelings and enhanced the more joyful ones. She often closed her eyes and let the beauty of it take her out of the melancholy she felt when Phoebe was angry or sulking about something, or when her cousin's grandparents came to call, doting on Phoebe and treating Julia like an unwanted guest, reminding her that her own parents and grandparents were long dead.

Julia stood talking, or, rather, listening, as Phoebe and two of her friends, who were just out in society and in their first Season, gossiped and giggled and drew attention to themselves.

More people arrived. Through the milling crowd, Julia saw Mr. Dinklage across the room. He bent toward two dowagers who held him in conversation. Julia smiled quite purposefully at him and nodded. He looked startled, suddenly straightening. He turned around to see who was behind him, looking over his left shoulder, and then his right, and then at Julia. She kept smiling.

Barely ten feet to Mr. Dinklage's left, Mr. Nicholas Langdon was staring at her with those strangely thoughtful brown eyes. The corner of his mouth went down even as his brow quirked up in an expression that was at once questioning and amused.

Julia's attention was pulled away by Phoebe and her friends asking her if she intended to dance.

"Of course, if someone asks me," Julia said, feigning a smile.

"I hope someone asks me," said one of the girls.

"I hope a *certain* someone asks me," Phoebe said archly.

The others giggled, and a blonde with pale eyes added, "I hope your certain someone—Mr. Nicholas Langdon—asks me too."

Everyone laughed except Phoebe.

"Don't look at me like that, Phoebe Wilhern. You have no reason to keep him to yourself, and he's the most handsome man here."

But Phoebe's lips remained pressed into a thin line, and she turned away from the group and walked with her nose in the air—in Mr. Langdon's direction.

The dancers got ready for the first dance as the music was already starting. Mr. Langdon had found a partner and was leading her to the floor. Phoebe changed direction and stood with an air of nonchalance by a group of young men.

Mr. Dinklage was still staring at Julia, his face suffused with a befuddled blush.

Sarah Peck's distressed countenance appeared in her memory. Hadn't Julia promised not to dissuade any respectable suitor? Wouldn't it be foolish of her to ignore a gentleman who was interested in her? A man with the means to marry her? Of course, she must explore her options, must give the man a chance to secure her affections.

She continued trying to participate in the conversation around her, but it quickly degenerated into a game to see who could bestow the highest praise on Mr. Langdon. Julia was wondering how she might extricate herself to go in search of more mature conversation, when she looked up to see Mr. Dinklage stepping hesitantly to her side.

"May I bring you some lemonade, Miss Grey?"

"You are very thoughtful, Mr. Dinklage. Thank you."

Mr. Langdon was dancing with a young lady, at that moment passing close to where Julia stood with the other young ladies bent on praising him. The girls didn't seem to notice his presence, however, and Mr. Langdon gave Julia a slight smile before turning back to his partner.

"Julia, didn't you hear me?"

"What?" Julia turned to Emma Holcomb.

"Are you getting overheated, Julia? Do you need to get some air?"

"You do look a bit flushed," another girl said.

"No, no, I am quite well."

"I was asking if you had ever been to Bath."

"Oh yes, once. It was lovely." Why did Mr. Langdon have such an ability to discompose her? She vowed not to pay him the least attention.

When the dance was over, Mr. Dinklage was hovering at her side. She took the drink from his hand. "Thank you."

She looked up to see her friend Felicity Mayson walking toward them.

"Felicity." Julia grabbed her friend's hand. "If I may, I'd like to introduce Mr. Daniel Dinklage."

They exchanged pleasantries, with Mr. Dinklage blushing, glancing away and back, and generally looking as if he'd never been in polite society before tonight.

But at least he wasn't overconfident and flirtatious.

Julia expected Mr. Dinklage to ask her to dance, but the three of them simply stood awkwardly looking at each other. The music was starting, and Julia wanted to dance, and with Mr. Dinklage. If she were to get to know him, she must dance with him at least once.

She gave Mr. Dinklage a crooked smile. His eyes grew bigger, and he swallowed, his Adam's apple bobbing. Finally, she resorted to asking, "Mr. Dinklage, do you dance?"

"Y-yes, Miss Grey, though perhaps not very well."

"I'm sure you dance well." *Well enough.* The music was starting. Couldn't he take a hint? She gave him her best sideways glance, well aware that Felicity was staring at her as if she had just sprouted horns.

"Would you do me the honor of dancing with me, Miss Grey?" he said.

I thought you'd never ask. "It would be my pleasure."

He led her onto the floor. Out of the corner of her eye she glimpsed Mr. Langdon but refused to look at him.

Mr. Dinklage's dancing was as halting and hesitant as the way he walked and talked. During the course of the dance, they said very little to each other until Mr. Dinklage said, rather breathlessly, "You look beautiful tonight, Miss Grey."

"You are very kind."

When the dance ended, Julia excused herself. Mr. Dinklage bowed politely, and Julia went to join Felicity, who was standing nearby.

Julia grabbed her friend's hand, and they moved away from the crowd so they could talk privately.

Julia told her about Sarah being sent away to be a governess elsewhere and her plea to Julia to find someone to marry.

Felicity frowned and shook her head. "I do not like to think of you throwing yourself away just because of what Sarah Peck said."

"I am not planning my wedding just yet, Felicity. I doubt his mother would look favorably on the match."

"If she doesn't, you can comfort yourself in the fact that you are far above him in appearance, talent, sense, and manners."

"But none of those things matter as much as having a few thousand pounds to my name, which I do not." Julia smiled in an attempt to make light of the situation. But Felicity of all people understood Julia's situation. She was the eleventh child of twelve, and though her father was a successful attorney from a family of landed gentlemen, Felicity would have very little in the way of a dowry. Her prospects were almost as slim as Julia's.

Two of Phoebe's cousins on her mother's side, Thomas and Walter Atwater, approached them and uttered the usual pleasantries. They were not particularly attractive, but they were young and unattached, and so Julia was glad when Mr. Walter Atwater asked, "Would you do me the honor of dancing with me, Miss Grey?"

"It would be my pleasure."

He led Julia onto the floor while his brother asked Felicity.

As they stood waiting for the dance to begin, just behind her she heard Mrs. Wilhern say her name. As her aunt was a little hard of hearing, she was talking in her loud, matter-of-fact way.

"Julia is a seemly sort of girl. It's a pity that she has attracted no eligible suitors, but if she does not marry, she will make a fine governess. She has less than three hundred pounds that her father left her, and I don't know who marries a girl with so little."

A fiery blush crept into her cheeks. Should she try to catch her aunt's eye to make her stop talking? Her aunt was not one to notice a subtle hint. Julia could only pray as Mr. Atwater led her through the motions of the dance. Unfortunately, instead of stopping, her aunt continued to speak loud enough that Julia could hear every word.

"Phoebe quite dotes on her, and I'm afraid we failed to make sure of a proper distinction between Julia's situation and her cousin's. Phoebe's rank, her fortune, and her rights are quite above what Julia can expect. Perhaps we shirked our duty to impress upon them both a consciousness of Julia's lower station. But Phoebe is such a headstrong girl and never liked to hear anything of the kind, and we indulged her."

By now, Julia wanted to run from the room, but Aunt Wilhern's voice droned on.

"I'm sure Phoebe won't need a companion anymore once she gets married. And goodness knows Mr. Wilhern and I have no need of her. We will try to find a suitable position for Julia. The family to whom she goes will be fortunate, since Julia can instruct in all the usual academic subjects, as well as music. She practices every day and is quite the proficient at the pianoforte and the harp."

Julia couldn't bear to look her dance partner in the eye. Of course, he could not have failed to hear every word.

Julia finally saw who Mrs. Wilhern had been speaking to—Mr. Hugh Edgerton and his mother.

Bad enough that her aunt should make such a speech to another matron like herself, but to a young man like Mr. Edgerton? What was her aunt thinking? But that was the problem; she talked without think-ing, oblivious to the impropriety of what she was saying.

Once again, it was their turn to promenade. Blindly, Julia took Mr. Atwater's hand and let him lead her through the middle of the two rows of dancers. She tried to look straight ahead, as if nothing had happened, and pay attention to the steps of the dance. But a stone crowded her chest, and she kept hearing her aunt's words, callously speaking of Julia being unable to attract a suitor, and of her aunt's intention to cast Julia off to be a governess as soon as Phoebe was married.

Tears gathered in her eyes, but she could not humiliate herself by crying in a public assembly. A lady should always be able to govern her own feelings.

Only making things worse was Mr. Atwater's halting way of danc-ing. He was worse even than Mr. Dinklage. Had he never danced before?

How painful to realize that her aunt did not consider her a member of the family at all, only a tool, a servant who would serve a purpose and then be discarded as unnecessary.

She was afraid to look at her partner, or to look anyone in the eye, and see her humiliation reflected back at her.

They changed partners in the course of the dance and she found herself with Mr. Langdon. She was captured by his deep-brown eyes before she had time to look away. But there was sympathy in them, in the gentleness of his expression.

He had heard what her aunt had said, and he pitied her. Her humil-iation was complete.

Neither of them said a word as they went through the movements of the dance. His fingers were gentle yet firm as he grasped her hand. She was grateful he didn't speak, but the hollow feeling came back into the pit of her stomach. How could Aunt Wilhern say such things about her at a party where so many others could hear?

Once she'd broken free from Nicholas Langdon's gaze, she couldn't bear to look at him again. *God, please help me get through this ball.*

Perhaps she could hide in the card room, or near the refreshments table. Or under it.

She could feel Mr. Langdon's eyes on her as he handed her back to Mr. Atwater, but she didn't look up at him.

When the dance ended, Julia excused herself, saying she needed some air. She walked across the large ballroom. Out of the corner of her eye she noticed Mr. Edgerton staring at her. He wore buff-and-brown-striped trousers with a waistcoat to match. With his larger-than-average height and build, his brown hair, and his wide-set eyes, Mr. Edgerton was considered handsome by some. But even though his was an old family, he had racked up considerable gaming debts and would need to marry someone with a fortune—which was why it was strange that he always seemed to seek Julia out at parties. She had long realized he felt a preference for her, but she assumed his debts would prevent him from pursuing her.

Julia forced herself to hold her head high as she slipped away and found a small sitting room. The window facing the street was not latched, so she crossed to the other side and opened it, letting the cool night air take the sting out of her cheeks.

Am I so alone and unloved? Destined to be a governess?

Beneath Phoebe's station, her aunt had said. She felt her face grow hot again. No wonder few men asked her to dance and none ever came to call on her. No doubt their families had warned them about young women like her, without dowries, desperate to make a good match. Certainly Mr. Dinklage's mother would make sure he did not pursue her.

Julia stared at the carriages going by on the street below. She pressed her hand against the window sash, letting the damp night air distract her. The lanterns and streetlights blurred as smoke from nearby chimney fires stung her eyes.

A tear rolled down her cheek. She quickly brushed it away and took out her handkerchief, dabbing at her eyes.

"Here you are."

Julia twisted around to find Mr. Edgerton behind her, almost touching her he was so close.

"I didn't hear you come in." She tried to move away from him, but she was trapped between the window pressing into her back, the desk beside her, and Mr. Edgerton in front of her.

"Forgive me for startling you." Mr. Edgerton's face was mostly in shadow, but his white teeth flashed in the pale light. "Are you well, Miss Grey?"

"Yes, of course. Only getting a bit of air." She tried to brush by him, but he moved closer and pressed her arm with his hand.

"You are upset about what your aunt said."

"I—I am well. I am sure my aunt . . ." She intended to say, "I am sure my aunt meant well," but that was not true. She did not think her aunt could have meant anything good by what she had said. She tried to think of something to say that would cause Mr. Edgerton to move out of her way, but the lump in her throat prevented her from speaking.

"I am very sorry."

He had taken her silence as an admission of her pain, as an invitation for pity. But the way he was touching her arm and preventing her from leaving the room made her heart beat uncomfortably. There was something in his pale eyes that put her on her guard.

"Excuse me," she managed to say. "I need to go, to return to the party."

He let go of her arm and moved aside enough to let her pass. But then he grasped her arm again. He whispered, "You do not deserve to be treated badly."

The look in his eyes reminded her that if anyone saw them alone in the unlit room, her reputation would suffer.

She pulled her arm out of his grasp. "I thank you for your kindness, but I have been away from the party too long." She turned and walked out of the room and into the hall.

She moved toward the ballroom and the safety of the crowd, the pounding of her heart stealing her breath. Unable to face the roomful of people yet, she slipped into the smaller room where a servant was serving lemonade to the ladies.

Mr. Edgerton's words and manner had been a direct result of what her aunt had said. He had not said or done anything particularly unseemly, but following her into the empty room, drawing so close to her, and touching her arm . . . a gentleman would not do such things to a lady who was respected and well connected, unless he intended to make an offer for her—or had nefarious intentions. Mr. Edgerton's debts made marriage to her impossible. Her stomach churned. Had her aunt's words made her vulnerable to men with immoral intentions?

She had always behaved with the utmost decorum. She was never indiscreet, never said things that could be misconstrued, and had always tried so hard to be above reproach. And now this.

This night was going terribly wrong.

CHAPTER FIVE

The guests were still dancing, the musicians still playing, as if her world had not just been turned upside down. She reached for a cup of lemonade, fighting to control her breathing, to push down her humiliation and compose her thoughts.

Felicity Mayson stood in the doorway. As soon as she saw Julia, she motioned for Julia to follow her to an unoccupied corner of the room. "I'm sorry for what your aunt said," she whispered.

Julia's heart sank. "I suppose everyone in the room heard her."

"Not everyone. But she was very wrong to say what she did. She must be jealous of you, and I suspect it's because you are so much prettier than Phoebe—and the fact that Mr. Langdon looks a great deal more at you than at Phoebe."

Julia shook her head. "No, no. I don't know why my aunt said those things, but Mr. Langdon isn't interested in me any more than he's interested in Phoebe."

"I've seen how he looks at you, Julia. I think it quite possible that she noticed it too."

Julia was holding her cup of lemonade so tightly the delicate porcelain was likely to break. She loosened her grip and shook her head again. "I don't think there was any malice intended, Felicity."

Felicity's blond brows drew together. "I don't believe she could say such things without at least some intentional malice."

"But if that is true . . ." Then her aunt did not have Julia's interests at heart and was not to be trusted.

Felicity gave her head a slight shake. "We won't argue the point, but you should get back out there and see if you can win Mr. Langdon. You'd be silly not to at least try."

Julia stared at her friend. "*Win* him?" First Sarah Peck, now Felicity. "I am quite sure Mr. Langdon never gave a second thought to me, except as someone to dance with."

"Perhaps. But remember when he got his sister to take your place at the pianoforte so he could dance with you?"

That *was* surprising. "He was being charitable. He also asked Sarah Peck to dance that night. He was simply afraid of running out of dance partners. My aunt has nothing to worry about, because I have nothing. Why would he ever choose me over Phoebe?"

"You're more beautiful, and you have much more sense and talent. There is no comparison."

"But she is more expressive and sociable. Everyone loves Phoebe."

"Mr. Langdon doesn't. Haven't you ever noticed that your cousin's eyes are small and her chin is rather weak?"

Julia shook her head. "I am not one whit prettier than my cousin. You are only saying these things because you are my friend, but I do not wish to speak ill of my cousin." Phoebe had always been a very pretty girl, had always garnered more compliments than Julia, but that could have been because Julia was only the poor relation, and no one wanted to promote the poor relation over the favored daughter. Phoebe's eyes were a trifle small, but she was still very lovely.

"Julia, I understand, but you are too modest. You are quite the handsomest girl wherever you go."

"You're only saying that because you're so sweet." *To me, but not to Phoebe.*

"Believe me or not, but don't give up your chance at happiness because of Phoebe and Mrs. Wilhern. Don't take your loyalty too far, Julia."

"And why shouldn't I be loyal? They took me in when I was an orphan, educated me, and gave me everything. Where would I have been without them?" Julia felt the tears well in her eyes and took a deep breath to dispel them.

"I am only trying to say that you mustn't let them treat you like you have no feelings—don't look now, but Mr. Langdon is walking toward us."

Julia's whole body stiffened.

"Miss Mayson. Miss Grey."

Julia turned to face him as Mr. Langdon gave them a small bow.

"Mr. Langdon."

"Miss Grey, would you favor me with the next dance?"

"Yes, of course."

Mr. Langdon nodded and excused himself.

"Oh, Julia!" Felicity clasped Julia's wrist. "He would never go looking for Phoebe to ask *her* to dance."

He would never have to.

Julia's mind was awhirl with conflicting thoughts. The music for the previous dance was ending, so Julia gave the servant her cup. Remembering Mr. Edgerton's earlier behavior, she whispered, "There are some things I must tell you. Will you be home tomorrow?"

"I shall wait for your visit with bated breath."

Julia went to join Mr. Langdon for the next dance.

Placing her gloved hand in Mr. Langdon's firm grip, she let him lead her onto the dance floor. This would be like any other dance with any other agreeable partner. She would enjoy the music, enjoy the dance, and focus on keeping her thoughts off her aunt's embarrassing speech. Thank goodness the dance was a reel, so they would be moving too quickly to engage in conversation.

Julia concentrated as she skipped and skimmed over the polished floor, trying to appear as if she were enjoying the activity, still unable to return the gazes of the other ladies and gentlemen who may have heard what her aunt had said. She avoided Mr. Langdon's eye too, at first, but eventually relaxed and nearly forgot, for a few moments, about her earlier humiliation.

He cut quite a dashing figure, straight and tall and yet graceful in his movements. He grasped her hand firmly to spin her around or to hold her hand high while she turned. He seemed almost to be studying her, and yet, not in an intrusive way.

Julia only hoped Phoebe was dancing with someone at this moment and that Felicity was wrong about him paying attention to her and inciting her aunt's jealousy. Such an idea must be ludicrous.

When the dance was over, Mr. Langdon bowed and thanked her. "Dancing agrees with you," he said.

Julia must have looked confused, because he said, "The activity brings out your smile and a healthy color in your cheeks, in a very becoming way."

Julia stared at him, unsure how to respond. She didn't want to be suspicious, but a sick dread rose up inside her. She would not have thought his words amiss on any other night, but tonight . . .

"Thank you. You are very kind. Please give my regards to your sister, Leorah."

"You may give them to her yourself, for she is just behind you."

Julia turned and found herself face to face with Mr. Langdon's younger sister. They exchanged civilities, with Leorah regretting that she wouldn't have the privilege of hearing Julia play and sing tonight. "You and my brother dance so well, it is a pleasure to watch you." They discussed which dances were their favorites. Leorah declared she liked a Scottish reel best, and Julia the cotillion, though she enjoyed all types.

The next dance began, and Mr. Langdon asked Phoebe to be his partner. *Thank goodness.* Julia loved her cousin and wanted what was best for her, and she hoped Mr. Langdon might grow to care for her. After all, it would be a suitable match on both sides. And Mr. Langdon asking Phoebe to dance might help Julia's aunt to no longer suspect that he felt an attachment to Julia.

As Julia and Leorah stood politely discussing various safe topics, Julia intermittently watched Phoebe, remembering what Felicity had said. For the moment, it didn't seem so unlikely that Phoebe might inspire Mr. Langdon's affections. He was smiling at her, looking much more interested than he had a few nights ago. He even seemed to take pains to speak to her at every opportunity during the dance. Perhaps Phoebe might win his affections after all.

A pang struck her, tightening her chest. If Julia had parents who loved her, if Julia had twenty thousand pounds . . . no, she could not let her mind go there. The very idea that she could feel jealous of Phoebe made her stomach churn.

Julia turned her attention away from Mr. Langdon and Phoebe and focused on what Leorah was saying.

Leorah had such an open temperament. Already Julia felt at ease with her, as if she could trust her. On a night when she had learned she couldn't even trust her own aunt to care about her and be discreet, it was comforting to make a new friend.

Leorah must have been feeling something of the same, for she suddenly clasped Julia's hand and squeezed it. "I like you, Julia."

Julia stared into Leorah's smiling face, startled at the girl's frank confession.

"You strike me as a sensible person, and sweet too. I shall visit you tomorrow, and we shall talk of tonight's ball."

"I would like that very much." Julia looked into Leorah's eyes and believed she saw that tomboy Mr. Langdon had spoken of, hidden behind a forced decorum. She only hoped Phoebe would not become jealous of her new friendship with Mr. Langdon's sister.

***

Nicholas had not been afforded a chance to ask Miss Grey any questions about her uncle—and he had not been inclined to, after the cruel way her aunt had spoken about her, and so publicly. But in dancing with Miss Wilhern, he planned to take advantage of the opportunity.

During a break in the dance, he asked Miss Wilhern, "Your father's estate is in Warwickshire, I believe. Is it very cold there this time of year?" It was an inane question, but he hoped it would lead nicely to the next one.

"Oh no, it is not so very cold in Warwickshire, but the roads are deplorable after the winter rains." She talked on while they waited for their turn in the round.

"The name Wilhern is of French origin, is it?" he asked when he finally got a chance.

"No, but my father does have some family from France. I'm afraid that branch of the family were all guillotined during Robespierre's Reign of Terror."

"How unfortunate."

"My father, at one time, was negotiating with various political leaders to get the lands returned to him, at least some of them, as he is the nearest surviving relative. But I haven't heard him speak of it for quite some time—at least a year."

"That is very interesting." *Indeed, most interesting.* He hadn't had to try very hard at all to find out what he wanted to know. But now that he had the information he wanted, he changed the topic of conversation, asking her favorite thing about London in the spring. It was all the encouragement she needed to talk on and on about parties and balls and shopping for new gowns.

He had probably shown too much interest in her—and he had been so careful not to show undue interest in any young lady—but it couldn't be helped. He needed to discover if her father had been the man behind his attack and the theft of the diary, or at least if he had a motive for betraying his country.

The code-breaking experts at the War Office had rather quickly deciphered the message of the diary after Nicholas had returned with the copy. The diary actually contained information about a plot to assassinate General Wellington and throw the British army into confusion, allowing Napoleon to sweep in and defeat them.

And now to find out that Robert Wilhern did indeed have a motive for helping the French—the recovery of his family's ancestral property.

This sort of work was much more enjoyable than trekking all over the Peninsula and getting shot. He could actually make a difference in this war—although he did feel more than a twinge of guilt for paying undue attention to Miss Wilhern in order to possibly uncover her father's traitorous activities. But surely his duplicity and ungentlemanly behavior was justified, since the fate of General Wellington, the army, and the country itself was at stake.

He even hoped Mr. Wilhern was the traitor he was looking for after hearing what Mrs. Wilhern had said about Miss Grey. The poor girl had turned white with embarrassment. Her aunt should have been protecting her instead of exposing her and her vulnerable situation. And then, his chest had burned at the way Edgerton had looked at her—like a wolf.

But he had to stay focused on the task at hand, which was to endear himself to Mr. Wilhern and his family, get as close to him as possible, and find out anything he could about what these traitors to England were planning. He couldn't afford to be distracted by the lovely Miss Grey.

***

Julia came down the stairs the next morning, ready to call on Monsieur and Madame Bartholdy, as she did every Tuesday. A servant started up the stairs but stopped when she saw Julia coming down.

"Miss Leorah Langdon is here to see you, miss."

"Show her into the drawing room."

Julia was already in the room when Leorah entered.

"Were you on your way out?" Leorah saw Julia laying aside her bonnet.

"I am in no hurry. I often call on my old tutor and his wife, Monsieur and Madame Bartholdy, on Tuesdays."

"Oh yes, Monsieur Bartholdy! You mentioned him last night."

"Would you like to accompany me? I'm sure he would be delighted to make your acquaintance."

"I would love to, but I cannot today. I have too many people I have to return calls to, but I wanted to see you."

"Shall I get Phoebe? I'm sure she would wish to see you." Phoebe would never forgive Julia if she spent time with Mr. Langdon's sister and did not tell her.

"Oh no, don't disturb her. I won't be staying, but I did want to know the title of that song you sang here a few nights ago."

They discussed music and songs, and Julia happily offered to let Leorah borrow some of her music.

After only a few minutes, Leorah politely took her leave, leaving Julia with a smile on her face.

No sooner had Leorah left than the servant announced Miss Felicity Mayson.

"Forgive me for being late," Felicity said, slightly out of breath, "but I quite lost myself in reading Mrs. Radcliffe's latest novel, *The Italian*. Have you read it, Julia?" Felicity asked.

"No. I read *The Mysteries of Udolpho*, but it was not to my taste."

"Ah yes, you are much too sensible to read such novels, Julia, but I confess, Mrs. Radcliffe's novels are my favorites."

Felicity's strawberry-blond hair perfectly suited her pale porcelain skin and green eyes. Men always took a second look at her but shied away when they learned she had no fortune. She never seemed to notice or care, and she was Julia's favorite walking companion.

"I suppose Miss Appleby did not want to join us."

"No, she's already had her morning walk and was frightened by there being too many men in the streets this morning. She's worn out from dodging their eye contact."

"Poor Miss Appleby," Julia said of Felicity's shy spinster aunt. "We must be off, then. The Bartholdys will wonder why we are so late." With that, Julia and Felicity set out for Bishopsgate Street.

While alone in the carriage, Julia quickly related to Felicity what had happened at the ball.

"Perhaps Mr. Edgerton is in love with you, Julia," Felicity said. "I know he made you feel uncomfortable, but perhaps he does not know the right way to flirt, or he was about to ask you to marry him but you left too quickly."

"Perhaps." Julia hated to falsely accuse anyone.

They had a nice visit with the Bartholdys, talking nearly the entire time about music and composers, perhaps Julia's favorite subject of conversation, and Madame Bartholdy served them her special cream cake.

When the visit was over, Julia's driver took them back to Mayfair, dropping Felicity off at her nearby house.

Once home again, Julia took off her gloves and bonnet and started up to her room. Phoebe appeared at the top of the stairs and hurried down so quickly Julia held her breath, fearing she would miss a step in her haste and fall headlong.

"Julia, where have you been?" Without giving her time to reply, Phoebe rushed on. "You'll never guess what Father has done. He has invited Mr. Langdon to come to dine with us in two days!"

Of course such a thing would thrill Phoebe, but why did Julia feel a sudden rush of breath into her lungs as her heart skipped a beat? She inwardly scowled and ignored her foolish reaction.

"You must help me flirt with him," Phoebe said, not even glancing at Julia as she clasped her hands together and continued to dance around on tiptoe, too excited to be still. "You must tell him my good qualities and make me seem more genteel than I really am. If you love me, you will help me secure his affections before he must leave again for the war, for I cannot bear to think he could go away without my having made an impression on him. Please say you will help me, Julia."

Julia looked into her cousin's blue-gray eyes, at the frightening desperation there, and whispered, "Of course I will help you."

What was she saying? She couldn't make Mr. Langdon fall in love with Phoebe any more than she could control her own destiny by marrying well to escape becoming a governess. "I shall do my best to mention all your best qualities, Phoebe, but please be reasonable. If he does not fall in love with you—"

"Oh, Julia, let's not speak of reason or realistic practicalities or anything of the sort. If I can make him fall in love with me, I shall, and if you can help me in any way, I will be grateful to you forever." Phoebe smiled with her entire face and then giggled and hurried back up the stairs.

CHAPTER SIX

Julia dressed with care for the dinner party. She'd seen a glimpse of the guest list and Mr. Edgerton was on it.

What were Mr. Edgerton's intentions? She would simply have to keep her distance and stay close to the rest of the party. Molly had come early to dress her and fix her hair. Julia wore a white silk dress, and Molly had decorated her hair with white ribbons and pearls. Ready before anyone else, Julia sat trying to read a book, her stomach flipping nervously every time she thought of Mr. Edgerton or Mr. Langdon, but for different reasons.

Phoebe burst into the room. "You are ready, I see." Her countenance fell when she looked at Julia. "You look beautiful. What did Molly do to your hair?"

"She said it was something new she learned. Don't you like it?"

Phoebe huffed. "Of course, but why did she fix your hair like that and not mine?" She pushed out her bottom lip.

"Shall I call Molly back?" Julia moved toward the bell pull.

Phoebe hesitated and then said, "No. I don't think I could sit still another minute." She wrung her hands and fidgeted with the lace on her dress.

"You look lovely. I'm sure you will not fail to please, but do not be so anxious."

Phoebe laughed, a nervous sound. "That will not be so easy, since all my happiness depends on whether I can inspire Mr. Langdon's affection for me."

Julia could repeat her usual words for Phoebe to not place so much importance on one man whose heart she had no control over and who had not shown very particular interest in her, but she bit her lip instead. Perhaps tonight would be different. Perhaps he would fall in love with her after all.

***

Nicholas would be paired with Miss Phoebe Wilhern for dinner, he had no doubt. The way everyone in the room was looking at them—Mrs. Wilhern with her large, languid eyes; Mr. Wilhern's small, foxlike eyes pinning first Miss Wilhern, and then Nicholas, with a searching look; even Miss Julia Grey, whose stiff shoulders were the only clue she was nervous, kept looking their way, hovering as if she wanted to help Miss Wilhern but was afraid to draw too near.

Miss Grey's uncomfortable air seemed to have as much to do with Edgerton's presence, however, as with Miss Wilhern's unerring attention to himself. When Edgerton drew near Miss Grey to offer his arm and walk her into dinner, she turned and cringed, her eyes widening as she hesitated to take Edgerton's proffered arm. She had no choice, however, just as Nicholas had no choice but to smile at Miss Wilhern and walk her into the dining room.

During dinner, Miss Wilhern talked nearly nonstop. Nicholas only had to glance her way and ask an occasional question to keep the conversation going. It worked out well, since his mind was more occupied with getting into Mr. Wilhern's study and looking for the diary than with Miss Wilhern's chatter.

"What do you do when you're not in town?"

Miss Wilhern was staring up at him, waiting for his reply. She had been asking him about his family's estate, Glyncove Abbey in Lincolnshire.

"I suppose I shall see little of Glyncove Abbey, now that I'm a lieutenant in the army," he said, hoping his regret did not show on his face. "Indeed, I haven't seen it these two years or more. But I once was fond of riding and shooting, like other young men."

"Have you always wanted to be an officer?"

He caught Miss Grey looking his way and was captured by her blue eyes shining in the candlelight. Her eyelids fluttered as she glanced away. Edgerton leaned down, bringing his face near hers, and she ever so slightly leaned away from him.

"I did not always want to be an officer," Nicholas admitted, turning his attention back to Miss Wilhern. "I had at one time intended to make the church my profession, but my father encouraged me to enter the army."

"I am sure you would have made an excellent clergyman." Miss Wilhern smiled at him. "But I must say, you look much more handsome in your uniform than you would wearing a pulpit gown."

Miss Grey shot her cousin a disapproving look.

"I probably should not say so, but it is true."

Nicholas couldn't hide his amused smile. Miss Wilhern's adoration might be gratifying in a base, shallow way, but she wouldn't make a very sensible wife. In fact, she rather reminded him of the fiancée who had thrown him over for an older, wealthier man. Certainly he had come to realize that losing her was a blessing in disguise, but the humiliation was not something that was easy to forget.

While Miss Wilhern was distracted by Miss Grey's look of reproof, he turned his attention to Mr. Wilhern and began a friendly conversation about shooting and other country pursuits.

"You must come to my estate after we go back to the country and shoot with me," Mr. Wilhern told Nicholas. "I believe my pheasants rival any in Britain."

Nicholas thanked him and said, if his duties would allow him someday, he should like to visit.

Miss Wilhern immediately claimed his attention again by exclaiming, "Oh yes! You must come to Wilhern Manor! You can shoot all you like and see our beautiful lake and gardens. I have the perfect horse for you, and we could go riding every day."

He pretended not to think her enthusiasm unwarranted and tried to sound polite but noncommittal. "That indeed sounds pleasant."

Soon dinner was over and the ladies adjourned, leaving the men in the dining room to smoke and drink.

A few minutes later, a footman came in with a note for Nicholas Langdon.

"Excuse me," Nicholas said, rising from his chair and taking the note. He walked out and stuffed the folded paper in his pocket. McDowell's signal came at just the right time.

Finding himself in a dark anteroom, he looked both ways. He didn't see or hear anyone coming, so he slipped out and headed in the direction where he hoped he would find Mr. Wilhern's study.

Men's laughter sounded behind him from the dining room he had just left, the men still sitting and telling amusing stories. He came to a closed door and carefully turned the knob. There was only a slight click when the door opened. He darted inside and closed the door behind him.

His heart was beating so hard it vibrated his chest. The room was dark, but enough light was coming through the windows to help him see the outline of the furniture so he wouldn't trip. He moved toward the desk at the other end of the room.

He bumped into a stool in front of a tall bookcase, making a slight noise as it scooted a couple of inches over the wood floor. He paused a moment and then continued to the desk. He opened the top drawer, but it was difficult to see what was inside. Thrusting his hand in, his fingers came into contact with what felt like several pens and a glass bottle of ink. He felt around some more, feeling papers. Nothing else seemed to be inside.

He closed the drawer and opened a smaller, deeper one on the right. He could see nothing in the dark drawer, but he put his hand in and encountered what felt like smooth leather. It was a book. His heart thumping harder than ever, he pulled it out and held it up to the light coming through the window.

It was similar to the stolen diary, but it was not the one.

Voices sounded from outside in the hall. One of them was a man's voice—Mr. Wilhern's.

His chest tightened as he dropped the book back into the drawer and closed it as quietly as possible. It gave a slight squeak. Nicholas held his breath.

Mr. Wilhern was still speaking in the corridor, just outside the study door. Should he try to hide? Or should he leave and claim that he had the wrong room, that he thought he'd been entering the retiring room? He moved carefully and silently toward the door. He wasn't sure there was anywhere to hide. So he waited.

The voice speaking with Mr. Wilhern was Miss Grey's. He tried to concentrate on what they were saying.

"Did you see anyone walking down this hall?" Mr. Wilhern demanded, his voice gruff.

"No, Uncle," Miss Grey answered. "But we heard a commotion outside in the street. I hope it is not—"

A quick explosion, like a gun blast, sounded from the front of the house. Then another and another. Mr. Wilhern's heavy footsteps sounded in the hall, growing fainter as he moved away from the door, no doubt to find out what was causing the noise.

Nicholas let out a pent-up breath of relief. That sound was McDowell setting off firecrackers in the street outside, to give Nicholas a distraction in case he needed it. But he had very nearly been too late. Did Miss Grey realize she had interrupted her uncle as he was about to come into the room and catch Nicholas going through his desk?

CHAPTER SEVEN

Julia placed her hand over her heart, which was beating as fast as the firecracker explosions outside.

Her uncle's study door was opening. She stared down the hall, straining her eyes to see who would emerge. But she already knew. Mr. Langdon had slipped into her uncle's study as she had been coming back from her room, to which she had retired to repair a bit of lace that had come unsewn from her cuff, to rejoin the ladies in the drawing room. The sight of him sneaking into her uncle's favorite room was so strange, she had frozen in place. After all, why was Mr. Langdon going into her uncle's study, alone, during a party? Was he lost? But if he'd made a mistake, he would have immediately come out.

A few seconds later, her uncle had stomped down the hall, a strained expression on his face. The look made a lump come into her throat, but when he stepped toward the study door, something caused her to call out to him and stop him. She'd stammered and then asked, "Have the men already rejoined the ladies? It seems very early for that."

She rarely made conversation with Uncle Wilhern. At first he didn't even look at her, glancing distractedly up and down the hall.

But then, he stared hard at her and asked her if she'd seen anyone walking in the hall.

Her answer had not been a lie exactly. She had not seen Mr. Langdon walking in the hall. She'd only seen a glimpse of him entering the study. She wasn't sure what made her withhold that bit of information from her uncle, except perhaps that she didn't want Mr. Langdon to experience her uncle's gruffness. He could be quite impolite when he was angry. At the very least, it would have been awkward for Mr. Langdon, and something made her want to protect him.

Now he was leaving the study. She peeked at him over her shoulder as he very gently closed the study door. He turned in her direction and his eyes met hers.

He froze in midstep. His mouth opened and then closed, as if he didn't know what to say.

"Miss Grey," he said and then cleared his throat. "I got lost looking for the retiring room, and then I heard some loud noises from the street outside." He closed the distance between them and smiled.

Something seemed to pass between them in that moment, as if he saw in her face that she knew he was not telling the truth. There was tension around his mouth as he stared into her eyes as if trying to delve into her thoughts, questioning whether she would reveal his secret.

"Nothing to worry about, I'm sure." She smiled up at his handsome face, cast partially into shadow in the dark hall. "I hope it didn't remind you . . ." She stopped herself. How ill mannered of her to bring up his injuries. But she had to finish her sentence. "Of the war."

"Not at all." He made a small gesture with his hand. "War memories do not plague me when I am in pleasant company."

He smiled benignly, but a flicker of some inscrutable emotion crossed his face, and she suspected, once again, that he wasn't being entirely truthful with her. Was he plagued with painful memories of the fighting, of getting shot and wounded, of his friends dying? How could he not be? A pang of sympathy pierced her chest.

He held out his arm to her. "I shall escort you back to the ladies."

She took his arm, a warmth steeling over her—which caused her to remember Phoebe and how jealous she would be to know that Julia had been enjoying Mr. Langdon's attention. Fortunately, he gave her a small bow just outside the drawing room door and left her there.

***

Nicholas had to be cautious not to excite Mr. Wilhern's suspicions. When he came back in from investigating the firecrackers in the street, Mr. Wilhern's brows were lowered and his jaw twitched. But he changed his expression as soon as someone asked him what he had found outside.

"Firecrackers. Only some mischievous lad, I suppose."

Once, after Nicholas had been staring down at his glass and glanced up, he'd caught Wilhern giving him a hard look.

After adjourning to the drawing room to join the ladies, Edgerton went straight to Miss Grey's side. His cheeks were flushed from too much drinking, but surely he wouldn't harass Miss Grey with so many people around.

Nicholas would keep an eye on him and make certain.

Other than making sure Edgerton behaved himself, Nicholas had no further agenda for the evening. He could not risk looking for the diary again tonight, though he still suspected Wilhern was the man who had sent the thugs to steal the diary from him. How strange to think a respected member of British society, a landed gentleman, could be a traitor to his country.

Nicholas would need to report to the War Office.

Miss Grey was leaning away from Edgerton. The man was obviously making her uncomfortable. And by the way her nose wrinkled, she could clearly smell the brandy on his breath.

During a sudden lull in the conversation, their host asked Nicholas, "How are your injuries healing?"

Almost everyone's eyes were on him now.

"Thank you, I am improving."

"How soon will you be returning to your regiment? The army doesn't normally allow its soldiers to be away from service for long."

"You are correct, sir." He thought carefully about his answer. "I am still healing, but I'm sure to be sent back to the Peninsula soon. For tonight, it is very pleasant to be enjoying the sort of company I shall be deprived of when I am back with my troop. I had rather hoped I might hear some music."

"Oh yes," Miss Wilhern exclaimed. "Julia can play and the rest of us can dance." She fastened her eyes on him.

His first thought was that Miss Grey would like to dance just as much as her cousin. At least Miss Grey sitting at the pianoforte would keep Edgerton from leaning too close to her and trying to have a private conversation with her, as he had been doing all night.

Miss Grey went to the instrument, and Nicholas could see that Miss Wilhern wished him to ask her to dance. He could hardly avoid it, so he did. The other young ladies were soon paired up, but Edgerton kept his seat—he was probably too inebriated to dance.

Nicholas danced once with each of the young ladies—all four of them—and then he sat next to Edgerton. The others soon sat as well, and someone asked Miss Grey to sing. Truly, her voice was one of the best he had ever heard.

He thought back to when she had seen him coming out of Wilhern's study. Would she tell his secret? If Wilhern had ordered those men to steal the diary from Nicholas, the man might realize that Nicholas was looking for it. He couldn't trust Miss Grey enough to confess what he was doing and ask her not to tell, so he simply had to hope that she wouldn't expose him.

After Miss Grey sang, the party began to break up, and people started to say their good-byes to Mr. and Mrs. Wilhern. Nicholas would have been the first person out the door, but he wanted to be sure Edgerton did not try anything untoward with Miss Grey. But by that time, Edgerton was almost falling asleep standing up, so Nicholas was able to take him in hand, usher him out the door, and put him in his carriage without much protest.

In regard to his goals, the night had not been very successful. But perhaps Miss Grey would prove to be a better ally than he had imagined.

CHAPTER EIGHT

Julia wandered down to the drawing room the next morning to play the pianoforte, where she often did her best contemplating.

As she sat at the instrument and began to play, she again pondered why Mr. Langdon had been in her uncle's study. Could it have had something to do with what she heard Mr. Edgerton and her uncle talking about at the ball a week ago? Something about a diary. His excuse of getting lost looking for the retiring room did not ring true.

Soon after, Mr. Edgerton had claimed her attention. She very much disliked speaking to anyone who had been drinking as much as he had, and she was aware that she should not allow herself to be caught alone with him. Mr. Langdon's presence had made her feel a bit safer. He was so gentlemanly, she imagined he had noticed Mr. Edgerton's inebriated state and was keeping watch.

Mr. Edgerton had told her, when no one else was listening, that he was not the destitute debtor that society's rumors had proclaimed him. "I am in a very fair way, or soon will be, to marry and purchase my own estate."

Could the reports of his gaming debts have been so inflated? Where could he have attained a fortune? Perhaps it was only the brandy making him say such things.

"Julia, may I speak with you a moment?"

Her uncle's voice brought her back to the present, and she stopped playing. He stood in the doorway, his brows lowered in a way that made her heart skip two beats.

"Of course."

"Come into the study with me."

She rose from the pianoforte and preceded her uncle.

Uncle Wilhern motioned for her to sit opposite his usual chair. Julia sat and forced her hands to stay still in her lap. Her uncle stared at her, unblinking. Normally he occupied himself with business when he was home, and he wasn't home that often. When they were residing in London, he spent a lot of time at his club, and when they were in the country, he was often shooting with a party of men, riding, or going to town on business.

Julia had always believed her uncle loved her in his own way. But had he ever felt any tender feelings for her, the kind a father would feel for a child? He never expressed any affection for her, but he paid little attention to his own daughter, and yet no one doubted that he loved Phoebe. He had taken Julia in, as his wife's brother's child, giving her all the advantages of a good education and good society. But now, observing him as he was observing her, she saw a coldness in his eyes that she never saw when he looked at Phoebe.

His stare remained hard as he stated, "It is my pleasure to tell you, Julia, that a gentleman has asked to marry you."

Julia sat still, trying to absorb the meaning of his words. "No one has declared himself to me." She swallowed. "Forgive me, Uncle, but I am astonished."

"Can you not guess the young man? Surely you have noticed his attentions to you."

Mr. Dinklage first came to mind, but she couldn't imagine him having the courage to speak to her uncle, and he was even less likely to brave his mother's disapproval. Mr. Langdon came unbidden to her thoughts, but of course, it could not be. He had shown no preference for her. Mr. Edgerton . . . yes, it must be he, although she wished it weren't. Oh, what could she say? Her uncle no doubt thought she would be foolish not to accept him. Her hands started to tremble.

"Since you will not venture a guess," her uncle said, pacing slowly from one side of his desk to the other, his hands behind his back, "I shall tell you. Mr. Hugh Edgerton. He is a gentleman and will be able, in a few weeks, to support you very well. He will arrive soon in anticipation of your answer."

"Uncle, I . . . I don't know what to say."

"What do you mean you don't know what to say?" The hardness crept into his voice. "You will accept him."

"I—I am sorry, Uncle. I am very sorry to disappoint anyone, but I cannot accept him."

Her uncle stopped and scowled at her from across his desk. "What? Can't accept him? You had better have a very good reason for refusing a gentleman whose interest in you is obviously earnest. He does you a great honor, as you have no fortune at all." He leaned over his desk, his eyes wide, his jaw twitching.

A trickle of perspiration made its way down Julia's back, between her shoulder blades. "I do not love Mr. Edgerton, and I have doubts about his character."

"What doubts could you have about his character?" His lip curled as his tone turned biting. "You, who have no other prospects at all. What reasonable objections could you have to his character?"

She could not avoid answering the question without appearing to defy her uncle. Her heart beat hard and fast against her chest. The thin muslin of her dress clung to her back and shoulders, even though the fire in the study was small. "He has done nothing perverse that I can say with conviction or that I know of personally. It is only a feeling that I have when I look into his eyes, that his thoughts are not those of a gentleman. And there are rumors of his gambling and debts. I do not wish to criticize any gentleman, but he also drinks too much . . . on occasion."

Was it her imagination, or had her uncle's eyes suddenly become bloodshot?

"And what if he does have a few vices? What gentleman does not have a few gaming debts and occasionally drinks too much? Are you so fine that you can look down your nose at the one man who is asking for your hand in marriage?"

Julia felt the blood drain from her face at her uncle's words. She could no longer meet his hard stare, and he turned his back on her.

Dear heavenly host, what could she possibly say? She'd rather become a governess than marry Mr. Edgerton. But her uncle's words made her feel as if she were being ungrateful by refusing to marry him. Perhaps marriage to the man would not be so terrible. But she could not resign herself to marry someone she felt no affection for, someone who filled her with mistrust. It was too abhorrent, the thought of giving herself, mind and body, to a man she did not love. She simply could not do it.

But the thought of her uncle being angry with her, thinking less of her than she had ever believed he could . . . Tears pricked her eyes.

She blinked and fought them back. This was no time to give in to weakness and emotional displays. Her uncle would respect her even less than he already did.

He went on, keeping his back to her. "I believe I know what is best for you, and it is my wish, as your guardian, that you marry this young man."

"Please forgive me, Uncle. You must know that I have always, and still do, wish to please you in every possible way that does not violate my conscience. I . . ."

"Your aunt and I took you in when you had no other place to go." He glanced over his shoulder at her.

"Yes, sir, and I'm very grateful to you and Aunt." The tears were encroaching again. "You have been the utmost in charity and kindness, and I—"

"I gave you all the same advantages my own daughter enjoyed."

"Yes, sir, and I am terribly mindful of that, very thankful and mindful."

"Then why do you defy me now with the insinuation that the man who wishes to marry you, and to whom I have already given my approval, is not good enough for you? Does that smack of gratitude, I ask you?"

Julia's face went hot, and her stomach sank. She clasped her damp hands together to keep them from trembling. "I never meant—"

"What high and lofty ambitions are you expecting out of life, Miss Grey?"

She forced herself to meet her uncle's hard stare. "I have no high and lofty ambitions. My aunt has made it quite clear that I have no choice but to be sent away to be someone's governess."

"I should think, if that be the case, that you would be very grateful for a gentleman's offer such as Mr. Edgerton's."

Perhaps this was why her aunt had made such humiliating statements about Julia. Perhaps they had planned to make her feel forced into marriage to Mr. Edgerton. But why?

"Do you doubt his ability to support you?"

"I doubt his ability to secure my affections. I regret that it is so, but it is, and it violates my conscience to marry someone I do not love and could not respect."

The way her uncle looked at her . . . her mind was flooded with the memory: She was seven years old and had only just come to live with the Wilherns. She was standing on the front lawn when her uncle's horse threw him. She'd been paralyzed with fear that her uncle might have been killed or seriously hurt.

Mr. Wilhern had picked himself off the ground and started beating the horse, repeatedly, with his riding crop. The horse screamed, over and over. Uncle Wilhern yanked on the reins until the horse reared, and still he continued beating him. Julia fell to the ground and covered her ears with her hands, squeezing her eyes tight.

That was where the nursemaid found her, trembling and crying.

"Julia! Get up off the ground," Betsy had said. "What are you doing? I've been looking all over for you."

She wasn't sure how long she had been crouching on the ground, but she had been trembling all over as she looked around. Her uncle and the poor horse were gone.

Now, as he glared down at her, Mr. Wilhern's face was the same shade of red it had been that day as he was beating the horse.

"I will advise you to think on this matter some more, to consider the inferiority of your life as a governess, the struggles and lowliness of your position compared to what you could enjoy as a gentleman's wife."

All her life she had striven to avoid her uncle's anger. Her heart was sinking, her stomach twisting, the painful manifestations of a guilty, utterly miserable awareness of her uncle's disappointment in her, as well as what she felt were his unjust demands. But what else could she do? She could not, would not, agree to marry someone she could not love or respect.

"You are determined to persist in this stubborn, ungrateful response, I see." His jaw twitched again, as he seemed to be grinding his teeth. He turned away from her abruptly. "I have raised you to think too highly of yourself, have given you too many advantages. But you will change your mind. In the meantime, I will inform Mr. Edgerton that you are considering his generous offer of marriage. You may go."

His refusal to accept her answer to Mr. Edgerton's proposal made her face burn even hotter. Should she tell him truthfully that she had no intention of changing her mind? The memory of his fury at that poor horse so long ago, and the same look in his eyes now, stopped her. Instead, Julia curtsied and hurried out of the room.

Her heart pounded as if she were that child once again, witnessing the uncontrolled fury of a man upon whose kindness she was dependent.

She ran up the stairs to her room, wanting to cover her ears and shut out his words and the sound of his voice, to close her eyes and blot out his scowl and cold stare.

Stepping inside her room, she closed the door and burst into tears. She kept her sobs as quiet as possible so no one—not Phoebe or the servants or her aunt—would hear.

CHAPTER NINE

"I won't be content unless I marry him," Phoebe said between sobs as she sat on the side of her bed. Her eyes were red, her cheeks blotchy, and tears dripped off her nose and jawline.

"Phoebe, it does no good to carry on like this. Please, don't cry so." Julia's heart squeezed painfully to see her dear cousin's distress. Phoebe's tears and obvious pain tore at Julia, but the poor man could love whomever he wanted. Why couldn't she accept that?

Phoebe clutched Julia's arm. "Please, Julia. Promise me you will help me. I can't love anyone else. I will never love anyone but Nicholas Langdon. There must be a way to make him love me. I simply will never get married if I can't have him. I'll die of a broken heart."

"Don't say such things," Julia said as sternly as she could. "Indeed, you should not."

Phoebe looked up at her, her lower lip trembling. Julia was reminded of Felicity's words about her cousin not being as attractive as she. Phoebe didn't look very pretty at the moment, even Julia had to admit. But no one looked pretty when they were sobbing without restraint.

"Listen to me, Phoebe." Julia sighed. She pulled a small chair up to the bed and sat down, taking hold of her cousin's arm. "You should not give your heart to someone who hasn't asked for it. You never know who may fall in love with you, or who *you* might come to love, if you are sensible and stop being so focused on one man."

"You don't understand, Julia." Phoebe shook her head and rubbed her nose with her soaked handkerchief. "You're not romantic. You're sensible and will marry a sensible man for sensible reasons. You don't understand love."

Julia was glad Phoebe wasn't looking at her at that moment, for she was afraid her expression would reveal her thoughts. Didn't understand love? And Phoebe did? This pining over a man she hardly knew? That was not love.

But did it matter whether Phoebe was truly in love or not? She thought she was, and she was making herself completely miserable over it. If it wasn't love, it was close enough, and Julia was heartily sorry Phoebe was in it.

"Julia, promise you will help me."

"I will help you if I can, but you can't force a man to have feelings for you." If only both she and Phoebe could fall in love with men who were in love with them, all their problems would be solved. Phoebe would not be sobbing over a man who seemed to feel no preference for her, and Julia would not feel pressured to marry a man who repulsed her.

Phoebe's chin trembled as she drew Julia's attention to her with an intense look. "You've always been the wiser one. But I simply can't stop loving him. I know I should, but I can't. You are my dearest friend, and I need you. Please promise me."

How could Julia say no? "I will do whatever I can, within reason, of course. But, Phoebe, I will exact a promise from you as well. Do you remember what the vicar said last Sunday in church?"

Phoebe shook her head.

"He said God expects us to trust him to help us make important decisions, that God will give us wisdom if we ask him. Promise me you will pray about this, that you will ask God to help you know how you should act and how to control these emotions. Pray for wisdom."

"I promise." Phoebe sniffed.

"Now dry your face and blow your nose. We'll go for a ride in the crisp spring air, and it will do you good."

"Thank you, Julia. I don't know what I'd do without you."

Julia smiled. "You'll always have me." *Until you marry and I become a governess.* Julia pushed the thought away, determined to be cheerful for Phoebe.

***

Sunday came around and Julia had not seen Uncle Wilhern since he had told her she must marry Mr. Edgerton. Mrs. Wilhern, Phoebe, and Julia waited for Mr. Wilhern by the front door to join them on their short journey to church, but his valet came down and said he was not to accompany them that day. Julia breathed a sigh of relief as they left without him.

Days crept by. Julia occasionally caught a glimpse of her uncle, or heard his footsteps on the stairs, and cringed.

Tuesday came round again and Julia and Felicity left the Wilherns' fashionable town house in Mayfair to visit Monsieur and Madame Bartholdy. Julia had something very particular to ask the Bartholdys, something that she hardly dared hope for.

Had you been a man, you could have become a world-renowned pianist.

So the great music master, Bartholdy, had said to her two years before. Had she been born in Austria or Germany, or been able to travel to the Continent, she might have been successful as a composer and performer. Vienna and Leipzig, Bartholdy said, would have welcomed a female virtuoso. She might have performed for kings and queens in palaces.

After exiting the carriage, Julia and Felicity walked down Bishopsgate Street toward the Bartholdys' building.

***

Nicholas strode purposefully through the East Side; he'd had his coachman let him out so he could walk the last half mile. He had gone to the War Office to report what he'd found—or rather his lack of findings—and they had encouraged him to continue to try to get close to Robert Wilhern and Hugh Edgerton, as they had other people checking into the other three gentlemen. They also encouraged him to go about his normal routine as much as possible.

And that was why Nicholas was walking down Bishopsgate Street on a Tuesday, to keep his regular appointment. He never saw anyone he knew in this part of town, so he was startled to see a well-dressed lady walking toward him, a lady who looked remarkably like Miss Grey. But that was ridiculous. What would she be doing in this part of town?

But the longer he watched her, the more he was convinced it was Miss Grey and her friend, Miss Mayson.

As he approached them, Miss Grey caught sight of him and her eyes widened. "Mr. Langdon! I didn't expect to see you here."

"Miss Grey." He tipped his hat. "I could say the same to you and Miss Mayson. May I escort you?"

"Of course. We are on our way to call on my old music master, Monsieur Bartholdy."

"But why are you walking? Why not take the carriage?"

"The coachman and I have an . . . um, understanding; I don't make him drive past the end of Bishopsgate Street, he picks me up in the same spot, and he doesn't mention to my aunt and uncle where I went."

Now she was smiling. The only problem was, he could hardly watch where he was going for noticing the way her smile transformed her countenance and made the sunlight, what little there was on this overcast day, sparkle in her eyes.

"Please excuse me," Miss Mayson said, "but I noticed a broken lace on my half boot when we were in the carriage, and I need to step into this shoe repair shop, just here, so that I might have it repaired."

"Of course. If I may be of assistance . . ."

"Oh no, I shall be able to take care of it. You and Miss Grey can keep each other company. I shall return in a few moments."

"Of course." Nicholas and Miss Grey were left alone on the street in front of the shoe shop.

He was about to try to start a conversation about the weather or the state of the roads, the usual safe topics, when he spotted little Henry Lee coming out of an alley, fixing his gaze on Miss Grey. The poor urchin was as dirty and ragged as usual, and Nicholas held his breath to see if she would react as most well-bred ladies would, with a screech of horror and then an order for the offensive child to get away from her. But as Henry approached, Miss Grey actually turned to him.

"Henry! How is your sister? Is she better?" She reached into her reticule and pulled out some coins before Henry could even ask and pressed them into his hand, obviously unconcerned about soiling her white glove.

"Aye, miss. She's much better now. No fever for at least a week."

Nicholas tried to catch the boy's eye from over Miss Grey's shoulder. He shook his head and winked at the boy.

"Well, if it ain't Mr. Lan—"

Nicholas shook his head again, frowning.

"Ah, I mean, who's the bloke with the shiny top hat, Miss Grey? Looks like a fine dandy gentleman if ever I saw one." Henry winked at Nicholas when Julia turned to glance his way.

She turned back to the boy. "Henry, do you know—"

"We should go, Miss Grey," Nicholas said, holding her elbow and urging her forward. "You never know when more of these little street urchins will be lurking, waiting to steal your reticule."

"That's true, Miss Grey," Henry added eagerly—too eagerly. "The bloke knows what he's talking about. You shouldn't trust street people like me. G'day, Miss Grey. Thankee for the shilling." Then Henry winked slyly at Nicholas. He was sure Miss Grey must have seen it.

"All done," Miss Mayson called out as she left the shop and joined them.

Nicholas hurried them both along until they had left the child behind.

"Do you know that boy, Mr. Langdon?" Miss Grey glanced up at him with suspicious eyes.

"Me? How would I know him? Now where did you say your Monsieur Bartholdy lives?"

"I didn't say, but it's just ahead, in the taller building there. That child knows you. But how?"

"Do you give that cheeky little blighter money every time you come here?"

"He knows I come this way every Tuesday. And don't call him a cheeky blighter. He's a dear little boy. He quite breaks my heart. He takes care of a little sister, and his mother too, and he's only eight years old himself. He's very brave," Miss Grey ended stoutly.

In addition to being a maestro on the pianoforte and having a voice like heaven itself, she also took pity on street urchins no other respectable lady would look at twice. He was almost afraid he was in danger of losing his heart.

Except for one thing: her uncle might be a traitor to England. He doubted Wilhern's niece, also his ward who owed so much to him, could possibly be as noble as she seemed. If given a choice between her uncle and her country, which would she choose? On the other hand, she might be useful in helping lead Nicholas to the other traitors who were helping her uncle.

"I thought young ladies' nursery maids warned them not to give money to beggars on the street." He tried to sound friendly and half teasing.

"They do. But not all ladies listen to their nursery maids." Miss Grey and Miss Mayson stopped in front of their destination. "Thank you, Mr. Langdon, for your escort."

"Shall I walk with you back to your carriage when you're done?"

"That won't be necessary. Good d—"

"I insist. I shall meet you back here in half an hour?"

"I suppose . . ."

"Half an hour, then."

***

The Bartholdys' maid led Julia and Felicity to the drawing room. Monsieur Bartholdy sat in his usual armchair with a shawl spread over his knees. Madame Bartholdy smiled and held out her hands. "Welcome, my dears," she said in her lilting foreign accent.

Julia didn't know much about where they had come from—it was even rumored that "Bartholdy" was not their real name—but she knew that Monsieur Bartholdy had been all over the world, playing for kings and potentates in places Julia had barely heard of. He had many souvenirs—a Russian samovar, silks from the Orient, tea sets from France, and beautiful works of art of every description. But the couple's furnishings were simple and well worn, as was their clothing, and Julia often worried about them having enough food.

Julia and Felicity clasped hands with Madame Bartholdy, and they kissed each other's cheeks. Then she went to Monsieur Bartholdy, and he held out his violently shaking hand. Julia squeezed it gently, stilling the shaking. His head shook as well. His eyes, though a bit faded, still looked at her with great intelligence.

"My dear"—his voice also shook—"have you two come to the 'Bartholdy Infirmary' to cheer up an old man and his wife? You both are prettier than ever. What have you been doing since last we saw you? Dancing and singing and breaking men's hearts?"

"Of course not."

Felicity and Madame Bartholdy had already begun their own conversation, so Julia answered Monsieur Bartholdy and smiled, knowing he was only teasing her. "I *have* been attending a lot of balls and parties this Season."

"And impressing everyone with your musical talent. Come, child. Play something for us. Play that piece you played for me last time, the one you wrote yourself."

"Do you truly want to hear that?" Julia felt pleased that he wanted to hear her own composition. She had wondered if it were any good. She was usually too shy to play her own songs for anyone but Phoebe and the Bartholdys, but if Monsieur Bartholdy thought it was good, then perhaps it was.

Julia sat down at Monsieur's pianoforte, which was always perfectly in tune. She felt her spirits rise as her fingers touched the keys. She allowed herself to feel the emotions of every measure, playing with feeling, as Monsieur Bartholdy had taught her.

When she finished, Monsieur Bartholdy was smiling, his eyes closed. Madame Bartholdy sighed dramatically. "Wonderful, *ma chère fille.*"

Monsieur Bartholdy fixed Julia with a fond gaze. "You are a great talent, Julia."

Now seemed like a good time to speak with him about what she'd been wanting to ask for months. "Monsieur Bartholdy, do you remember how you once said that if I were a man, I could play for kings?" She paused and took a deep breath. "Do you think it will ever be possible for me . . . to perform?"

Monsieur Bartholdy's smile faded. He sighed, frowned, and shook his head. "In England, I believe it is impossible. But in France, in Italy, Austria, and Germany . . . perhaps. Perhaps."

"I only need a chaperone." Julia swallowed. "Would it be possible for you two to accompany me, for you to take me to Europe?"

He looked at her sadly. "My traveling days are finished, unfortunately." He seemed to be thinking. "Perhaps if your uncle and aunt understood and supported your ambitions, were willing to promote you, perhaps they could take you to the Continent. I could write some letters for you, and some doors might open." He gazed at her with pity in his eyes. "I'm afraid I cannot think of any other way for it to work out for you, *chérie*."

She suddenly wished she had not asked him, could take the words back. She was angry at herself for wanting something that could never be. It wasn't as though her dearest wish was to perform, but if she were never to marry, performing would be a more preferable way to support herself than becoming a governess.

Monsieur had once broached the subject with Mr. and Mrs. Wilhern, when Julia was thirteen years old, and asked if they would be willing to take her, or allow Monsieur Bartholdy to take her, on a performance tour of major European cities as a young prodigy. They had refused, as though the very idea was insulting. Julia had developed the impression from them that a young lady performing was disgraceful. But why should it be so?

"It isn't fair," Madame Bartholdy said, getting up and walking over to Julia. She laid her hand on Julia's shoulder. "But one never knows what the future holds."

"If I weren't . . . as I am," Monsieur Bartholdy said, "I would risk it. We would take you, Madame Bartholdy and I. You are of age now."

"It is no matter," Julia hurried to say. "As Madame Bartholdy says, we don't know the future. God may have plans we know not of."

Monsieur nodded. He had indicated more than once that he was not a strong believer in God. But Julia had always professed to be, and at times like this, wasn't a Christian supposed to have faith? God could do anything, after all.

CHAPTER TEN

Julia had been very surprised to see Mr. Langdon in this part of London. Amongst the poorer people walking the streets, he was anything but out of fashion with his buff-colored breeches, white shirt and cravat, and rich brown waistcoat and jacket that matched his eyes.

And when he appeared in front of Mr. Bartholdy's house as she and Felicity were departing, she could not help but smile, even though smiling at him seemed somehow disloyal to Phoebe.

"Mr. Langdon," she acknowledged.

"We meet again, Miss Grey, Miss Mayson. May I?" He stood between them and offered an arm to each.

She placed her gloved hand on his arm, and Felicity took his other arm, and they continued on their way together.

"Mr. Langdon, please pardon me for saying so, but it seems extraordinary to find you walking here in this part of town. You must admit, this is nowhere near your home in Mayfair."

He gave her a sidelong glance, raising his eyebrows at her. "Like you, Miss Grey, I have friends in unexpected places."

"I see."

He obviously wanted to be mysterious, and it vexed her that he was building her curiosity. Perhaps she could trick him into giving her more information.

"How did you meet Henry?"

His mouth twisted as he smiled wryly. "Henry who?"

Julia eyed him from lowered lids. She was as convinced as ever that he knew exactly who Henry was. "Henry's mother must be a terrible drunkard to let her children run wild that way. Probably has no morals at all. Poor children, having to suffer for their parents' sins."

Mr. Langdon was scowling now and avoiding her gaze. She almost laughed out loud but held her breath instead, waiting to see if he would reveal something.

"Not all poor people are poor due to their own excesses and sins, Miss Grey. 'Tis a misconception all too common amongst those of the upper class."

"Oh?" she baited him.

"Yes, and—" He looked at her and stopped. She hastily wiped the expectant look from her face, but it was too late.

Mr. Langdon stopped short and turned to face her, forcing Julia and Felicity to stop too, which was quite impolite of him.

"What do you know of Henry's mother?" he demanded.

"I could ask you the same question. Really, Mr. Langdon, your manner is quite discourteous. Your sister, Leorah, would be shocked at your ungentlemanly manners, no doubt, just as Felicity and I are."

"Leorah is never shocked by my impolite manners, when I am indeed impolite."

"Again, I ask you," Julia insisted, "what do you know of Henry's mother?"

Mr. Langdon stared into Julia's eyes. She couldn't understand it, but the longer she looked at him, the harder it was to breathe. His features, his look, his manner, everything together was affecting her strangely. Her throat constricted, and she blushed.

How good it was that Phoebe could not see them, and that Felicity was here to make it a bit less awkward.

"I cannot lie to you, Miss Grey." His voice was low and deep. Did he always talk like this? "Truly, I know all about Henry and his mother. As I suspect you do as well." He frowned at her, as though in rebuke of the way she had tried to trick him.

"Yes." Julia swallowed, unable to form a coherent enough thought to say more.

Mr. Langdon took her hand and placed it on his arm again, turned, and began walking down the street as though they had never stopped. "Henry's mother, as you probably know very well, was ill for several months, and while ill, she lost her home. Being a poor widow, she was forced to move in with her sister, whose small living quarters were hardly large enough for herself and her own children. Henry and his sister are accustomed to taking care of themselves as well as their sick mother, as she is still unwell. You were right, you know," Mr. Langdon said quietly, looking straight ahead. "Henry is a very brave boy."

Julia stared up at him, not watching where she was going, holding on to Mr. Langdon's arm. What was she to think of the man now?

"How do you know so much about Henry?" Julia asked.

"I met Henry through a friend." The self-assured smile was back. "As I said before, both of us have friends in unexpected places."

She felt a stab of guilt for being the recipient of Mr. Langdon's smiles. Phoebe would give anything to have him smiling at her like this. But of course, Mr. Langdon could have no interest in Julia. He needed to marry well. If he married Phoebe, he *would* be marrying well.

Julia must never let his friendly smiles and beguiling brown eyes make her lose her head—or her heart, as Phoebe and many others had.

"Where is Henry? He usually meets me on my walk home. You didn't send him away, did you?"

"Henry is well. I gave him a little errand to perform."

She wanted to ask Mr. Langdon what kind of errand he'd sent Henry on. Men could be so thoughtless. Perhaps he'd sent Henry somewhere dangerous. After all, these streets were not safe for children. She'd heard of young boys getting captured by ill-intentioned scoundrels set on making thieves out of them for their own gain or forcing them to do dangerous jobs, like searching the bottom of the Thames for valuables or trolling for coins in their bare feet amidst broken glass and all manner of hazardous objects. Sometimes unsupervised children were run over by carriages and maimed or killed. Ladies weren't supposed to know of such things, but anyone who didn't deliberately turn a deaf ear could not help but hear of them. The stories twisted Julia's heart. She didn't like to think of any child suffering, especially Henry.

"You won't have sent him far away, will you? You know the dangers for young children—"

"Of course, Miss Grey. I was careful not to send him on any dangerous intrigues down dark alleys."

"I didn't mean to imply—"

"Forgive me for teasing you, Miss Grey." Mr. Langdon turned his most disarming smile toward her. "I sent the boy with some money to buy a goose and some bread for his mother."

"Oh." She wanted to calmly tell him, "That is very kind of you," or "So good of you, sir," but her throat closed, and she found herself blinking rapidly as she thought of the proud look on Henry's face, and the joy and gratitude on his sister and mother's faces, when he brought home a goose.

Why would Mr. Langdon be concerned about Henry? She'd never known a gentleman who cared a whit for the poor children running around the streets. The sight of them evoked either embarrassment or anger from the upper classes, and Julia had never once seen anyone show them any charity. The general consensus seemed to be that they were of a baser sort of humanity, that the poor didn't deserve any better because their situation was the result of immoral choices and "bad blood," an inborn evil. But Julia couldn't feel this way, especially not about the children. Perhaps it was because she was an orphan herself. She didn't believe children were to blame for their situation in life, and they deserved the compassion of those who were able to help them.

She could not recall their rector ever encouraging compassion for the poor, and she had seen her uncle shake his fist at a small boy who had walked up to him once on the street and asked for money to buy bread. Her uncle had yelled, "Get away, little beggar, before I call the constable!"

And yet her uncle had taken Julia in as an orphan. Certainly the charity of polite society was highly selective.

So why would Mr. Langdon be any different? He was a charming young man who dressed well and was fond of dancing. He'd never wanted for anything in his life, his future had never been in doubt, and his every need had been anticipated and provided for by his wealthy family and by a house full of servants. Why would he care about Henry and his poor family?

Julia eyed him silently.

"Your cousin Miss Wilhern told me your uncle has interests in France." He made the statement without looking at her.

"Yes, I believe he does have claims to a large property owned by some of his mother's family."

"His mother was French?"

Felicity was looking straight ahead during all of their conversing, but Julia knew she was listening to every word.

"Yes. But I do not believe the French government will ever release the property to my uncle. They are not disposed to turn anything over to an Englishman."

"No, I don't suppose they are. So you believe he will never be able to gain control of this family property?"

Why was Mr. Langdon questioning her so about such a thing? "I do not—that is, I am not very familiar with the business."

"No, of course not."

She glanced up at him. He suddenly turned to Felicity and began asking after her brothers, two of whom were near Mr. Langdon's age.

"Tom is still at Eton, is he not?"

They spoke of her brothers and their plans for the future.

"I saw your Mr. Dinklage yesterday," he said, suddenly turning back to Julia.

"Why do you call him *my* Mr. Dinklage?"

"Don't look so guilty, my dear. Come, if you are engaged, you may tell me. I shan't spread the news abroad."

Julia glared at him. The man *was* incorrigible. "I shall tell you precisely what you are entitled to know, Mr. Langdon, which is precisely nothing." He was being abominably uncivil. She was being uncivil as well, but he deserved it.

"You are right, of course. But Mr. Dinklage told me"—Mr. Langdon lowered his voice and leaned toward her—"that you are the loveliest young lady of his acquaintance, and if it is in his power to make you his wife, then he will most certainly do so."

Julia's cheeks heated. *How very indiscreet of Mr. Dinklage.*

Julia made no comment. She could feel Mr. Langdon's eyes boring into her, but she refused to look at him as they walked.

They arrived at the next street over from Bishopsgate. The Wilherns' coachman was waiting for Julia and Felicity there.

Mr. Langdon had a look of regret on his face. Was he sorry for teasing her about Mr. Dinklage? Or was he sorry that she might marry another?

Staring into his warm brown eyes did strange things to her heartbeat, but she was captured and couldn't seem to look away.

"Good day, Mr. Langdon."

He grabbed her hand and squeezed it, warmth seeping through her glove. "Good day, Miss Grey." He handed first Julia and then Felicity into the carriage, and they set off.

CHAPTER ELEVEN

Another ball. Nicholas entered and caught himself looking around the room—not for Mr. Wilhern or Mr. Edgerton, as he should have been, but for Miss Grey.

Unfortunately, he wasn't looking for her so he could discover more about her uncle's possible involvement in betraying his country to the French. He simply wanted to see her and talk to her again.

He was not in a position to take a wife and therefore should not be showing a preference for any girl. Besides, hadn't he promised himself he would never become enamored of a girl with little or no fortune? Especially after his disastrous engagement to Henrietta, who was now the widowed Mrs. Tromburg.

"Nicholas," his father had said many years before, when he was only sixteen, "be wise and make an advantageous match. Don't be a dupe and marry beneath you like your Uncle George."

Nicholas's father, as the oldest son, had inherited the family's manorial estate and extensive grounds and properties, including a London town house, while his younger brother, George, had died a pauper. George Langdon had no inclination for the military, and he had an abhorrence of becoming a clergyman. When he failed to make a great match, marrying a penniless tutor's daughter, Nicholas's father had been forced to support him the best he could, as his brother George was quite proud and didn't make it easy. He resented his brother's help, even while requiring it to keep his children from starving.

Nicholas had no desire to be like his uncle, God rest his soul. He intended to be completely self-sufficient and never ask for or accept anything from his brother. He had even thought of becoming a mission worker and remaining unmarried like his friend John Wilson, who helped the starving poor of London's East Side. But if he did marry, it wouldn't be to a mercenary girl who cared more about a man's purse than his character. And though Miss Grey might be compassionate to poor destitute street children, she had proved to be at least somewhat money minded when it came to marriage, based on the way he had seen her smiling at Mr. Dinklage.

Already Miss Wilhern had spotted Nicholas and was coming his way. At least she had better taste in men than her cousin.

Perhaps he was being hard on Miss Grey. Perhaps he wouldn't be if she were trying to flirt with him instead of Mr. Dinklage. But no matter. He had come here to dance, not to find a wife—to dance and spy on Mr. Wilhern. Therefore he was free to enjoy himself. He must simply avoid forming any attachments.

To prevent the inevitable flirting and desperation in Miss Wilhern's eyes, he asked her to dance right away.

Miss Wilhern smiled and talked while they danced and seemed to be trying to amuse him. He gave her a smile for her efforts and then caught sight of Miss Grey talking with his sister, Leorah.

Across the room, Mr. Dinklage looked even more uncomfortable than usual. Why wasn't he hovering around Miss Grey, as he normally was? But then he saw the reason. Mr. Dinklage's mother, who rarely attended social events, was sitting against the wall, glaring first at Miss Grey and then at her son.

Someone had no doubt told Mrs. Dinklage of her son's and Miss Grey's preference for each other. What would Mr. Dinklage do now? But Nicholas felt no pity for the man. If he loved Miss Grey, he would not allow his mother to look at her that way. No, he would let his mother know that he would marry Miss Grey no matter what. And if his mother disapproved, he would join the church or purchase a commission in the military. But somehow, Nicholas couldn't imagine timid Mr. Dinklage in a soldier's uniform.

What would Miss Grey do? Would she ignore Dinklage? Or carry on with her flirtations as though his mother were not watching them with hawk eyes?

Miss Wilhern was looking suspiciously at Miss Grey now, and he realized he was being rude by ignoring his partner. He focused his attention on Miss Wilhern for the rest of the dance.

***

Julia was hoping this ball in the crowded assembly rooms would somehow erase the terrible memory of the last ball, when her aunt had humiliated her and Mr. Edgerton had frightened her.

So far, her hopes had been dashed as she tried her best to ignore Mr. Dinklage's mother, who was staring hard at Julia every time she glanced her way. Mr. Dinklage looked quite uncomfortable. Perhaps he wouldn't even speak to her.

She didn't feel as if she owed Mr. Dinklage anything, neither loyalty nor even particular civility. And if his mother was going to glare at her all night, Julia would show her that she was not intimidated by her cold stares and was quite capable of pretending not to even see her. But if Mr. Dinklage could marry her, despite his mother's glares, and if she were able to feel some affection for him, her troubles would be over, as far as her uncle's pressuring her to marry Mr. Edgerton.

At present, Julia was enjoying a conversation with Mr. Langdon's sister, Leorah.

"Julia, I must teach you to shoot a bow and arrow. Archery is such fun."

"I'm not sure I would recommend my sister as a tutor," Mr. Langdon said over Julia's shoulder.

"Why ever not?" Julia asked, turning to include him in the conversation, guiltily realizing she had hoped he would come and join them.

"My brother enjoys maligning me," Leorah said, "but he can't say anything against my archery skills, as I'm a much better shot than he is."

"Yes, but she often gets bored with shooting at a target and ends up shooting birds and small animals."

Julia almost laughed. "Is this true?"

"My brother loves to exaggerate. I haven't shot any game in several years, not since I was a child. But I have to admit, it is much more fun to shoot at a moving target than one sitting still."

Julia did laugh then. Mr. Langdon smiled down at her. She shouldn't be laughing with the man. She would simply have to focus on Leorah and not laugh out loud. But whenever she was with Leorah and her brother, the siblings always seemed to end up talking about each other—and making Julia laugh.

"I would be willing to try archery, if you were willing to teach me," Julia said to Leorah. "What other pastimes do you enjoy?" She could hardly wait to hear what Leorah would say.

"I detest sewing and needlework of every kind," Leorah answered, forcing Julia to clamp her hand over her mouth to keep the giggle inside. "I'd rather have a hot poker in my eye than sit and try to sketch a landscape. And I am negligent of practicing any musical instrument. But I do love a good gallop through the countryside. I have the most wonderful black stallion, Buccaneer, back home in Lincolnshire." Leorah leaned in conspiratorially. "He has as much spirit as any other stallion, but he loves me dearly. In fact, Bucky won't let anyone else ride him." Leorah sighed. "I can't ever imagine loving a man as much as I love my sweet Buccaneer."

"Really, Leorah. The things you say." Mr. Langdon was frowning, but there was a twinkle in his eye as he gazed down at his sister. "Your husband will require quite a strong constitution. I pity the man."

"Why should I ever have a husband?" Leorah tossed her head. "I plan to live with you and your wife and make sure she stands up to you and never allows you to get away with anything."

Mr. Langdon grunted and scowled. Julia was hard-pressed not to laugh again. She closed her eyes and took a deep breath to stop herself.

"Look, now," Mr. Langdon said. "You've scandalized poor Miss Grey."

"Not a bit," Julia replied. "I find Miss Langdon's attitude refreshing." Julia smiled at her new friend.

"You see?" Mr. Langdon looked at his sister. "You have been a bad influence, and now Miss Grey will ride roughshod over poor—over her own husband someday."

Of course he had been about to say "over poor Mr. Dinklage." Julia pretended not to notice his insinuation. "I think it a very good thing for a woman to have gumption and spirit like your sister, and I will not hear a word against her."

"Gumption and spirit, you call it? Her governess called it wild abandon and disregard for decorum."

Leorah laughed, obviously enjoying her brother's accusations and not the least bit repentant.

A young man was walking toward them, his eyes fixed on Leorah. Julia nodded in his direction. "I believe that gentleman wishes to speak with you."

Leorah turned, and the man asked her to dance. She accepted and excused herself.

Mr. Langdon looked at Julia. "Would you do me the honor, Miss Grey?"

Julia nodded and let him lead her onto the floor. She would dance her one dance with Mr. Langdon and be done with it.

The dance was a reel, so they didn't have much of an opportunity for conversation, but even when they did, they didn't speak. Julia thought it safer not to, and Mr. Langdon didn't seem to be in a talkative mood either—although the way he was looking at her made her feel flattered and nervous at the same time. But he did not look at her in the way of Mr. Edgerton, who made her feel exposed and uncomfortable, or Mr. Dinklage, whose expression was one of painfully repressed longing. Mr. Langdon's look made her feel . . . pretty.

Eventually she would have to face Mr. Dinklage as well as his mother, so for now she was content to enjoy silent camaraderie with Mr. Langdon.

When the dance was over, he took her hand and led her back to where the older ladies and chaperones were seated. He stared into her eyes and said softly, "I wish you well, Miss Grey."

"Thank you, Mr. Langdon. And I you."

He seemed to see someone over her shoulder, and his lips quirked upward in an ironic smile. He gave a quick nod to her and turned to leave.

"Miss Grey."

Julia turned to find Mr. Dinklage standing behind her. "Good evening, Mr. Dinklage."

"Good evening. I wonder if you would be so good as to allow me to introduce you to my mother."

"Of course." She placed her hand on his arm, and he led her to where his mother was sitting. Julia's dread increased as she drew nearer to Mrs. Dinklage, whose eyes were locked on her in a cold, disagreeable expression.

Mr. Dinklage must have been feeling the same thing Julia was, for his steps were halting and reluctant, and she wished he'd just get on with it.

"Mother, I'd like to introduce Miss Julia Grey. Miss Grey, this is my mother, Mrs. Mary Dinklage."

"How do you do?" Julia curtsied, but the woman still looked as though she'd bitten into a walnut shell.

"So this is Julia Grey. Who was your father, Miss Grey?" She spoke the name as if it were distasteful.

"Major William Grey, Mrs. Dinklage, of the eighth Infantry. My guardian, Mr. Robert Wilhern, is married to my aunt, my father's sister."

The old woman's top lip seemed to shrug but without exposing her teeth, as if her shoes were pinching her toes.

"My son says you play and sing very well."

Julia did not comment.

"Do you prefer my son, Miss Grey?"

Julia was shocked into speechlessness by the woman's question.

"Because my son has formed an attachment to you that I find . . . disadvantageous. My son shall inherit his family's ancient estate. The good name of Dinklage has survived centuries, Miss Grey. Who are the Greys? The Wilherns are a fine, old family, I'll grant you, but you have no fortune, no parentage, no—"

"Excuse me, ma'am, but if it is your wish to insult me, I would prefer you do it in private. At present I am not inclined to discuss my family with you. You will excuse me." Julia dropped a quick curtsy and walked away.

CHAPTER TWELVE

Julia's knees knocked against each other as she walked. Her hands shook so violently she hid them in her skirt.

Never had Julia spoken in such a way to anyone, especially someone so much older! She could barely see where she was going as she walked away from Mr. Dinklage and his indignant mother.

She suddenly felt a hand on her arm and turned to see Felicity Mayson by her side.

"Good for you, Julia." Felicity squeezed her arm.

"You heard? Did anyone else hear?"

"I don't think so. But, Julia, I fear you will never be allowed to marry Mr. Dinklage now."

What would Sarah Peck say? No doubt she would be upset that Julia had thrown away a chance to endear herself to Mr. Dinklage's mother.

"I'm not sure any man is worth having a mother-in-law like that."

Felicity pursed her lips in agreement as the two of them moved toward the refreshments table.

She didn't feel anything for Mr. Dinklage. Was she a fool? But she knew she had done the right thing. She was proud of herself for standing up to the woman, and Leorah would be proud of her too. Perhaps now Mr. Langdon would stop teasing her about Mr. Dinklage.

She didn't like hurting Mr. Dinklage, and it made her remember how Sarah had said it would be better to marry any available respectable man rather than become a governess. She had certainly destroyed the possibility of gaining Mrs. Dinklage's approval. If she didn't marry Mr. Dinklage, what other choice did she have, besides Mr. Edgerton? There were no other men offering for her hand. But then, perhaps Phoebe was nowhere near marriage either. If she could have a few more Seasons, Julia might meet another such Mr. Dinklage, but someone who would inspire her affection and regard, someone who was free to marry her.

"Why aren't you dancing?" Julia asked Felicity.

"No one asked me. Perhaps one of your admirers will ask me."

Julia frowned as she sipped her lemonade. "What admirers?"

Felicity used her fingers to tick them off. "Mr. Dinklage, Mr. Edgerton, Mr. Langdon—"

"Sh! Don't even say such a thing," Julia whispered. "He isn't interested in me. If he were, he'd dance with me twice instead of only once."

They both smirked.

"Here comes one of them." The smile disappeared from Felicity's face. "Mr. Edgerton."

Julia clenched her teeth. She would not stand up with the man. She didn't care if she had to be uncivil to him.

"Miss Mayson. Miss Grey." He nodded to each of them and then flashed his even white teeth at Julia.

"Mr. Edgerton." Felicity greeted him, but Julia remained silent. An astute man might understand the hint, but Mr. Edgerton turned to Julia.

"Miss Grey, will you do me the honor of dancing the next set with me?"

"I do not wish to dance at the moment. You will excuse me."

He stared at her, his small eyes narrowing slightly. "I hope you are not unwell, Miss Grey."

"I am well. I simply do not wish to dance." *I wish to talk to my friend Felicity and not to you.*

A flash of something unexpected, something like desperation mixed with longing, crossed his face. He turned to Felicity. "Will you do me the honor, Miss Mayson, of dancing with me?"

Hesitating, looking at Julia, Felicity agreed. When Mr. Edgerton turned, she gave Julia an apologetic look.

Julia smiled and nodded—and was left alone to contemplate her future.

Julia had received her first letter from Sarah Peck. She had described her new employers as "cold and contemptuous," her pupils as "naughty and spoiled," but the oldest son, she said, was "handsome and congenial."

Not too congenial, I hope.

Was that to be Julia's future? Spending her spare time exchanging letters with Sarah Peck about the dangers of employers' older sons becoming too familiar?

***

"Mr. Dinklage is gone." Phoebe closed the door behind her as she entered Julia's room, where Julia sat at her tiny desk in front of the window, writing to Sarah Peck.

"Gone? Gone where?" Julia put down her pen.

"To Derbyshire with his cousins. Maria Cotter says it was to get him away from you! I told her she was a liar and to keep her mouth shut." Phoebe pulled up a stool and sat down beside Julia. "Is it true?"

Julia sighed. "I'm afraid it is, in all probability."

"Why, Julia? You weren't in love with him, I'm sure."

"No, I wasn't in love with him."

"Was he in love with you?"

"He may have believed himself to be."

"Julia! Why didn't you tell me? Are you so afraid of gossiping that you won't even tell your secrets to *me*? Did he ask you to marry him?"

"No, Phoebe, he did not. His mother did not approve of me, it seems."

"The little coward. Afraid of his mother! It would have been such an advantageous marriage for you, Julia." She stared at the wallpaper, resting her cheek in her hand. "But I must say, I can't abide the thought of you married to him. He isn't handsome enough for you, and he's even losing his hair."

Julia frowned. "It hardly matters how much hair he loses, especially since I am not to marry him in any case."

"How can you be so dispassionate about it? Did you want to marry him?"

"I confess I had hoped to . . . for the space of five seconds. But I was never in love with him."

"He should be heartily ashamed of himself for liking you and then running away simply because his mother disapproved."

"He could hardly marry without her approval, Phoebe. Since his father died, his mother holds the power to disinherit him." Although secretly Julia thought he could have stood up to his mother and eventually changed her mind. The truth was, he hadn't wanted her enough to fight for her.

Perhaps it was ungracious of her to think so, and she would not admit these thoughts to Phoebe.

"Are you always so perfect, Julia? Do you never think of yourself above others? Do you not feel slighted by his ungentlemanly behavior?"

"It was my own fault. If anything, *I* have wronged *him*."

Phoebe raised her eyebrows and crossed her arms. "How?"

Julia shook her head, remembering again how she had deliberately tried to flirt with Mr. Dinklage because of what Sarah Peck had said.

"I should never have smiled so much at him and encouraged him to ask me to dance when I didn't have a strong attraction to him. It was wrong of me, and I'm afraid I've hurt him worse than he has hurt me."

"Only because you flirted with him? Julia, this is too much. How can you blame yourself? Everyone flirts. Flirting isn't a crime."

"But a young lady should never try to gain a man's affections by flirting when she feels no attachment to him. It is wrong. I would not take it lightly if a lady did that to my brother, for instance."

"But you don't have a brother, Julia."

"No, but if I did . . . The point is, a lady shouldn't go around breaking hearts and treating men's affections lightly."

Phoebe looked up to the ceiling and sighed dramatically. She stood and walked in a circle in the space between Julia's bed and dressing table. She continued her circular path while she talked. "You exasperate me, Julia. It's as if you were born good, born an old woman rather than a girl."

"That isn't a very flattering thing to say."

"Then admit that you enjoyed flirting with Mr. Dinklage."

"On the contrary, I felt guilty and afraid that someone would read my thoughts and call me a hypocrite." *Or at least a flirt who was only after the wealthiest husband, as Mr. Langdon most assuredly thought.* "After all the times I told you not to flirt or give attention to any man without great discretion . . . and yet there I was, flirting with a man I wasn't even sure I would accept should he ask me to marry him."

Phoebe laughed. "I guess you aren't perfect after all." She smirked, and Julia had a sudden urge to tweak her nose.

"No, Phoebe, I'm not perfect. But I suppose I can be thankful Mr. Dinklage's mother didn't approve of me, so that I wouldn't have to admit to him that I don't love him and don't wish to marry him."

Phoebe threw her arms around Julia. "I can't imagine any man not falling in love with you. I'm sure I love you as much and more than I could love any sister." She pressed her cheek against Julia's.

Julia's heart swelled with love for the impulsive girl. She was the one person in all the world who actually loved her.

Phoebe released her. "I must go. I am going riding with Maria Cotter and her brother in an hour."

"Even after you called her a liar?"

"Oh, she never minds what I say. Besides, she said she would look like a ninny going riding with only her brother."

Phoebe opened the door to find a servant in the hall, who curtsied to her and then handed Julia a letter.

"For you, miss."

"Good-bye, Julia." Phoebe skipped down the hall.

Julia closed the door and focused on her letter. It was from Sarah. Julia opened it and started to read.

> *My dear Julia,*
>
> *I am getting to know my new pupils and enjoying teaching them—mostly. The boys are not very scholarly or interested in books, but one of the daughters, Catherine, is a sweet-tempered girl who likes to please me. Her brothers, however, make her cry at least once a day. They can be so trying.*
>
> *Truly, I was very lonely in my first days here and missed you and Phoebe and the rest of the Wilhern household most keenly. However, my employer's son, Mr. William, has been very attentive to me. Can you believe we are the same exact age, born on the same day? He brings me little gifts—nothing that I shouldn't accept, lest you scold me, dear Julia—a flower from the garden or some printed papers. He is home from school and hopes to become a barrister in a year or two. I've never met anyone so humble and sweet. He doesn't mind that I am a governess. He seems to enjoy my company and seeks me out*

when I'm in the garden taking my walk in the mornings. I must confess, I look forward to our conversations more than anything, and I'm certain my life would be one long drudgery if not for Mr. William. Therefore, you mustn't scold me, Julia. I just cannot do without this innocent distraction, for it is completely innocent.

And now I am most anxious to hear how things stand between you and Mr. Dinklage. It is my greatest wish to receive a letter from you saying that you have been able to engage Mr. Dinklage's affections, and he yours, and you are to be married as soon as the banns have been read.

God bless you, Julia, for your friendship to me.

Yours devotedly,

Sarah Peck

"Oh, Sarah." That her friend could be so imprudent as to form an attachment to her employer's son. She must write immediately and put her friend on her guard.

But perhaps the man did have feelings for Sarah, and perhaps those feelings would translate into a proposal of marriage. It wasn't completely unheard of. Although Julia couldn't remember a single instance in which a gentleman's son had married a governess. All the stories she could remember had ended in the ruination of the governess's reputation. Story after story crossed her mind of a governess who had fallen for the charm of her employer's son—or some other gentleman—who had then taken advantage of her and left her heartbroken and ruined.

If Sarah thought being a governess was bad, how much worse off would she be once her character was defamed to the point that she would no longer be accepted in a respectable home?

But Julia was thinking too far ahead. Sarah surely wouldn't do anything so imprudent. If the man didn't have honorable intentions toward her, she would not fall for his trickeries. Sarah was a morally upright girl.

Still, her letter gave Julia enough alarm that she vowed to, as kindly and gently as she could, write a letter that would warn Sarah of the dangers of being too familiar with her employers' son. It was worth the risk of straining their friendship.

Julia turned back to the letter she had already started, dipped her quill in her ink pot, and prayed her words would be as well received as they were meant.

CHAPTER THIRTEEN

The Season was well underway. Phoebe had been despondent the past few days as Mr. Langdon had not been amongst the guests at the last two balls they'd attended. Had he returned to his regiment in the Peninsula?

The next Tuesday, Julia scanned the street for Mr. Langdon's familiar face as she and Miss Appleby, Felicity's spinster aunt, who was taking Felicity's place as her visiting companion, made their way down Bishopsgate Street to visit the Bartholdys. She wasn't *hoping* to see Mr. Langdon, precisely. She was only curious, for Phoebe's sake, and wanted to find out if he had quitted London or would be turning up at the next ball. But did this explain the way her heart fluttered when she saw a hat ahead that looked like Mr. Langdon's? The way she held her breath until she saw it wasn't him after all?

It didn't mean anything. Why would she *want* to see a man who had such a penchant for teasing her, especially about Mr. Dinklage? Certainly Mr. Langdon had learned by now that Mr. Dinklage had thrown her over because of his mother's disapproval, and that Mrs. Dinklage had sent him away for the rest of the Season to keep him safe from her.

Safe from me. How ludicrous. But if he married Julia and was cast off by his mother, she would settle the estate upon his younger brother, and he who had been destined for wealth would forever be poor—because of her.

She'd never truly wanted him. So why had she flirted with him?

"Believe me, Mr. Dinklage," Julia muttered under her breath, "you are safe."

"Did you say something, Julia?" Miss Appleby asked.

"No, I was only . . . no."

"You seem very preoccupied lately. Are you sure all is well?"

"Oh yes, very well, Miss Appleby. And you? How are your new spectacles working for you?"

"Very well. I can read much faster now."

Julia nodded, her mind going back to Mr. Dinklage and why she had flirted with him.

It was because she was afraid. She wanted security, respectability, and safety from poverty. So how could she blame him for wanting the same things, things only the retaining of his wealth could give him? No, she did not blame him.

"Oh, Mr. Langdon," Miss Appleby cried.

Julia drew in a quick breath as she looked up into Mr. Langdon's dark eyes.

"Miss Appleby. Miss Grey. Forgive me for startling you." Though Julia noted that the way the corners of his mouth quirked upward did not indicate remorse.

"How strange that we should meet you here again, Mr. Langdon. Do you have, er, business in this part of town?" Perhaps her question was impertinent, but Julia hoped he would tell what he did there.

"I do, Miss Grey." He smiled.

When it became clear that he wouldn't say anything more, she said, "But you will not tell us what that business is."

"I think it best that I not. Perhaps someday . . . perhaps."

She would *not* let her mind speculate on what he meant by that.

Ahead of them on the street, a commotion seemed to be moving their way. Julia had been warned by the coachman that an unruly mob could crush and maltreat her if she went down this street unescorted, but nothing of the sort had ever come close to happening. But as the noise increased, three men emerged into view, all of them holding on to each other, stumbling, and singing a bawdy drinking song in loud, slurred voices.

Mr. Langdon tightened his grip on her elbow. The three men were almost upon them, but because of the number of people surrounding them, there was nowhere to go to get out of their way. One and then another of the men focused his bloodshot eyes on Julia and Miss Appleby, the only well-dressed young ladies on the street, leering grins spreading over their faces. The man in the lead licked his lips.

Mr. Langdon stepped in front of Julia and Miss Appleby, who began making mewling sounds and muttering, "Oh dear, oh dear. Heaven help us."

"Well, look 'ere, me lads," one of the men said. "There be ladies in our midst." He peered around Mr. Langdon's shoulder at Julia.

"Move along, gents," Mr. Langdon said in a friendly voice. "My sisters and I need to pass."

Julia forgave him the lie and even silently blessed him for it, under the circumstances.

The inebriated man's saggy jowls drew up in a face-splitting grin. "A real gentleman it is, bless me soul. What say you, lads? Should we let 'im and 'is sisters pass?"

The strong smell of spirits invaded Julia's nostrils, and she covered her nose with her gloved hand.

"P'raps they that come this way should pay a toll to them what lives 'ere," the man's companion added, swaying precariously and lolling against the other man's shoulder.

"Move along, and step aside for the ladies." Mr. Langdon's voice sounded different, firm, with an edge of warning.

The supposed leader of the three inebriated men glanced to the left and right at his friends. "I s'pose this 'ere gentleman thinks 'e can best the three of us. Shall we show 'im what 'earty fellows we be?"

"Aye, aye!" they roared.

The man in the lead held up his fist and took a swing in their direction.

Mr. Langdon leaned away from the drunken man, who missed his mark entirely. The would-be assailant was thrown off balance by his exaggerated swing and began to stumble to one side. His openmouthed friends caught his arms to keep him from sprawling to the street.

The crowd backed away to avoid the potential brawl, and Mr. Langdon gracefully sidestepped the men and ushered Julia and Miss Appleby along in front of him.

Once they were past them, Mr. Langdon turned to tip his hat at the ragged accosters.

"Excuse us, gentlemen."

The three men gaped stupidly at them. Mr. Langdon, Julia, and Miss Appleby walked briskly. Julia glanced backward, but the men were moving along down the opposite way.

"Thank you, Mr. Langdon."

"Oh yes, you quite saved us, Mr. Langdon. I was so frightened, I nearly fainted. We are so obliged to you." Miss Appleby pressed a hand to her throat.

"Think nothing of it, ladies."

A warmth spread over Julia at the sound of his voice and the smile on his lips. Other men might have refused to speak to the drunken men and forced their way past them. Some might have yelled for the nearest constable and made an even bigger commotion. Others might have physically beaten the weaker, inebriated men and left them bleeding in the street. No one could have faulted these actions. But Mr. Langdon had left the ragged men their dignity—what little they could claim—while protecting her and Miss Appleby quite gallantly.

There was no look of haughty pride on his face, only a calm confidence.

But why was he again strolling through this part of town? Julia had heard it whispered that men sometimes came to the East Side of town for licentious activities. The question remained: What was he doing here?

There seemed only one way to find out; she would have to follow him.

"I do believe we have arrived at your destination, ladies. I shall return to escort you back to your coachman in half an hour."

"Oh no, that won't be neces—"

"I must insist, I'm afraid, after our little incident a moment ago. And so I shall return." He tipped his hat to Julia and then waited for her to ring the bell at the Bartholdys'. She did so and then smiled and nodded farewell to Mr. Langdon when the servant let her inside.

As soon as the servant closed the door, Julia impulsively whispered to Miss Appleby, "Please tell Monsieur and Madame that I shall return in a few minutes."

Before Miss Appleby could protest, Julia quickly let herself back out the door just in time to see Mr. Langdon turn the corner to the right. She followed after him, hurrying quietly to the corner, peeking around it, and then scurrying after him while keeping her distance.

What would she tell him if he caught her? She could tell him the Bartholdys sent her on an errand. But no, she couldn't tell him a blatant lie.

He walked to the next corner and turned right again. A brick building was straight ahead. It looked to be an old residence, its façade crumbling. A sign over the door read Children's Aid Mission. Mr. Langdon strode up to the door, opened it, and went inside.

Children's Aid Mission? What was Mr. Langdon doing at a charity mission for children? She could hardly imagine.

"Miss Julia!"

Julia spun around to see Henry Lee at her side. She pressed her hand against her chest to keep her pounding heart from running away as her face heated guiltily.

"Henry. You startled me."

"I was on my way to the mission. I come here every day."

"And Mr. Langdon? Does he come here every Tuesday?"

"Course. Mr. Langdon comes to play with us lads. He is a most excellent ball player. Have you come to play tea party with the girls?"

"I'm afraid not, Henry."

She glanced up to make sure Mr. Langdon wasn't watching her. She didn't see him anywhere, so she turned her attention back to the little boy. He had such large brown eyes. Even with one tooth missing in front, and his clothing worn and faded, he was an adorable child.

"Henry, why does Mr. Langdon come here to the mission? I don't quite understand . . ."

"He comes to play ball with us, as I said, miss." Henry looked quizzically at her, cocking his head to one side and then nodding like a wise old man, as if a new thought had come to him. "Now you say it, I do think Mr. Langdon and Mr. Wilson, the parson who runs the mission, are old chums. Mr. Langdon wants to help his friend, I s'pose, and he likes playing with us, so he comes here to the mission. He gives us a few coins sometimes too. He's a good bloke, Miss Julia."

Julia swallowed the lump that had formed in her throat and hurried to say, "Oh, I'm sure he likes playing with you very much, Henry. You are a fine lad, to be sure."

"Miss Grey."

Julia jumped and whirled around. Mr. Langdon stood just behind her, an accusatory half frown on his lips.

CHAPTER FOURTEEN

Though Mr. Langdon frowned, a glint of humor sparkled in his eye. A red-haired gentleman stood beside him.

"I was—" Julia tried to catch her breath. "I was talking with Henry, but I must be going back to the Bartholdys'—"

"Miss Grey, may I introduce my friend and the director of the Children's Aid Mission, Mr. John Wilson." Mr. Langdon spoke the words stiffly, as though suppressing his true thoughts.

Julia forced herself to be composed and nodded, meeting Mr. Wilson's clear blue eyes. "How do you do?"

Mr. Wilson bowed. "The pleasure is mine, Miss Grey." Amusement and surprise flickered over his boyish face. "I shall leave you two to converse." He looked down at Henry. "Shall we see what mischief the other children are getting into?"

Henry nodded and took Mr. Wilson's hand as they walked toward the redbrick building.

Julia felt her face tingling as she delayed meeting Mr. Langdon's gaze for as long as possible.

"You were spying on me." The surprise in his voice was unmistakable. "Miss Grey, this is most shocking. I had thought your purpose for coming to the East Side was to visit your dear music instructor, Mr. Bartol—"

"Mr. Langdon, you overstep your bounds with your insinuations." Julia drew herself up with as much fake dignity as she could muster.

"Come now, Miss Grey. You must admit to following me. What were you hoping to discover?" His look was piercing.

She felt herself blushing furiously. Of course, he had caught her, and she'd be lying if she denied it, but it was most ungentlemanly of him to say so. Should he not be flattered that she had followed him? She might have expected him to tease her and laugh at her silliness in following him. Instead, he looked at her as if she had truly done something wrong.

"Hoping to discover? Why, nothing. That is, you would not tell me your business in the East Side, and I did not know any other way of finding you out." She longed most fervently to disappear, or to at least wake up and find that she had been dreaming. Why had she let her curiosity get the better of her?

"Now that you have found me out, and now that you know where I go . . ."

"I shall not speak of it," Julia said quickly. "If that is your wish."

There was a spark of suspicion in his eye, reminding her of how he had snuck into her uncle's study. But even though his purpose here today was innocently visiting a mission to play with children, that certainly was not what he had been doing in her uncle's study. Was he involved in something nefarious? Was that why he looked at her with suspicion in his eyes now? Or did he have a good reason for sneaking into her uncle's study?

"Thank you, Miss Grey." He touched her hand, curving his fingers lightly around hers, and lifted it to his lips.

He was not like the other privileged gentlemen of the ton that she was acquainted with. She couldn't imagine any one of them playing with poor children, or going through her uncle's study, for that matter. "Will you tell me why?" she whispered.

"Why?"

"Why you come here to play with children?"

His gaze was intent as he seemed to be searching her face for something. "I come to see my friend, Mr. Wilson, and because the children enjoy seeing me. I rather like seeing them as well." Then he took hold of her hand again and placed it on his arm. "Let me escort you back to the Bartholdys'."

They walked in silence for a few moments before Mr. Langdon said, "I think you, Miss Grey, of all my acquaintances, might understand."

Of course *she* understood. She was an orphan. She was an object of pity at best, scorn at worst, almost as surely as these little neglected children whose lives he tried to brighten. Did he pity her the way he pitied these children? For some reason, the thought made heat rise to her cheeks again. But she was being silly. She had been educated and given a life of privilege and leisure. Her circumstance was blessed beyond anything these poor children of the East Side experienced. He probably was only referring to her friendship with little Henry.

When they arrived back at the Bartholdys' home, Mr. Langdon stopped Julia a few feet from the door. "Were you truly so curious to see where I was going?" He was smiling again in his teasing way.

Julia smiled too, pretending to make a joke of it. "I suppose I must have a bit of a craving for espionage. But you left me no choice but to spy upon you, since you were so stubbornly determined not to share your secret with me."

His brown eyes were warm and probing at the same time. "This is a new side of you, Miss Grey." His shoulders lifted as he took a deep breath. "A pact," he said, holding out his right hand to her, "never to divulge the other's secret."

Julia and Mr. Langdon shook hands like two gentlemen sealing a business agreement. So why then did the touch of his hand send warmth all the way up her arm and make her dwell on things that could never be?

***

Yet another ball. Perhaps it was only the rain that made Julia dread exiting the coach and entering the town house of their hosts for the evening, Mr. and Mrs. Fortescue, who were trying to get their two daughters married off. But she could avoid neither the ball nor the rain.

Phoebe sat across from her, adjusting her bonnet, while Aunt Wilhern sat in the corner, looking more alert than she had all day. Her aunt and cousin alighted, and Julia followed.

The Fortescues stood at the head of the receiving line, smiling as though they were anxious to please but not sure how to go about it. They had invited every eligible oldest son in London, as well as a few younger sons with good prospects for either the church or a military career. They'd only invited the Wilherns, Julia, and the other young ladies so as not to be talked of badly—and as bait for all the gentlemen.

Julia would, of course, be as pleasant and agreeable as she always was, no matter what she was thinking, as polite society dictated.

She glanced around the room and was pleased to see Felicity Mayson not far away. But a moment later, Mr. Edgerton turned from speaking to Felicity, and a smile spread across his face as he locked eyes with Julia.

Felicity turned back to Mr. Edgerton, no doubt to distract him so Julia could lose herself in the crowd. Julia quickly set out to do just that.

She worked her way through the press of people, exchanging polite greetings with acquaintances but continuing to move, as though she had an important destination. She took a moment to glance behind her, but she didn't see Mr. Edgerton.

When she turned around again, she bumped into someone. "Excuse me, I'm terribly—"

"Excuse me, Miss—" Mr. Dinklage stopped when he saw to whom he was speaking. He swallowed, his Adam's apple bobbing, and his cheeks went pale and then just as quickly turned red.

"Mr. Dinklage. Good evening. I trust you are well?"

He swallowed again before saying, "Miss Grey. I am well, I thank you. And you are well? And your family?"

"We are all well. How very kind of you to ask."

Mr. Dinklage blinked repeatedly and seemed unable to look her in the eye. "I must go . . . to get some refreshment . . . for my mother." He blushed even redder at the reference to his mother, and she believed he would have sunk beneath the floor if he could have.

"I bear you no ill will, Mr. Dinklage," Julia said softly. "Let us be friends. Shall we?"

Finally looking her in the eye in a most grateful way, he grasped her hand. "Thank you, Miss Grey. You are too good, I am sure." Tears seemed to well up in his eyes. "Better than I deserve. Please forgive me."

"There is nothing to forgive."

Julia gave a tug on her hand, hoping to escape the man before too many people noticed them talking so quietly or overheard them. Besides that, she didn't want to see him cry.

Finally, he let go of her hand.

"Excuse me," she said as she turned away from Mr. Dinklage and nearly bumped into—

"Mr. Langdon." She couldn't help smiling but then saw that he was eyeing her with raised brows.

"Miss Grey."

Would he tease her about Mr. Dinklage? He seemed about to but instead said, "Would you do me the honor of dancing the next set with me?"

Julia nodded but then immediately felt guilty at the pleasure his asking her to dance afforded her. She must not appear to enjoy his company so much. She tried to suppress her smile and behave as she would if she were dancing with any other gentleman present.

His hand was warm on her back, his other hand firm but gentle on hers as he pressed it. Her cousin Phoebe would be devastated to know that Julia thought about Mr. Langdon every day, even when she tried not to, and that on Tuesdays, Julia looked forward more to meeting him on the street than to actually calling on the Bartholdys.

Forgive me, God.

Julia took her place on the dance floor opposite her handsome partner, for he was especially well looking tonight with his dark coat and snow-white neckcloth against his sun-darkened skin and side whiskers as black as a chimney sweep's.

Something caught Julia's eye, and she glanced to her right. Aunt Wilhern sat with such a scowl on her face that Julia was assaulted with a stab of guilt.

The joy instantly drained from the dance. Did Aunt Wilhern think Julia and Mr. Langdon were being flirtatious? He certainly never wore that smile when he danced with Phoebe. What if her aunt and uncle believed Mr. Langdon was enamored of Julia? Would her uncle cast her out of the house? Even Phoebe wouldn't defend her when given a choice between Julia and Mr. Langdon.

Mr. Langdon danced masterfully, graceful for one so tall and broad shouldered. Julia watched his face but refused to smile back at him. She pictured him married to Phoebe, the two of them content together. If such an event took place, Julia would be practically his sister. In that event, she could speak freely with him, friend to friend, and not even her Aunt Wilhern could criticize or resent her then. That thought was not unpleasant.

But of course, the idea of his marrying Phoebe was not quite as far-fetched as it had once seemed. He did sometimes seem to show a bit of a preference for her cousin. Therefore, Julia would need to be extra careful how she conducted herself with the man. She couldn't control the way he looked at her, however, and the way he was looking at her could very well be the reason for her aunt's scowl.

As soon as the dance was over Julia would get well away from him. Her aunt couldn't possibly be angry with her for simply dancing with the man. He danced with many young ladies. It wasn't as if he had asked to dance with her a second time.

He gave her a questioning glance, and as they waited for their turn, he observed, "You don't seem to be enjoying the dance. You are not unwell, are you?"

"Oh no, I am well. That is, I am enjoying the exercise."

"But not the company?"

"Don't be silly." Julia gave him a small smile. "You are a very pleasant partner, Mr. Langdon, as you well know."

"Were you disturbed by seeing Mr. Dinklage? Forgive me if my question is impertinent."

Was that what he thought? "Mr. Dinklage is an acquaintance I am pleased to hear well of. As you know, he had hoped we would be more than mere acquaintances, but that is not to be, and it is just as well, as we would not have suited each other."

"Oh no?"

"No."

"He didn't seem as convinced of that as you."

"But that does not signify." Julia lifted her chin a notch. "All has ended as it should have."

This was somber subject matter, which was just as she could have hoped. She didn't want her aunt to see her laughing and smiling at Mr. Langdon. Let her see them both looking rather grim.

"But poor Mr. Dinklage. How will he ever recover sufficiently to love again?"

Julia coughed to cover up the laugh that threatened to escape. Something about his tone amused Julia in a most uncompassionate manner. *Oh dear.* The thought of Mr. Dinklage in a decline, unable to recover for love of her, was certainly nothing to laugh about. She felt a return of her guilt when she remembered the tears that had welled up in his eyes a few moments before.

"Mr. Langdon, you are being unkind."

"Am I? Forgive me for my insensitivity to poor Mr. Dinklage." He made a moue of mock remorse.

Julia had to force herself to look away. He was so naughty! How could she laugh? How could she not?

The dance ended, and Mr. Langdon escorted her toward the row of dowagers where her aunt sat. Phoebe accosted him with some question while Julia excused herself and moved away.

Felicity was coming toward her, her eyes fairly sparkling.

"Felicity, what is the news I see on your face?"

Taking hold of her arm, Felicity whispered, "Mr. Edgerton and I were just having a most interesting conversation—about you."

"Oh, Felicity, you know I cannot abide the man."

"But he had the most complimentary things to say about you, Julia. He said you were the loveliest lady of his acquaintance and that he only wished you would deign to speak to him. He praised your intelligence, your musical talent, and your gracefulness. Perhaps you should at least dance with him."

"Felicity," Julia leaned close, not wishing anyone to hear her words, "My uncle has put a great deal of pressure on me to marry Mr. Edgerton. But I do not wish to marry him."

"Because of his reputation for gaming? Perhaps that has been exaggerated."

Julia shook her head at her friend. Felicity was too kindhearted to believe evil about someone without indisputable proof.

"Even if that were so, there is still the matter of his drinking too much. Not only that, but there is something in his eyes that I do not like. You remember what happened at the other ball, where he followed me into that room and made me uncomfortable. I cannot marry him." Julia was careful to keep her voice down.

"Perhaps he did not intend to make you uncomfortable. But if you do not wish to marry him . . ." Felicity frowned and bit her lip. "Surely your uncle will understand and will not force you."

"It was almost frightening, the way he accused me of being ungrateful for not marrying the man. He is very set on the idea." Julia's heart was starting to pound just thinking about the terrible conversation.

Felicity shook her head and continued chewing on her lip. "Do you think Mr. Edgerton is so very bad? Perhaps you should at least dance with him."

"I would not have thought he could make you his ally so easily, Felicity. He must have sounded convincing, but I'm afraid I do not wish to be near the man. I cannot marry him, and I could never fall in love with him. You should believe me, for I know it is so."

"I am sure you are very sensible, Julia, but he spoke of you in the most glowing terms."

Suddenly, a young man Julia was not acquainted with came and asked Felicity for the next dance. She agreed and excused herself from Julia.

Julia was relieved to see Mr. Langdon escorting Phoebe to the dance. She only hoped Phoebe didn't get upset over him asking Julia to dance first.

Julia stood near her aunt in an out-of-the-way spot so she could observe the guests without being obvious. Her uncle was no doubt smoking and swapping stories with the other men in another room. Her aunt sat listening to two older women, looking thoroughly bored.

Aunt Wilhern suddenly turned and caught Julia's eye. "Julia, will you fetch me some lemonade?"

"Of course, Aunt." Julia hurried to obey her aunt's request, catching a glimpse of Phoebe's radiant face as she smiled up at Mr. Langdon.

Julia hurried to the side room where the refreshment table was set up and retrieved the lemonade. As she turned to take it to her aunt, she had to stop to prevent a collision with Mr. Edgerton.

"Miss Grey," he said in a most intimate-sounding voice. His smile was almost feline, like a cat staring at a mouse.

I am no mouse. Julia's spine stiffened. "Excuse me, but you are blocking my way."

"Forgive me, Miss Grey." Still he didn't move. "I have been hoping to speak with you."

"I do not have the time. I must take this lemonade to my aunt. Excuse me." Julia did her best to let her voice convey firmness while hiding the fear that rose inside.

Mr. Edgerton took hold of her arm. She couldn't jerk away or she would spill the cup of lemonade in her hand. He leaned even closer. "I will not let you go, unless you agree to meet me in the courtyard."

"I will not." Julia's voice shook. *How dare he!* Oh Lord, it was starting again. If he could convince her to meet him in the courtyard, he could possibly force her into a compromising situation so that she would be practically forced to marry him. Who could she turn to for help without making a scene and creating gossip?

"Unhand me this instant," she said as quietly as she could.

"Can't you see that I adore you? Your uncle has insisted you marry me. Will you defy him?"

"You are no gentleman!" She glanced around to see who might be watching them. No one seemed to pay them any attention. Indeed, few people were in the room besides the servant who had served her the lemonade, but she was sure the maidservant was listening to every word.

Mr. Edgerton only gripped her arm tighter. "You should be reasonable. Nothing good can come of your resistance."

"Mr. Edgerton, you will unhand me this moment, or I shall call my uncle to defend me."

He let out a chuckle. "Your uncle is nowhere near. Come with me." His voice was coaxing as he pulled on her arm, causing the lemonade in her cup to slosh, nearly spilling.

Julia had no choice; she would be forced to throw the lemonade in his face and cause a ruckus the entire party would hear of. But when she tried, his grip was too tight. She could do no more than slosh out a few drops onto the floor.

Her face burning and her breath coming in hollow gasps, Julia said, "I will never meet you, in the courtyard or anywhere else. You are a fiend, and if you do not let go—"

"Excuse me, Mr. Edgerton." Mr. Langdon strode quickly to her side. "But you are detaining my dance partner." Mr. Langdon gave Mr. Edgerton a withering look, his jaw twitching.

Mr. Edgerton let go of Julia's arm. Mr. Langdon took the cup of lemonade from her hand and calmly set it on the table. He held out his arm to her and led her away from the red-faced Mr. Edgerton.

They arrived on the dance floor just as the music started, and Julia blinked the traces of tears from her eyes to see Mr. Langdon's face. His brows were lowered and his jaw set in a rock-hard line. Then, as they began to engage in the steps of the dance, his expression softened. "Are you all right, Miss Grey?"

"Yes, I thank you." She mustn't think about how grateful she was to Mr. Langdon or she might cry. Instead, she concentrated on her anger and loathing for Mr. Edgerton.

A lady never showed emotion at a public gathering. How many times had she lectured Phoebe on this very matter? But Phoebe never had to worry about men like Mr. Edgerton trying to force her to meet him in the courtyard, or her father trying to force her to marry someone she could not love.

Oh dear Lord!

It suddenly hit her like a boulder against her chest—Mr. Langdon had already danced with her! She was dancing with him for the second time that night.

CHAPTER FIFTEEN

Julia's panic rose. Mr. Langdon never danced with anyone a second time. Everyone would see. Julia's aunt, Phoebe, and everyone else would say he was singling her out. The gossip would spread from one end of the party to the other by the end of the dance.

Julia glanced around her. Was she imagining it, or was everyone staring at them and whispering?

And she had forgotten about her aunt's lemonade. There Aunt Wilhern sat, scowling darker than anything Julia had seen before. Nearby, Phoebe watched them, a stricken look on her face.

Oh, this couldn't be happening. It must be a nightmare. She had dreamed this nightmarish moment before. It must be a dream.

But there was Mr. Langdon looking down at her with a strange expression on his face. She could feel the warmth of his fingers as he took her hand and guided her through the steps of the dance.

Should she run away? No, that would draw even more attention to the two of them. Was it possible that Mr. Langdon didn't realize what he had done? He had made her the object of all his admirers' jealousy, not to mention drawing speculation from every woman, young and old, in the room. But that would be nothing, was nothing, compared to what her cousin and aunt must be thinking, how hurt Phoebe must feel, hurt and betrayed.

Oh, the tears that would flow tonight. How the Wilherns would hate her.

"If I may ask," Mr. Langdon said quietly as they waited for their turn in the round, "what was Mr. Edgerton saying to you?"

Must she repeat that horrible man's words? "He was . . . he was being most ungentlemanly." She would remain dignified and only state the facts. She must pretend a coolness she didn't feel. "I have made it quite clear to Mr. Edgerton that I do not wish to accept his advances, but he actually laid a hand on me in a most ill-mannered way and insisted I go out to the courtyard with him. I am afraid I shall have to tell my uncle about his behavior."

Of course, she wasn't at all sure she would mention the incident to her uncle. She was almost as afraid of her uncle as she was of Mr. Edgerton, and Mr. Langdon might not even believe that she was entirely innocent in the matter. But for the moment, she must remember that she was in a public place, with a man her cousin was violently in love with. She must behave with cool decorum until she could finish this dance and plaster herself to Felicity's side for the rest of the ball.

"You should tell your uncle about Edgerton's behavior. I shall speak to him as well. And if he troubles you again, I wish you to tell me."

If they had been alone, or walking down the street toward the Bartholdys', she might have said, "You, Mr. Langdon?" in a teasing tone. But as she was, at the moment, trapped in a second dance with the much-desired Mr. Langdon, with Mrs. Wilhern and Phoebe looking at her as if she had just dashed Phoebe's only hope for love and happiness, she set her face and eyes straight ahead and said woodenly, "You are very kind."

During another lull in the dance, he asked, "Are you well, Miss Grey? You look pale."

Perhaps he still didn't realize. "Do you not know what everyone is whispering? I was too distracted at first to realize, but you already danced with me earlier, Mr. Langdon. You are dancing with me a second time."

She half expected him to look startled, to be shocked at his blunder. But instead, he smiled. "Are you worried about that? Does it bother you so much?" She feared he would laugh out loud.

"Well, I—" She couldn't very well say, "Phoebe will be heartbroken, and everyone will be gossiping that you intend to marry me!" Although it was the truth. "I didn't know . . . you were aware . . ."

"I suppose the gossips will be speculating on our upcoming nuptials. Forgive me if I've put you in an awkward position, Miss Grey." At least he finally realized the seriousness of what he had done.

At the end of the dance, Mr. Langdon thanked her, bowed to her with a tiny frown, and walked away. Was he angry with her? No, he probably regretted having danced with her a second time to get her away from Mr. Edgerton.

Julia nervously scanned the room for Phoebe. Her gaze flew to where Mrs. Wilhern had been sitting, but she was standing and walking away. Where was she going? Would Julia be left at the dance all alone, abandoned?

***

Nicholas had thought Miss Grey would be flattered that he was dancing with her a second time. She would realize how fond he was of her. He had half expected her to blush and look pleased. He *wanted* her to blush and look pleased.

Instead, she'd been horrified.

He could hardly blame her. It was rather thoughtless and indiscreet of him. He never danced with a lady more than once at a ball. It was not wise to do so, to create gossip and speculation, or false expectation in the lady. But her horror was quite extreme. Was there someone else whose attentions she wanted to claim? Or perhaps she was only afraid of upsetting her cousin Miss Wilhern.

He had been glad to save her from Edgerton, and asking her to dance was the first excuse he thought of for extricating her. If there was anything that excited his anger, it was a gentleman trying to take advantage of a lady.

Edgerton had become dissolute, given to gaming and dissipation since he left school. It made Nicholas's blood boil to see Edgerton holding Miss Grey's arm and speaking to her in that intimidating manner. It would have made him angry to see any gently bred girl treated that way, but Miss Grey . . .

He had wanted to tear Edgerton apart.

He admired the way Miss Grey cared about her old tutor, Monsieur Bartholdy, how devoted she was to her cousin, as well as the kindness she showed Henry. He even had a notion that she had begun to admire him as well. Perhaps he had been mistaken. Besides, as long as he was investigating her uncle, who seemed very likely to be involved in something nefarious, possibly even high treason, he should not think of Miss Grey as a possible marriage partner. It was foolish in the best of circumstances, since neither of them had any fortune.

He watched Miss Grey walk toward her friend, Miss Mayson. The two young ladies stood talking, their heads close together. What was she telling her? About her horror at Edgerton's overbearing conduct toward her? Or her fear of the gossipmongers who saw Nicholas dance with her a second time?

Just then, Edgerton caught his attention. The man was leaning against the wall, coolly staring at Miss Grey and Miss Mayson.

Nicholas strode over to Edgerton. "What do you think you were doing in there, treating a lady that way?"

Edgerton curled his lip in a sneer. "Do you mean Miss Grey? She is soon to be my wife. I may treat her any way I wish."

"What do you mean? Has she accepted your proposal of marriage?" Nicholas said.

"No, but she will. Her uncle, Wilhern, will persuade her to accept me."

"Why would her uncle do that?" Heat bubbled in the pit of his stomach. What kind of man forced his ward to marry someone she did not wish to? Oh, he knew it was done in order to secure a fortune and to improve a family's prospects, but why Edgerton? He did not have a large fortune, and his debts were enormous.

Edgerton feigned a shocked expression. "Do you not think it is the most advantageous match Miss Grey could make? For an orphan of no fortune? Her uncle simply wants what is best for her. And why do you want to know, Langdon? Do you have designs on her yourself?"

"You once told me your father would never sanction any bride who doesn't bring a substantial fortune. Why would your father allow you to marry Miss Grey?"

"Perhaps Wilhern is willing to give me a large sum if I marry her and save her from the terrible fate of becoming a governess."

That didn't seem likely, not after the way Miss Grey's aunt had spoken of her.

"Then why grab her and manhandle her the way you did just now?"

Edgerton opened his mouth and then closed it, glancing down as if examining the toe of his boot. "I don't know. I . . . I wanted to speak to her alone, but she refused to go to the courtyard with me. The truth is, Nicholas, I do love the girl." He looked up and grimaced. "I'm sorry if I upset her, truthfully. I have never been very good at wooing. I intend to marry her, but she doesn't quite fancy me yet."

Nicholas debated with himself what to say to Edgerton, whether to believe he was sincere. Finally he said, "She will never fancy you if you treat her in such a way." His stomach sank at the thought of poor Miss Grey trying to make herself love a man like Edgerton simply to please her uncle and avoid becoming a governess. "But if you ever treat her in that reprehensible way again . . . she is a friend of my sister's, and, as such, you are never to go near her again unless you are sober and ready to treat her like the lady that she is."

Edgerton looked askance at him. Finally, he used his elbow to push himself off the wall. "Very well, I shall take your advice. Any other tips you might have to make her want to marry me?"

Nicholas clenched his teeth. He didn't want to be giving Edgerton pointers on how to woo Miss Grey. He still wanted to punch him in the face. "No."

Miss Grey still stood talking with Miss Mayson. Had Nicholas harmed her situation with her family, with her aunt and uncle and cousin, by dancing with her twice in one evening? Though he hated Edgerton for pointing it out, Miss Grey probably was a bit desperate to avoid becoming a governess. But would she be desperate enough to marry Edgerton?

Either way, Nicholas could not help trying to see that she would get home safely. There was something almost sinister about the way her guardians, the Wilherns, treated her.

Nicholas had no desire to dance anymore that night, but while Miss Grey spoke with her friend, he turned and asked the first girl he saw, pasting a smile on his face and vowing that no one would say he favored Miss Grey or was paying her undue attention.

CHAPTER SIXTEEN

As Julia walked away from the dance floor, the crowd around her blurred. Thankfully, she noticed Felicity subtly waving her over, so she headed in the direction of her friend.

The hand she reached out to Felicity was shaking.

"Julia!" Felicity said in an excited whisper. "Mr. Langdon danced with you *twice*."

"Please don't speak of it," Julia whispered back. "Just imagine what Phoebe will say, what my aunt and uncle will think."

"Oh." Felicity's mouth hung open in realization. "I didn't think about that. But do you believe Mr. Langdon is in love with you?"

"No, no. At least, I hope not." *That's not entirely true.* "Phoebe would never forgive me. How could I betray her that way?"

"You wouldn't be betraying her, Julia. Mr. Langdon hasn't shown any undue interest in Phoebe, hasn't led her to think he had any intentions toward her. She will simply have to get over her infatuation with him and learn to be happy for you."

"Felicity, he hasn't exactly asked me to marry him! He only danced with me a second time. Now everyone will think—oh, what will I do if my uncle casts me out?"

"He wouldn't do that." Felicity squeezed her hand extra hard. "You are getting upset for nothing."

Her aunt and uncle loved Phoebe, but she wasn't at all sure they loved her. To them, she was only a poor relation.

A servant walked up to Julia and bowed. "I beg your pardon, Miss Grey."

"Yes?"

"Mr. Wilhern asked me to inform you that he and Mrs. Wilhern are waiting for you in the carriage."

Julia felt the blood rush from her cheeks. Her uncle must be furious.

"Julia?"

She glanced up at Felicity.

"Don't worry." A crease between Felicity's brows showed that even she was worried, perceiving the seriousness of her situation. "I will call on you tomorrow."

"Thank you." Julia tried to squeeze her friend's hand, but she seemed to have lost strength in her limbs. Still, she must walk, must put one foot in front of the other and obey her uncle and make her way to the carriage without crumpling to the floor. She must not create a disturbance. A well-brought-up girl never did so if she could help it. She must behave properly. After all, if she were going to have to make her way by becoming a governess, a spotless reputation would be essential to her survival.

***

As soon as the set was done, Nicholas thanked his partner and turned to see Miss Grey leaving the ballroom.

He followed her, though at a far enough distance as to not seem as though he were following her. He tried to look nonchalant as he went, barely glancing at her to make sure she was still in front of him. When she went to get her wrap, while no one was looking, he slipped outside.

The Wilherns' carriage was there, waiting. At least they were taking her home. He should probably go back inside. There was nothing else he could do. But something made him slip into the shadows by the front door, into a small alcove where there was just room enough for a small bench and a potted bush. Miss Grey emerged from the house only a few feet from him and proceeded down the front steps to the waiting carriage.

As she reached the door of the carriage, a footman stepped forward to open the door for her. He took her hand to help her in. For a moment, the footman's face was illuminated by the carriage's lantern. Nicholas gasped.

The Wilherns' footman was one of the men who had attacked him and stolen the diary.

***

Julia collected her wrap and ended up at the carriage, hardly knowing how she got there. A footman helped her into the equipage, and Julia sat in the only available seat, next to her uncle, facing her aunt and Phoebe, who was leaning on Mrs. Wilhern's shoulder.

Mrs. Wilhern was fanning Phoebe's puffy face with a handkerchief. Julia's cousin sniffed and shuddered, sniffed and shuddered, reminding Julia of a small child.

Of course Phoebe was upset. Mr. Langdon had singled Julia out, whether he'd meant to or not. He probably only did it because he could think of no other discreet way to save her from Mr. Edgerton, but they would all blame Julia for Phoebe's upset.

Her aunt's face was a cold mask. Julia sensed the anger and tension in her uncle's body, even though she didn't dare look at him. Her heart quaked within her, and she focused her eyes on the window of the carriage. How her aunt and uncle must hate her for upsetting their beloved daughter! Would they force Julia to leave immediately? Where would she go?

Perhaps they would allow her to explain. But as the carriage lurched and started slowly on its way, carting the four of them down the street, no one said a word.

What explanation could she offer? She could tell them that Mr. Edgerton had accosted her and Mr. Langdon had asked her to dance only to extricate her. But somehow, the thought of telling them of Mr. Edgerton's untoward behavior made her even more afraid. What if her aunt and uncle didn't care that she was frightened of Mr. Edgerton or that his behavior was indecent? They were already angry with her for not accepting his marriage proposal.

She had always tried to avoid any hint of impropriety. What good had it done her?

Julia took a deep breath to compose herself. She must conduct herself with ladylike dignity, now more than ever.

Her mind tormented her with imaginings of what her uncle would do or say when they arrived at the Wilherns' London town house. The silence seemed to roar at her, louder with each passing moment. When they were nearly there, Mr. Wilhern cleared his throat.

"Tell me plainly, Julia. Has Mr. Langdon made an offer of marriage to you?"

"No, of course not." Julia's voice sounded hoarse. She struggled to say, "I have no reason to believe he has any designs of that nature . . . for me."

She stopped to catch her breath, which had deserted her, as Phoebe looked accusingly at her from red-rimmed eyes.

Mrs. Wilhern humphed. She stroked her daughter's head the way she usually stroked her pet pug dog's.

Julia's stomach sank and twisted by turns. "Phoebe, you know—"

"Quiet," her uncle commanded gruffly. "We have arrived. Not a word in front of the servants."

Phoebe sniffed. Her father exited the carriage and then handed Phoebe out first. Mrs. Wilhern left next, and then Julia's uncle took her trembling hand.

"I will speak with you in my office," he growled in her ear.

Julia walked into the house and made her way to her uncle's office, feeling one minute as if her knees were made of wood and the next as if they had turned to jelly and would collapse beneath her.

She stood waiting for her uncle to enter. Was this how the French nobles had felt when they faced the guillotine, waiting and knowing they would be executed but not knowing how much they would feel it?

After what seemed an eternity, her uncle entered and closed the door behind him. He turned his back to her and said nothing.

"I am sorry, Uncle, for how it must have seemed, but I beg you to believe that there is no attachment between Mr. Langdon and myself. I am sure he has no intentions of marrying me. You must believe that I would never hurt Phoebe. She means everything to me." Julia had to stop, as her tears were choking off her voice.

Still, her uncle didn't turn around. She took out her handkerchief and tried to mop away the tears before he could see them.

"Julia," he said in a steady voice, clasping his hands behind his back. Silence reigned for a few more moments before he turned around to face her. "I know I don't need to remind you of where you would be if it weren't for my taking you in."

"No, sir, and I am most grateful to you and Aunt Wilhern. Most sincerely grateful, with all my heart." She spoke quickly, trying to get in the words of gratitude.

"And now I will tell you something else that you already know." His voice was cold, like a hollow drumbeat. "Phoebe wishes to marry Nicholas Langdon and says she will not be content until she does."

He seemed to be waiting for a response, so she answered, "Yes, sir."

"Do I need to ask you to ensure that you not only do nothing to prevent that from happening but that you do your best, as much as it is in your power, to make certain Mr. Langdon thinks well of Phoebe?"

"No, sir. I mean, of course I want him to think well of Phoebe."

"Good." He stared at her from cold black eyes. "Then we understand each other."

Julia bit her lip to keep it from trembling.

"You may go to your room, or if you think it best, you may go to Phoebe and assure her that even if Mr. Langdon were to ask you to marry him, you most definitely would not accept him. I still intend for you to accept Mr. Edgerton's proposal of marriage. And there will be dire consequences if you do anything to encourage Mr. Langdon's attentions."

"Yes, sir."

***

"But why did you dance with him a second time, Julia?" Phoebe sat propped against the pillows in her bed, a soggy handkerchief clutched in her fist. "You knew it would hurt me and that he would think you had designs on him. You should have refused." Phoebe turned her tear-streaked face away from Julia.

"You know I would never hurt you." *God, help me convince her.* "I simply didn't realize he had asked me to dance a second time. Probably he didn't realize it either." He probably *did* realize it, as he wasn't a man to do anything thoughtlessly. But Julia was desperate enough to tell Phoebe whatever would please her.

"I didn't remember that I had already danced with him."

Phoebe turned to give her a disbelieving, openmouthed look.

"I was trying to avoid that odious Mr. Edgerton."

"Julia, you shouldn't call him odious just because you do not wish to marry him." Phoebe gave her a self-righteous look.

"I hope I am not so ungracious to call him odious on *that* account. He has made untoward advances that I have not thought it proper to discuss."

"Julia, I'm not a child!" Phoebe sat up straighter, as if the subject interested her. "Did Mr. Langdon rescue you from him?" Her voice was an awed whisper.

"I wouldn't put it in those terms." This information seemed to placate her cousin, but Julia knew instinctively to downplay anything romantic Phoebe might make of the situation. "He simply was finding a reason to extricate me—quite literally—from Mr. Edgerton."

"Did Mr. Edgerton put his hands on you?" Phoebe's damp eyes were wide now.

"He had hold of my arm and wouldn't let go. He tried to convince me to go outside with him."

"What did Mr. Langdon do?"

"He told Mr. Edgerton that I was to dance the next dance with him, so Mr. Edgerton had no choice but to let go of me."

"That is just like Mr. Langdon, to save you like that."

It was, wasn't it? "I only hope he was the only person at the ball who noticed what Mr. Edgerton was doing."

"What was he doing, Julia? Did he have the audacity to ask you to . . . to go away with him?"

"He insisted I go with him to the courtyard outside. I refused, but he wouldn't let go of my arm."

"Perhaps he's so in love with you he became wild with wanting to convince you to marry him, Julia!"

"I don't think that is quite accurate." Julia sat down on the side of the bed, and it already felt as if things were back to normal between them. "Besides, everyone knows his family insists they will not sanction his marrying anyone but an heiress, because of his debts."

"Oh yes, but Father says he has done away with that problem."

"What do you mean?"

Phoebe shrugged her shoulders. "Father told me he is giving Mr. Edgerton a rather large sum to marry you, which will be enough to cover all his debts."

"But why would your father do that? Why does he particularly wish me to marry Mr. Edgerton?"

"It is rather strange." Phoebe's forehead wrinkled. "I had not thought Father intended to give you a dowry, but . . ." She shrugged again. "Wouldn't marrying Mr. Edgerton be better than becoming a governess? I know you do not particularly like him, but is he so terrible?"

Julia bit her lip, hard. How would Phoebe feel if she were in Julia's position and someone asked her the same thing?

She turned away before Phoebe should see the look of anger and resentment that must surely be on her face. Did Julia not deserve happiness or love? Was that what everyone was telling her?

Phoebe said quietly, "Father wishes you to marry Mr. Edgerton. He told me so himself. He believes Mr. Edgerton would make you a good husband, as he sincerely admires you and wants to save you from becoming a governess."

Julia kept her back turned as hot tears slipped from her eyes. She quickly wiped them away with her fingers and drew in deep breaths to chase the salt drops away.

"But I don't suppose you have to decide now." Phoebe sounded nonchalant. Just as Julia was gaining control and forcing back the dam of moisture, Phoebe said, "So you have no intentions toward Mr. Langdon?"

Julia turned to face her cousin. Phoebe was displaying her pouty look, as she tucked her chin to her chest and looked up at Julia.

"None whatever." Julia's voice sounded dull and flat.

"And you don't think he has any toward you?"

"Of course not. Anyway, he has no fortune, he is a sensible man, and he would never desire me over you." Julia tried to smile but felt the corners of her mouth trembling.

"Oh, Julia, I knew you could never want the man I love." Phoebe sprang forward and threw her arms around Julia.

Her embrace caused a gnawing in Julia's chest, and she barely returned the hug.

Julia pulled away. "Do something for me, Phoebe."

"Of course."

"Tell your father that you know there is nothing between Mr. Langdon and me, that you know I have no intentions of betraying you in any way, and that I will do anything I can to maneuver Mr. Langdon's affections in your direction."

"Oh, will you, Julia?"

"Of course." Julia ignored the painful knot in her chest.

If Julia could not have a love of her own, at least she could see Phoebe happy. And Mr. Langdon would be her cousin, practically her brother, if he married Phoebe.

CHAPTER SEVENTEEN

Julia took breakfast the next morning with her aunt and Phoebe. Her aunt said no more than was necessary, but Phoebe made a show of speaking with Julia as much as ever, no doubt to reassure Mrs. Wilhern that all was forgiven.

Forgiven. How could Julia help being a little resentful of her relatives for making her feel as if she had committed a sin by allowing herself to dance a second time at a ball with an eligible young man? How different things would be if Julia had a family who loved her as much as the Wilherns loved Phoebe.

But such thoughts would only make her bitter. It was perfectly right and fitting for parents to want the best for their daughter. They couldn't be expected to care as much for a niece as for their own child.

A manservant entered the room and presented the morning's post to Mrs. Wilhern. She shuffled through the letters and handed one to Phoebe and one to Julia.

Julia's was from Sarah Peck. She had wondered if her friend was angry with her after Julia had reported what she had said to Mrs. Dinklage, destroying any hope of a marriage between Julia and Mr.

Dinklage. She had also worried she had offended her friend by warning her against becoming so familiar with her employer's oldest son.

Julia placed the letter in her pocket, quickly drank her tea, and hurried upstairs to read it. Once in her room, she sat by the window and unfolded it.

> *Dear Julia,*
>
> *I am sorry I have been a bad correspondent of late. I must tell you that I hardly have any time of my own. When I am not teaching the older children, I am amusing the younger ones. I do not have a single friend in the household besides Mr. William, as the housekeeper is an irascible old complainer, and the other servants treat me as if I think I am better than they are. I confess, I do not crave their company either. And since William is away most of the time, I find myself wishing for a Julia to talk to, or a Phoebe, someone who neither looks down her nose at me, nor thinks me too high-minded—a companion to make my evenings less dreary.*
>
> *Such is the life of a governess, Julia. You probably think I blame you for what you said to Mrs. Dinklage. I was rather dismayed at the way things ended for you and Mr. Dinklage, but I wish I had been there to hear you give that insufferable woman a rightfully earned set down. She deserved it, I have no doubt, for you are such an even-tempered, docile person, Julia. You are everything that is gentle and good, and you deserve the best of men.*

Julia had to put the letter down for a moment and dry her eyes with her handkerchief. *Docile.* Yes, she had thought being docile and good and everything society dictated a young lady should be would gain her the love and favor of her aunt and uncle, and of a good man. She was realizing now that she quite possibly had got it all wrong.

She went on reading. At this point in the letter, the color of the ink was slightly different, the handwriting more hurried and messy.

Julia, since writing the above I have left the employ of the Smithermans. You will blame me, no doubt, for my weakness. In truth, I blame myself. I know I behaved foolishly. And now I fear I shall be ruined forever. Julia, I have run away with William to London, have given myself to him completely. And now I believe he has abandoned me, for he did not come back last evening, and I am alone, with very little money and nowhere to go.

I have no excuse. I believed myself in love with him. I was desolate, desperate to feel loved, to truly live and not be entombed in my own loneliness and the scorn of other people. I believed he might love me enough to marry me. I was too foolish for a woman of twenty-four years. I should have known better, did know better. You tried to warn me, and you were right. I should have listened to you. But, Julia, he offered me the chance to escape. The things he said to me . . . I believed he was sincere. I should have known better. Forgive me, Julia, for I don't think I can ever forgive myself.

Forgive me even for writing to you, but you are almost my only friend in the world. I shouldn't burden you with my sin, with my ruin, Julia, but if nothing else, this should serve as a lesson for you. Please don't ever do as I have done, for I have earned myself the scorn I so desperately wanted to escape. If I thought my situation bad before, it is utterly worse now. And please do not feel

you have to continue your correspondence with me. If you do not write to me, I shall understand.
    Yours sincerely,
    Sarah Peck

"Oh, Sarah!" Julia checked the return address. She didn't recognize the street name. It was probably in a part of town worse than where the Bartholdys lived. What must Sarah be feeling?

"Why didn't she listen to me?" Julia had warned her about becoming too familiar with the oldest son. Now he had ruined her and obviously didn't care. Fiendish man! Oh, what wouldn't she say to him if she were to encounter him on the street! To abandon a sweet, loving girl like Sarah! It was unpardonable.

The man was a villain, but he was not the first gentleman to seduce a governess or servant and then abandon her. There were countless such stories on the lips of the gossips at every ball or party. "Mr. Theodore Richards, oldest son of the Richards family in Shropshire, has run away with the family's governess, a Miss Little. Mrs. Richards is furious, for she has four younger children who are running wild, and she hasn't had a moment's peace since the trollop of a governess left."

Of course, if it had been a gentleman's daughter rather than a governess, it would have been treated in a much more serious manner. There would have been talk of him being made to marry the girl. The papers would have mentioned it discreetly, only giving the first letter of their names. But a governess . . . no gentleman would be expected to marry a governess, and the papers wouldn't even deem it worthy of mentioning.

The gentleman goes on his way as if nothing ever happened. He is full able to make a suitable match. But the governess's reputation is forever ruined.

Julia sat down at her writing desk at once and took out a sheet of paper, pen, and ink.

She began: *Sarah, please write to me and tell me where you are and how you fare. You know I will help you in any way I can! Please do write to me.*

What could Julia offer her? If only she could offer her a home! But it was impossible. Mr. and Mrs. Wilhern would never allow her in their house. If Julia had married Mr. Dinklage . . . it would have made it possible for her to help her friend. She would have at least been able to send her enough money to live somewhere decent.

Perhaps she *had* been selfish and thoughtless not to try to endear herself to his mother. Perhaps if she had, Mr. Dinklage would have been allowed to marry Julia, and Julia could have benefited not only Sarah in her dire situation but others as well. Perhaps she could have persuaded her husband to help Mr. Wilson in his mission to help the poor children of the East Side, like Henry and his sister, to help fund the Children's Aid Mission.

Julia clutched her chest, feeling as if she was choking. No, she couldn't think such thoughts. She couldn't go back and change things, nor was she certain she would if she could. She must focus on what to say to poor Sarah.

She wrote: *I have a little money, which I will gladly give to you. Perhaps you can advertise for a new position, somewhere in the country away from London and Sussex where no one knows of this and it can all be hushed up.*

Unless, of course, she was with child.

Julia quickly finished her letter and hurried to take it to the post herself. A short walk would soothe her nerves.

***

Instead of walking to the Children's Aid Mission on the East Side that Tuesday and running into Miss Grey again, Nicholas went to speak to McDowell at the War Office. They strategized how to catch Wilhern passing information to the French. They were nearly certain he was the traitor, since Nicholas had identified his footman as one of the men who had attacked him and stolen the diary.

"You must find a way to get back inside the Wilhern house," McDowell said. "Get back into his study and see if you can find anything to show us what they are plotting and how they are getting the information out of the country. You said Wilhern's daughter is in love with you. Flirt with her. Get another invitation to dinner."

Nicholas hesitated. "I don't like making the girl think I have an interest in her when I don't. It goes against my grain."

"You are a very honorable man, Nicholas, but there is too much at stake here. It appears someone is trying to find out Wellington's exact whereabouts so they can kill him and turn the tide of this war. We need to find out what they know and how they are getting their information. We need answers."

Nicholas had a strong aversion to leading a young lady to assume he felt more for her than he actually did. But it seemed insignificant when compared to the outcome of the war. After all, he had a greater duty to his country.

Which is how he ended up walking toward the Wilhern house, wondering how to show enough interest to get invited to their home without giving Phoebe the idea he might want to marry her. Especially since he actually preferred her cousin Miss Grey's company and conversation—much preferred.

He also had an idea that he might be able to find out more information from Miss Grey. At present, she might not be feeling terribly loyal to her uncle.

CHAPTER EIGHTEEN

Miss Appleby accompanied Julia on her usual Tuesday visit to the Bartholdys, which was cut short due to Monsieur Bartholdy feeling unwell. All the way down Bishopsgate Street, her darting eyes betrayed her, as she couldn't help searching the street ahead for Mr. Langdon. When she did not see him, she wasn't sure if she was relieved or disappointed.

She arrived back at the town house and found Phoebe and Mrs. Wilhern entertaining Leorah Langdon in the drawing room.

"Julia! How good to see you!" Leorah jumped from her seat and clasped her hand.

Over Leorah's shoulder, Julia caught a glimpse of her aunt's scowl. Her aunt normally didn't leave her room until after noon and therefore didn't know Julia went out every Tuesday to visit her old tutor. Would she ask her where she'd gone?

Julia quickly sat down, wishing she knew how to downplay Leorah's enthusiasm at seeing her. "It is a lovely day for a walk," Julia said to fill the silence.

"Oh?" Mrs. Wilhern said. "Where did you walk to, Julia?"

Julia fidgeted with her gloves. "I walked to—to call on friends."

Phoebe, who knew of her secret visits to the Bartholdys, interjected, "Julia is a great walker, and she and Miss Appleby love to visit friends together, especially in the mornings, don't you, Julia?"

"Oh, nothing out of the ordinary—"

"So you visited Felicity Mayson," Mrs. Wilhern said, the scowl never leaving her face. "How is her mother? I heard she was not feeling well."

"Oh, I didn't visit Felicity today, although you are right, Aunt. I do often visit her, and sometimes she accompanies me on visits." She picked at a loose string on her skirt. Julia felt her face turning red at her aunt's scrutiny. Finally, she decided it was better to voluntarily tell the truth. "Miss Appleby and I have been to visit Monsieur and Madame Bartholdy."

Mrs. Wilhern's upper lip curled. "Why in heaven's name? The Bartholdys, indeed."

Her scornful tone made Julia's spine stiffen.

"I hope you do not make it a habit of walking in such a neighborhood. It won't reflect well on your character if you are attacked or molested in such a street as theirs."

My character? Julia felt an argument rising inside her breast, but she quelled it and replied, "Yes, Aunt Wilhern." She hoped her aunt didn't ask if the coachman had driven her there. She didn't want to get him in trouble.

Phoebe began asking Leorah about her family, no doubt working the conversation around to her brother, and Julia sighed in relief at the change in topic. As soon as Leorah left, she hoped to run up to her room with the excuse of changing her clothes before her aunt asked her any more questions.

Phoebe was expressing a desire for Leorah to come for a visit to their country house in Warwickshire when the Season was over in a few weeks. As the Langdons' home was in Lincolnshire, Leorah said it was possible she could come for a short stay. Phoebe's entire face lighted up with excitement. Of course, Julia knew Phoebe was thinking of having her father invite Leorah's brother to come with her.

Phoebe and her single-minded pursuit of Lieutenant Nicholas Langdon.

When Leorah rose to take her leave a few minutes later, Julia regretted she had been too nervous to enjoy her visit. As Julia squeezed Leorah's fingers in farewell, her friend said, "Do come and call on me. We are but a short walk from here."

The invitation had been given to Julia and appeared not to include Phoebe. Of course, Leorah meant nothing uncivil, only that Julia was more her friend than Phoebe. Julia was quick to say, "Of course, Phoebe and I will come, very soon. You may depend upon it."

But before Leorah could make a move toward the door, Nicholas Langdon was announced. He entered the room.

Leorah eyed her brother with a mixture of surprise and suspicion. Phoebe's pale cheeks turned pink as she seemed to be standing on her toes, and Aunt Wilhern rallied to sit up straight.

Nicholas bowed and smiled at everyone around the room in turn. "My sister was not leaving, I hope."

"I was," Leorah admitted, "but I can stay a bit longer, and then you can escort me home."

They all sat down again and began to talk of the weather, the subject that always seemed safest when one is nervous. After a few moments, they spoke of politics, another rather safe topic amongst fellow Tories.

"Mr. Langdon," Mrs. Wilhern said, "won't you and your sister join us for dinner next Thursday evening?"

Mr. Langdon look pleased, almost relieved. He agreed to come, and he only stayed a few moments more before declaring that he would escort his sister home.

No sooner had Leorah and her brother gone, Phoebe watching them walk down the street from the sitting room window, than she began exclaiming to her mother how wonderful she was for inviting them to supper. Phoebe immediately added that it would be perfect if Leorah went back with them in the fall to Wilhern Manor. Surely her mother could persuade her father to have a hunting party and invite Mr. Langdon. He could have no objections.

"What luck that Julia was able to secure a friendship with Mr. Langdon's sister!"

Mrs. Wilhern turned a cool eye on Julia, as if she believed Julia had had other designs when she'd made friends with Leorah.

Julia excused herself as quickly as possible and hurried up to her room. One thing was certain: she could not call on the Bartholdys in the next few weeks. She only hoped her uncle didn't discover her visits and become angry with her.

Julia made her way up the stairs and to her room. She closed the door behind her and found a letter for her on the dressing table from Sarah Peck.

She snatched it up and tore it open.

Dear Julia,

I urge you not to try to see me. I wouldn't want your reputation to become tainted by association. I fear now that there is no hope for me to ever be thought respectable again, for I believe I am with child. I am ruined, and I have no one to blame but myself. I do not even blame William. He was only doing what men do. I was the foolish one, and I alone will bear the shame and reproach.

Oh, Julia, I pray you will never know the wretchedness I feel!

Julia, if you know anyone—and I can't imagine how you would—anyone who might help me, or if you've ever heard of a home for girls in my condition and situation, a place where I might be away from society and have my baby in safety, please write to me and tell me. Perhaps you might have read of some Christian place of that sort in the paper, a charity poor house where I might work out my stay. Nothing is beneath me now. I can sew or clean or do laundry. But I must get out of this place or I fear I shall end up sinking, giving in to despair and doing harm to myself.

It is selfish of me to even write these things to you, Julia, you who are so unsullied by the world and who always strive to be good and proper and follow all of society's rules. But I don't know where else to turn for help.

Pray write to me soon, even if you have no help to offer me. Your letters are my only companions.

Yours ever,

Sarah Peck

Julia sank into a chair, her knees shaking as she imagined herself in Sarah's situation. She must help her—there was no question about that—but how? She knew of no such place, a place of charity for girls who found themselves in Sarah Peck's position. If there were such a place, how would she find it? Who could she ask without raising suspicion and causing a scandal for which her aunt and uncle would never forgive her?

Suddenly, she saw the face of Mr. Langdon's friend, Mr. Wilson, with his friendly expression and kind eyes. Of course! His charity mission helped children, but might he not also know a place where someone in Sarah's situation could receive help? Surely he would. She determined to ask him as soon as she could. She only had to be careful to go at a time that would not excite Mrs. Wilhern's suspicions.

Perhaps Providence had led her to meet Mr. Wilson just at the right time. And now Providence would give her a way to help poor Sarah.

In the meantime, she took out pen and paper to write to Sarah and tell her she had every hope of finding just such a place for her, if only she could wait a few more days.

***

"Julia, come here."

Julia arrived home from posting her letter to Sarah to be greeted by her aunt's command.

Her heart fluttered. She laid aside her bonnet and entered the sitting room. "Yes, Aunt Wilhern?"

Her aunt sat in the corner of the settee, stroking her little gray-and-black dog while it rested in her lap, its eyes half closed.

"Julia, you have been calling on Monsieur Bartholdy in an unsavory part of town." She fixed Julia with a baleful stare. Mrs. Wilhern's eyes, which protruded slightly, struck Julia, not for the first time, as resembling her pug dog's.

Aunt Wilhern seemed to be waiting for Julia to speak, so she answered, "Yes, Aunt. Miss Appleby and I, and sometimes Felicity, call on Monsieur and Madame Bartholdy on occasion."

"I believe you call on them every Tuesday. Is this true, Julia?"

"Yes, Aunt Wilhern." The poor coachman must have been forced to disclose the truth. What would her uncle do to him? "It isn't Coleman's fault, Aunt. I asked him to take us, and he—"

"I won't tell Mr. Wilhern about any of this if you promise me not to visit there again."

"But why?"

Mrs. Wilhern frowned at the question. "I do not want a niece of mine, with only that half-addled spinster, Agnes Appleby, or her niece, Felicity Mayson, as a chaperone in that part of town, and neither would Mr. Wilhern."

"But, Aunt, please. I enjoy my visits with them, and I am perfectly safe, I assure you." God would take care of her, and her aunt need never know about the incident with the three drunken men Mr. Langdon had maneuvered them around.

"Julia, I am not accustomed to having my word questioned."

By Phoebe, yes. By me, no. "Forgive me. May I pay one more visit to the Bartholdys to say good-bye?"

"You can say good-bye in a letter." Her aunt's tone was firm. She had stopped stroking the pug, and her hand rested on its neck, clutching the skin in a way that made the dog's eyes open wider.

What would she tell the Bartholdys? How would she explain? And worse, how would she speak to Mr. Wilson at the children's mission about a place for Sarah, now that her aunt had ordered her never to go there again? Did she dare defy her aunt?

She certainly didn't want her uncle to know. She shuddered at the thought.

"One more thing before you go. Mr. Langdon and his sister, Leorah, are to dine with us next Thursday. Phoebe has her heart set on marrying Mr. Langdon, and I expect you to do anything in your power to secure your cousin's happiness."

"I have no intention of endangering Phoebe's happiness. Phoebe knows I would do anything for her."

"Good." Mrs. Wilhern closed her eyes so long, Julia wondered if she had nodded off. But she opened them again and said, "I give you leave to go."

Julia retreated to her room. *Haven't I done everything that was expected of me? Haven't I tried to obey every instruction?* She closed her door behind her.

All her careful striving to adhere to society's rules had built a foundation for her life that was shaky at best. At any moment, it would crumble beneath her.

CHAPTER NINETEEN

Three days later, Nicholas waited just down the street from the Wilherns' town house, hoping to see Miss Grey emerge from the house—alone for the short walk to fetch Miss Mayson or Miss Appleby for their morning constitutional—and come his way. He could not wait very long or he would look suspicious. Unfortunately, there were no shops nearby he might duck into and pretend to browse while he secretly watched her house.

He strode to a tree by the street and stood pretending to examine his sleeve. How long could he stand here without being noticed? Finally, he started down the street, passing the Wilherns' house. He kept his head facing straight ahead but watched for any movement at the house to his left.

He kept walking until he was well past the house. But before it was completely out of his sight, he turned and walked back that way. Just as he was nearly parallel to the Wilherns' town house again, he was rewarded with a feminine figure opening the door and walking down the three steps to the street. She wore a simple blue bonnet and a blue-and-white spencer. She turned to walk in his direction and stopped short. "Oh. Mr. Langdon."

He bowed, tipped his hat, and offered her his arm. "May I walk with you?"

"Why, yes, I was just going to call on my friends, Miss Felicity Mayson and Miss Appleby, for our morning walk."

"Ah yes." Nicholas didn't have a lot of time, as Miss Mayson's home was very near.

"Is something wrong, Mr. Langdon?"

"I was just thinking of something Mr. Edgerton told me yesterday."

Julia stiffened and her mouth opened in hesitation. "Mr. Edgerton? Was it something to worry you, Mr. Langdon?"

"It was only that he said he had asked your uncle's permission to marry you, and your uncle had said yes, but that you had not agreed to it." He waited a moment, but when she did not speak, he said, "I was concerned that you were—forgive me if I am being impertinent—that you were being coerced by your guardian."

He leaned forward slightly to catch a glimpse of her face underneath the rim of her bonnet. Her face was pale, and she quickly turned away.

"Miss Grey, you may confide in me. I promise you I am very discreet, and I may be able to help you, if you are in need of assistance in the situation." Though she must wonder how he could possibly help her.

They reached the street corner, and as no one was around, he stepped in front of her and faced her.

She was obviously distressed, though she was biting her lip trying to hide it. Would she open her thoughts to him? He needed her to tell him if she knew anything. His heart clenched in his chest. If only he could help her, not just extract information from her.

"I have noticed the way Mr. Edgerton singles you out," he said gently, "but I would not think your uncle would accept him for you, since Mr. Edgerton has no fortune except what he has gambled away."

"That is what I thought as well," she said. He had to lean down to hear her. "But my uncle believes Mr. Edgerton is coming into a large sum of money soon, and he wishes me to marry him."

But why push her so hard to marry Edgerton? Unless her uncle owed some sort of obligation to Edgerton. And the fact that Edgerton was supposedly coming into a large sum of money convinced him—Edgerton must be in on the spying scheme with Wilhern.

"Perhaps," she went on, her voice a bit shaky, "my uncle is trying to do what is advantageous for me. He is trying to keep me from being . . . from being a governess." Her lip trembled and she caught it between her teeth as she blinked rapidly.

Nicholas's chest ached at the painful sight of her trying to convince herself that her uncle was acting in her best interests, that he was pressuring her to marry Edgerton because he wanted what was best for her.

"Perhaps," he said, trying to say it as gently as possible, "there is some other explanation for your uncle's wishing you to marry Mr. Edgerton."

"What do you mean?"

He had to word this very carefully. "I do not wish to malign your uncle, but is there anything, anything at all, that you have witnessed lately, anything unusual in his behavior, that might signal you to believe that he will benefit in some way from your marriage to Mr. Edgerton?"

A thought seemed to dawn on Miss Grey; recognition spread across her face, and then she frowned. "Mr. Edgerton does seem to visit my uncle a lot at odd hours. I've seen him coming out of my uncle's study. Also, I overheard them once at a party talking about a diary, but I did not think—what? Is there something significant about a diary?"

"Does your uncle know you overheard him?"

"He did not see me." Her pretty blue eyes were wide and her lips parted. She looked frightened. He wished he could assure her she had nothing to worry about, that he would protect her.

Could he trust her? Should he tell her? Her help could be extremely valuable and could save thousands of British soldiers, including General Wellington, but it would also put her in danger.

Two young ladies and a gentleman were walking toward them. At least one private coach had already passed them on the street, so he held out his arm and she took it. They began walking as if they were out for a morning stroll. Not very many people were out this early, but he did not want to start any gossip mills churning.

When they had politely nodded to the oncoming ladies and gentleman and passed them, Julia asked quietly, "Mr. Langdon, is my uncle involved in something nefarious?" She glanced up at him, and there was a determined set to her jaw. The fearful look was gone.

They had made their way to Hyde Park. A path led them along a row of trees, with the grassy open area on their other side. He wished they could sit to have this conversation, so he could look into her eyes. But they were probably less conspicuous if they kept walking.

"Miss Grey, you may not realize it, but your uncle is in so much debt, he is on the verge of losing his estate, Wilhern Manor, in Warwickshire."

"I had noticed there seemed to be a lot of creditors calling on my uncle."

"That could be one of the reasons . . . it appears your uncle is involved, along with Mr. Edgerton, in a crime."

"What sort of crime?" She turned to look at him.

Surely he could trust her. Surely she would not betray him, with that sweet, innocent, slightly horrified look on her face. But was he being gullible? If she were trying to fool him, wouldn't she have just such a look on her face? Was she acting? Or was she really as good and kind and noble as she seemed?

He remembered her kindness to Henry and the way Miss Grey's aunt and uncle had treated her.

"If your uncle and Mr. Edgerton were involved in espionage, in the betrayal of their country and yours, would you help me?"

Her face went white as lamb's wool.

"If your uncle is helping France in a plot to kill General Wellington, will you join in our efforts to stop him? Will you choose your loyalty to crown and country, to England's sons fighting on foreign soil, over your loyalty to your uncle?"

She had stopped and was staring up at him, a little color already coming back into her cheeks.

"I can give you some time to think about it, but remember, many lives are at stake. Your country—"

"Yes. I will do it."

Her blue eyes stared into his, round and wide and luminous. Her jaw was firmly set, but her lips . . . her full, perfect lips were slightly parted in an expression that matched the vulnerability in her eyes—frightened yet determined. His heart skipped a beat, and he swallowed the lump in his throat.

He should *not* be thinking about kissing her at a moment like this.

***

Julia stared up at Mr. Langdon. She could barely breathe as she made the commitment to spy against her own uncle, the man who had taken her in and given her a home when she was only an orphan. Her uncle had provided her with an education and allowed her to grow up with his own daughter. But he was a traitor.

"You believe me, then?" Mr. Langdon gazed down at her with those brown eyes.

How could she not believe him? Besides, it all made sense, even why her uncle wanted her to marry Mr. Edgerton. "If I marry Mr. Edgerton, I cannot lawfully accuse him or be a witness against my husband, and therefore I would be unlikely to implicate my uncle either."

"That is true. You are very clever, Miss Grey." He gave her a look of admiration. But then he sobered. "Are you afraid of your uncle? Do you think him capable of . . . harming you?"

The memory of her uncle beating his horse rose up before her, followed by the look on his face when she told him she would not marry Mr. Edgerton. "I believe he is capable, yes. But I shall not let him know I suspect anything." She did her best to give Mr. Langdon a confident smile, but the corners of her mouth didn't quite succeed in obeying her.

What was she getting herself into?

"So as to lessen the risk of anyone discovering our alliance, we need a way for us to exchange messages without ever encountering each other or being seen in each other's company."

He walked over to an old gnarled oak tree beside the patch. Its trunk was enormous. Mr. Langdon glanced all around. It was still so early that the only people around were grooms exercising the horses, and only a few of those in this one corner of the park. He stepped up to the tree, so close to it that Julia could only see what he was showing her by stepping quite close to it herself.

He stuck his hand in a knothole in the trunk of the tree and pulled out a rock about half the size of his fist.

"Whenever you need to get a message to me, put it in this hole and cover it with this rock. I shall check it every morning and every evening. This should be safer than using servants to carry our messages for us or coming to each other's homes to deliver them."

Julia nodded. "I always take my morning walk before any of the family is awake."

"Perfect. Now let us go before anyone sees us."

She took his arm and they started back through the park's entrance, which was only a few steps away, and back onto the street.

"If you ever feel yourself to be in danger," he said, "do send me word or come to me."

"I shall be careful not to give my uncle cause to be suspicious of me, and in the meantime, I shall listen for any information I can discover."

"Yes, try to intercept any messages your uncle might receive, and see if you can eavesdrop when Mr. Edgerton comes to visit your uncle. But be careful."

Again, Mr. Langdon stopped and his intense eyes gazed down at her. The concern in them nearly stopped her heart. Did he truly care what happened to her? Did anyone care about her, orphan girl that she was? Phoebe cared, but . . . if she knew Julia was spying on her father, even Phoebe's love would grow cold. Julia could lose everything, the only things she had—her uncle's support, her cousin's love, and her own good standing in society—if her uncle were to be found guilty of treason.

But how could she not give Mr. Langdon her help? How could she not do all she could for her country? If many of her countrymen's lives depended on her, she would do whatever she had to do to save them. How could she not?

"You are not having second thoughts?" he asked as they continued walking down the street leading them back to her home as well as Felicity Mayson's.

"No. I am willing to do what I can."

There was a crease in his brow.

"What are you thinking?" Julia asked.

"This could be very dangerous for you. But if you find yourself in danger, you will tell me, will you not?"

"Of course." Julia imagined her uncle's fury if he should ever discover that she was plotting against him. Her heart skipped a beat.

"The messages you encounter will probably be in code." Nicholas Langdon spoke quickly. "They will look like words, but the words will not make sense. Whenever possible, copy down the letters exactly and then leave the original where you found it. If you need to leave me a direct message, or I you, the War Office will be known as 'our mutual friends.' The traitors will be spoken of as 'the relatives in Kent.'"

Julia imprinted this information in her mind.

"You understand?"

"Yes."

They made their way back to Grosvenor Square and passed right by her Uncle Wilhern's town house. As they began meeting up with other people on the street, Julia deliberately made her expression one of polite calm, even smiling at passersby. Mr. Langdon appeared perfectly calm himself as he stopped in front of Felicity Mayson's door.

"Good day, Miss Grey." He tipped his hat to her.

She nodded and knocked at her friend's home as she did nearly every morning.

Julia and this man shared a secret now, a dangerous secret. But even if the secret were not discovered, neither Julia's nor Phoebe's lives would ever be as they had hoped, because her uncle and guardian, and Phoebe's father, was a traitor to England.

CHAPTER TWENTY

It was Tuesday. Julia sat writing another letter to Sarah. The risk of her aunt's wrath was too great to try to sneak away to keep her regular visit to the Bartholdys. Sarah, in her last letter, had spoken of her fear as her small amount of money dwindled. Julia wrote to say she hoped and believed she would be able to find a safe place for her soon.

Once, during her first Season in society, Julia had hoped a certain gentleman was on the verge of proposing marriage to her. When she heard he had proposed to a widowed lady nine years his senior because of her fortune, Sarah had held Julia's hand and cried with her. Phoebe had gone to bed, but Sarah had sat up with her, assuring her she was too lovely and sensible a girl to be passed over for very long. She was sure Julia would find a worthy match and would then be glad that this unworthy gentleman had thrown her over for someone else.

Julia couldn't let someone as kind as Sarah down. She must try to sneak away tomorrow and make her way to the children's mission to speak with Mr. Wilson.

A light knock sounded at her door, and Julia looked over her shoulder to see Phoebe clutching a letter.

"Julia, did you know about this? Can it be true?" She stared at Julia with a look of astonishment.

"What? Can what be true?"

"It's about Sarah." Phoebe came toward her, holding out the letter.

Her heart in her throat, Julia took the letter from Phoebe and saw that it was addressed to her aunt. "Do you have Aunt Wilhern's permission to read her letter?"

"She gave it to me."

Julia's heart beat faster as she read aloud, "I am sorry to tell you— you probably have already heard it from someone else—but Robert Smitherman's son has run away with their governess, who is none other than Miss Peck, whom you employed until recently, if I am not mistaken."

Julia's stomach felt sick. She glanced at Phoebe, whose lips formed a thin line. "Keep reading."

Julia swallowed and then continued. "Miss Peck and their son, Mr. William Smitherman, went to London more than a fortnight ago. The governess took everything she owned without any explanation at all, and now poor Mrs. Smitherman is frantic to find a new governess. And as for the son, he still hasn't come home but has been persuaded to leave the girl and go back to Eton and resume his studies. His mother is very put out with him, but boys will have their mischief. I do hope, for the sake of your precious daughter, Phoebe, and Miss Grey, that no one will think she had been a bad influence on your own young women. Phoebe and Julia are such good girls, to be sure, most proper and agreeable, and should weather this little squall with no lasting damage. We shall hope no one else hears of it."

Julia skimmed the rest of the missive, which spoke no more of Sarah and what had become of her, as if she didn't matter. It was signed *Mrs. Brumley*, whom Julia remembered as the doughy wife of a country gentleman in Derbyshire.

The fact that Mrs. Brumley knew of these events only proved to Julia that the news of it had no doubt reached enough people to prevent Sarah from being able to find another respectable post, either now or in the future.

"Julia, did you know about this?" Phoebe crossed her arms and stared at Julia.

"I am afraid I did."

"Why did you not tell me? I am not a child, you know. I am only two years younger than you."

Her words made Julia recall something Sarah had once said several years ago. *Phoebe may be only two years younger, but you were born older than she will ever be.*

"Sarah didn't give me permission to share her situation." Julia handed the letter back to Phoebe. "I am sorry. It is not a happy event, in any case, and I would have spared you if I could."

"You needn't have *spared* me. Besides, Mother is incensed. She says neither of us is ever to see Sarah again or even correspond with her."

Julia lowered her voice to a whisper. "Did she have you tell me this?"

Phoebe nodded.

So Mrs. Wilhern was using Phoebe to tell her not to associate with Sarah. Did she think she could turn Phoebe against Julia too, to cause the two of them to disagree about Sarah? Would her aunt intercept Sarah's letters? Would she discard them before Julia could read them?

Julia would have to use another way to communicate with Sarah. Her heart pounded at the thought of her aunt and uncle finding out that she was defying them, that she was sending Sarah letters against their direct wishes.

But how could she turn her back on Sarah when she had no one else? Besides, she was already defying the Wilherns by agreeing to spy on her uncle.

Julia glanced over at her desk and saw the letter she had been writing to Sarah. Quickly, she pulled her blotter paper over it so that Phoebe wouldn't see. Would Phoebe betray her to Mrs. Wilhern? Probably not, but she didn't want to put her cousin in a position where she might be tempted to lie to her own mother.

"Julia?"

"Yes, Phoebe. This is a lesson for us both. We cannot be too careful. We must . . ." Julia recognized that she was on the verge of either saying things she didn't mean or saying what she really thought—the former would be hypocritical and the latter would be unwise. Phoebe looked aghast. "Julia, neither you nor I would ever do something like that! But Sarah . . . Sarah always did wish she were not a governess. You are not so poor as Sarah, and we are both sure to get eligible proposals, maybe this very Season. I shall marry Mr. Langdon, and you shall marry . . . I don't know who, but someone worthy, I am certain. Perhaps Mr. Edgerton." Phoebe looked at Julia out of the corner of her eye, rather slyly.

Had her father influenced Phoebe to try to persuade Julia to marry Mr. Edgerton? Julia stared at Phoebe. "You know I have no wish to marry Mr. Edgerton. And I will have but two hundred thirty pounds if I marry, and there is certainly no guarantee anyone will—"

Julia stopped herself and turned away, taking a deep breath and attempting to force down the anger that was creeping into her voice. "Perhaps everything will work out the way we both hope." She forced a small smile.

"I was just speaking to Father. You must know that Mr. Langdon is coming to dinner on Thursday." Phoebe became more animated as she spoke, her eyes growing rounder with each word. "Father shall ask him to come to Wilhern Manor when we go back to the country when the Season is over."

Julia suddenly remembered the other important matter she needed to turn her attention to. "Phoebe, where is your father now?"

"Father? I believe he was about to leave to go to his club." Her smile stretched across her face again. "I must go speak with Molly about how to arrange my hair for Thursday." She took a few steps toward the door and then turned and smiled at Julia. "Don't worry. Once Nicholas and I are married, one of his friends will do for you, Julia, I am sure of it!" Then Phoebe rushed out of the room.

Julia shook her head and turned her mind back to her more immediate concerns. She would wait a few more minutes until she was sure her uncle had left to go to his club.

Her mind went back to Sarah and her dilemma. Julia sat back down at her desk and stared at her letter. She must speak with Mr. Wilson at the Children's Aid Mission. Julia might have spoken to Nicholas Langdon about Sarah's situation, but it seemed an awkward subject to broach with him. Mr. Wilson, however, must be accustomed to seeing such problems, and therefore he was her best hope of finding a safe place for Sarah. She could write him a letter, but when he replied to her, what would her aunt think of Julia receiving a letter from a strange man? Mr. or Mrs. Wilhern might even open it and read it.

No, she must speak with him in person. Tomorrow she would take the risk.

Julia went into the hall and listened for her uncle's voice or footsteps. Not hearing either, she walked downstairs to the small room where her uncle kept his riding crop, walking stick, and the hat he wore when he rode his horse. All three were missing.

Julia went back up the stairs, hoping not to encounter anyone who might ask her what she was doing there.

She hurried back toward her uncle's study. Voices came from behind her, two of the servants talking, so Julia kept walking until she reached a sitting room. She went inside and then waited for the servants to pass.

Her heart was hammering in her throat as she stepped back out into the corridor and walked as soundlessly as possible to the door of her uncle's study. She tried the doorknob. It was locked.

What could she do now? Would the key that fit her own room also fit her uncle's study? Probably not. If he would take the time to lock his door, and if there were incriminating documents in his study, then he would take care that the lock and key were unique from others in the house.

Where did he keep the key?

His valet, Rogers, would probably have it on his person. But since Mr. Wilhern was away, might the valet leave his key ring in his room while taking his leisure elsewhere?

Julia hurried up the stairs to the top floor. She vaguely remembered someone saying that the male servants' rooms were at the west end, while the female servants slept at the east end. What would she say if someone saw her here? What excuse could she possibly give? She would say she was searching for Betsy, the upstairs maid, because she had misplaced something and thought Betsy might know where it was.

The corridor was bare and did not look like the rest of the house. The floor sagged in places, and the walls were dull and bare of wallpaper or paint. Which door could be Rogers's?

Three of the doors were the same distance apart, with a fourth and fifth closer together. Could the closer doors be single rooms instead of for multiple occupants?

Julia stepped forward, listening at the first door. Her heart was beating so hard it seemed to affect her hearing. Still, she didn't hear anything, so she tried the doorknob. It turned freely and opened, creaking slightly.

"Anyone there?" Julia said softly.

No one answered. She entered the room. It was very neat, with everything in its place. Surely this was Rogers's room, as he seemed like such an immaculate and meticulous person. And there, on the wall near the small, narrow bed, was a metal ring of keys.

She could hardly breathe, her chest was so tight, but she walked toward the ring, reached out, and took it carefully in her hand, trying not to rattle it too much. She held it tight to her breast and turned to hurry away. She stepped out into the corridor and closed the door behind her and then scurried toward the stairs.

Still no one was around as she made it safely to the first floor with the keys in her hand.

She reached the door and quickly tried the first key. It did not fit. Her hands shook as she tried the second one, the metal keys rattling against each other.

Someone was coming. Footsteps sounded from the back stairs.

Julia hid the keys in the folds of her skirt and turned to walk down the corridor. She met Betsy, who dropped a quick curtsy.

"Good morning, Betsy."

"Morning, miss." Betsy continued down the corridor.

Julia slipped into the sitting room, closing her eyes and pressing her hand against her chest where she could feel her frantic heartbeat. When she had caught her breath, she stepped out into the corridor and made her way back to the door. Not sure which keys she had already tried, she fumbled until she managed to insert one into the lock. It wouldn't turn. She tried another and another. Finally, after the fifth one, she was able to turn a key in the lock. It clicked and unlocked the door.

Julia pulled out the key, held the ring close to her, and entered the room, closing the door behind her.

Her knees were weak as she pressed her back against the door, peering around her in the semidarkness of the room. Even though it was morning, this room faced west and the windows therefore let in very little light. But Julia's eyes adapted quickly, and soon she was moving toward his desk.

Several papers lay stacked there. Julia looked at them, but mostly they were receipts for household items and lists of recent expenses. Nothing looked important.

She opened a drawer and began looking through it, lifting out ledgers and loose papers, but nothing resembled a secret message or code. She did her best to put things back the way they were. Finally, she remembered that desk drawers sometimes had false bottoms where one might conceal something thin, a few sheets of paper, for instance.

She opened another of her uncle's drawers and felt around the bottom of it. Suddenly, her finger touched a tiny knob, which she pressed, causing the bottom of the drawer to swing down. When it did, a paper fell out, folded into fourths.

Julia picked up the paper and unfolded it. She tried to read it, but it did not make sense. There were letters on the page, but they only formed nonsense.

Julia sat down and took a sheet of her uncle's paper. She picked up his quill pen and dipped it into the ink and began copying the sheet as quickly as possible. She forced her hand to steady and her mind to concentrate. After what seemed like a very long time but was probably only a few minutes, she finished.

Julia folded the original piece of paper and put it back in its hiding place in the drawer. She quickly folded the copy she had made into a very small square and held it in her palm. Too nervous to look anymore, she closed the drawer and stood up, grabbing the keys off the desk. She strode to the door and listened. Not hearing anything, she carefully opened the door.

She looked both ways in the corridor and then stepped out and closed it behind her. She still had to take the keys back to the valet's room. She started toward the stairs and then remembered she ought to relock the door.

Her heart pounded as she went back and started fumbling with the keys, making them jingle in the stillness of the empty hallway. Finally, she found the right key and locked the door and then hurried away, clutching the keys against her thigh to keep them quiet.

On the top floor, Julia moved quickly to Rogers's room, hung his keys where she had found them, and turned to leave. If anyone found her now, she'd never be able to explain what she was doing in her uncle's valet's sleeping quarters. She hurried to the door and stepped out, closing the door behind her.

She practically flew through the corridor and down the servants' stairs to her own room. She went inside and fell across her bed, still breathing hard, her hands trembling, and a dampness on her forehead and her back.

Spying was quite the most terrifying thing she had ever done.

CHAPTER TWENTY-ONE

Two days later, as dinner and the hour of Nicholas Langdon's arrival drew nearer, the excitement in the Wilhern household grew apace until Julia was certain she could feel it in the air. Phoebe had started getting herself ready hours earlier than she usually would. Her hair had been curled and pinned and poked and teased and supplemented by false locks, and it now lay piled high and highly adorned, with a few wisps dangling by her ears. These wisps flew wildly about as she rushed into Julia's room and slammed the door behind her.

"Julia, do you think this is my best dress?" Phoebe flung her arms out by her sides in a desperate gesture.

The pale mint green was very becoming to Phoebe's complexion. "It is a good color for you. You look lovely and glowing."

"Oh, but do you think I should wear my pink one with the green sash? Or maybe my white one with the seed pearls sewn into the bodice. I want to look perfect."

"Phoebe, you look very well indeed, believe me. I don't think you should give your dress another thought. Besides, men don't pay nearly as much attention to dresses as we ladies do." Although Mr. Langdon was more observant than other men.

"Julia, you always think I look well." Phoebe sighed in frustration.

Unable to think of anything to say that Phoebe would believe, Julia turned back to the mirror. Molly had promised to come and arrange Julia's hair after she finished with Mrs. Wilhern. But if Molly didn't arrive soon . . .

"Julia, do you think Mr. Langdon will think I'm pretty?"

Julia looked into Phoebe's eyes, which were at once hopeful and anxiety ridden. They were a blue-gray color with pale lashes framing them, and her hair was fit for a princess. Julia couldn't help but think Phoebe's good complexion and high spirits would cause everyone to overlook any trifling faults in her appearance. She was a loyal, sweet girl, and Julia truly wanted her to be happy.

But thinking of Phoebe marrying Nicholas Langdon made Julia's stomach churn.

"Phoebe, you look lovely, as I said before. Now stop doubting yourself."

"It isn't that easy." Phoebe's lip and chin trembled as tears brightened her eyes. "You don't feel things the way I do, Julia. You don't understand how difficult this is for me."

Two tears, one from each eye, slid down Phoebe's face as she turned to leave.

Julia tried to think of something to say, something that was both truthful and calming to Phoebe, but she could not.

***

The maid took so long to come that Julia began to arrange her hair herself. She gathered it up, one strand at a time, and pinned it in place.

Two days earlier, after searching her uncle's office, Julia had calmed herself, walked quickly to the park, and found the oak tree with the knothole. She stuffed the copy she had made of the coded message she found in her uncle's desk into the hole and covered it with the rock and then walked back home without encountering anyone she knew. Perhaps this spying would not be as difficult as she had thought.

"Oh, Miss Julia, forgive me." Molly rushed into the room and quickly took up a handful of pins. "Mrs. Wilhern kept me so late, even though I reminded her—twice—that you were waiting for me to see to your hair. But your hair is easy. I shall have it looking presentable in no time, but I am afraid you will be late."

"No matter, Molly." It was better this way. Julia would not be there when Nicholas Langdon and his sister, Leorah, arrived and therefore would miss any awkwardness—and that stab of embarrassment she always felt for Phoebe when she greeted the object of all her hopes, Mr. Langdon.

Julia pictured how he would look, with his frock coat and top hat and walking stick, as he approached their door. His dark hair would be draped just so across his forehead, his snowy white neckcloth tied according to the latest fashion, and his manner and expression everything a gentleman's should be.

Why did he have to be so perfect?

Even if he wore a tweed coat and scuffed boots and no neckcloth at all, he'd still have that breathtaking smile, those warm brown eyes.

Oh dear. She was over-romanticizing the man, just like Phoebe. After all, he was putting her in danger, asking her to risk everything to help him spy on her uncle. A gentleman never endangered a lady. Did he think less of her than Phoebe? Is that why he had asked her to spy on Mr. Wilhern instead of asking Phoebe? No, logically Julia was the better choice, as she was only his niece, not his daughter. Besides, she couldn't imagine Phoebe being able to set aside her emotions long enough to see that England's future was more important than her own. But that was understandable. Difficult enough to spy on your own uncle and guardian but infinitely more painful to spy on your own father.

Molly yanked one last strand of hair into place. She thrust in the last pin, poking Julia's scalp.

"Ouch!"

"Forgive me, Miss Julia." Molly pulled out the offending pin and repinned it. "Do you need help with anything else? I promised Sally I would help her in the kitchen."

"You may go, Molly. Thank you."

There was nothing left to do except go down and join the dinner party. Julia took a deep breath, clasping and unclasping her hands. "God, help me not to pay too much attention to Mr. Langdon, and for love and mercy, please let him not pay too much attention to me."

By the time Julia entered the drawing room, Andrews, the butler, was announcing dinner. Julia waited for her escort into the dining room as the guests were paired two by two. An older Member of Parliament was there, along with Nicholas Langdon and Leorah. Phoebe, of course, was escorted by Mr. Langdon.

Julia's cheeks heated as Mr. Edgerton approached her. Of course. She should have known her uncle and aunt would invite him to be Julia's dinner partner.

"Miss Grey." He held out his arm to her. "You look very lovely tonight."

She took his arm and allowed him to lead her to her place.

The meal seemed to last forever. She sat beside Leorah, who divided her attention between Julia and Phoebe. Mr. Edgerton sat on Julia's other side. He was very polite and spoke to her in a more mannerly way than he had in the past. Perhaps he was actually trying to woo her instead of relying solely on her uncle's domineering influence.

Phoebe was her usual vivacious self. Mr. Langdon seemed to listen to most of her chatter, and Leorah was frequently drawn into Phoebe's conversation with Mr. Langdon as well. Julia made polite but very formal and reserved replies to Mr. Edgerton's attempts at conversation.

Halfway through the courses, Julia glanced up, and her gaze was captured by Nicholas Langdon's keen eyes, compelling her to look back.

Just beyond him, at the head of the table, Julia noticed someone watching their exchange—her uncle.

Julia quickly looked down at her place setting and lifted her fork to her mouth with a dainty bite of goose liver. She chewed slowly, staring down at her plate. The goose liver felt like dirt and ashes in her mouth. She swallowed, forcing it down her throat, and then reached for her glass to stop herself from choking.

Had Mr. Langdon found her note? He said he would check the oak-tree hiding place every morning and evening. She only wished he could have told her he found it and what significance it was.

When the ladies withdrew to the drawing room, Phoebe focused her attention on Leorah, talking to her of all the things they might do when she and her brother came to Wilhern Manor at the end of the London Season.

Finally, the men joined them in the drawing room, and Julia purposely avoided making eye contact with Mr. Langdon. Mr. Edgerton sat near her. She smelled the strong drink on him, but she also smelled the mint he had chewed to try to cover it up, and he did not seem as inebriated as he had the last time he had dined with them.

Phoebe turned and scanned the faces of everyone in the room. She had that gleam in her eye as she asked, "Does anyone object to having some music and dancing?"

There were hardly enough people for dancing. Their only guests were Mr. Langdon, Miss Langdon, Mr. Edgerton, and Mr. Waterhouse, the Member of Parliament. But Mr. Waterhouse suddenly stood and said, "I shall play so that the young people can dance."

"Oh, Mr. Waterhouse, you know how to play? How very kind of you," said Phoebe.

He made his way to the pianoforte and began to play a lively tune.

Mr. Langdon might have known that Phoebe meant to dance with him. That must be why he asked her to dance right away. A tiny pang stabbed Julia's chest as she illogically wished he had asked her instead.

Now she'd be forced to dance with Mr. Edgerton—although if she was honest, that was not the reason for the pang. At least she could pass him on to Leorah after the first dance.

When Mr. Edgerton asked, "May I have this dance?" Julia did not bother to argue. But she managed to avoid Mr. Edgerton's touch until the dance started. He clasped her hand in his, which somehow felt warm and moist, even through their gloves.

Mr. Langdon held Phoebe's hand lightly, a gentlemanly distance between his body and hers.

As they moved around the room to the music, Julia tried not to show her dislike of Mr. Edgerton. When it was over, Julia said, "Do ask Miss Langdon to dance. She is sitting all alone."

Julia quickly sat down. Happily, Mr. Langdon broke his own rule by standing up again with Phoebe, while Mr. Edgerton danced with Leorah. Now Phoebe could not say that the only person Nicholas Langdon had danced with more than once in one evening was Julia.

For the next dance, Mr. Edgerton asked Julia again, and Mr. Langdon continued to dance with Phoebe, who looked as happy and simpering as Julia had ever seen her. There was no doubt she was enjoying herself and that she felt the significance of Mr. Langdon's attentions toward her.

Finally, when that dance was over, Mr. Langdon excused himself from Phoebe as Mr. Waterhouse began playing yet another dance tune. He came toward Julia and Mr. Edgerton.

"Pardon me, but I should like to dance this one with Miss Grey, if she is willing."

Julia was almost afraid to look him in the eye, afraid everyone could see their secret in the way they looked at each other.

But when they faced each other on the floor as the dance was starting, he said in a low voice, "I took your message to our mutual friends. They were very pleased."

"It was helpful to them?"

"Yes, indeed."

They started to move through the dance and were no longer able to speak. Julia forced herself to behave exactly as she had with Mr. Edgerton. She kept her expression bland and did not meet his eyes any more than was necessary, but she could feel his gaze on her quite often.

When that song was done, her uncle said to Phoebe, "That is enough dancing. You will wear out our guest, Mr. Waterhouse."

Phoebe said, "Julia can play for us. You don't mind, do you, Julia?"

So Julia spent the rest of the night playing, while Mr. Langdon danced the rest of the evening with Phoebe, and Mr. Edgerton danced with Leorah. Mr. Waterhouse conversed with his host, Mr. Wilhern.

When their guests were finally leaving, Mr. Langdon said his farewell to Julia. "Thank you for playing so beautifully for us." He squeezed her hand as his brown eyes delved into hers. "Good evening, Miss Grey."

"Good evening, Mr. Langdon."

But Phoebe grabbed Nicholas Langdon's arm and drowned out Julia's farewell as she exclaimed, "Mr. Langdon, do not forget that my father has invited you and Miss Langdon to sit with us in our box at the theatre in three nights. You will be there, will you not?"

Phoebe's voice trailed off as she walked with him to the door.

Of course, she supposed Mr. Langdon was only paying attention to Phoebe to make sure her father continued to invite him to his home. She should *not* feel attacked by jealous thoughts of whether Nicholas Langdon actually preferred her to her cousin.

***

The following day, Julia hoped Mrs. Wilhern would sleep until midmorning and not make an appearance until the afternoon. Mr. Wilhern had left early on a trip to the country and wasn't expected back for a few days.

Julia made ready to go to the Children's Aid Mission to speak with Mr. Wilson. With the aid of Providence, neither her aunt nor her uncle, nor even Phoebe, would ever find out. She would leave early, walk down the street and fetch Felicity, take a hackney coach, and be back before anyone knew she was gone.

Her heart beat hard against her chest as she thought about what her aunt and uncle would do if they knew. When she and Felicity had ventured far enough away from her home, she approached a hackney coach and driver and asked him to take her to Bishopsgate Street in London's East Side.

The driver held the door for them as they climbed inside, and then he closed them in.

"Why are we taking a hackney coach, Julia?" Felicity's eyes were wide as they sat inside the strange coach.

"Because I'm not supposed to be going to the East Side."

Felicity stared hard at her in the dim light of the closed vehicle.

"Aunt discovered that I had been going every Tuesday to visit the Bartholdys, and she forbid me to go again. She said it was not a respectable place for her niece to go. But I am not going to the Bartholdys'. I'm going to the Children's Aid Mission to speak to their director about a place for Sarah. You do not mind going with me, do you?"

"Of course not. My parents are not as fastidious as your aunt."

She only hoped Mr. Wilson would be in and she could speak with him right away. She shouldn't even run across Mr. Langdon, since it was an hour earlier than her usual Tuesday run-ins with him. She should be able to talk with Mr. Wilson and depart again in a matter of minutes.

The hired coach smelled of stale smoke and body odor. But dwelling on the possibility of a way to help Sarah made it bearable.

"You are such a good friend to come with me," she said to Felicity, who squeezed her hand.

The small closed carriage came to a stop. Julia didn't wait for the driver but opened the door herself and climbed out, just as he was stepping down from his driver's perch. They were only a hundred feet from the mission.

"Shall I come back for you, miss?" The driver tipped the brim of his hat up. Then he eyed Julia up and down.

"If you could wait for me I'll only be a few—"

"No, miss." He shook his head.

Julia handed him his fare for the ride there. "Could you come back in ten minutes?"

"I'll be back in half an hour." He nodded as if this was the time she had requested.

Julia frowned, but the man was already hopping nimbly onto his seat and setting the horses in motion again.

They walked briskly toward the narrow alley where she knew she would find the Children's Aid Mission's redbrick building. She stepped up to the door and knocked.

A girl of about twelve opened the door. She was wearing an apron and holding a bucket in one hand. "May I help you, miss?"

"Yes, thank you. I am looking for Mr. Wilson. Is he in?"

"Not at the moment, miss."

Julia's heart sank. What was she to do now? "Is there someone else I might speak with, someone in charge of the mission?"

"You mean Mr. Wilson. There's no one else in charge."

"Do you know when he might return?"

"No, miss. He didn't tell me." Her eyes suddenly brightened. "Perhaps you might speak with Mr. Langdon."

"Good morning, Miss Grey. Miss Mayson."

Julia spun around. She pressed her hand to her chest in surprise. "Good morning. I wasn't expecting to see you."

She was standing so close to him she could see the thickness of his black eyelashes, the warm brown of his eyes, his perfect features, and his squared chin. There was a strange intimacy between them, as if they knew each other's thoughts.

Was it her imagination or was he leaning toward her? His smile was truly heart-stopping as he focused solely on her. It was almost like looking into the sun—blinding and overwhelming.

Then his eyes clouded a bit as he asked, "May I be of assistance?"

"I came to speak with Mr. Wilson, but apparently he isn't in."

"Is it a matter you could discuss with me?"

"Oh no." Julia had no wish to explain Sarah Peck's situation to Mr. Langdon. "I am sorry, but I had a question that only Mr. Wilson might be able to answer."

"I see."

But it was clear that he did not see. After all, what business could she possibly have with his friend, the poor clergyman in charge of this charity mission? Felicity stood beside her, chewing her lip.

"Please forgive me, but . . ." Julia fought to think how to explain. "I wanted to ask Mr. Wilson about a way to help a friend."

He gestured toward the door. "Won't you come inside?"

Julia glanced at the open doorway. The young girl had disappeared. "No, we can't stay."

"Can I walk you to the Bartholdys'?"

"We're not going there today."

He fixed her with a penetrating gaze.

"Our hired coach won't be coming for us for almost half an hour," Felicity reminded Julia.

Julia winced inwardly at the confused look on Nicholas Langdon's face. But if she could trust him with her life, perhaps she should trust him with Sarah's secret.

CHAPTER TWENTY-TWO

Nicholas couldn't help staring at her. What strange business was this? Miss Grey was his contact with the Wilherns, risking her life to spy on her own uncle, though there could hardly be any benefit in it for herself. And now she was here, wanting to speak to John Wilson, a man she hardly knew, on behalf of a friend. What could she want with Wilson that she would not want to tell him about?

"Shall we take a walk, then, while you wait for your coach?"

Miss Grey took one of his arms and Miss Mayson took the other. As they walked along the alley toward the wider, cleaner Bishopsgate Street, she suddenly stopped and faced him.

"I have a request to make of you, Mr. Langdon."

The back of his neck prickled as he saw desperation in her eyes. She blinked and it was gone.

"You may ask anything of me." The polite words were what any gentleman might say to a lady in such a situation, an almost rote response. But in this case, with this particular lady, he was afraid he meant them.

"Please don't tell anyone I was here today. It is of the utmost importance that my visit be kept strictly secret."

"Of course. We both know the importance of keeping secrets."

She nodded and looked away, as though suddenly remembering. "Yes. Yes, that is true."

They resumed walking and Nicholas noted the simplicity of her hair, which was thick and looked soft and silky enough to line a nest with. Looking at her profile, he could see her lashes were exquisitely long. And she had the most perfect lips—he could hardly help noticing. Best of all, she had a certain innocent sweetness in her expression, along with a determined strength he had failed to discern until recently.

"Why don't you tell me what you needed to speak to Wilson about? He is a good friend. I can ask him your question and tell you his answer later today."

"I suppose that would be all right." She bit her bottom lip. "I suppose I may tell you, if you promise not to tell another soul."

"I most solemnly promise not to tell another soul. Besides John Wilson." Curiosity was eating him up, didn't she know? He gave her what he hoped was his most sincere expression.

She seemed to study his face, and gradually, she softened and didn't look quite so worried.

"Excuse me, Julia, Mr. Langdon." Miss Mayson moved away from them. "I want to go in this shop to look for a special sachet for my mother's birthday. I shall return in a few moments."

When Miss Mayson had gone, they stood outside the shop, and Miss Grey took a deep breath and said, "I came to ask Mr. Wilson if he knows of a safe place, perhaps some type of charity mission, where a woman might live . . . if she had ruined her reputation and had nowhere else to go." She spoke so softly, Nicholas found himself leaning down to catch her words as they walked along. But then, when what she had said sank into his consciousness, he tried not to look as surprised as he felt.

"This young woman needs a place to go immediately, or as soon as possible."

She couldn't mean herself. Could she? "Has something happened with your uncle? Is he trying to ruin you?"

"Oh no, it isn't for me." Miss Grey pressed her hand against her chest and shook her head slightly. She looked him in the eye. "My friend is a kind and loving person, but she made a mistake and is desperate for somewhere to go until she can have her child. She has no relatives to turn to for help. Although it is true that once my uncle finds out what I have been doing and is brought to justice, I will not have anywhere to go either and will be in a similar predicament. But I am not speaking of myself in this instance."

She looked away, and he realized even more fully what he had been asking of her.

***

Julia did not want Mr. Langdon to think she was asking for his pity. She knew what she was getting herself into by spying on her uncle, but she wanted to do it. It was her duty to the Crown and to her country. Besides, whether she helped spy or not, once her uncle was found out, she'd have nowhere to go and her reputation would be tainted by association.

Julia spoke swiftly as they walked. "I was hoping that Mr. Wilson, as a clergyman and the head of a charity mission, would know of a place for my friend. But perhaps it was unfair of me to tell you, for you will wonder of whom I am speaking."

"No, Miss Grey." He stopped her with a firm hand on her arm and turned to face her. "I am very glad you have told me so that I might be able to help. And as for wondering who she is . . . we all have sinned and fallen short of God's best. I have no right to pass judgment."

"That is most kind of you, Mr. Langdon. Thank you. This person is in great need, and I seem to be her only friend in her desperate situation. I don't want to see her further hurt. I am sorry I had to reveal these things to you and rely upon your secrecy, but her need is urgent and immediate."

"You may depend upon me to keep this information with the utmost discretion and to share it only with Mr. Wilson. And I can offer this assurance—that although I do not know the particulars, I do believe Mr. Wilson will know exactly where this young lady may find a safe place to live, at least temporarily."

"Oh, Mr. Langdon, you can't know how much relief this brings." Julia pressed her hand to her heart as such a rush of air filled her lungs that she became lightheaded. "I will write to my friend immediately. But how will you—or Mr. Wilson—get the information to me? How must I instruct my friend to act?"

"In our usual place, of course," Mr. Langdon said, a grave look in his eyes that caused her stomach to flutter. "I will let you know what your friend must do."

"Thank you, Mr. Langdon." Tears filled Julia's eyes, and she swallowed to force them away. "You are very kind."

He stared at her as if he were trying to discern something from her expression, as if he was looking right through her, into her thoughts. Though, if her aunt and uncle found out that she was helping Sarah and had defied them by coming to the East Side today, she very well *could* be in need of a place to live.

Felicity exited the shop and came toward them. "They had the very thing." She smiled, showing her perfect teeth, and held up her wrapped parcel.

Mr. Langdon and Julia congratulated her and turned to walk back toward the place where they would meet the coach.

Julia was staring at Mr. Langdon's profile when she became aware of snorting horses and a carriage stopping just behind her. Turning, she saw it was the driver who had driven them there.

"Here is our hackney."

"Allow me." Mr. Langdon helped Felicity in first, then Julia, holding firmly to her hand and placing his other hand beneath her elbow.

He closed the door behind her, and then, out of the window, she saw him pay the driver. As they drove away, he held her gaze with solemn eyes and a grave expression.

Most people would think ill of her simply because she associated with and was trying to help a young woman whose morals had been compromised.

But Nicholas Langdon was not like most people.

***

Very early the next morning, Julia put on her pelisse and her largest bonnet and walked to the park. It was a damp, foggy morning, so she encountered very few people, which was good, since walking alone in London was not a proper thing for a young lady.

She went straight to the oak tree and put her hand inside the knot-hole. Under the rock was a piece of paper. Julia drew it out and continued walking, hiding the paper in her palm. When she had walked several more feet, she turned and faced the trees. Julia quickly unfolded the note and read silently:

> *Have your friend come with her belongings to the Children's Aid Mission at noon on Monday. All is well and will be well.*

Julia quickly stuffed the note into her reticule, which was hanging from her wrist, and made her way toward home, her heart soaring inside her chest. Now she just had to get word to Sarah.

As soon as Julia entered the front door, Phoebe exclaimed, "There you are! I was wondering if you'd gone for a walk."

"I'm surprised to see you up so early."

"I couldn't sleep. You haven't gone for a long walk, have you?" Phoebe glanced down at Julia's shoes and then reached out and touched Julia's cheek. "You look a bit flushed."

"No, I did not go far. Would you like to walk with me? We can take a turn around the square."

Phoebe nodded. Julia waited while Phoebe put on her gloves, bonnet, and a light spencer to guard against the morning chill. With their parasols in hand, they set out. Julia vowed to write a letter to Sarah as soon as she got home and post it that very day to make sure Sarah received the information in time.

Julia peeked down at her reticule where she had placed Mr. Langdon's note, which might as well be a sleeping snake. As soon as possible, she would have to burn it. If Phoebe or Mrs. Wilhern ever found out Nicholas Langdon had written her a note . . . it didn't bear thinking of. But then, how would they know *he* had written the note? He had not signed it. Still, if someone recognized his handwriting or somehow guessed it, she would never survive the wrath of the Wilherns.

***

The next day was Sunday, and as Julia was changing after the morning church service, a knock came at her door. Molly quickly finished buttoning the back of Julia's dress and hurried to open the door.

Mr. Wilhern stood in the doorway. "Molly. Let Miss Grey know I wish to see her in my study as soon as she is able to come down."

Julia stayed in the back of the room. He glanced at her quickly before turning and walking away.

Her heart thumped inside her. What could her uncle want? Had he discovered, somehow, that she had rifled through his desk, copied the coded message, and given it to Nicholas Langdon?

"Shall I finish your hair, Miss Grey?" Molly asked.

"I'll just pin it." But Julia's hand shook as she lifted a pin.

"Let me." Molly sat her down and quickly finished pinning her hair.

"Thank you, Molly."

There was nothing left to do but go downstairs and see what her uncle wanted with her.

Her shoulders and neck ached with tension as she approached her uncle's study. She could not go on forever before being caught, so she needed to find out something definitive, something that would help the War Office capture Uncle Wilhern and everyone else working with him, so as to thwart their evil plans.

She entered her uncle's study, and he stood up immediately from his desk.

"Come here, child."

His brows were lowered, but he did not look especially angry. He fixed her with a penetrating stare. "Julia, you are like a daughter to me. I wish to always keep you near, and I know Mrs. Wilhern and Phoebe feel the same. And here we have a very eligible young man who wishes to marry you. He has even agreed to drink less just to please you. Surely you noticed the difference when he was here two nights ago."

"Yes, Uncle. I suppose he has also come into the fortune you mentioned."

"Very soon he will." He narrowed his eyes at her. "It is wise of you to think of such things, my dear, as you have no fortune of your own." He paused a moment and then continued, "Does this mean you have decided to accept Mr. Edgerton?"

Julia swallowed. If she said no, her uncle would be furious and would possibly start making plans to send her off to work as a governess, washing his hands of her. If she said yes, it would be a lie, but it might buy her more time.

"I am still uncertain."

"What are you uncertain of?" His face began to turn red. "Do you think anyone else wishes to ask for your hand? Do you have prospects I know nothing of?"

"No, of course not. There is only Mr. Edgerton. I believe if he continues to behave the gentleman, as he did at dinner two nights ago, I shall . . . I shall accept him." Her breathlessness betrayed her nervousness at having to tell the lie.

"He is coming to speak with me in a few minutes. Would you like to sit with him for a bit, to see the fruit of his intentions and his efforts to make his behavior more pleasing?"

Nothing would be more distasteful. "If you wish it, Uncle, of course I shall."

Mr. Wilhern looked genuinely pleased. "After we finish our meeting, I shall take him to see you in . . . ?"

"The front drawing room."

He nodded. "Very well, very good."

Julia took that as her cue to leave. She turned to go, and as she did, she suddenly wanted very much to know what Mr. Edgerton and her uncle might have to talk about. How could she listen in on them without them knowing? Her eye caught on a large wardrobe near the door. If she could conceal herself inside it, she could probably hear every word they said. And then when they left to go to the front drawing room, she could step out and follow them without them seeing her and be just a few seconds behind them.

But it would only work if her uncle left the study before Edgerton came.

Julia walked down the corridor and stepped quietly into the sitting room, which was across the hall and only a few feet from her uncle's study. Finding a book lying on a table, she picked it up and started reading.

After several minutes, she heard footsteps. Julia approached the doorway and peeked out. Her uncle was walking toward the front of the house. In a moment, she heard masculine voices.

Julia darted into the corridor and scurried in through her uncle's study door. She opened the large wardrobe, mentally rehearsing what she would say if she were caught, and then stepped inside the piece of furniture.

CHAPTER TWENTY-THREE

Julia squatted underneath the lowest shelf, where she was forced to stand on top of stacks of papers. She balanced herself with her hands against the side and back panels. Her heart pounded and her shallow breathing made her dizzy, but she concentrated on not moving, keeping every muscle taut. *Breathe, Julia. Don't faint.*

The roaring in her ears was so loud, she wondered if she would even be able to overhear what her uncle and Hugh Edgerton were saying. She opened the door just a tiny crack and waited.

After a few moments, she heard voices.

". . . She is softening. I think she can be persuaded." She recognized her uncle's voice. "Just don't get drunk—you know she doesn't like that. Say something flattering, and for goodness sake, smile at her and don't look so despondent when you see her." Her uncle went on. "She has always been a compliant girl, even timid and obedient. I was shocked when she stubbornly refused to give in. But she will accept you, I am sure. And once you are married, use a firm hand with her and she will submit to you. She has not the spirit to defy anyone."

The roaring in Julia's head suddenly grew too loud. *I will never marry Edgerton. Never,* she railed inwardly, her stomach churning. *Compliant. Has not the spirit to defy. Wouldn't he be surprised?*

She had to calm herself and listen for something more important.

Mr. Edgerton mumbled something that Julia didn't quite hear. She clenched her eyes shut, focusing on easing the slight cramp in her ankle by shifting her weight to her other foot.

"Now what do you have for me?" she heard her uncle say.

"We have the final man in place," Edgerton said.

What did he mean by that? A rustle of paper and a brief silence, as if a document had been exchanged and her uncle was looking it over.

"The four of them will need money to bribe a few officials to get them to the front lines, to Wellington," Edgerton said.

Wellington. "Mm, yes, I have it here. And each of them knows what to do?"

"They have their forged documents, and once the deed is done, they will scatter over the Continent, at least for a year or two."

"Good."

Once the deed is done. He must mean once they assassinate Wellington. Julia had to get their names! If she could get the names of these four men and get them to Mr. Langdon and the War Office, they could capture them before they set sail, thereby foiling the plot to kill Wellington. Were they named on the paper Edgerton had given her uncle?

Julia leaned her body slightly forward, trying to see through the tiny crack in the wardrobe door. There. Her uncle was folding a piece of paper and placing it on his desk.

"There's extra money there for their ship passage. If everything else goes as planned, it should all be over very soon, and you'll have your coinage. Still have your eye on that estate in Warwickshire?"

A mumbled reply.

"Julia and Phoebe will want to be settled near each other. It's a good choice." Her uncle affably slapped Mr. Edgerton on the back. "Come. Miss Grey is waiting for you in the drawing room. Remember, smile and be pleasant."

As the two men walked toward the door, moving out of her line of vision, Julia eyed her uncle's desk. She waited until she could no longer hear their footsteps and then pushed the wardrobe door open. She stepped out with one foot but tripped as she tried to pull her other foot out.

The floor came rushing up, but she caught herself with her hands just before her knees hit the polished wood floor. She sprang upright.

She hurried to her uncle's desk, her knees cramped and her ankles burning. She grasped the paper and folded it smaller. Having no reticule or even a pocket in her skirt, she stuffed it into her bodice and down the left side and then rushed out of the room to meet her uncle and Mr. Edgerton in the drawing room.

She slowed her pace. How must she look? Was her hair out of place after crouching in the wardrobe? No time to repair it. She must try to slow her breathing. She touched her hot cheek with the back of her hand, keenly aware of the paper stuffed down her bodice.

Her uncle was just walking out of the drawing room when she arrived.

"Julia, there you are. I thought you would be waiting for us."

"Forgive me, I had to . . . retrieve something."

"Never mind. Mr. Edgerton is here to see you."

Julia forced a smile, but it trembled on her lips. She ducked her head demurely as Mr. Edgerton reached for her hand. Just as he kissed her gloved hand, she heard the slight rustle of the paper in her bodice.

"How nice to see you, Mr. Edgerton," she said quickly. "I trust you are well today."

"Yes, I am very well." He did smile, but almost as an afterthought, no doubt remembering her uncle's words to him. "And you, Miss Grey?

Are you well?" He looked at her curiously, his forehead suddenly wrinkling as he studied her.

"Oh yes, of course, I am very well. I have had my morning walk already and feel very well. But you look as though you don't believe me."

"Forgive me, Miss Grey. Of course I believe you. You only look a bit . . . flushed."

"Oh no, I am well, I assure you. I perhaps got a bit heated as I was rushing back to the drawing room just now. A lady always prefers a bit of color in her cheeks to being too pale, don't you think?" She was coming across as almost giddy and enthusiastic—too enthusiastic.

"Indeed." Mr. Edgerton's smile was quite genuine now. "You look very beautiful, Miss Grey, with a bit of color in your cheeks. In fact, I don't believe I have ever seen you looking so well."

Or paying so much attention to you either. But it seemed necessary to put on this show. She did not want them suspicious that she had taken the paper. But what would her uncle do when he discovered it missing? It was a terrifying thought. Perhaps she could read it quickly and deliver it back to his desk before he realized it was missing. But she had folded it two more times. He would surely notice that.

Mr. Edgerton was saying something about her playing and singing. ". . . sounded just like an angel. My mother's very words."

"Oh, how very kind," Julia said, again looking down, trying to appear modest. "But you mustn't flatter me. Phoebe does enough of that, but she is the dearest girl in the world and I could never do without her." It was the kind of thing ladies often said to make themselves appear kind and flirtatious at the same time, but it was simply the first thing that came into Julia's distracted mind. "I do love my cousin Phoebe. We are quite devoted to one another."

"Yes, of course. And I . . . I do not want you to think that I . . . well, that I would not be accommodating to the two of you living near each other."

The awkward look on his face was actually the most earnest one she had seen, and it stirred a strange mixture inside her, of pity, guilt, and horror—pity that he obviously wanted to marry her so much, which could never happen. Guilt that she was flirting with him while hoping to turn him in to the authorities for treason to the Crown. And horror at the thought of putting herself in this man's power, of marrying a man who seemed to have no qualms about betraying his own country.

Julia did not reply, pretending to be too abashed.

Her uncle jumped in with some comments about the weather and the roads, and eventually Julia nearly forgot the paper in her bodice, though it was sticking her in the side.

The visit seemed to be winding down. Mr. Edgerton stood. "May I call for you tomorrow? I should like to take you riding in my new curricle."

Julia hesitated. It was the last thing in the world she would want to do, but at the moment, she could hardly think past getting this note read and returned and reported to Mr. Langdon.

"If my uncle does not object, I accept."

A smile spread over Mr. Edgerton's face, making him look boyish—a great contrast to the fact that he was betraying king and country for money.

Now that he was leaving, Mr. Edgerton moved slowly, taking Julia's hand and kissing it. She kept her facial expression steady so as not to cringe.

"Until tomorrow," he said, no doubt thinking he looked and sounded gallant.

As soon as he and her uncle left the room, Julia moved to the doorway and passed out behind them. They went toward the front door and she crept back toward her uncle's study.

She could not let him catch her in the study, so she ducked into the sitting room. Snatching the note out of her bodice, she unfolded it and quickly scanned it.

Names. She had to write these down. She scurried to the tiny desk in the corner of the room and jerked open the drawer, taking out the inkpot, pen, and a sheet of parchment. Quickly she wrote down the four names, deeming them the most important information, and then tried to quickly convey the rest of the information in the paper—mainly the ship's name and date of departure.

Julia's hand trembled as she folded the paper again and hid it against her skirt. She stepped back to the door and looked out. Her uncle was nowhere to be seen. But he could appear at the end of the corridor at any moment. Her heart stole her breath the way it was pumping so hard, but she dashed out into the corridor and slipped into her uncle's study, running to the desk and laying the now wrinkled and creased paper where she had found it.

Her heart pounded even harder as she made it to the doorway. Footsteps sounded at the end of the corridor. She skittered back toward the sitting room and rushed inside.

Her uncle was coming down the corridor. Had he seen her? She couldn't imagine he missed seeing her. She grabbed the paper she had copied the information onto and tried to fold it, crumpling it in her haste, and shoved it into her bodice. Was her uncle coming into the sitting room? Would he ask her what she was doing? Or would he go into his study and see the paper and know that she had read it?

Her stomach churned at the thought of her uncle coming and finding her here, demanding her to tell him what she had done.

What should she do? Should she calmly leave the sitting room and go up to her room? Or should she hide herself here and hope he had not seen her?

She waited, listening. Only silence filled her ears. Finally, footsteps sounded just down the corridor. Her uncle was leaving his study. Were the steps coming closer? Or moving farther away?

They were moving away. She stepped to the doorway and peeked out. Her uncle's steps were fast. Was he angry? Did he realize someone had seen the incriminating paper?

Julia waited until he was out of sight and quickly hurried up the stairs to her room and closed the door behind her.

She placed her hand over her bodice. If she hid the paper in her room, her uncle could search and find it. But if she kept it in her bodice . . . surely he would not search her person. Her face burned as she remembered the way he had beaten his horse, the rage in his eyes. Would he look at her the same way? Would he realize she'd had just enough time to find the paper, read it, copy it, and replace it in his study? Would he be up here in her room to question her at any moment?

If only she could run and give the note to Mr. Langdon before her uncle could find it.

Not knowing what else to do, Julia threw herself across her bed and squeezed her eyes shut. "God help me," she whispered. Who else could help her? Who could she turn to? Mr. Langdon was a respectable man. If she ran to his home right now and begged him for shelter, both their reputations would be ruined. He'd have to turn her away. His mother and sister would be horrified, and Phoebe would never forgive her.

And how would Phoebe feel when she realized Julia had been spying on her father? Her father would be tried for treason. He could be hanged. Phoebe's future would be ruined.

Tears squeezed out the corners of her eyes. No, she could not cry. She had to get this paper to Mr. Langdon. As soon as she thought it safe, she would have to walk to the park and put it into the knothole in the oak tree.

A knock came at her door. She sat bolt upright, placing her hand over the paper in her bodice. "Yes? Come in."

Her uncle opened the door. "Julia?"

"Yes, Uncle Wilhern?"

The look on his face was hard and suspicious, but didn't he always look like that?

"I think you should marry Mr. Edgerton right away."

"Right away? Oh."

"You have no objections, do you?"

"Oh no, but when you say right away, do you mean—"

"I mean by the end of the week. He plans to get a special license."

"The end of the week?" How could she put him off? He would become even more suspicious. "That is so soon. What will . . . what will I . . ." In her panic, tears stung her eyes.

"I wish it. It is to be on Friday. I will see to the arrangements." His jaw was hard and his eyes black and cold.

Julia's stomach turned inside out.

"You do not object. Good. I have made up my mind and will not change it. Friday. It is your wedding day." He seemed to grit his teeth together. "And, Julia, if you betray me . . ."

He knew. Her cheeks tingled as the blood drained from her face. "Betray you, Uncle? Of course not. Whatever could you mean?" *God, please let me look innocent.*

He stared hard at her. "Then you are willing to marry Mr. Edgerton on Friday?"

Her breath came in shallow spurts, pulsing in her lungs. "I am." What else could she say? She had no choice but to agree. But if she agreed too readily . . . she allowed two tears to fall onto her cheeks.

At first her uncle merely stared. Finally, he said, "Think of how happy you are making my friend Mr. Edgerton."

Was that supposed to be comforting? She let another tear fall.

"Well, then, I shall leave you. But do not forget your ride with Mr. Edgerton in the morning."

Julia found a handkerchief on her night table and wiped her cheek.

Her uncle gave her one last penetrating look and then left the room.

CHAPTER TWENTY-FOUR

Julia allowed the tears to come freely. She had never realized what a relief it was to cry. Perhaps Phoebe had discovered this quite some time ago, which was why she cried so often.

After several minutes of letting the tears flow, Julia finally wiped her face and poured herself some water, all the while aware of the paper stabbing her under her arm beneath her clothing.

Julia wandered about the room. Would it be safe to deliver her note to the message tree now? Or should she wait? No one ever noticed her in the mornings, but her uncle might follow her if she left now.

She pulled the paper out of her bodice and stuffed it in her reticule. She took up her bonnet and went downstairs.

No one was around. No one asked her where she was going. With any luck, she could get to the park and be back within ten minutes, and no one would even know she had left the house.

She arrived at the park, making her face a picture of contentment and calm. It was the hour when many people were out, taking the air, walking or riding, and she was forced to acknowledge several people before she turned the corner to find her tree.

She approached it and slipped the paper out of her reticule and then placed it into the knothole.

She had done what she could. But anything could happen. Someone else could find her paper. Her uncle could realize what she had done, could easily imagine that Nicholas Langdon was her contact. After all, Mr. Langdon had been the one in possession of the diary. Not only that, but he was staying in London a suspiciously long time after his recovery from his injuries.

What if her uncle had followed her and seen her put the paper in the tree? Or Mr. Edgerton? They'd make sure Mr. Langdon never received the information. Perhaps they would even kill Julia—and Mr. Langdon.

She had to stop these racing thoughts. She concentrated on breathing and walking and not thinking.

When she was nearly home again, a man turned the corner and was walking toward her. Julia's breath went out of her, and she stumbled.

It was Nicholas Langdon.

He caught sight of her when she was still several feet away, and he smiled.

She approached him. They were actually in sight of the Wilhern house. Anyone looking out of the front windows might see them. People were passing them on foot and in carriages.

"Mr. Langdon."

"Miss Grey." He tipped his hat to her and then leaned his head toward her. "Forgive me for saying so, but you are looking a bit pale. Are you unwell?"

"There is something for you at the park," she said as blandly as possible. Should she risk telling him that her uncle was planning to force her to marry Mr. Edgerton on Friday? Of course there was nothing he could do, and she did not want anyone seeing them talking.

He kept his eyes trained on her face, as he said quietly, "Are you in danger, Miss Grey?"

What could she say? "No. You should go. It's very important." She smiled to put him at ease and so no one would suspect that their conversation was anything but polite and appropriate.

"Thank you, Miss Grey." He said the words carefully. "If the worst happens, you will come to my home, to my sister, Leorah. Promise me."

"I shall try my best." She had to blink quickly to push back the tears.

He clasped her hand in his.

"You should go before someone sees us." When he looked reluctant, she said, "The best thing you can do for me is to take the note to our mutual friends and convince them to act upon it immediately."

"I shall leave you word, if I possibly can."

"Good day, Mr. Langdon." Julia watched as his fingers let go of hers. She forced herself to continue the short distance to her front door.

As she entered the front vestibule and began removing her bonnet, her uncle stepped from the front sitting room. "Was that Mr. Langdon I saw you speaking with?"

"Yes. I took a short walk to the park, and he—"

"Is there something between you and Mr. Langdon? What were you talking of?" Uncle Wilhern's eyes were narrowed, a sharp look in the small dark orbs.

"Nothing very particular. He . . . he asked after my health."

Her uncle stared at her. Julia began pulling off her gloves. "If you have no further need of me, Uncle, I shall go up to my room."

"Just a moment." He seemed to be thinking, and then he said, "I want you to go and tell Phoebe you'll be marrying Mr. Edgerton on Friday morning by special license."

Julia hesitated, but only for a moment. "Of course. I tell Phoebe everything." She held her head high as she walked toward the stairs and started up. When she reached the top of the landing, she looked over her shoulder. Her uncle was still eyeing her. But at least he had not left the house and followed Mr. Langdon to the park.

Julia headed toward Phoebe's room, knocked lightly on it, and entered.

Phoebe sneezed violently.

"Phoebe, what is the matter? Are you unwell?"

"You know I am never unwell." Phoebe wrinkled her nose, a peevish tone in her voice. "But I do feel a bit feverish."

Julia stepped toward her and placed her hand on Phoebe's brow. "You are very warm. I think you do have a fever."

"Well, I refuse to be sick." Phoebe crossed her arms. "Don't tell Mother, or she will make me go to bed."

"Perhaps you should go to bed, Phoebe."

"Not only will I not go to bed, but I want to go for a walk. Come, Julia. Let us walk to the park and see who is out and about."

The last thing Julia wanted to do was go for a walk with Phoebe and run into Mr. Langdon as he was retrieving her note.

"I am not in the mood for a walk, Phoebe, but I did come to your room to tell you something important." How well did Phoebe truly know Julia? Surely she would realize Julia had no desire to marry Mr. Edgerton.

"Phoebe, I have agreed to marry Mr. Edgerton. We shall be married by special license on Friday morning."

Phoebe's eyes grew wide. Then she sat down abruptly on the side of her bed. "You have accepted Mr. Edgerton? You are marrying on Friday?"

No. "Yes."

"When did you accept him, Julia? Why did you not tell me?"

"I only accepted him today. Your father wanted me to accept him."

"Mr. Edgerton is handsome. I am sure you will be content with him, Julia, as long as we can be settled near each other. I believe Father said Mr. Edgerton would buy an estate near Wilhern Manor so we could be close."

Carefully, Julia said, "You think I will be happy with Mr. Edgerton, then?"

"I think so." Phoebe suddenly placed her hand against her chest. "I am not feeling well. I think . . . I feel feverish." She coughed and then moaned. "Fetch Mother. I think she will want to send for the doctor."

Was that all Phoebe had to say about the matter? But perhaps she was very sick after all.

Julia turned and went to fetch Mrs. Wilhern.

In four days she would be Mrs. Hugh Edgerton, as far as her uncle and Phoebe knew. But if her uncle and Mr. Edgerton were not apprehended on charges of treason and plotting to assassinate General Wellington before then, Julia would run away. She could go to the Bartholdys, but they were poor and she did not want to be a burden on them. They were kind and would take her in for a short while, but that was certainly not a long-term solution.

She had overheard someone speaking of a governess position in the country, the Atherton family in Suffolk, who had six children. And suddenly, she was desperate enough to wish for that position, a way to make her own living and escape her uncle and Mr. Edgerton. She would write to Mrs. Atherton today about the position.

Mr. Langdon had said he would help her if she found herself in danger, but she didn't think he meant this sort of trouble. She would see him tomorrow night as they were all attending an assembly. Perhaps she could let him know that time was running out for her.

***

The next morning, Julia pulled the covers up to Phoebe's chin.

"I can't be sick." Phoebe peevishly swatted at the blanket.

"You are coughing, you have a fever, and your nose and eyes are too red to fool anyone into thinking you are well."

Phoebe threw her head down into the pillow and burst into tears. "I'll miss seeing Mr. Langdon at the assembly tonight. It's not fair."

"If you don't rest and get well, you'll miss the trip to Bath later this week, and your aunt and uncle and cousins will be very disappointed in not seeing you."

Julia handed Phoebe a handkerchief. "You'll only make your head hurt by crying. The physician said you must not upset yourself. You must drink your tea and take your medicine and you will be better in a few days. But if you don't, it could go to your lungs, and that could be dangerous."

Phoebe blew her nose loudly and turned her head away. "You won't go tonight without me, will you, Julia?"

"No, of course not." Julia tried not to sound disappointed. "Your mother and father will stay home as well, I'm sure." Truly, it was best she did not see Mr. Langdon any more than was necessary. She didn't want her uncle to see her talking to Mr. Langdon again. Besides, if Phoebe suspected even half of what Julia felt when she saw Mr. Langdon . . .

"Get some sleep." Julia squeezed Phoebe's arm. "Send for me if you want me to come and read to you."

Phoebe sniffed but didn't answer. Julia slipped out and went to her own room to secretly pack a bag, in case she had to leave in a hurry.

***

Julia had hoped when she went to bed early that she would feel better in the morning.

Phoebe's fever had only lasted a few hours, and after three days she seemed to be recovering from her cough, but Julia's throat hurt, her head ached, and a cough had started deep in her chest. That morning, she woke herself up coughing. Her whole body ached. Mrs. Wilhern and Phoebe would not be awake for quite a while longer, so Julia lay in bed, praying she wasn't getting sick. Now, of all times, when it was only two days until she would have to escape by whatever means necessary from marriage to Hugh Edgerton.

Julia lay in bed for hours before the maid, Anna, came in and asked if she was unwell.

"I'm afraid I am. When Phoebe wakes up, will you tell her?"

"Yes, miss."

Anna didn't even ask her if she could bring her anything. Mrs. Clay, the housekeeper at Wilhern Manor, would have made a fuss over her, bringing her special tea and broth and informing Mr. and Mrs. Wilhern immediately.

Julia got up and poured herself a glass of water. After two sips she was coughing again. She crawled back into bed.

Phoebe burst into the room. "Julia, you cannot be sick! A woman cannot be sick on her wedding day. Do you think you shall be well by Friday?" She stared down at her.

"I am sure I don't know." Julia winced at the pain in her chest.

"You are not so very sick, are you, Julia? We are supposed to go to Bath immediately after your wedding to Mr. Edgerton."

"I'm afraid I am," Julia rasped, just before an attack of coughing bent her over and violently shook her. "If I am very sick, perhaps we shall be forced to postpone the wedding." A wisp of hope invaded her aching chest.

"But perhaps it is only a cold and you will be well enough by tomorrow."

"I do not think—" Julia was seized with such a fit of coughing that she couldn't finish her sentence. She sat up in bed and coughed so long and hard that tears ran down her cheeks and her chest burned as if with fire.

"Poor Julia. You are quite ill, aren't you?" Phoebe patted her on the back until she was done.

"Will you . . . ring for . . . some tea?" Julia rasped.

"Of course. That will make you feel better."

Phoebe sat on the edge of her bed, chattering about how much she would miss seeing Mr. Langdon at all the balls if they should go to Bath as planned. When the tea arrived, Phoebe stood.

"I shall go to Mother at once and beg her to go to Bath without me and let me stay and nurse you, Julia."

"I would dearly love for you to stay with me, but—"

"I shall tell Mother at once." Phoebe turned to hurry from the room.

Julia wanted to stop her, but she began to cough again and couldn't say a word until well after Phoebe had closed the door behind her.

After Julia had drunk her tea, Phoebe walked back into the room, her head and shoulders drooping and her face dejected.

"Mother won't hear of me staying. She says if you are too sick to marry Mr. Edgerton on Friday, then we will go to Bath early and leave a servant here with you. I am so sad, as I shall dearly hate to go an entire fortnight without seeing you and Mr. Langdon."

"A fortnight isn't so terribly long."

"Of course it is. It is *terribly* long." Phoebe sniffed and sank down beside Julia.

Julia refrained from telling Phoebe not to cry. Speaking might make her cough again. Besides, she felt like crying herself at the prospect of being sick when she needed her strength to get away from Hugh Edgerton.

"I don't understand why I have to spend two weeks of the Season, especially when it is almost over, in Bath, of all the boring places in England." A tear, followed by another, fell from Phoebe's eyes and into her lap.

Julia said nothing. She couldn't remember the last time Phoebe had cried and she hadn't comforted her, but she didn't even feel like trying today.

"I shall not have any fun in Bath, for who is in Bath this time of year?" She looked up at Julia. "Someone must take care of you. You are sick, Julia, and I well remember how miserable I was. I am not entirely well as yet."

Phoebe coughed a bit, and her tears quickly dried as she turned her attention back on Julia. "You always did bear your illnesses better than I. You're so patient and hardly ever complain. But perhaps you will recover as quickly as I did."

"Yes, perhaps so." And in that case, her bag was already packed and hidden in the back of her wardrobe.

***

Julia spent a miserable day in bed, feeling worse and worse as the day wore on.

When Phoebe returned, Mr. Wilhern was just behind her, a severe look on his face.

"Julia, Father and I came to inquire how you're feeling. Are you able to come down to dinner?"

"I do not think so." Speaking brought on a violent attack of coughing.

"You no doubt have the same malady Phoebe had," Mr. Wilhern said. "Only a cold. Stay in bed and you will be well by Friday."

"Yes, Uncle."

CHAPTER TWENTY-FIVE

Julia woke herself up during the night, coughing and feeling feverish. When Phoebe came into her room the next morning, she asked, "How do you feel? Any better?"

Julia shook her head.

"You do not look well at all. Shall I tell Mother to send for Dr. Alcott? Do you think you have a fever? Your cheeks look very flushed."

Julia tried to speak but was overtaken by a coughing fit.

"Poor Julia. I shall go tell Mother." Phoebe hurried out of the room.

Instead of her aunt, Mr. Wilhern came into the room again with Phoebe. "Are you sick?" he asked without preamble. "Or is this a ploy to avoid marrying Edgerton tomorrow?"

"Father!" Phoebe stared, openmouthed and wide eyed. "How can you be so unfeeling? Julia is obviously very sick." She stepped to Julia's bedside and laid her hand on her forehead. "She's burning up with fever and has a horrendous cough."

Mr. Wilhern appeared unmoved. "Very well. Since she is so sick, we shall postpone the wedding until we return from Bath."

Phoebe again stared at her father with an open mouth. She slammed her fists on her hips. "Father, you shall owe Julia an apology when you realize how sick she is."

Julia observed them through a haze of pain and fever. All she could think of was that she was not sure she could escape Mr. Edgerton tomorrow, as sick as she felt.

"Julia," Phoebe said, leaning over her, "you will try to get better, won't you? I cannot bear it if something should happen to you."

Julia began to say, "I have every intention of getting better," but a fit of coughing cut her off, leaving her too exhausted to do anything except nod her head.

"Mother is choosing a servant to tend you. She says I must not come in here anymore, as you may be contagious, but I shall pray for you."

"Thank you," Julia rasped, managing a smile for Phoebe.

***

Julia quickly realized she shouldn't lie on her back or the coughing would be worse. She lay on her side for a while and then propped herself up with pillows.

Kitty, one of the kitchen servants, came into the room with a tray of tea, waking Julia from a light sleep.

Julia tried to sit up higher and took the proffered cup of tea with trembling fingers.

"I will come again to see if you are better, after the family has gone."

"Gone?"

"Yes, the family is going to Bath. They decided to go a day early."

So they would not even pretend to be concerned about her. No matter. At least she had the great relief of not having to marry Hugh Edgerton tomorrow—although her uncle would no doubt usher her to the altar just as soon as she was well again.

***

Julia slept fitfully. The night felt like a bad dream as she was frequently awakened by her cough and the pain in her chest. She was relieved when it was over and the sun peeked through her window, although she was still exhausted and feverish.

Her chest hurt more than ever, and even her ribs and her back were starting to ache from all the coughing. When the latest fit was over, she leaned forward, trying to breathe. Her chest felt as if it were being squeezed by a giant fist. She couldn't draw in a complete breath. She sucked in air as hard as she could, but her chest felt so tight. The pain was excruciating. Was she dying?

She lay back against the pillows. As she struggled to breathe, she could hear a rattling sound coming from her chest.

Julia forced herself to get up and walk about the room. Perhaps she would feel better after moving around.

Rather than feeling better, her head began to pound and her vision began to spin. She saw black spots. She went back to the bed as quickly as possible and fell across it, lying there on top of the blanket.

While she lay waiting for her vision to return and her heart to stop jolting inside her, she prayed, *Dear God, if I die, please take care of Phoebe when her father is apprehended for treason. Send her a kind gentleman to marry her and take care of her. And if possible, let her never find out that I helped send her father to prison. And please . . . let Mr. Langdon find happiness. He is a good sort of man.*

***

Nicholas waited for his sister to finish her breakfast. She was eating exceedingly slowly this morning.

He had not seen Miss Grey in several days, not since the day she had delivered the information that had been so valuable. They now had enough to arrest Robert Wilhern and Hugh Edgerton, and they could stop the four men who were being sent to kill General Wellington. But they were waiting to apprehend them until the actual date of the ship's departure as they endeavored to gain as much information as possible on those who were helping Wilhern and Edgerton on the Continent.

In the meantime, had something happened to Julia? He had heard Phoebe was sick and that was why they had not attended the assembly more than a week ago, but that did not explain why he had not seen them since. Finally, Nicholas approached his sister.

"Leorah, accompany me to the Wilherns' so that we might call on Miss Wilhern and Miss Grey."

Leorah eyed him suspiciously. "And which of the two are you so interested in? And if you say Phoebe Wilhern, I will not believe you."

"Well, as you have settled the matter in your own mind, I wonder you should ask me. Come. Don't keep me waiting."

"I shall not go with you at all if you take that imperial attitude with me, brother." Leorah crossed her arms and set her chin in that stubborn way of hers.

Best to placate her. He wanted to see Miss Grey.

"Leorah, pray, be a dear," he said, emphasizing *dear*, "and join me in paying a visit to our mutual friends, Miss Wilhern and Miss Grey."

"That is a bit better, although I detected insincerity in your voice."

"You must surely be mistaken."

Leorah readied herself, and they were soon off. In five minutes, they were being invited into the house by a young, rustic-looking servant.

"We would like to call on Miss Wilhern and Miss Grey, if they are at home."

The young woman looked relieved to see them. "The Wilherns went to Bath. Miss Grey is home, but she is very sick."

"Sick?"

The urge to bolt upstairs seized Nicholas, and it was with difficulty that he controlled himself.

"Is she very unwell?"

"I'm sorry to say she is, sir. Her fever is very hot, and she was talking out of her head this morning."

"May we see her?"

The servant girl led them up the stairs.

"Why was the doctor not called? Who is in charge here?" Nicholas didn't care that he sounded strident.

"I am the only one here. Mrs. Wilhern gave the other servants the week for a holiday."

When they were almost to the second floor, Nicholas nearly tread on his sister's heels. She turned to face him.

"Nicholas, you can't go in."

"Why not? Oh, go on, then." He shooed her up the stairs. "Quickly, and tell me how she fares so I can go for Dr. Alcott."

Leorah followed the maid inside the room.

Nicholas paced outside the door. In a few moments, Leorah stuck her head out. Her eyes were wide as they latched onto him.

"Run and fetch the doctor. Julia is terribly ill. Make him hurry." Then she shut the door in his face.

He raced down the stairs two at a time. He hurried home, just one street over, running most of the way and praying, *Don't let her die.*

He fetched his horse and rode to Dr. Alcott's. When the doctor's housekeeper announced that he was in and would see him momentarily, Nicholas most fervently thanked God that he wasn't out on a call.

The doctor was older, with deep crow's feet at the corners of his eyes. "Mr. Nicholas," Dr. Alcott greeted him. "What can I do for you?"

"I need you to come right away. A young lady, Miss Julia Grey, is very ill."

Nicholas waited for him to collect his bag and get in his curricle. He chafed silently at the slowness of Dr. Alcott's horses.

At the Wilhern house, Nicholas opened the door without even knocking and led Dr. Alcott up the stairs.

Leorah opened the door as they reached the top, ushered the doctor inside, and then closed the door again, shutting Nicholas out.

Waiting outside her door, he heard coughing. He gasped at the terrible violence of it. It was as if she were choking, and she sounded very weak.

He waited, pacing back and forth. The Wilherns had left her here, without even a proper servant to care for her. Had they realized she was spying on him? Were they trying to kill her? Perhaps Wilhern had poisoned her.

He considered knocking or calling to Leorah to come and tell him something. Could Leorah be assisting the doctor? He had no doubt his sister could do anything she was called on to do, but . . . why didn't she come out and tell him what was happening?

"Leorah," he called from just outside the door. "Is there anything I can do?"

A few moments later, he heard footsteps approaching on the other side, and then the door opened to Dr. Alcott, with Leorah just behind him. They came out into the hall.

The doctor's gaze was direct. "She has pleurisy and an infection of the lungs. It is very serious, and she needs expert care—hot liquids and as much of the right foods as you can get her to take. You'll need to get more than one servant, someone who's experienced with nursing, to help watch her night and day."

Nicholas and Leorah looked at each other. "Cora," they said at the same time.

"We shall take her home. Our old nursemaid, Cora, will care for her." Nicholas was already taking a step toward the stairs to go get the carriage.

"No, she mustn't be moved," the doctor said firmly. "She is too weak."

"Then I will fetch Cora. She and Polly can come and stay and care for her here."

"That is a good plan." The doctor and Cora had often consulted each other when anyone in Nicholas's family had been sick.

"You said she has pleurisy and a lung infection? How soon will she recover?"

"With proper care, she may recover, but it could take quite some time."

May recover? "How long?"

"She will be in bed at least three weeks, I would estimate, if she recovers. And once she does, she could have a reoccurrence. Sometimes the lungs are weakened to the extent that they continue to be inflamed every time there is a change in the weather. If so, it could greatly shorten her life."

The doctor looked as though he were speaking of a rise in the cost of tea, instead of the uncertain fate of the sweetest, loveliest girl in England.

"But we will hope for better things. She is young, and, I daresay, quite strong. She could recover and never have a second bout of it. However, she must guard her health, as all ladies should, by wearing something around her neck in cool weather." The doctor scowled. "Ladies' fashions these days present a mortal danger. Exposing their shoulders and necks, wearing these thin muslin gowns in all kinds of weather—it is a wonder they aren't all dying an early death." He gave Leorah an accusatory look.

"Remember," he continued, addressing Leorah now, "she needs nourishing food, not just broth, as often as you can persuade her to eat. She must regain her strength, and she must not be left alone. I cannot imagine what Mr. and Mrs. Wilhern were thinking. A grievous neglect, to be sure." He humphed as he turned to leave. "Send for more laudanum and my special cough remedy when that runs out," Dr. Alcott called over his shoulder.

"Of course." Addressing Nicholas, Leorah said, "I'll be here until you get back with Cora."

He nodded and then hurried to catch up with the doctor, who was staring down at his feet as he descended the stairs.

"Pray, send your bill to me."

"Nonsense. I'll send the bill to Mr. and Mrs. Wilhern with a stern note telling them they should take better care of their niece, poor girl."

Nicholas could think of a few stern words he'd like to send them as well.

He made haste to ride back home and fetch Cora and Polly. When he told them both of Miss Grey's terrible illness and how she had no one but the scullery maid to take care of her, they both clucked their tongues and muttered diatribes about the poor dear's wretched lack of care and then hurried to collect enough things to stay away from home for a few nights.

"I will take very good care of her, don't you worry, Mr. Nicholas." Cora gazed at him with obvious compassion in her gray eyes. She even reached out and squeezed his arm.

Were his feelings so apparent? He'd thought he was hiding them, but Cora knew him too well. It hardly mattered who knew his strong regard for her if she should . . . But she would not die. She would recover. God would not let her die.

When Nicholas arrived at the Wilhern residence with Cora and Polly, he left the two of them with Kitty, who would show them where they could put their things. Then he climbed the stairs two at a time to Miss Grey's door. He knocked softly and then opened it.

He couldn't see Julia because the bed curtains hid her face, but Leorah walked toward him. "Are Cora and Polly here?" she whispered.

"Yes. How is she?"

"She's sleeping."

He walked toward the bed, determined to see her before he left. He pushed the bed curtain aside. Her face was pale and there were dark smudges beneath her eyes. But with her hair all about her face in a riot of dark, silky strands, she still looked beautiful. As he stared down at her, he became aware of a soft wheezing, and then a rattling, at regular intervals and realized the sound was coming from her chest as she breathed in and out.

"The poor thing is worn out," Leorah whispered behind him. "So weak she couldn't sit up. The coughing has kept her awake, but the doctor gave her laudanum to help her sleep."

Nicholas couldn't take his eyes off Julia. *God, please make her well. Make her strong. She is too beautiful, too brave and good, too young, to die.* She was far superior to any of the Wilherns, in character and every other way.

In fact, she was far superior to any girl he had ever met.

CHAPTER TWENTY-SIX

Nicholas paced the room, staring out the window where twilight had already fallen. Had the Wilherns deliberately left her here, alone, knowing she was ill?

But was Nicholas any better? He had left her in harm's way and had gone days without ensuring she was still safe. Of course, it was dangerous for him to show any undue interest in her, but he should have been more attentive. He would not make that mistake again.

After Henrietta had run away and broken their engagement, he'd never thought he could feel so much for a woman again. But he hadn't even known what love was then. Love had been little more than his attraction to a pretty face and a lovely smile and what he had thought was that lady's innocence and artlessness. He had been easily duped. But Miss Grey was much more than a pretty face. She had sense and understanding, moral fiber and compassion. He did not like remembering how she had attempted to influence him to like her cousin, while at the same time trying to attract that insipid Mr. Dinklage. But how could he blame her? Julia's family had assured her she was destined to be a governess. It wasn't as if Nicholas had expressed any particular interest in her—or had much to offer her. He had vowed not to marry for quite a while.

He sat down at the pianoforte. How many times had Miss Grey sat at this instrument? How many hours had her fingers touched these keys and brought forth music? He sat on the bench and ran his hands over the instrument. Then he noticed the music. These were Miss Grey's own original compositions. He'd never known she wrote her own music.

"Mr. Nicholas?" Cora stood in the doorway.

He leapt out of his seat. "Is she better? May I see her?"

"I believe she is a little better after her long sleep." Cora moved slowly up the steps, pausing to look back at him. "We persuaded her to eat. It is a mercy and a blessing, for she can't get her strength back without eating. Even her color is better."

Nicholas was anxious to see for himself, so anxious that he passed Cora on his way up the stairs, unwilling to wait for her.

Inside Miss Grey's room, which was rather dim as her bed was shaded from the light of the fireplace, he called out softly, "It is Nicholas Langdon. May I come in?"

There was a hesitation and then a soft, "Yes."

He stepped to her bedside, and Miss Grey smiled up at him, making his heart thump hard against his chest.

"I am so sorry to have been such a bother to you and Leorah . . ." she began. She stopped and took a heaving breath, as if it were both painful and difficult to breathe.

"Please, Miss Grey. You could never be a bother. And pray don't talk if it pains you."

She motioned weakly toward her throat, as if to apologize for her difficulty. Nicholas grabbed her hand in both of his, causing a look of surprise to flit over her face. He leaned over her.

"We will take care of you. You shall get the best care possible. Our own physician shall call every day, and Cora and Polly will stay here with you as long as you need them."

She stared up at him, her lips parted and tears in her eyes, as if he had grown wings and a halo. Was it so hard to believe that someone could show her kindness and want to take care of her? His heart clenched inside his chest. But then, noticing her eyelids beginning to droop, he suspected that Cora had given her some medicine and that she wouldn't be able to stay awake much longer.

***

Julia stared up at Mr. Langdon, the laudanum starting to pull her under again. She should ask him what was happening with the War Office and the information she had acquired for them. Instead, her heart fluttered at the sensations coming from his hand holding hers. It couldn't be improper, since she was so sick.

He looked as if he hadn't shaved in two days, but the dark shadow it created on his chin and above his lip was rugged and masculine and not without appeal. He stared down at her so intensely, she imagined she could feel his eyes delving into her own, infusing her with his compassion and warmth. His hand was so strong, and those brown eyes . . .

"Thank you," she rasped, her eyelids closing.

Cora came into the room. Julia heard her voice as if it were coming from far away. She was in danger of saying something foolish if she spoke. But she forced her eyes back open so she could look at him again. He was still leaning over her, still holding her hand. His grip was warm and gentle.

Cora was saying something about her falling asleep, that sleep was good for her. She tried to stay awake for him. She hadn't thanked him properly for bringing Cora and Polly and saving poor Kitty from caring for her by herself. But she couldn't make her mouth work. She took one last look at him through half-closed eyelids.

A moment later, something soft and warm pressed against her forehead. It felt like a kiss.

**

After three days, Julia was still so weak she could hardly walk across her room before becoming exhausted. At least she no longer thought she was dying.

Leorah and Nicholas Langdon had called on her every day. They would talk to her and tell her not to speak, as talking made her cough. Finally, on the third day, Leorah left the room to go fetch a book for her, and Julia was alone with Nicholas Langdon.

He leaned closer to her and spoke softly, his beautiful brown eyes fixed on hers.

"Does Mr. Wilhern suspect that you are spying on him? Is that why they left you here with hardly anyone to take care of you?"

"He was suspicious after I took that paper and copied it. I believe that is why he told me I had to marry Mr. Edgerton by special license last Friday. But I got sick and . . ." She smiled. "I was given a reprieve."

"He would have forced you to marry Edgerton?" Mr. Langdon ran a hand down his face.

"I would not have." She paused as a coughing fit came upon her. Thankfully, it wasn't as violent or as lengthy as before.

While Julia was coughing, Mr. Langdon's brow creased.

"Don't talk. I know the coughing is painful." And as she stopped coughing, he asked, "Is there anything I can get for you?"

She shook her head. "I would have run away rather than marry Mr. Edgerton."

"What if you could not have escaped? I cannot let them make you marry him. Perhaps I could make arrangements for you to go to the country in secret."

Of course he must understand that secretly sending her to the country would alert the Wilherns that something very suspicious was going on, and it could ruin Julia's reputation as well.

"When will the War Office people act?" she asked. "If they would apprehend my uncle and Mr. Edgerton . . ."

"I think they will wait a bit longer, as they want to be certain they know who their fellow conspirators are. It is an easy thing to arrest the four men as they board their ship to the Continent, but apprehending everyone else involved at the same moment so that they do not flee . . . that is a bit more difficult."

Julia nodded. But it was very inconvenient for her. And yet . . . she dreaded the awful moment when poor Phoebe's father would be charged with treason. No doubt all his assets would be seized, and Phoebe would become fatherless and penniless at the same time.

Which was why Julia had sent a letter inquiring about the governess position in Suffolk. Phoebe's Bath relations would surely take her in, or some of her other relations, but Julia would need to have a position to go to right away.

But this was not Mr. Langdon's responsibility, nor even something he needed to know. To tell him would be to ask for his help, and that would be improper—a young unmarried woman asking the help of a young unmarried man who was wholly unconnected to her.

"But I promise," Mr. Langdon said, leaning even closer to her, her heart fluttering at the concern in his eyes, "I shall keep a closer watch on you. I would never forgive myself if your uncle did something evil to you."

He stared down at her hand lying on the coverlet. His hand moved toward it, as if about to clasp hers, and then stopped. "I want you to know that—"

The door opened. Mr. Langdon withdrew his hand and sat back, a strange look on his face, as Leorah came into the room and held up the book.

"I found it. It was in the music room." She paused, staring at her brother, and then smiled a slow, knowing smile. She stepped forward and gave the book to Julia. "I hope you will be well enough to enjoy reading it."

"I'm sure I shall. Thank you."

The atmosphere was suddenly awkward as Leorah seemed to look at her brother with both amusement and approval. But surely Leorah knew that her brother could not have an interest in marrying Julia. He had no fortune, and Julia was destined to be a governess. But Leorah was the kind of person to believe that anything was possible. Julia's life had taught her to be more practical.

***

Two days later, Leorah was sitting by Julia's bed. Leorah said some cheerful words about the weather and the fact that the Season would soon be over and she would be returning to her family's country estate in Lincolnshire.

But Julia was thinking about how much Leorah and Mr. Langdon had done for her. They had even loaned their footman, Barnes, to spend every night in the house so that they were not without a male protector.

"I am so grateful to you, Leorah," Julia said, "and to your entire family, for all you have done for me while I've been sick."

"You are a most delightful girl, Julia, and it is my pleasure to take charge of you—mine and my brother's, Cora's, and Polly's. If you thought for a moment that we do not wish to care for you as our very own, then you are gravely mistaken." She said these last words so softly, so tenderly, that Julia couldn't help but believe her. But had Leorah truly meant to include her brother when she said they were pleased to take charge of her? Julia hadn't seen Mr. Langdon for the last two days.

"People may hear of my illness. Word could get back to Mr. and Mrs. Wilhern, and they will wonder why I haven't written."

"You are not well enough to write, Julia. Depend upon it, when they discover how seriously ill you have been, and how you were left nearly alone in the house, they will be wracked with remorse."

Would they? She had always longed for their love, had tried so hard to earn it by being good and prudent and respectable, by helping Phoebe in every possible way, by showing she was grateful to them for taking her in and providing every advantage of society and education.

Now the prospect of their love was impossible, as she had betrayed them so completely by turning over evidence of Mr. Wilhern's treasonous activities.

"You must rest and recover from this. When you are quite well you shall come visit me in Lincolnshire, and I shall visit you and Phoebe in Warwickshire."

Julia expressed her joy at the prospect of the visits, but of course, it could never be.

***

Later that week, while Julia continued her recovery, Leorah regaled her with a story from the day before, of how she had ridden her horse in Hyde Park and almost run down a somber-looking gentleman. He'd seen her coming and had sprung out of the way as if he were certain she meant to do him harm. In doing so, he had lost his hat, which went rolling into the path of an oncoming carriage. The man had been furious, accusing Leorah of being wild and completely without propriety.

"Truly, I was sorry to have caused him to spoil his hat," Leorah said, "but he looked as if he could afford a new one. Besides, he had plenty of time to move out of my way. He shouldn't have jumped aside so suddenly as to lose his hat. My horse wouldn't have hit him if he'd only stood still. When he insulted me in that haughty manner, I ceased to feel sorry for him."

Julia laughed quietly, and it didn't even cause a coughing fit.

What would it be like to be Leorah, completely free and easy with her manners and behavior, unafraid of what anyone might say about her conduct, unfettered by society's rules when they seemed silly to her? Julia had never felt free and easy a day in her life. She had always concerned herself with society's rules, obeying and conforming so that her aunt and uncle would approve of her, paying the utmost attention to what she said and did to ensure she had the best chance at an advantageous marriage. And yet how little benefit it had been to her.

Still, Julia couldn't quite imagine throwing caution to the wind and behaving like Leorah.

At one time, she had thought her decorous behavior was the only kind that would please God. But she couldn't imagine God being displeased with Leorah. Leorah was kind and good and completely without artifice or ill will. She was energetic and didn't always conform to polite society's idea of how a young lady should conduct herself, but perhaps those things had nothing to do with achieving God's approval. Didn't God see inside a person's heart and judge them for their thoughts and motives? God's ways were not man's ways. It was starting to seem obvious to her that polite society's rules and God's requirements were completely different.

Leorah demonstrated how the gentleman had walked across the street and picked up his hat, and the scowl on his face when he stared at it and then at Leorah. Julia was sitting in bed, propped up by pillows and laughing, when Phoebe burst through the door.

"Julia!" Phoebe cried. "Leorah wrote to us that you were unwell. Oh, Leorah." She turned to Leorah and clasped her hands. "Thank you so much for taking care of Julia!"

Leorah said, "Julia was gravely ill with a lung infection, but she is much better now, as you can see."

Mrs. Wilhern stood in the doorway. She did not proceed any farther into the room, and she had the thin-lipped look of disapproval that used to make Julia's heart sink.

Phoebe turned her vivacity on Julia and said, "You do look a bit pale, Julia, but not so very sick."

What answer could she make to that?

"You said the servants had all deserted her except the scullery maid," Mrs. Wilhern stated, one hand on her hip and the other poised in the air by her shoulder, as if she were being fitted for a gown.

"Yes, that is correct," Leorah said.

"The servants are all here now. I've just seen them for myself."

Julia nearly gasped as her aunt questioned Leorah's word.

"Well, Mrs. Wilhern," Leorah stated, unintimidated, "that was not the case seven days ago when I found Julia here so ill she was hallucinating, burning up with fever, and without anyone to attend her except a kind scullery maid named Kitty."

"Oh dear!" Phoebe cried, covering her mouth with her hand and staring down at Julia with wide eyes.

"She was quite alone, she and Kitty, until I discovered her plight and my brother brought our physician. Dr. Alcott was most concerned and told us that she was very seriously ill with pleurisy and a lung infection, and her recovery was by no means certain." Leorah stared straight into Mrs. Wilhern's eyes.

Mrs. Wilhern's expression did not change, but she said, "I am concerned that the servants would vanish in such a manner and leave Miss Grey alone. It shall be dealt with."

"I hope you will take note of the loyalty of Kitty." Leorah continued to stare, unblinking, at Mrs. Wilhern. "She deserves to be rewarded."

Julia didn't think her aunt seemed at all interested in rewarding Kitty.

"Mrs. Wilhern, I'm happy you are here at last." Dr. Alcott stood behind Mrs. Wilhern with his medical bag.

Julia could easily imagine how her aunt felt about him saying "at last."

Her aunt turned to face the doctor. "Dr. Alcott. How do you do?" Mrs. Wilhern's tone was cold, her eyelids lowered over her eyes.

"Very well, madam. Your niece here has had a very serious illness, but she has turned the corner, so to speak, and is recovering well now."

"Her illness was serious, you say?" Mrs. Wilhern asked with a condescending look.

"Indeed. When I first saw to her, after Mr. Nicholas came and fetched me, had she not improved, I believe she could have been dead in less than twenty-four hours."

"Good heavens!" Phoebe exclaimed. "And Mr. Langdon came and fetched you?"

"Mr. Nicholas found me at home and I came immediately. Which was fortunate indeed, for she had no proper servant to care for her. But Miss Leorah and Mr. Nicholas saw to everything, as you know by now, I'm sure."

A momentary silence followed his speech. Then Mrs. Wilhern said, "We shall leave you to attend Miss Grey. Come, Phoebe."

Leorah left the room as well, with a backward glance at Julia. She was biting her lip and her brows were lowered, as if she were fighting back a retort.

Julia forced back her own thoughts and answered the doctor's questions.

CHAPTER TWENTY-SEVEN

An hour after the doctor left, a knock sounded at Julia's door, and Aunt Wilhern entered the room.

"I am pleased you are getting well, Julia." But Aunt Wilhern didn't smile or look particularly pleased. She stepped toward the bed, though remained nearer the door than Julia.

"Thank you, Aunt. I feel much better."

"I want you to know that, contrary to what some gossips are saying, I did not intend to leave you alone to die in this house while we all went to Bath." Her eyes were in their usual half-closed state, and Julia couldn't tell if her aunt was looking at her or not.

"Of course not," Julia said quickly.

"And I did specifically instruct Anna to stay with you and care for you until you were well enough to join us in Bath, for I never imagined you had more than the small cold that Phoebe had just got over."

"Of course. I wouldn't—"

"And since Anna deserted you, I have sent her away. She no longer works here. Kitty the scullery maid is to take her place in the kitchen."

This would be a promotion for Kitty. "Thank you so much for rewarding Kitty in this way."

"And she shall have extra pay for helping you while you were sick."

"Thank you, Aunt Wilhern."

"Phoebe and I are leaving now to call on Mr. and Miss Langdon, to thank them for assisting you and for sending for the doctor."

"That is very good of you."

Aunt Wilhern nodded and turned to leave.

A few hours later, Phoebe came in to tell Julia all about their call on the Langdons. Mr. Langdon had been on his way out, but when he saw them, he had stayed and talked to Phoebe.

"And you will never believe what happened." Phoebe's face was alight, her small eyes round and her mouth open.

"What?"

"Mother asked him and Leorah if they would promise to visit us this winter in Warwickshire, and Leorah said she thought perhaps she would be able to, and Mr. Langdon said the same. What do you think of that? And when he comes, Father will offer him twenty thousand pounds to marry me. I could be married before next spring."

Julia's heart skipped a beat. Would her uncle actually approach Mr. Langdon about marrying his daughter, dangling her dowry in front of him as incentive? Perhaps he already suspected—or knew—that Mr. Langdon was spying on him. Of course Uncle Wilhern would want him to marry his daughter—to ensure that he would not ever testify against him.

Aside from all that, it was simply amazing that Phoebe was content to have her father offer her in marriage to the man, referencing her twenty thousand pounds as an inducement.

Julia listened as Phoebe talked for ten minutes about how handsome Mr. Langdon was, about his height, his grace and presence on the dance floor, his impeccable taste in clothing, and what the other girls of her acquaintance had said about how handsome he was. In all her ecstatic ramblings, she said not one word about his character.

Because she didn't know anything about his fine character, his compassion, or his sensibleness and sensibility. She didn't know of his work at the Children's Aid Mission on behalf of the poor. What would Phoebe say when she found out about that? And perhaps more importantly, Phoebe didn't know that he was doing his duty to his fellow officers and his country by finding evidence of her father's treachery.

"He told me how glad he was that you have me to talk to while you are sick. He said I must make you smile and keep you company as much as possible. Do you think he likes me, Julia?" Phoebe looked at her with wide, pleading eyes.

Julia shifted against the pillows behind her back. She cleared her throat and then reached for her cup of tea. "Of course." She took a sip. "What else did he say?"

Phoebe looked disappointed at Julia's answer. She frowned and then continued, "He asked me about my trip to Bath."

Because he is polite.

"And he asked if we were coming to the ball tonight and said that he would be there." Phoebe arched her eyebrows and smirked.

He was making small talk.

"And he asked about you a lot, what the doctor said yesterday, if you were still coughing, and if you were out of bed yet." She frowned. "Sometimes I wonder if he prefers you, Julia. Mother thinks the same thing."

"Don't be silly." Julia picked at the fringe on her dressing gown. "He was only being kind. You know how thoughtful he is."

"Yes, but he did ask particularly about you, Julia." Phoebe's lips formed a pout.

"He knows how sick I was, and yet he hasn't come to visit me, has he?"

"No."

"Well, then." Julia searched her mind to think of another topic. "You never told me much about your time in Bath, Phoebe. You said your cousins were well. How many balls did you attend?"

"I attended two balls, where I was introduced to so many people I could never remember all their faces and certainly not their names, and two dinner parties, which were tedious beyond belief. Even you would have complained. We went to a concert because Lydia insisted—you remember Lydia—but it was even more boring than the dinner parties, although you would have liked the concert, Julia."

Yes, she would have very much liked to go to a concert or the theatre, but her aunt and uncle and Phoebe rarely went. Theatre was not to their taste, and Phoebe despised concerts. She said it made her want to scream to have to sit in one place for so long and not make a sound. And the music was never to her liking. Besides, music was made for dancing, Phoebe said, and simply sitting and watching the musicians play was excruciatingly dull.

"I did see Mr. Dinklage in Bath. At first I couldn't remember who he was. Can you believe it? He seemed quite altered, thinner. He said he had been very ill himself. He also seemed pleased to see a familiar face. He didn't know a soul in Bath and was only there because his mother wanted to take the waters, and she was in such poor health that she kept to her room. He did ask after you, Julia, but the look on his face was so wistful and pained. I do believe he will always regret you."

"He will forget me."

"Julia! It isn't like you to be heartless."

"I'm not being heartless. He threw me over for his mother."

"Oh, Julia!" Phoebe laughed quite raucously. "What a funny thing to say! But I suppose it is true." She shook her head. "He was never handsome enough for you."

"I am sorry I flirted with him, poor man, but I don't think I ever would have married him."

"Oh, of course not." Phoebe flipped her wrist in a dismissive gesture. Then she smiled as her mind caught on something more interesting. "The Langdons will soon be going back to their own country estate, and as soon as you are well enough to travel, we shall go home to Wilhern Manor. Then we will await Leorah and Mr. Langdon's arrival." Phoebe clasped her hands and squealed. "Is it not too wonderful?"

Julia merely smiled.

"But I am disturbing you, and you need your rest to get well. Do get well quickly, Julia, for as soon as Mr. Langdon leaves London, there can certainly be no reason for us to stay here."

"Indeed."

"What? I do declare, Julia, you talk even more softly now than you did before your illness."

"I promise to try to be well as soon as I can."

"Ah, Julia. You are so good to me." Phoebe squeezed her hand. "I don't know how I could ever do without you. Whenever Mr. Langdon and I are married, you must come and stay with us at least half the year."

Phoebe was already skipping toward the door. "Rest well, Julia."

As Phoebe closed the door behind her, Julia allowed herself to contemplate the contrast between Phoebe and Leorah. She had often thought the two of them similar. They were both full of life and energy and high spirits, but where Leorah refused to follow society's rules because she found them ridiculous, Phoebe didn't follow them because she refused to check her own recklessness. When she wanted something, she didn't care whether it was appropriate or not. Wherever her impetuous emotions led her, Phoebe followed.

Leorah, on the other hand, though spirited and lively, was also sensible. Julia couldn't imagine her allowing herself to throw caution to the wind and fall in love with a man who had shown her no encouragement. Leorah would marry sensibly—but for love—or not at all.

***

A few days later, having been informed that Felicity was coming that morning, Julia ventured downstairs and was sitting in the drawing room when her friend arrived.

"Are you sure you're warm enough?" Felicity asked as soon as they were settled near each other and Phoebe had run out of the room to fetch something.

"Yes, thank you." Julia pulled the shawl around her neck, as her doctor had cautioned her to do—to avoid exposing her throat to cool air.

"I wanted to be sure and see you before you leave for the country. Phoebe says you are all to leave as soon as you are well enough to travel."

"Oh, I do wish you could come with us." And she wished she could tell Felicity that she wasn't likely to be going anywhere with the Wilherns, as her uncle would most likely be going to prison soon.

"But we are destined to stay in town. London is so dirty and disagreeable in winter." Felicity sighed but kept smiling.

Felicity's father had gained his fortune through trade and was still employed as a merchant. They had a fashionable house in town but no house in the country. Julia would have loved to invite her friend to visit her, but the Wilherns' country house would be confiscated as soon as her uncle was arrested for treason.

"Perhaps you will be mistress of your own country estate someday and can ask me for a visit then." Felicity smiled archly.

"That hardly seems likely at the moment."

"Does it not?"

Julia eyed her friend. "What are you thinking of, pray tell?" Then she had a nervous suspicion that she already knew the answer.

"Did I not hear that it was Mr. Langdon who flew down the street after the doctor for you? That he stayed all day, pacing about, to hear how you were faring?"

"Did you?" Julia found herself breathless at the thought of Mr. Langdon so concerned for her.

"Now don't turn pale," Felicity said, starting to fan Julia's face.

"I am well. But I believe you are mistaken, Felicity."

"Am I?"

"Yes. Mr. Langdon is believed to be Phoebe's suitor."

Felicity gave her a dubious look, raising her brows and quirking one side of her mouth. "After the way he spoke to you and looked at you when we went to the Children's Aid Mission . . . I would not be surprised if he did not ask you to marry him very soon."

Julia would not, could not, allow herself to hope for anything concerning Mr. Langdon.

A servant announced Miss Leorah Langdon at that moment. She came into the room with a bright smile and wearing an even brighter yellow spencer, which heightened the beauty of her dark hair and eyes.

Julia gave Felicity's hand a quick squeeze of warning, hoping she understood not to talk anymore of Mr. Langdon.

Leorah greeted them both warmly. As initial niceties were being exchanged, Felicity asked, "And is your family well, Leorah?"

"Oh yes, quite well. No, that is not true." She frowned a bit. "My brother has been quite ill."

Julia felt all the blood drain from her face. Poor Mr. Langdon! Had he contracted her illness? Would helping her cost him his health, or even his life?

"Oh, I mean my oldest brother, Jonathan, not Nicholas." Leorah smiled at Julia and squeezed her hand reassuringly. "Forgive me for my carelessness."

Felicity was grinning at her, and Leorah's look was more of compassion. She said softly, "No one who knew Nicholas could help but love him."

Julia forced a smile, her face still tingling as she determined not to dwell on Leorah's words. "Shall we have some tea?" Julia rang the bell.

Phoebe bounced into the room, exclaiming in exaggerated terms her joy at seeing Leorah. "What a happy group we are!" Phoebe cried, clasping her hands.

Phoebe talked excitedly with Leorah, and Felicity leaned her head close to Julia's and whispered, "Mr. Langdon will never love Phoebe, no matter how much she wants him to."

Julia gave Felicity a horrified look, and her friend said no more. The tea was brought in, and Phoebe played hostess by moving closer to pass out the tea things.

Phoebe dominated the conversation, and Julia's thoughts whirled inside her head. She remembered the expression on Leorah's face, how she had looked almost sad as she had squeezed Julia's hand. Perhaps she knew how Julia felt about her brother but knew also that her brother couldn't ask Julia to marry him.

Besides, Julia had a legitimate worry, now that she was getting her strength back and her aunt and uncle were back from Bath. Her uncle would surely insist she marry Mr. Edgerton immediately. In fact, now that Mr. Edgerton had the special license—as she assumed he had already acquired it—her uncle could take her straight to the church on any given day and force her to marry the man at a moment's notice.

"Don't you think so, Julia?" Phoebe asked. All three young ladies were staring at her.

"What?"

"The roads to Wilhern Manor. They're the best roads in that part of England. Leorah and her brother will have no trouble at all traveling to visit us this winter."

"Oh, certainly, the roads are very good."

"Julia, should you go back to bed? Are you feeling ill?"

"Oh no, I am well. I think tomorrow I shall be well enough for a short walk."

"Oh, I shall tell Mother!" Phoebe clapped her hands. "We shall be in Warwickshire very soon, in less than a week, I am sure, and then you shall come and visit us, Leorah. Your brother promised most faithfully."

"Of course, Phoebe."

Julia did not miss the conspiratorial smile Leorah sent her way. She hoped Phoebe did not notice it.

CHAPTER TWENTY-EIGHT

Julia sat at her desk replying to a letter from Sarah Peck, who was sending her letters through Felicity from her new home.

A knock came at her door. Julia turned to see her uncle entering.

She hastily covered the salutation of her letter with a second sheet of paper.

"Julia. You are nearly well, I see."

"Good morning, Uncle. I—I have not entirely got my strength back yet. But Dr. Alcott says I should make a full recovery."

"That is very good news." But the cold way he eyed her belied his words. "Now that you are better," he went on, "I trust you are willing for your marriage to Edgerton to take place soon."

"Of course." *What day? Tell me what day.*

"At the moment, Edgerton is away—that is why he did not come to visit you when you were ill—looking into an estate he is thinking of purchasing in Warwickshire."

Julia feigned a look of pleasure at hearing he was to acquire an estate in the same county as Wilhern Manor.

"Will he return soon?"

"Yes, I daresay. Very soon."

Good. He would be back in time to be arrested, along with her uncle, for treason.

"When he does return, he will want to marry right away."

"Yes, I imagine he will."

Her uncle continued to eye her. He suddenly stepped toward her with a menacing, twisted smile. Grabbing her arm, he yanked her to her feet.

"You showed that paper to Nicholas Langdon, didn't you?"

Aware of his painful grip on her arm, a thousand thoughts raced through her mind.

He jerked her closer. "Answer me."

"I don't know what you are talking of." She tried to clear her mind of fear, to think coldly and logically. "Uncle, you are hurting me."

"Don't play innocent. You are the only one who could have taken it."

"Taken what?"

He glared at her from eyes as black as night. "I am not a man to be trifled with. I will not allow you or anyone else to get in my way." He tightened his grip on her arm, squeezing so hard she cried out.

"Be quiet," he ground out.

Suddenly, her door opened and Phoebe entered without knocking, as she often did.

"Father!" Phoebe cried. "What are you doing?"

Her uncle released her and stepped back. "Nothing at all. Julia and I were only having a discussion about when her marriage to Mr. Edgerton would take place. Isn't that right, Julia?"

"Yes." Julia rubbed her arm where her uncle had so cruelly held her.

"Phoebe, leave us for a few more minutes while we finish our discussion."

"Julia, are you well? Father, what is this?"

"Phoebe, do as you're told," he ordered in a harsher tone than Julia had ever heard him use with his daughter. His tone softened a bit as he amended, "You may come back in a few minutes."

Julia kept her back turned and soon heard the door shut. When she turned around, Phoebe was gone.

Her uncle was glaring at her. "You will not speak a word of this to Phoebe. You will not leave this room until Edgerton returns tomorrow to marry you. And if you do, I shall make you rue it."

Would he beat her the way he had beaten his horse all those years ago?

But her next thought was, *He is afraid.* He realized she had taken the incriminating paper, and he had to keep her quiet. Otherwise he never would have threatened her like that. He was afraid, as well he should be, since treason was a crime punishable by death.

"Do I make myself clear?"

"Yes, Uncle Wilhern." She glared at him, stare for stare.

Finally, he turned away and left her room.

Julia examined her arm. It ached terribly where her uncle had dug into her soft flesh. Bruises were already appearing on the white skin on the underside of her arm, one for each of his cruel, biting fingers.

How dare he physically bully her! She closed her eyes, trying to keep the hate from overwhelming her.

A timid knock came at her door. Julia took a deep breath, let it out, and called, "Come in."

Phoebe stuck her head in. "Is Father gone?" She came inside, closed the door behind her, and then hurried across the room to Julia. "What was that about? Was Father threatening you? Surely he wouldn't . . . Is he forcing you to marry Mr. Edgerton?"

How much should she confess to Phoebe? Her cousin would despise her when the truth came out, when she discovered that Julia and Mr. Langdon, the man Phoebe hoped to marry, had conspired to put her father in prison and change her privileged life forever. Julia's heart suddenly ached with the imminent loss of her closest friend.

"Phoebe, I . . . I am still not feeling entirely well. Your father was speaking to me about Mr. Edgerton. He believes my marrying Mr. Edgerton is for the best." Julia kept her face turned away. Phoebe was not the most perceptive person, but Julia didn't want to risk her reading her expression.

"I am sure that is true, Julia. Mr. Edgerton is handsome. At least you won't have unattractive children."

Was that truly Phoebe's first thought?

"Uh, yes. Will you do something for me, Phoebe?"

"Of course."

"Will you let me know when Mr. Edgerton arrives back in London, if you hear anything? Or if you hear anything of him?"

"I will, Julia. But don't worry. Mr. Edgerton is a gentleman, and Father told me he truly loves you. You will be content with him, and Father also said he is buying an estate in Warwickshire. We can visit each other every day, nearly, and everything will be as it always was."

A sudden attack of tears had Julia blinking rapidly and nodding.

"It will all be well," Phoebe said, squeezing her arm comfortingly.

Julia gasped in pain, as Phoebe had squeezed the place where Mr. Wilhern had bruised her.

"What is it?"

"Nothing."

"Marriage to Mr. Edgerton will not be bad. You will see."

A lump in her throat suddenly choked off her air, but Julia fought it down and simply nodded, trying to smile.

"Will you come down to dinner?"

"No, I think I need to rest."

"I shall have your dinner sent up to you, then."

Julia nodded, not trusting herself to speak.

After Phoebe left, Julia walked to her window and looked out on the street below. If only she could get a note to Mr. Langdon. He might be in danger. After all, they were ridding themselves of Julia. Forcing her to marry Mr. Edgerton would prevent her from testifying against him, and, consequently, Mr. Wilhern. Now that he knew of Mr. Langdon's involvement . . .

But it was much too dangerous to try to write to Mr. Langdon, and even if her uncle had not forbidden her to leave her room, someone might follow her.

Just then, a man who was slightly hunched approached their front door, looking quickly back the way he had come and then over his shoulder, as if trying to see if anyone was following him. Then he disappeared into the house.

Surely this man was meeting with her uncle. What if he were bringing information that Nicholas needed?

Julia slipped out of her room and hurried down the stairs to the floor below. As she reached the corridor that led to her uncle's study, she heard male voices. She stood still and listened. They were coming from farther down the corridor, near the front door.

Julia might only have a second or two. She ran the few feet down the corridor, which felt like a few hundred feet, and darted in through the open doorway of Mr. Wilhern's study.

Quickly, she swung open the door of the wardrobe and stepped inside, squatting and closing the door behind her. She closed her eyes and tried to calm her breathing and her pounding heart while she waited.

She heard footsteps coming closer. Two men passed by the crack in the door of the wardrobe. One was her uncle and the other was the man who had approached the front door just moments ago.

Julia kept her eye up to the crack as her uncle pulled a folded piece of paper out of his pocket.

"Take this," he said, "and deliver it to Nicholas Langdon. I've forged his friend John Wilson's signature and handwriting, asking him to come tonight to the Children's Aid Mission at eight o'clock to help him with something urgent. Then you must be at the corner of Bishopsgate Street and Halfmoon Alley no later than seven thirty. Wait on the opposite side of the street and shoot him from there."

Shoot him.

The breath rushed out of Julia's lungs, but she focused on not making a sound.

"Are you sure you will remember all that?" her uncle asked.

"Of course." The man repeated all that Mr. Wilhern had told him, ending with, "and I'll shoot Langdon from across the street and then run like the hell hounds are at my heels."

"Good. And don't come back here. I'll come to you."

"Yes, sir."

Just at that moment, Julia's foot slipped, and she caught herself with her hand, making a slight noise against the side of the wardrobe. Had her uncle heard her? Her heart seemed to stop beating as she waited.

"I'll walk you to the door," her uncle said, and their footsteps retreated out of the room.

She waited another moment and then opened the door and stepped out.

"Julia." Her uncle stood in front of her, his lip curled in an angry smile. "So that is how you found my note." He grabbed her arms with both hands and drew her forward, within inches of his dark eyes. "Who did you tell about the note? Nicholas Langdon?"

"No, no!" *God, forgive me for the lie.*

"Did you write it down? Did you write down anything that was in the note?"

"I don't know what you're talking about."

"Shall we change our plans?" The man who had met with her uncle was still standing there, and Julia noticed the deep pockmarks on his cheeks.

"No." Her uncle turned his head to address the pockmarked man but did not loosen his grip on her arms. "It's more important than ever to kill Langdon tonight."

"But why?" Julia cried. "He doesn't know anything. And Phoebe will be heartbroken. She might even do herself harm."

"She is young and silly," Mr. Wilhern said harshly. "She'll fall in love with the first man who smiles at her. We've come too far to let you and Langdon ruin all our plans."

"Please. You do not need to kill Mr. Langdon. He doesn't know anything. You'll be found out if you do."

"If Edgerton were not about to marry you to shut you up, I'd kill you myself. That is how ruthless I am, Julia Grey." He ground out the last few words through his clenched teeth. "You will not stop us, do you hear?"

He shook her back and forth until her vision grew blurry. When Julia blinked and was able to focus again, she saw he had let go of one of her arms and was holding a knife.

"Go." He nodded at the pockmarked man. Turning back to Julia, he pressed the point of the knife into her side.

"Let's go. If you make a sound, I shall stab you and leave you to bleed to death. Edgerton can marry you tomorrow, if you're still alive."

Julia could do Mr. Langdon no good if she were dead, so she walked silently while her uncle forced her up the stairs to her room. She saw no one the entire way. He pushed her inside and locked the door from the outside.

CHAPTER TWENTY-NINE

Julia put her hands to her head. If only she had not made that noise and her uncle had not found her. But it did no good to regret that. She had to think. There had to be a way out, or a way to get a message to Mr. Langdon.

She ran to the window. She could always watch and wait for him to pass by and yell out to him. But her uncle could catch her and do harm to Mr. Langdon without waiting until tonight. Besides, he might not walk by at all.

Perhaps Phoebe would find her locked in her room and help her escape. But that was unlikely. Her uncle would have thought of that and was probably at this moment telling Phoebe a lie about Julia. Maybe he was sending Phoebe somewhere on a visit that would keep her out of the house until at least tomorrow. Once he'd had Nicholas murdered and could get Julia officially married to Mr. Edgerton, he'd make sure Julia and Mr. Edgerton were sent far away on their honeymoon, so that Julia could not tell Phoebe anything until much later.

No doubt her uncle had plans to move his family to the Continent as soon as his plot was completed. But what about Wilhern Manor in

Warwickshire? Would he abandon it? Nicholas had said her uncle was greatly in debt and would probably lose the estate to creditors.

Julia walked to the door and tried to open it. It was locked, as she knew it would be. Was there a way to open it? Perhaps she could force it open. But with what?

She went back to the window and opened it. Three floors off the ground, she'd be killed or badly injured if she jumped. She couldn't climb down, as there was nothing on the façade of the building to hold on to.

Perhaps she could get a message to someone.

Quickly, she scribbled a note that read, *Please open the door. Julia.*

She ran to the door that connected her room with Phoebe's. They had both agreed, several years before, to keep the door between their rooms locked, for privacy's sake. The problem was that Phoebe had the only key.

She shoved the note through the crack under Phoebe's door and then knocked softly.

There was no sound. She knocked again. Still nothing.

Of course her uncle had known she would knock on this door and try to get help from Phoebe.

Julia leaned against the door.

"What are my options," she said softly to herself. "I can sit here listening for someone to come into Phoebe's room and then knock on the door and beg them to open it. Or I can wait and listen at the other door, the one to the corridor, and knock on the door when I hear someone walking by. Or I can open the window, call down to whomever is passing by, and hope they will be willing—and able—to come inside and save me."

The first option seemed unlikely to work, since probably no one would be entering Phoebe's room. The last option seemed likely to fail, as her uncle would hear her, or would intercept the person coming in to save her. The second option seemed the best of the three.

Julia stood and walked to her own door. As she did, she passed the bell pull.

Of course! She could ring for a servant. Could it be that her uncle had forgotten such an easy and common way of getting assistance? A servant would hear the bell and come to see what she wanted. It was not often—very rare, in fact—that she ever rang for a servant.

Should she try it now? Or wait until her uncle had decided she was being docile and would accept her fate?

It was now two o'clock. Still pondering, she sat down against the door to the corridor and laid her head against it to catch any sound she could.

After a few minutes of sitting, dwelling on what would happen to Mr. Langdon if she did not warn him, she was overcome with nervous energy and jumped up. There had to be another way. There must be something she wasn't thinking of.

She wandered over to her old trunk, which she had brought with her after her parents had died and which had contained all her possessions at that time. She had not looked inside it in years.

She opened it and rummaged around inside, finding a Bible, a *Book of Common Prayer*, and several other items, including baby clothes and a black iron cross.

She picked up the cross, having never paid much attention to it before, and turned it over in her hand. The cross was heavy and seemed very old. It was a little larger than her hand and would make a good weapon if she had to defend herself. And now that she thought of it, she could probably use it to break the lock on one of the doors.

Walking over to the window, she sat down and stared out at the street below, cradling the cross in her hands.

So now she had a fifth option—break through the locked door herself. The thought gave her a feeling of power.

But it would be best to wait until closer to eight o'clock before trying to escape. If she escaped too soon, her uncle might discover it in time to find another way to kill Mr. Langdon.

Footsteps approached on the other side of her door. She hid the heavy cross in the folds of her dress, against her outer leg, and covered it with her hand.

A key scraped in the lock. The door swung open and her uncle entered.

"Julia. I am glad you are taking this so well. You always were a very sensible girl."

"What do you want?" She turned her face away from him, unwilling for him to see her feelings in her expression.

"I came to tell you not to try to ring for a servant. I have disconnected your bell. Also, I have sent Phoebe away. She thinks you went riding with Leorah Langdon without her. She is furious with you and so has gone on an outing with her mother. They will spend the night at her cousin Dorothea's tonight. I just wanted to let you know, so you wouldn't hope for Phoebe's intervention."

His voice was hard and cold, his face expressionless.

"If you cooperate, I shall encourage Mr. Edgerton to treat you well once you are married. If you do not cooperate . . . Mr. Edgerton listens to everything I tell him. He is quite swayed by me. If I tell him you are an obstinate, stubborn sort of girl, it will be easy for me to persuade him that treating you with kindness is a mistake, that he should be harsh in order to secure your love and obedience. Do I make myself clear?"

Julia refused to even look at him and made him no answer.

After a long pause, he said, "Everything will turn out all right for you. Edgerton will have a fortune, and you and Phoebe will be settled near enough for frequent visits. What more could a girl of no fortune and no parents hope for?"

Heat rose into her face. *What more could a girl like me hope for? Marriage to a man I could never respect and friendship with a spoiled, selfish girl like Phoebe?*

Was that truly what she thought of Phoebe? Had Julia's feelings for her cousin changed so drastically?

Soon—very soon—Julia would be free of Phoebe, for good or ill, but she could never hate the one person she had grown up loving.

As soon as she escaped and was able to warn Mr. Langdon of the attempt on his life, Julia would take the post chaise to her new position. She had been accepted as a governess by the Athertons in Suffolk. They had younger children who had been without a governess for some weeks. Mrs. Atherton was quite eager for Julia to come to them as soon as might be.

The terrible fate of becoming a governess, which Sarah Peck had so dreaded for Julia, seemed infinitely better than staying and marrying Mr. Edgerton, even though he would have a fortune after helping to arrange the assassination of England's best general.

Her uncle finally interrupted her thoughts.

"I shall leave you now, Julia. You never should have interfered in my business. But it shall all turn out well in the end."

He closed the door behind him.

***

Julia had been in her room for hours. No one had come to her rescue. She had run out of water and had not eaten anything since breakfast. But she felt strength—nervous energy, more like—running through her limbs and emboldening her. She was ready to escape, however she might be able to.

It was now nearly six thirty. She wanted to give herself enough time to reach Mr. Langdon before he left his home to make his way to the East Side and Bishopsgate Street.

Suddenly, she heard the scraping of metal in the lock on her door again, and it opened. Her uncle stood balancing a tray of food. "I did not want you telling Edgerton I mistreated you, so I brought you something."

He looked almost cheerful as he set the tray of food and drink on her small table.

Julia said, "That is kind of you," in a bland voice. She was becoming quite good at this espionage thing, disguising her feelings and such.

She walked over and pretended to be interested in the food. She even lifted a piece of bread to her lips and took a tiny bite so he could see her chewing.

"I shall leave you to eat. But I am nearby . . . if you need anything."

Of course, they both knew he wasn't nearby in case she needed anything, but rather, in case she tried to escape. Julia nodded and watched him leave, hearing the key grating in the lock as he once again locked her in.

Julia took a larger bite of the bread to try to settle her stomach, but it only made her feel more queasy. She put it down and took a sip of tea—and realized how thirsty she was. She drank the entire cup and then poured herself another and drank it as well.

"Thank you, Uncle."

She could do this. Her uncle thought she was a "good, sensible girl" and that all she could wish for was Mr. Edgerton as a husband. If he did not yet realize it, then he was about to discover that she was not the timid six-year-old he had brought home to be a companion for his own overindulged little girl.

Julia went and picked up the heavy iron cross. She went to the door that separated her room from Phoebe's, since he might be watching her door, raised the cross, and whacked at the lock. It made a loud sound.

"God, please don't let him hear. Please help me."

She struck the lock again. Nothing happened. The lock was also made of iron, apparently, and her striking it with the cross was not having much of an effect.

Perhaps she could pick the lock.

She hurried to her dressing table and found a hairpin. She ran back to the door and stuck the hairpin in the lock. After jiggling it and forcing it past something that clicked, she felt the lock give way, and the door opened.

Her heart soared. She took the heavy iron cross with her and hurried through Phoebe's room to her door. But when she tried to open it, it was also locked.

Again, Julia went to work on the lock with the hairpin. But after several minutes, she put down the cross so she could work the pin with both hands. Still, it did not open.

How late was it getting? Would she be too late to save Mr. Langdon? Her hands were sweating and she wiped them on her muslin dress.

Julia could feel her composure slipping as she worked more frantically at the lock. "God," she whispered, "I know I rarely pray except in church. Perhaps it is wrong to only pray when I am in trouble, but I need help. Please, please do not let Mr. Langdon die." She bit her lip as she kept working at the lock. She whispered in desperation, "Please help."

An idea came to her to use two hairpins instead of one. Julia sprang up off the floor and ran to her dressing table to grab a second pin. She rushed back and continued working at the lock, this time using two pins. In less than a minute, she heard the telltale click as the lock opened.

She grabbed the iron cross off the floor, jerked the door open, and ran out into the corridor. Thinking to take the servants' stairs at the back of the house, she turned to her right and saw her uncle standing just outside her door, his eyes wide.

"Get back here," he growled.

CHAPTER THIRTY

Julia turned and ran toward the front stairs, her heart pounding sickeningly.

"Get back here, Julia!" Her uncle's footsteps pounded behind her.

She clutched the heavy cross as she ran. *Oh God, help me. I don't want to strike my uncle with this cross, but please don't let him catch me.*

Her skirts were tangling around her legs and slowing her down. She could feel her uncle getting closer but did not dare turn around to look.

She reached the stairs and ran down them two at a time.

"You can't get away."

Julia imagined she felt his breath on her neck. She turned her head just as he lunged for her, his hands reaching.

She screamed, stepping quickly to the other side of the stairs.

Uncle Wilhern brushed against her arm as he lost his balance. He fell headfirst down the stairs. He finally came to rest at the bottom, lying on his side. His eyes were closed, and he did not move.

Julia ran the rest of the way down the stairs, avoiding his motionless form as she held up her skirt with one hand.

She darted out the front door and down the steps in the direction of the Langdons' town house.

***

Julia knocked on the front door of the Langdon home while staring back down the street. She was breathing so hard, when the servant answered the door, she could barely speak.

"Is Mr. Nicholas Langdon at home?"

The servant, a middle-aged woman, stared at her with her mouth open. "No, miss. Mr. Nicholas has gone from home and did not say when he might return."

"It's very important." Julia stopped to swallow past the dryness in her throat. "I need to speak with him, if he is at home."

"Upon my honor, miss, he left just two minutes ago. He took the carriage. Old Bailey drove him."

"Thank you." Julia ran from the door, hurrying down the street to the next street over, where she could always find a hack for hire.

Oh, why had she not got there sooner? Why did he have to be gone?

She slowed, unable to run anymore. Soon she came upon a carriage and driver. "Please, sir, can you take me to Bishopsgate Street?"

He tipped his hat and quoted her a price. Fortunately, she always carried a few coins sewn into the hem of her skirt, to keep it from flying up immodestly in any gust of wind. It should be enough.

The young driver handed her in.

"If you please, sir, I am in a hurry."

"I'll do my best, miss."

Soon they were off, riding down the street at a fast pace.

Julia ripped the hem out of her dress and removed enough coins to pay the driver. And then she had several minutes to think while they rode through the evening streets. The sun had not yet gone down. Surely it could not be very late. Mr. Langdon must have gone somewhere else first, because it would not yet be half past seven when she arrived at the place where her uncle's evil friend was assigned to wait and shoot Nicholas Langdon.

But what if she were too late? No, no, she could not think like that. She would make it. She would get there in time. She must.

An image of Nicholas Langdon lying in the street, a bullet through his chest, rose vividly in her mind. A pain, as if she had been shot herself, streaked through her.

Ruthlessly, she shoved the image away. He would not be shot. He would not.

The carriage arrived at Bishopsgate Street in less time than usual. Julia watched out of the window until they were near the place where the pockmarked man was supposed to wait.

She could not let him see her, she suddenly realized. He knew what she looked like.

Julia rapped on the side of the carriage to get the driver to stop. "Let me out here."

He stopped the horses. Julia opened the door herself and sprang out. She gave him the money and then noticed him staring at the iron cross in her hand. He must think she was daft. Truly, she wasn't sure why she was still clutching the thing. But she hurried away down the street.

She had come away without even her bonnet, without a shawl or anything of the sort. Without anything to hide her face, the man across the street would see her.

She slipped into the nearest door, a shabby little shop that sold candles and other household odds and ends. Through the shop window she could see the place where the pockmarked man would be waiting. No doubt he was hidden in the shadows of the alley, waiting for Nicholas Langdon to walk by. Would he have his coachman let him out at the end of Bishopsgate Street, as he always did, and walk the rest of the way? Or would he have him drive closer tonight?

She needed to be able to see when he arrived. She slipped out the door and back onto the street, shielding her face with her hand. She stepped into another shop, quite close to the corner of the street where the Children's Aid Mission was located. Standing at the large front window, she would surely see Nicholas Langdon as he walked this way, before he reached the corner.

She looked back and forth, examining every face that came near. She also searched the opposite corner, looking for the pockmarked man. Was he waiting in the shadows of the alley, between those two buildings? It seemed the most logical place.

She continued to search down the street for Nicholas Langdon. But what if he came from the other direction this time? Every nerve in her body seemed to be just beneath the surface, stretching, ready to leap out and stop Nicholas Langdon.

"Miss, may I help you with something? I need to close the shop."

The baker—she suddenly noticed this was a bakery—stood at her elbow.

"Oh. No, thank you. I was just . . . No, thank you." Julia stepped out the door—and saw Nicholas Langdon coming. From the opposite way. He was nearly to the corner. A man across the street was stepping out of the alley and raising a gun.

"Nicholas!" Julia screamed his name and ran as fast as she could, just as a loud report sounded from across the street.

She felt herself slam into Nicholas Langdon's chest. A second loud blast came from the same place. Julia dropped her cross. It fell to the street with a metallic thud.

Her knees weren't holding her up, but Mr. Langdon's arms kept her upright against his chest.

Nicholas Langdon was pulling her into the smaller street, toward the mission.

"You must hurry and get away. They are trying to kill you." She forced her knees not to buckle. "Go, quickly. The shooter will find you."

"Be calm. Some men tackled him and took his gun away." He held her at arm's length and looked her up and down. "Oh no." His face held a look of horror as he stared at her midsection.

"What is it?" But she suddenly knew. A sharp pain stabbed her side. Another pain was pulsing through her hand. Blood stained her white dress.

"You've been shot." Nicholas Langdon scooped her up in his arms, holding her tight against him. He started at a fast walk toward the Children's Aid Mission building.

"Don't take me to the mission. That is the first place they will look."

"Where, then?"

"To the Bartholdys'. Do you remember where it is?"

"You need a doctor." He suddenly groaned.

"What is it? Are you hurt?"

"No! Julia, you've been shot! Oh God, please don't let her die."

"I won't—" She gasped at the pain in her side. "I won't die. It is nothing, I am sure." She glanced down but could not see her wound, as her injured side was pressed against his stomach.

He was striding very fast, almost running, as though she weighed no more than a child.

People were exclaiming all around them, and those on the street stood back to let them pass, staring very pointedly at her.

She lifted her hand. It was indeed quite bloody. But at least all her fingers were present.

"I do not think I am injured very badly. I think I can walk."

He only glanced at her, his brows drawn together, and kept up his fast pace.

Soon they reached the Bartholdys' tiny house. "Knock," he ordered.

Julia knocked on the door with her uninjured hand. Nicholas Langdon tried to open the door, but it was locked.

A servant opened to them. She stepped back when she saw Mr. Langdon holding Julia.

Everything around her became a bit hazy. He laid her on a settee and knelt beside her.

"Bring something to staunch the bleeding," he ordered. Was he angry? He sounded angry. Madame Bartholdy was running around in such a distracted way, calling out instructions to their servant. Julia was hardly aware of anything but Nicholas Langdon hovering over her, his face contorted with obvious anguish.

Nicholas stared down at Julia's side, pressing his hands against it.

"You are spoiling your gloves." It was the only thing she could think to say as the bright-red stains spread over his fingers.

"Send the servant to fetch a physician." He glanced up at Madame Bartholdy.

"Yes, of course," she said in her thick accent. Then she turned to give instructions to the poor servant, who looked as if she might faint.

"Are you in much pain?" He was staring down at her in that intense way of his, his brown eyes quite close to hers as he continued to press his hands into her side—until Madame Bartholdy brought a bundle of cloth bandages. He took them and pressed them against the wound.

"Not if you wouldn't press so hard."

"I am sorry, but I don't want you to lose too much blood."

Everything seemed like a dream and not entirely real.

He leaned quite close again and said, "How can I ever forgive myself? Oh, Julia, why did you do it?"

The pain—and his calling her by her given name, Julia, instead of Miss Grey—seemed to wake her out of her dreamlike state. She had been shot. *Oh dear.* And she had screamed his Christian name just before the first shot came.

She gazed up into his tense face. "I thank God you were not hurt, that I reached you in time."

Madame Bartholdy suddenly knelt beside him. "Let me do that. You comfort Miss Grey."

Nicholas Langdon moved closer to where Julia's head lay on the settee. The pain was suddenly so sharp she was having trouble catching her breath.

Mr. Langdon snatched off his soiled gloves and threw them on the floor. He picked up her injured hand, took up one of the cloth bandages, and wiped at the blood.

"It looks as if he only nicked the side of your finger, here." He showed her and then he ripped the cloth into a long strip and wrapped it around the wound, tying it in place.

"Whatever you were holding, it must have stopped the bullet from hitting my chest."

"My parents' cross."

"What? A cross?"

"The surgeon is coming," the servant announced, running back into the room. "I found him walking this way. He was on his way home from another call."

"There are no physicians nearby, but a surgeon may do almost as well," Madame Bartholdy said apologetically.

An older man came in the door and made his way toward them, finding a table to set down his bag.

"The second bullet must have struck your side," Nicholas Langdon said. "Do you know who did it?"

"I don't know his name. He had pockmarks on his face and brown hair. My uncle told him to shoot you. He sent you the note. It was not from Mr. Wilson at all. I was so afraid I wouldn't get there in time." Her last few words came out as a whisper.

Nicholas Langdon bent and kissed her wrist and then stood as the surgeon drew near and began asking questions.

Monsieur Bartholdy said, "Mr. Langdon? Come. We men are not needed for this next phase of the operation."

Where was Monsieur Bartholdy taking him? But when the surgeon cut a hole in the side of her muslin gown, Julia was glad he was gone.

The surgeon washed away the blood. "Glory be. This is but a flesh wound. The bullet merely scraped you, child, and kept going. You shall require no more than a bandage." He shook his head, smiling. "You are a very fortunate young lady."

Only a flesh wound. That was good. She waited impatiently as he applied some kind of salve to the wound and then bandaged it with Madame Bartholdy's help.

"Madame Bartholdy," Julia said, reaching for that lady's hand, "please tell Mr. Langdon that he must get away from here. He could still be in danger."

"You can tell him so yourself," she said cheerfully, laying a thin shawl over Julia to ensure her modesty. "I'll go get him."

"Now, miss, I think you will be well." The surgeon was packing up his things. "Change your bandage once or twice a day and do not do anything strenuous for several days."

"Oh, I must pay you." She could not allow the Bartholdys to bear the expense.

"I will take care of it," Nicholas Langdon said as he strode toward her. He and the surgeon spoke quietly with each other in the corner of the room for a few moments before he came toward her.

"You must go." Julia tried to sound as urgent as possible. "My uncle may try again to kill you."

"Won't he also come looking for you?"

"Yes, but he won't kill me." *He will only force me to marry Mr. Edgerton.* "You are the one in danger."

"I do not think he will attempt to kill me a second time in one night. But I must go now and speak to the constable. I saw some men overcome our shooter and capture him, just after the second shot."

"Oh. But what if—"

"Do not worry." He grabbed her uninjured hand and held it firmly between both of his. "I shall return for you very soon. First I must make sure your uncle is arrested—tonight, so he cannot harm you or me again."

"But you do not know who else may be out there, trying to kill you."

"Hush, now."

She was so aware of his bare hand holding hers. What did he mean by it? For him to hold her hand without gloves . . . it was very improper. But she suddenly didn't care, for the first time in her life, what was proper or improper. She loved this man with all her heart.

But that was precisely why she should not allow him to hold her hand. He could not marry her, after all.

He seemed about to say something else when a knock came at the door.

"Nicholas?" came a man's voice from behind them. "I heard you— or a lady—were shot. What has happened?"

Mr. Wilson came toward them, his eyes roving from Mr. Langdon to Julia lying on the settee.

"This lady, Miss Grey, was hit by a shot fired at me, I'm afraid." Mr. Langdon looked down at her, his expression very serious. "But now I must go and see what I can do to have our assailants arrested. Would you stay here while I'm gone and make sure the lady is safe?"

"Yes, of course."

Madame Bartholdy was standing over Julia, smiling. "You should rest, my dear. The surgeon said to give you a few drops of this to help you sleep." She held a small bottle and a glass in her hand.

Julia tried to catch a last glimpse of Mr. Langdon as he walked out the door. *God, keep him safe.*

CHAPTER THIRTY-ONE

Julia awoke to a bit of light spreading on the floor from some unseen window. Where was she? She recognized the Bartholdys' sitting room and realized she was lying on their settee amidst a comfortable cocoon of blankets. Then the events of the day before came back to her.

Her side pained her a bit as she sat up. But it was only a flesh wound, the surgeon had said. Her finger was still wrapped in the bandage Nicholas Langdon had tied on and did not hurt at all. But she must have dropped her cross when the bullet had hit her finger. She wished she could have it back, wished she had not dropped it, but at the time, it was the last thing on her mind.

Had Mr. Langdon and the police apprehended the men responsible for shooting at him, including her uncle?

"I have to go." Julia pushed herself up, feeling the pull of the bandage on her side and a twinge of pain.

"Where are you going?" Madame Bartholdy sat up straighter from the armchair where she sat covered with a thin blanket. She smiled pleasantly.

"Madame Bartholdy. Thank you for caring for me last night and staying with me. I seem to have slept all night. Do you know if Mr. Langdon was able to . . ."

Footsteps sounded in the corridor, and then the man in question stood in the doorway.

"Miss Grey, Madame Bartholdy," he greeted them politely. He turned to Julia with a slight crease in his forehead. "How are you feeling this morning?"

"I am very well, thank you. Just a flesh wound." She smiled.

"I retrieved this for you. At least, I think it is yours." He held out her heavy iron cross.

"Oh yes! Thank you. It belonged to my parents. I brought it with me to use as a weapon, in case I needed it."

He reverently laid it in her lap. "I thank God that you did. It saved my life."

Julia caressed the cross. It was not decorative or beautiful, just a plain iron cross, but tears pricked her eyes at how grateful she was to it for saving Nicholas Langdon's life.

"And you?" she asked. "How did you fare last night?"

He looked a bit rumpled and was still wearing the same clothes he'd had on the evening before.

"I was able to convince the War Office that it was time to apprehend the man behind the shooting last night. However, Mr. Wilhern was not at home when they went to arrest him. He must have fled. They will keep looking for him. But they were able to capture the man who fired the shots. They have also arrested the four men listed on Mr. Wilhern's note, who were booked on the ship with false identification as soldiers bound for the Peninsula. Their plan to assassinate General Wellington has been thwarted, thanks to you, Miss Grey."

His gentle smile warmed her heart. "And thanks to you, Lieutenant Langdon."

"And I am alive thanks to you, Miss Grey."

"I shall go check on breakfast." Madame Bartholdy stood, smiling, and left the room.

Now that they were alone, Julia was not sure where to look or what to do. The last thing she wanted was for Mr. Langdon to feel obligated to her in some way. But how could she say so without sounding very rude?

"I need to go." Julia threw off the blanket covering her but then remembered she was not suitably dressed, as her dress had a gaping hole in the side. She made sure the shawl was wrapped around her middle. "I do not want to be a burden to the Bartholdys."

"You may come and stay with me—with my family, Leorah and my mother. They would be very glad for you to visit."

"The truth is, I have been accepted as a governess for a family in Suffolk. The Athertons. I will need to travel there right away."

"A governess?" He was staring at her as if she had just told him she was growing a mermaid's tail.

"I must provide for myself now." She felt the heat rise into her cheeks. Of course, he could not be her friend, not now that she would be a governess. She would no longer be in his social class.

"But you are injured. You do not need to go today."

"I think it is best if I do. My uncle may want revenge against me, and he could possibly try to harm me or the Bartholdys if I stay here. And he or Mr. Edgerton could easily find me at your home. No, I believe I must go."

"Is there anything I can do to assist you?"

Julia hesitated.

"I shall retrieve your things from your uncle's house. If you will only give me the name of the place, I shall see that your things are sent there."

She should probably refuse, since he would have to pay for her trunks to be sent, but she felt intuitively that he would be hurt if she refused. Besides, if he did not help her, she was not sure how it might be done.

"That is so very kind of you. The direction is Suffolk, Donnerly Hall."

"Did you say Donnerly Hall? The Athertons?"

"Yes."

"I know them, a little. I shall come and visit you there."

"Oh no. That would not be proper."

The expression on his face changed.

"That is, you could not visit a governess. You . . . it is not done." If he only knew how much it would hurt her to leave him, to think of never seeing him again. But of course, she could never tell him that.

He turned his face away from her. What was he thinking? Julia could not bear to think he was angry with her. Perhaps he was regretting that he could not ask her to marry him. She hoped it was that. But at the same time, she did not want him to feel the pain that was sitting in her chest at that very moment, like a one-hundred-pound bird with its talons digging into her heart.

"I shall very much miss our alliance," she said, hoping to sound cheerful, "and our secret hiding place in the tree at the park." She couldn't help but smile. "And please do say good-bye to Leorah and tell her how sorry I am I cannot take my leave of her myself. I shall miss her spirit and fearlessness."

Suddenly, he turned to face her. "I shall see you again. When all of this is finished—" He walked closer and knelt in front of her, lifting her injured hand. He caressed it, running his thumb over her knuckles, and then kissed it, his lips warm against her skin.

The air rushed out of her lungs. What bliss it would be to be married to this man. She reached out and touched his hair and then immediately pulled her hand back. But he snatched it and kissed it too, his head bowed over her hands.

Someone was coming. He let go and whispered, "God be with you." He stood and left the room.

Monsieur and Madame Bartholdy both came into the room.

"What a handsome young man," Madame Bartholdy said with a smile. "And very honorable."

"Yes." Julia pressed the back of her hand to her cheek. Handsome and honorable and utterly wonderful.

CHAPTER THIRTY-TWO

Julia had been at the Athertons' estate in Suffolk for a few weeks and had not heard from Nicholas Langdon. When she had first arrived, she was afraid the Athertons would refuse her and send her away, if they had heard about her uncle's treasonous acts against the British crown. But they apparently had not heard and welcomed her with a cold dignity and a bit of relief at having procured a governess at last.

Julia, however, lived in fear that they would hear stories from London that would convince them of her ruined reputation. After a week, Mrs. Atherton called her into her sitting room.

"Miss Grey, it has come to my attention that your uncle, Mr. Wilhern, is suspected of being a spy for the French and has fled the country. Your aunt and cousin are living with relatives now. Is this true?"

"I only know that he is suspected of being a spy."

The woman stared at her. Finally, she said, "I suppose a girl cannot help her relations. I had been told your reputation was exemplary. You have not been corrupted by your uncle, I hope?"

"No, ma'am. I assure you I have not."

This seemed to satisfy Mrs. Atherton, and she sent Julia back to the schoolroom.

Now, after three weeks at Donnerly Hall with the Athertons, Julia had settled into a routine. Mornings were filled with teaching her charges reading, writing, and arithmetic—or at least attempting to. Afternoons were for music and language instruction for the older children.

In the evenings Julia was free. She often walked about the extensive grounds of the estate or stayed in her room, reading or doing some other solitary activity. She thought often of Phoebe and prayed that she would not be too miserable and would not despise Julia too much. Julia had rarely ever been without Phoebe's company, so it was strange not to be able to talk to her or even write to her, since she did not know with whom she was staying.

There was no one else in the house near Julia's age, except some of the servants. But none of them would speak more than a monosyllable to her—except the children's nurse, who was at least fifteen years older than Julia and rather coarse in her sentiments and conversation topics. However, Julia was more than willing to overlook some lack of education and niceties simply to have someone to talk to, someone who didn't look at her as if she resented Julia's slightly higher position, as the other servants did.

The family members, the mother and the older daughters, all spoke to Julia as if she were too low to deserve to breathe the same air. As the governess, she seemed to be in a class all her own, as Sarah Peck had also found herself—a very lonely place, with no possibility of making a friend who would treat her as an equal.

Julia often sat in her room overlooking the stable, watching people come and go. She was not allowed to go where she pleased. She could not play on the pianoforte at odd times of the day as she had been wont to do when she lived with the Wilherns. Most importantly, she must take care to avoid the master of the house, Mr. Atherton, for he was friendlier with her than anyone else in the house—much *too* friendly.

In fact, Julia had begun to fear the sight of him, with his fleshy, flushed cheeks and his habit of prowling about the corridor near her room, obviously having overindulged in drink. He had not been bold enough to touch her, but he had been much too eager to have a private word with her in the corridors of the large house. She had always managed to escape him with some excuse or another, but she feared she would need to find a new position soon before he became bolder.

That was why Julia was writing to her friend, Felicity Mayson, to ask her the name and the direction of the school Felicity and her sisters had attended when they were younger. If she could secure a position at such a school, at least she could make friends with the other teachers and not constantly feel as though someone were either looking down on her or thinking she was looking down on them. She could live with the other teachers as an equal.

Julia had written to Felicity more than two weeks ago and told her about her situation. Felicity had written her back. Julia now read her letter again:

> *My dear Julia,*
> *I have been hearing the rampant gossip going through London. How much of it do you know? Do you know your uncle has fled the country to avoid being imprisoned for treason? Some say he plotted to assassinate the Prince Regent and the entire royal family. Others say he sold military secrets to France in exchange for having his substantial debts paid off. Mr. Edgerton was taken to the Tower of London and then, a few days later, was set free. Everyone wondered if he was a traitor too, and he has not been seen in London since he was released. Julia, what do you know of all this?*
>
> *Forgive me for my morbid curiosity. You only told me that your uncle is in some trouble and you must care*

for yourself now, and that is why you took a position as governess. I am very sorry that this has happened, but thank you for continuing our friendship. I cannot help but think your situation will change. You are the best person I know.

You asked me about Phoebe. I hear she and her mother are living with cousins in London and that Phoebe was seen walking in Hyde Park and crying. It is only too bad that she never listened to your advice to be more discreet with her emotions. But I have also heard that Mr. Dinklage has been visiting her often. Perhaps he can cheer her up. His mother died, you know, about a week after you left. Now he is free to marry whomever he wishes.

Please write to me soon, and, if you wish to enlighten me as to who is guilty of what and what might happen next, I promise not to tell another living being.

Your discreet and loving friend,
Felicity Mayson

Julia trusted Felicity not to tell anything she would not want shared, but it little mattered anymore. The truth would come out about her uncle eventually. Apparently they did not have enough evidence to punish Mr. Edgerton for his role. But that only meant that he never did get his large sum of money from the people in France who were trying to kill General Wellington.

It was actually somewhat of a relief for Julia to be so far removed from the drawing-room gossip of privileged society. As a governess, she might as well be thousands of miles away in Jamaica or Barbados or America.

Felicity mentioned Phoebe crying in a public park and not listening to Julia's advice. But as Julia looked back on it, perhaps she was the foolish one, at least to some extent. Julia had put so much pressure on herself and on Phoebe to follow society's rather arbitrary rules, when she should have been following "the only good and perfect law of liberty and of love," which the rector had spoken about in church this past Sunday—God's Word.

What if Phoebe did cry openly when she was sad? She had a right to be sad, and anyone who criticized her for it simply wasn't being loving. Being overly emotional might be unwise, but being unloving was a failing indeed.

Julia had it at least partially wrong, trying to control Phoebe, and trying too hard to conform to the world's views of good and bad, but God in His mercy had taken care of her anyway. She might never be married, but at least she had food and clothing and a roof over her head, as well as a few friends, including Felicity.

Julia quickly finished her letter to Felicity, asking her for the information about the school she hoped to apply to, and went downstairs to give her letter to be posted.

The sun was going down, but it wasn't too late to go for a short walk around the gardens. As she was passing the dining room, she overheard Mrs. Atherton speaking. Julia stopped in the dark corridor, out of sight of the dining room, and listened.

"Mrs. Henrietta Tromburg, a recent widow and my old friend's daughter, is coming for a visit. I want the red room cleaned and polished before her arrival tomorrow afternoon. And remember that she is still in mourning, and warn the maids not to be chattering and giggling away as they are so fond of doing."

The children would be much more likely to disturb Mr. Langdon's former fiancée than any of the servants, who were terrified of Mrs. Atherton. Besides, by now Mrs. Tromburg would only be in half mourning.

"I am planning a small house party for her, and I have invited several guests. They should arrive a week from today, so we will need all of the extra rooms aired and cleaned by then. And I must try to send the new governess away. She is far too handsome and elegantly dressed. Everyone will mistake her for a guest instead of the governess."

Julia's heart thumped hard against her chest at hearing herself spoken of.

"I don't know if she has anywhere to go, mum," the housekeeper, Mrs. Farnsworth, replied.

Mrs. Atherton made a grunting sound. "Well, then, I will warn her to stay out of the way when the guests arrive. But if I had known she was as fair of face as she is, I never would have taken her on."

Julia moved as quietly as possible the rest of the way down the corridor, her knees a bit wobbly at the thought of being caught eavesdropping. She made it to the door and went out into the pale light of the waning day.

She walked around the garden, enjoying the cool, clean air and the soft sounds of nature, trying to clear her heart of the unsettled feeling that had lodged there after hearing that Nicholas Langdon's former fiancée would be arriving the next day, and that a whole houseful of guests would be here in a week.

Julia shook her head. It hardly affected her. But she couldn't help but wonder if Mr. Langdon would be interested in renewing his offer of marriage to the woman he had fallen in love with years ago, now that she was a widow. Didn't people always say that first love was the strongest? And if Mrs. Tromburg had only a small jointure to live on after failing to produce an heir, then perhaps Mr. Langdon would marry her out of pity—and because he still loved her.

These thoughts weren't making Julia feel any better. Since it was growing quite dark, she went back inside and up to the safe haven of her room.

***

Julia's young pupils stood at the window, staring down at the carriage below, as Mrs. Tromburg alighted and made her way to the house.

"May we please be allowed to go and greet her?" little Elizabeth, the six-year-old, asked.

"No, I'm afraid not."

"Oh please, Miss Grey!" The older girl and even some of the boys joined their voices to Elizabeth's.

"Your mother would not be pleased at all with that, I am sure. Now, if you are good girls and boys, I shall allow you to have extra gingerbread at teatime, and I will ask your mother's permission to let you go down, in an orderly and genteel fashion, to greet Mrs. Tromburg then. She will be tired from her journey, and you had much better greet her when she is rested."

"But it is *three hours* until tea!" Elizabeth said it as if it were three years.

"No need to worry, Miss Elizabeth. You will still be alive and well in three hours."

When teatime came, Julia walked the children toward the drawing room. The boys hung back, seeming shy at the prospect of meeting a young lady, but the girls started to run. Julia couldn't get their attention without yelling. No matter. They wouldn't want their mother's guest to think they weren't ladylike, and they would slow down when they reached the drawing room.

"Come along, boys." Julia shooed the boys in front of her.

Julia entered but stood near the door, knowing she was only wanted to watch the children, not to join them for tea. The young widow was sitting near Mrs. Atherton and smiling at the girls. She greeted each of the children formally but pleasantly.

The children seemed awed by her, even the boys. Julia had to admit, Mrs. Tromburg was quite beautiful. Her hair was a vibrant blond, her eyes bright blue, and her skin was clear and fair. Her hair was perfectly arranged and her dress immaculate. She didn't look the least worse for having traveled most of the day.

While they had their tea, Julia found a book and sat near the door, observing their visitor discreetly while the children entertained her with their stories and questions. Julia was impressed with their good behavior. They normally weren't nearly so well mannered.

When tea was over, the nursemaid came to fetch the children, as their instruction was over for the day. Julia stood to leave as well, but Mrs. Tromburg called out, "Won't you stay a few moments, Miss . . . ?"

"Miss Grey," Mrs. Atherton supplied.

The two women looked completely comfortable as they waited for Julia to approach. She made her way toward them, feeling dowdy in the dress she had taught in all day.

"I know you as the Wilherns' ward. You were at a ball I attended, I am sure of it. How do you like being a governess?"

Julia tried not to notice the snide look in Mrs. Tromburg's eyes. "I have very worthy young pupils, I thank you."

Mrs. Tromburg smirked. "And I see you were able to regain your health after Mrs. Dinklage prevented you from marrying her son. It is always a shame when young love is thwarted."

"I am sure I don't know what you mean. I was never in love with Mr. Dinklage." Julia pretended a coolness she did not feel.

"Oh, forgive me. I meant no harm." She waved her hand nonchalantly.

Of course you didn't. "Will that be all you require?"

"One moment. Mrs. Atherton. Won't you allow Miss Grey to join us for the dance when all your guests arrive next week?"

They both looked at Julia's employer, who wore a smile.

"If you wish it, my dear, of course."

"Miss Grey must miss such amusements now that she is earning her living."

Julia gave Mrs. Tromburg a fake smile, curtsied, and left their presence. She was thankful they allowed her to leave without asking her if she would attend, for she wasn't certain her reply would have been at all civil.

***

The next day, Julia received the information she'd requested from Felicity. She immediately wrote to the school, desperate as she was to escape from her present position. She felt like a rat, always hiding, working hard to teach children who had no desire to learn and then scurrying back to her room to avoid Mr. Atherton's attention.

When the guests began arriving a week later, Julia still hadn't received a reply from the school.

The children ran to the window as the third carriage arrived. Julia sighed. The children weren't listening to a word she was saying, and the older ones had done almost none of the work she had given them. The arithmetic lesson she had prepared would only be an exercise in frustration. But she had an idea.

"Children, since it is such a fine day, why don't we all put on our hats and bonnets and go out into the garden for a botany lesson?"

They turned brightened expressions toward her and cheered.

"But you mustn't run off. You must all stay with me, and we shall collect specimens to bring back with us so we can have a scientific study of the most interesting plants and insects."

"If I catch a lizard, can we study that?" young Timothy asked. He was one of the sweetest of the children. She only hoped his father and mother's indifference, coupled with extravagant indulgences, wouldn't make him as bitter and heartless as some of his older brothers and sisters.

"I don't think you'll find any lizards now that the weather is cooler, but if you do, yes, you may catch it and we will study it. We shall come back to the room and look for him in one of our many books." The Athertons had spared no expense in providing the children with books on both plants and animals, full of drawings and descriptions of creatures from England and around the world.

The children rushed to find their outerwear, and Julia helped the little ones with their light jackets and bonnets. She did her best to keep them quiet as they all trooped down the servants' back staircase to avoid the front of the house where the guests were arriving.

As they reached the ground floor and the children began running outside, a familiar voice, coming from the direction of the front door, caused Julia to pause midstep.

"Thank you, it is good to see you again as well."

The deep, masculine voice sent a shiver across her shoulders.

Someone exclaimed, "Nicholas Langdon!" and Julia's fears—or were they hopes?—were confirmed.

Her heart pounding, she followed the children outside, realizing the voice that had said Mr. Langdon's name in such delighted tones was his former fiancée, Mrs. Tromburg.

CHAPTER THIRTY-THREE

Nicholas hurried up to his room where his valet, Smith, was putting away his things. He watched where Smith put the portfolio, and he picked it up and looked through it, making sure its contents were still in order. Satisfied that nothing was damaged or missing, he laid it across the desk by the window, which overlooked the gardens.

Movement outside caught his eye.

His heart skipped a beat at the sight of Miss Grey amongst a group of children in the garden behind the house. She was bending over a little boy's outstretched hand, as though carefully examining something he was showing her.

His gaze followed her as she straightened and herded the children in front of her, and they all moved farther away, around the tall hedges and out of sight.

He grabbed his hat.

"Just a moment, sir." Smith came over and adjusted Nicholas's neckcloth. Nicholas was still wearing his coat, and he dashed out and took the back stairs two at a time. He walked out into the garden, putting on his hat as he went.

***

Even as Julia tried to listen to the children, keep an eye on all of them, and encourage them to find interesting leaves, flora, and fauna, her thoughts were racing. *Nicholas Langdon is here.* Certainly he couldn't be here to see her, even though he had said he would visit. Most gentlemen wouldn't want to speak to her now that she was a governess.

She would be expected to keep out of the way. Would he even see her? Julia had heard what Mrs. Atherton had said about wanting her out of sight, and in spite of Mrs. Tromburg saying she wanted Julia to attend the ball, she had no intention of actually attending. The woman would surely find a way to humiliate her.

"Miss Grey, look at this!" It was Timothy again. He held up his hand, and lying across his palm was a long-dead dragonfly, its wings mostly intact.

"That is a beauty, Timothy. If you like, you can put him in my bag here"—Julia held out her canvas bag—"and we will take him inside and look for him in our books."

Timothy was still staring at the insect in his hand. After a moment he said, "May I look at him a bit longer?"

"Of course."

Timothy was about the same age as little Henry back in London. Julia didn't suppose she would ever see Henry or his sister again.

Hearing the rustling of dead leaves behind her, Julia turned to see which of the children was approaching her. But it wasn't a child at all.

"Mr. Langdon."

"Miss Grey."

Julia felt the heat rise to her cheeks, driving away any chill from the autumn wind. *Oh God, I don't know what to say to him.* His beautiful eyes and sun-browned skin . . . she couldn't help remembering how close he had held her when he'd carried her to the Bartholdys'. Had that only been a few weeks ago?

"Have you been well?" he asked.

"Yes, I've been very well."

"All healed, then?" There was a small smile on his lips. Oh, how handsome he was. It almost pained her to look at him. Could she trust her own judgment? If so, she would say his expression was one of tenderness and concern. Her heart missed a beat.

"Yes, I thank you. And are your family all in good health?"

"Yes, thank you. My sister was happy to receive your letter. She sent a reply with me." He reached into his pocket and pulled out not one but two letters and held them out to her. "There is a second letter from your friend Sarah Peck. Mr. Wilson asked me to bring it to you."

Julia accepted the letters, wishing it were proper to clasp the hand that held them out to her. "I am most grateful to you." She lifted her head and let herself be captured by his dark-brown gaze.

"You remember our mutual friend, Henry Lee, don't you?"

"Of course."

"It seems he will be attending school."

"School! Oh, that is wonderful." Julia clasped her hands, unable to suppress her joyful smile.

"A benefactor has paid his tuition."

"I am so pleased. Oh, that is just what he needs. And how is his family? Are they well?"

"His mother was well, last I heard, as was his sister. I shall tell them you asked about them when next I see them."

"Oh, thank you. I would like that very much."

Mr. Langdon was giving her such an intimate smile that her heart fluttered, stealing her breath. She tried not to stare.

"And your friend," he said, lowering his voice a bit, "Miss Peck is well. If you would like to send her a letter, I will be very happy to take it to Mr. Wilson, who will see that she gets it."

"That is so kind of you. I would like that above anything."

"Mr. Wilson has been very impressed with her industry. She has been helping tend the sick in her, ah, special school, and now that it is becoming harder for her to do that, she has been making blankets and shawls to give to the poor."

Sweet Sarah Peck. God was taking care of her, giving her something useful to do. What a blessing. "I am so glad. Thank you for telling me."

"Yes, and from my knowledge of John Wilson, I am not so sure he hasn't lost his heart to her." He smiled and seemed to lean toward her. "He revealed to me two weeks ago that he intends to marry her."

"Truly?" Julia's heart lifted to the ceiling at the thought of Sarah happily married, and to a man of integrity and kindness like Mr. Wilson! "Oh, I do hope it is so. She is such a worthy girl." She realized immediately that most people would see irony in her statement, but Nicholas Langdon did not seem to.

"And very pretty, as Mr. Wilson has told me."

Oh, it was too wonderful to think of Sarah married and happy and taken care of. *Oh God, let it be so.*

A couple that Julia did not know walked by. When they had passed, Julia took up the subject again. "Mr. Wilson and Sarah Peck were together often, did you say, at the mission?"

"Not at the mission, but when they were helping the sick in the home where Miss Peck and several other young ladies are living. He was very impressed with her willingness to help. He said her gentle nature was evident and that she is the very sort of woman he could wish for in a wife, notwithstanding the mistake she made. And the fact that she has a friend like you, Miss Grey, is also a testament to her character."

Mr. Langdon's head was bent toward hers, and his gaze was unwavering from her eyes. His voice was gruff, barely above a whisper. "I understand it quite well, I'm afraid. He was captivated by her sweetness and beauty. He saw his future in her eyes."

Julia suddenly found it hard to breathe. "Sarah is a very pretty girl with a . . . a good heart. She will make him a good wife."

Julia's heart was full to overflowing as she looked into Mr. Langdon's handsome, smiling face. How kind, how good, he was. *I love you, Nicholas Langdon.*

"Why, Mr. Langdon! What are you doing out here?" Mrs. Tromburg rounded the end of the hedgerow. Another lady walked beside her.

Julia quickly hid her letters inside the canvas bag with the leaves and beetles the children had collected.

"Mrs. Tromburg." Mr. Langdon acknowledged her, reluctantly it seemed—or perhaps Julia imagined it.

Mrs. Tromburg claimed his arm in a most possessive manner, as if she were entitled to have him escort her wherever she wanted to go.

One of the children was tugging on Julia's velvet jacket, so Julia turned to Elizabeth.

"Is this a good leaf, Miss Grey?"

"Oh yes, that is a very fine leaf, Elizabeth."

"And I found these as well." The little girl showed her the contents of both her fists.

Behind her, Julia heard Mrs. Tromburg say, "I insist you let me show you my favorite spots in the Athertons' gardens." She led Mr. Langdon away.

Julia was once again alone with the children.

As soon as she got them all inside again and occupied with school-work, she would read her letters. And she would go over in her mind every look on Nicholas Langdon's face, every nuance in his eyes, until . . . until she had driven herself to distraction wondering what he was thinking.

***

Julia and the children came back in the house and set to work—or at least, Julia set to work trying to interest the children in setting to work—finding all their various leaves and flowers in the sketchbooks and color illustrations in the children's schoolroom. After an hour of trying to keep the children occupied with this and their other studies, during which they either ran back and forth to the window, pulled each other's hair, or otherwise fought with and distracted each other, their nurse came in and announced they were to have a holiday from studying for the rest of the day. Their mother wanted them all to take a bath and put on their best clothes and present themselves to the guests in the evening.

The children screamed and yelled "Hooray!" until Julia's ears rang. But she slumped in relief at being given her own holiday. She was free to go read her letters.

She grabbed them from where she had placed them on the top shelf of the bookcase and hurried to her room. Closing herself inside, she crawled into bed, feeling cozy as she opened Leorah's letter first.

> *Dearest Julia,*
> *I cannot tell you how welcome your letter was to me. Thank you for writing, even though I am normally a very bad correspondent.*
> *I cannot fathom why my addlepated brother has allowed you to become a governess. He should have forced you to come and stay with us. I don't know why he concerns himself so much with propriety. But I shall not pain you with any more mentions of him.*
> *I must say that I cannot believe what your Uncle Wilhern was about. I hope you do not mind that Nicholas has told me all, for I shall never repeat it. But to resign yourself to be a governess—you are too good and too talented and too wonderful a lady to be teaching a passel of*

brats to read and write and embroider cushions. You are much more of a lady than I will ever be, Julia, and I do not mind telling you that I look up to you as the model of sweetness and gentility. You must come to me as soon as you get a holiday. You must spend your time with me, and if those people, the Athertons, ever treat you badly, you must come and live with me. Mother and I are quite independent, and we do as we please. Father never prevents us from getting our way. But do not worry. I don't let it go to my head.

You are no doubt shocked at my manner of speaking, Julia, as you are so much gentler than I have ever been, but you must take my advice and speak your mind more often. It is good for the soul, I assure you, to tell people exactly what you will and will not allow.

I am not a very accomplished letter writer, as you will have guessed by now, but my point was entirely to beg you to come and let me pamper you as my own dear friend just as soon as you are able. You are expected, Julia.

Your humble friend,
Leorah Langdon

CHAPTER THIRTY-FOUR

During the reading of Leorah's letter, Julia found herself gasping and chuckling by turns. Julia went back to read the beginning, where Leorah had said, *I cannot fathom why my addlepated brother has allowed you to become a governess. He should have forced you to come and stay with us. I don't know why he concerns himself so much with propriety.*

Julia closed her eyes as the emotions overwhelmed her. Oh, the sight of him today, looking kind and handsome and attentive. Then he had been commandeered by Mrs. Tromburg. Had he gone with her because he was ashamed to be seen talking to a governess? Julia didn't think so, but yet he did not refuse his former fiancée. Though she had not given him much choice in the matter.

Pulling out the second letter, this one from Sarah, she held them both against her cheek, breathing in their smell, no doubt the smell of Nicholas Langdon's coat pocket, until she shook her head at her foolishness. Sighing, she opened Sarah's letter and began to read.

> *Dear Julia,*
> *You will not believe what I have to tell you, for I am married, to the most wonderful man in the world, John*

Wilson! You have met him, so I do not need to tell you how kind and good and handsome he is. We were married rather secretly two days ago with only his mother and sister to witness. Can you believe they are not ashamed of me? John will adopt the baby as his own when he or she is born, in about four more months. I cannot imagine why he loves me, but he does. It is a miracle.

And in this miracle, Julia, you are the angel. You were the means by which I met John. I was in love with him almost as soon as I saw him, before I even had time to think or stop myself, but I never would have met him had it not been for you and your great kindness.

I do hope someday that you will be as happy as I am. I won't be able to bear it if you aren't, because you deserve it so much more than I. Oh, Julia. If only you can find another such a man as my John, someone good and loving and giving. If you do find him, he cannot help but recognize his equal partner in you.

Julia had to stop reading to wipe the tears from her eyes. Rather than finding such another man, Julia had become a governess, the same fate Sarah had begged her to avoid.

Sarah went on to say how happy she was and how she looked forward to seeing Julia as soon as she was able to come for a visit, hoping the Wilherns wouldn't prevent her from visiting her friend when they found out she was married.

So Sarah did not know what had happened, that Julia's uncle had fled the country and caused Phoebe to be dependent on the kindness of her relatives. And Mr. Langdon must not have told them, or else he had told Mr. Wilson, who had not told his wife.

At least Sarah was happy. Julia could be happy for her, to know she would be loved and cared for as only a husband could. *Thank you, God.*

Julia went to put both letters away when she noticed something on the floor, something white and flat, in front of her door. It might have been there when she'd come in and she hadn't noticed, as she'd been so preoccupied with her letters. It appeared to be another letter. Sometimes the butler shoved her letters under her door when the post came.

On opening it, she saw it was from the director of the school she had written to.

> *Dear Miss Grey,*
> *I am writing to inform you that we would be most inter-*
> *ested in employing you for the position of music teacher in*
> *our school, as soon as you are able to come. The salary is*
> *modest, but you will be provided a private room, as well*
> *as all your meals.*

She could leave. She had another position.

Even though Leorah had assured her she could come and stay with her, it could never be a permanent solution. Besides, due to her feelings for Mr. Langdon, it wouldn't be proper. This position at this school was the best Julia could hope for. Now she could leave Mr. Atherton's lecherous, roving eyes and Mrs. Atherton's condescending arrogance.

But first she would need to give notice.

Julia went to her desk and wrote a quick note, asking Mrs. Atherton to allow her to leave her employ in one week. *I am sorry to only give a week's notice,* Julia wrote, *but the other position is open now, and I do not want to risk losing it.*

After ending it with the proper sentiments, Julia folded the letter and went in search of Mrs. Atherton.

Julia went downstairs and heard feminine voices in the music room. The door was open, and when Julia looked in, she found Mrs. Atherton standing in a small group, speaking with Mrs. Tromburg and Mr. Langdon. Julia hesitated and then kept walking past the doorway rather than interrupt Mrs. Atherton and her guests. She only hoped no one had seen her walk past. She would simply have to give the letter to Mrs. Atherton later.

"Miss Grey, wait."

Julia turned to see Nicholas Langdon hurrying toward her. Her heart seemed to rise into her throat as she waited for him to catch up to her.

"Did you need something?" he asked.

"I only wanted to give this letter to Mrs. Atherton. Would you give it to her?"

"Won't you come in and give it to her yourself?"

"No, I don't think I should. I don't want to disturb her while she is with her guests."

He stood quite close to her. "Julia, I need to speak with you. I have something—"

"Nicholas Langdon, you said you would play a duet with me." Mrs. Tromburg was calling to him from the doorway of the drawing room. "What are you doing? You promised."

He looked annoyed. "As I was saying—"

"I must go, but I would like to speak with you." Julia didn't want to keep him standing in the dark hall with her. "We can speak later." She handed him the letter and hurried away before he could say anything else.

Julia spent a quiet evening in her room. She couldn't help wondering what Mr. Langdon was doing; how his time was being monopolized by the young widow, Mrs. Tromburg; and whether her beauty would be able to charm him a second time.

***

The next morning, just as Julia was getting the children settled down to their schoolwork, someone knocked on the schoolroom door. Julia got up and opened it to Mrs. Atherton.

"I came to tell you, Miss Grey, that there is no need for you to stay another week. You may leave any time you like. In fact"—she raised her eyebrows and looked down her long, pointed nose at Julia—"I would prefer it if you would leave early tomorrow morning."

"You don't want me to finish out the week with the children?"

"No. The carriage will be made ready for you at dawn. You may collect your salary from Mrs. Farnsworth."

Painfully aware that the children were just behind her and hearing everything their mother was saying, Julia nodded, meeting Mrs. Atherton's disdainful stare. "Thank you, Mrs. Atherton. Would you like to explain the situation to the children, or shall I?"

Mrs. Atherton looked momentarily nonplussed and then waved her hand in the air. "Just as you please. Tell Nellie to look after them." With that, she turned and walked away.

Taking a deep breath, Julia closed the door and faced the children. They were all reacting to the news according to their dispositions. Some of their expressions were blank, as if they had already stuffed down and hidden their feelings about having to say good-bye to another governess. Elizabeth was starting to cry, the first big tear rolling down her cheek. Julia gathered her up in her arms and sat on the floor with her in her lap.

"Come here, children." Some of them sat with their heads down, but Timothy drew closer to her, as if hoping she would hug him too. She reached out and put an arm around him, holding him to her side.

"I'm so sorry, but I must leave you." She felt the tears damming up behind her eyes. "You are all intelligent, wonderful children, and I want you to know that I have come to care for you all very much in the short time I have been here. You are very important, and I will be praying for each of you, every night before I go to sleep, that you will grow up strong and healthy, and that you will be kind and good adults who care about other people, just the way God cares about you."

They stared at her as if she were speaking another language, their eyes round and bright.

"Why are you leaving us?" Timothy asked. "Were we bad?"

"No, of course not. You weren't bad. I don't want to leave you, but I must. It is not your fault. If I could, I'd take you all with me."

"You could take me." Timothy's face suddenly lit up. "No one would know I was gone. I once fell asleep in the cupboard and slept there all day, and Nellie didn't even notice I was gone. You could take me with you, and I could come back when I was a grown-up man."

Julia smiled. "I do wish I could, Timothy. Your mother and father wouldn't allow it. Besides, your brothers and sisters would miss you."

The others chimed in with either agreement or disagreement with her statement.

Julia got their attention again. "I want you to promise me that you will study diligently and obey your new governess, and be respectful of your nurse and your parents."

Nellie came in and clapped her hands. "Come along, then. It's a fair day to run around in the sun. Don't waste it."

Reluctantly, it seemed, the children stood and went to find their hats. Little Elizabeth put her arms around Julia's neck. "You were my best governess of all," she whispered next to Julia's ear.

Julia smiled at her. "You are a brave girl, Elizabeth. I hope to see you again, perhaps when you are a young lady, all grown up. Yes?"

Elizabeth nodded. Julia wiped the girl's chubby cheeks with her handkerchief, and the child went to find her things. Julia stood and watched them all leave with their nurse.

***

Julia had the rest of the day to pack up her things and say good-bye to the other staff members. Most of them hadn't been very friendly to Julia, so she only bid a few of them farewell.

This was her last chance to speak to Mr. Langdon. She could not go away without telling him good-bye. And even though she was only a teacher at a girls' school now, part of her longed to tell him how much she cared about him.

Julia stood at her window, absently staring at the stable yard. She saw a man dismount and hand the reins of his horse to a groomsman. There was something familiar about the man. As he spoke to the servant, he turned his head and looked up at Julia's window. She gasped and covered her mouth.

Hugh Edgerton grinned up at her.

CHAPTER THIRTY-FIVE

Nicholas hung back, hiding himself just outside the door of the drawing room. How had Edgerton wrangled an invitation to this already overcrowded house party?

Edgerton started toward the door, glancing around as if making sure no one would see him leaving the drawing room. Nicholas quickly ducked into the library, waiting in the shadows until Edgerton passed, and then he followed him, making his footsteps as silent as possible and staying as far back as he could without losing sight of him.

Edgerton headed for the back stairs. Nicholas stayed well behind him, letting him go around the curving wooden steps. He started up after him, stepping gingerly so as not to make any loud footfalls with his boots. He soon realized Edgerton hadn't stopped on the first floor, as he could still hear his boots on the stairs above, but had headed up the next flight, to the rooms. When he heard him knocking on someone's door, Nicholas flew the rest of the way up.

"Who is it?" came the muffled voice from inside, and Nicholas knew it as Miss Grey's.

Edgerton didn't say anything, only knocked again. Nicholas surged forward and Edgerton swiveled to face him and held up his hands. "What—?"

"Stay away from Miss Grey."

Edgerton glared at him. "What gives you the right?"

"Because I know what you and Wilhern did. Do you wish me to blacken your name even more than you have done yourself? Stay. Away. From Miss Grey." Nicholas leaned menacingly toward him.

Edgerton backed away, still holding his hands up as if to ward off a blow. "Very well, very well. I'm staying away." He continued to back away and finally said, "May I leave now?" He gestured toward the stairs, which were behind Nicholas.

Nicholas stepped aside to let him pass and then watched him go all the way down and out of sight. Finally, when he could no longer hear Edgerton's steps and all was quiet, Nicholas stepped up to her door.

"Miss Grey?" he called softly. "Are you there?"

"Yes, I am here. Thank you for chasing him away."

"You are most welcome." There was so much more he wanted to say, but it was hard to speak when he could not even see her, and when others might be coming up or going down the stairs at any moment and hear them.

He pressed his forehead against the door, imagining her on the other side. "Will you come to the ball tonight?"

"I cannot."

"You will be my special guest. I will make sure no harm comes to you." He pressed his palm against the door and closed his eyes. *Please say yes.* He imagined that he was pressing her warm hand instead of the cold wooden door, imagined her eyes sparkling back at him. It was agony to be so close to her and yet not be able to see or touch her.

He held his breath as he waited for her answer.

***

Julia approached the door, wishing she could open it, thinking of him on the other side. But as the governess, it would be improper to be seen talking to Mr. Langdon in the doorway of her bedroom. She pressed her hand against its hard surface, longing to be closer to him. "I do not believe Mrs. Atherton will want me at the ball."

"I will get permission from Mrs. Atherton."

How could she explain? *Your former fiancée, Mrs. Tromburg, would only find some way to humiliate me.* Besides, he would be ridiculed for dancing with her.

She swallowed and said, "I must leave soon. I have a new position."

"Come with me now, to the garden." There was an edge to his voice. "I need to speak to you."

"I will be there in five minutes."

"I'll wait for you at the north side of the hedge." His voice sounded eager and oh so dear.

Julia quickly washed her face, put on her bombazine spencer, and then grabbed her bonnet. Taking a quick look, the mirror showed a pale, wide-eyed girl. "Give me strength, Lord. No matter what happens." Tying her bonnet under her chin, she hurried from the room, down the stairs, and out the back door.

Julia walked toward the north side of the hedge. She kept her head down to avoid the strong wind that was forcing her eyes to water. As she rounded the end of the tall hedgerow, she glanced up, expecting to see Mr. Langdon alone. Instead, she saw Mrs. Tromburg standing in front of him. The two of them were talking, their faces close together.

Julia's stomach churned and her cheeks burned. Had he summoned her here to see *this*?

Just then, Mrs. Tromburg stood on tiptoe, her hand reaching up as if to caress Mr. Langdon's face.

Mr. Langdon stepped away from her, and his eyes fell on Julia.

Mrs. Tromburg turned around, also catching sight of Julia, and smiled her widest smile. "If it isn't the governess!" she called out.

Julia was an imbecile to believe Mr. Langdon might care for her, might even ask her to marry him. Julia turned and hurried back toward the house.

***

Nicholas took a step toward Miss Grey, about to call out to her, when Henrietta caught his arm.

"What do you want with her?" She gripped his arm tighter. "Don't be a fool, Nicholas. Marry me and I will make you happy, I swear."

He looked down at Henrietta, really looked at her. Was she mad to offer him marriage? Her words repulsed him, but at the same time, the desperation on her face evoked pity. She had little to live on now that her husband had died. She must be frantic to find another husband.

"I am sorry, but I cannot marry you."

"What will become of me? Surely there is still some love for me in your heart."

She lifted her hand toward his chest, but he sidestepped out of her reach.

"I do not love you. I'm sorry." He started walking toward the house. Did he still have time to catch Miss Grey?

"I don't believe you," she called after him.

He didn't look back but broke into a run, not seeing Miss Grey anywhere. She must have gone inside.

As soon as he walked in, Mrs. Atherton stopped him. "Mr. Langdon, I was just looking for you. I wanted to speak with you about the parish here at Donnerly and the living that has become vacant. Mr. Atherton and I are trying to decide whom to offer it to. Can you tell me of any worthy rectors who might be interested? I wanted to get your opinion of some of the candidates."

"Mrs. Atherton," he broke in when she finally paused to take a breath, "may I speak with you about this later? I am in a hurry—"

"Oh no, for I only have a minute myself before I have to go get ready for the ball, and you do as well, for it is getting very late. Believe me, it will only take a moment."

Nicholas clenched his teeth and followed his hostess into what appeared to be her husband's office. There she listed what seemed like a hundred prospective clergymen for the vacant living.

"Mr. Langdon? Are you listening?"

"Mrs. Atherton, I wholeheartedly recommend Mr. Killigrew. I know him personally, and he is an honorable man, and now I believe we both of us have barely enough time to get ready for the ball, so I bid you good day until then." He bowed formally but quickly.

"Oh, of course, Mr. Langdon. You must get yourself dressed and ready, and so must I."

He left the room as she was still speaking.

**

Julia made it to the house without Mr. Langdon even calling out to her. She went more slowly up the stairs to her room, hoping he might catch up to her. After all, the tête-à-tête he was having with Mrs. Tromburg might not have been his doing.

But what if Mr. Langdon had asked Julia to meet him there so he could tell her that he was marrying his former fiancée? Julia quickly closed her door behind her.

It made sense. He had once loved Mrs. Tromburg, had once planned to marry her. And she was very beautiful. Julia could understand how a man could be blinded by beauty and artifice and marry someone who was completely wrong for him. He wouldn't be the first man to succumb. And besides, he might feel badly that she had been left with such a small jointure, hardly enough to live on.

It was silly of Julia to think he might want to marry a governess with no fortune or connections. An orphan whose guardian was a traitor. Unloved and unlovable.

Julia felt dizzy and realized she'd hardly eaten anything all day. So she closed her door and went down to the kitchen to see if the cook and kitchen maid would be more polite than usual when she asked for tea. After all, it was her last day.

***

Nicholas reached Julia's door. Finally. He knocked but there was no answer. He knocked again and called softly, "Miss Grey." Still nothing.

Someone was coming, so he started back down the stairs and passed a maid going up. She smiled flirtatiously at him as she passed.

Either Miss Grey was too angry to answer his knock, or she wasn't in her room. And he was running out of time before the ball. He would simply have to write her a note and shove it under her door. He couldn't stand outside her room all evening. The servants would be talking about it, and so would the guests, by tomorrow morning.

He simply had to speak to her. He couldn't wait. In case he didn't see her at the ball, he would write to her and ask her to meet him, first thing tomorrow morning.

CHAPTER THIRTY-SIX

Julia brought her tea up to her room to eat in peace and silence, but somehow, the room seemed lonelier than ever. The tea was comforting, and she sipped it slowly while staring at her bag and trunk, already packed and waiting to leave with her at dawn.

She had missed her chance to speak to Mr. Langdon in the garden, so perhaps she would attend the ball after all. It could be the last time she would ever see him.

Perhaps she should also write him a letter. In a letter she could thank him, and also apologize to him, and wouldn't have to fear what he would say or how he would look.

She went to her tiny desk and began to write:

> *Mr. Langdon,*
> *Please don't think me too forward for writing you this letter. I am sorry I was not able to speak with you, as you expressed a wish to, but I must leave at dawn, at Mrs. Atherton's orders, to go to my new position as a teacher at the Cumberland School for Girls in Kent. Because of this circumstance, I hope you will excuse me.*

I very much wish to tell you that I was most grateful for your help when I was so very sick, for loaning your servants to care for me, and the many kindnesses you showed me. I also wanted to thank you for taking care of me when I was injured, for paying the surgeon, and for having my trunks sent here for me.

Forgive my impertinence, but allow me to tell you that I have long admired you as the best and most honorable man of my acquaintance. I tried to avoid you and even, for a while, tried to think badly of you, all because my cousin Phoebe fancied herself in love with you. I tried many times to check her from recklessly setting her heart on marrying you but without success. But that is no excuse for thinking ill of you or for hiding my own admiration for you. For, Mr. Langdon, I confess that I love you.

Julia chuckled a bit hysterically at what she was writing. She could never give such a letter to Mr. Langdon! It was impossible, ridiculous. But it felt oddly refreshing to put her true thoughts and feelings on paper. Therefore, she continued:

I love you, and my intense feelings for you first began, I believe, when you asked Sarah Peck to dance, rescuing her from sitting all alone that night so many months ago when no one else gave her the least notice. You were all grace and style and handsome vitality, but I didn't want to believe you were anything but a flirtatious dandy. As I learned more about you, I found I couldn't disdain you. Truly, you were kind and good and everything a Christian gentleman should be. You cared about the poor, and you helped orphans and those in dire circumstances. You showed courage, wisdom, and restraint, and you were

*not afraid to act on behalf of others. Even though I was
helplessly in love with you, I continued to tell myself I
wasn't, that you and I were nothing more than friends.
Phoebe begged me to help her make you love her, because
otherwise she could never be happy, and I was foolish
enough to say yes to what she asked. I couldn't believe then
that you could ever love me or want to marry someone
in my situation.*

*As I am now a penniless governess, without family or
connections, I know my love for you is even more hopeless.
And so, I will be gone in the morning and must bid you
adieu forever. I love you too well to wish you anything but
happiness and the best that God can possibly afford you.
May God be with you always.*

Julia's tears fell on the paper, as she signed, *Your faithful friend and
fellow spy, Julia Grey,* at the bottom.

Foolish, silly letter. A sensible, proper young lady would never give a
man such a letter. No, Julia must write him a practical letter, something
that she could actually give to him when she left in the morning.

Julia took out another sheet of paper and began to write again:

Mr. Langdon,

*Forgive me my impropriety in writing this personal letter
to you, but I wanted to say how sorry I am that I was not
able to speak with you, as you expressed a wish to, in the
garden. I must leave at dawn, as Mrs. Atherton orders
me to do, to go to my new position as a teacher at the
Cumberland School for Girls in Kent. I hope you will
excuse me.*

*I also wish to thank you for your service to me when
I was sick, as well as your kind attention when I was*

injured a few weeks ago on Bishopsgate Street. You have been a charitable friend, and I am grateful. You are a most worthy gentleman, deserving of every good thing God might provide for your happiness. Therefore I wish you all of God's blessings, including health, joy, and long life.

There. That was not too forward. It conveyed a proper regard and thanked him for all he had done for her, while apologizing for not being able to speak with him in private as he had wished. But it did more to hide, rather than reveal, the extent of her feelings.

Her first letter conveyed the truth, and if she were brave like Leorah, she would give him the first letter. Part of her wanted to. Part of her wanted to open her heart to him and be completely honest.

No, it was too bold. He would think her improper. She would give him the safe letter and save herself the embarrassment of having said too much.

She signed the second letter and folded it, writing *Mr. Nicholas Langdon* on the outside, just as a piece of paper slid under her door and scooted across the floor at her. She walked over and picked it up, unfolding it and reading:

Miss Grey,
Please do me the honor of meeting me in the garden in the morning at nine o'clock. I must speak with you. I greatly regret not being able to speak with you this afternoon, but I was inexorably detained for half an hour by two different people, and when I knocked on your door, there was no answer. Forgive me for my boldness, but I beg you not to leave for your new position without giving me the opportunity to speak with you.
Your humble and obedient servant,
Nicholas Langdon

Her heart skipped a few beats at the urgent tone of his letter. But she would be gone well before nine o'clock in the morning. She could not possibly meet him. Mrs. Atherton had ordered the carriage to take her away at dawn.

Perhaps she could find a way to speak with him tonight at the ball. Mrs. Atherton might be furious, but it might be worth it to dance with Nicholas Langdon one last time.

Yes, that was exactly what she would do.

Julia went and dug through her trunk until she found her best ball dress, the blue silk trimmed in silver embroidery. She pulled it out. The puff sleeves were a bit wrinkled, and the lace collar was not standing up as it should, but it would look well enough after she put it on and fluffed it a bit.

Already she could hear people laughing downstairs. Did she have the boldness to do this? To go down and join the ball as if she were just another guest? Perhaps she would not be able to speak to Mr. Langdon even if she did go to the ball. If that were the case, Julia could slip the letter—the safe one—under his door tonight, before she went to the ball. He would surely see it when he went back to his room, and if he still wished to speak with her, he could find her before she left. After all, the ball would last almost until dawn.

But she didn't know which room belonged to him.

She quickly put on the ball gown, which took longer to do by herself, and then hurried out of her room, down the back stairs to the kitchen, and found the scullery maid, Ellie, shoving firewood into the large stove. Cook was barking orders, sending the various other servants scurrying. No one was idle; everyone looked intent and red faced as they scurried about in the heat of the basement kitchen.

How would she get Ellie's attention?

Julia watched and waited for Ellie to come into the hall. She heard Cook order the maid to help wash some vegetables. When she finished that task, she sent Ellie to make sure the fire in the music room was burning high.

As Ellie was hurrying past her with a basket of coal, Julia followed behind. "Ellie, will you do something for me if I promise to help you with your work?"

"I'm afraid I can't at the moment, Miss Grey." She continued her brisk pace without even looking back. "Cook and Mrs. Farnsworth would have my head if I stopped the slightest moment tonight, what with all the company in the house and the ball tonight and all the work that has to be done. And it wouldn't be proper for you to do my work. I'm sorry, miss, but I can't stop for even a moment." And she didn't stop as she hurried into the music room, Julia on her heels.

"But all I need is to know"—Julia lowered her voice so no one else would hear—"which room belongs to Mr. Langdon."

Ellie knelt in front of the fireplace in the music room and refilled the coal grate. "He's in the room at the top of the stairs, second door to the left."

"Is that the main stairs or the back stairs?"

Ellie was already hurrying out of the room and headed back toward the kitchen. "Come back after the ball starts and I'll show you."

"Oh, thank you, Ellie." Julia went back up to her room to dress her hair.

When she heard the music begin to play, she crept back downstairs to look for Ellie. On her way to the kitchen, she spotted movement in a darkened alcove.

Julia stopped and plastered herself against the wall, hoping whoever was there would leave. Gradually two people came into focus, locked in an intimate embrace. A throaty, feminine laugh came to her just as the two broke apart, and Julia recognized Mrs. Tromburg and Mr. Edgerton.

Julia held her breath, hoping they wouldn't see her. Mr. Edgerton whispered something in Mrs. Tromburg's ear, and then they turned and walked down the corridor away from Julia.

Mr. Edgerton and Mrs. Tromburg? It hardly concerned Julia. She only had to find Ellie. At least perhaps this meant Mr. Edgerton would leave Julia alone tonight.

It took several minutes, but Julia finally found Ellie, a grim and tired expression on her face. She was holding a long, lit candle in her hand. As soon as she saw Julia, she said, "Help me light the sconces upstairs?"

"Yes, of course."

"Come with me."

Julia followed her up the stairs, three flights from the basement, and Ellie pointed to a door. "That's Mr. Langdon's room."

"Thank you, Ellie. I am very grateful to you."

"Here." Ellie handed her the lit candle. "Light all the sconces on this floor and I'm much obliged to you, Miss Grey. And I will miss you when you're gone. Yours was the kindest, prettiest face one was likely to encounter in this house."

Julia smiled back at the young girl, who couldn't be more than fifteen but spoke like someone much older. "Thank you, Ellie."

Ellie was already hurrying downstairs to more work.

Julia proceeded to light the wall sconces one by one. When she finished, she walked toward her room to fetch her letter to Mr. Langdon.

She had tried to be so prudent, to conform to society's every rule for young ladies. Now, what she was contemplating was against all the rules she'd once believed in.

Whether she was able to speak to Mr. Langdon at the ball or not, she still wanted to give him the letter. She might not be able to say what she wished to at the ball. She should deliver the letter now while no one was in the hallways.

As she entered her room, she stared down at the two letters. One of them said everything she longed to tell Mr. Langdon, the truth of her feelings and her situation. The other letter was the one polite society said she should write—if indeed she should write to Mr. Langdon at all. Which one should she give him?

Of course, the prudent Julia would give him the more formal letter. But what if she took Leorah's advice and stopped conforming? What if she said exactly what she felt, for once? What if she followed her heart and concentrated only on obeying God's rules, instead of society's rules?

Julia snatched up both letters and headed back down the corridor toward Nicholas Langdon's room. When she reached his door, she stared down at the two letters—the long one that said everything and the short one that said so little. Her hands trembled. Impulsively, she shoved the long one under his door and hurried back toward her room.

And ran right into someone.

"Miss Grey!"

"Mr. Atherton."

He was holding her arms as she regained her balance.

"Excuse me, sir. I was on my way—"

"Julia, I have just been hoping I would find you."

Julia stepped back, firmly pulling away from his grasp. She held back a nervous laugh.

"I must go now." She tried to look and sound firm as she tried to step around him. He leaned to the side and prevented her.

"You do not need to go now. Stay and speak with me for a few minutes. I've been wanting to have a private talk with you, and Mrs. Atherton tells me you will be leaving us in the morning." His manner was more forceful than usual, his saggy cheeks red from whatever spirits he had been drinking.

He suddenly moved in closer and ran his hand down her cheek.

Julia recoiled, stepping back. He grabbed her arm and held her fast.

"Let go of me, sir. You may not touch me." Her voice was taut as heat rose into her face. She wrenched herself free of his grasp, but he caught hold of her other arm.

"You are just a governess," he hissed. "How dare you defy me?"

Instinctively, Julia lifted her foot and stomped down on his, causing him to let out a tiny howl.

He loosened his grip, which was all Julia wanted, and she ran past him, up the stairs, and to her own room. She slammed the door behind her and locked it. She went and pulled on her heaviest trunk and then pushed it up to the door and sat on it.

Her hands shook like leaves in a storm, but she had escaped him. Could she risk going to the ball? What if she encountered Mr. Atherton again?

Perhaps it was best she stay in her room after all. Her heart sank. What if she never saw Nicholas Langdon again?

***

After the third dance, Nicholas began looking around for Edgerton. He wasn't dancing, he wasn't in the room with the refreshments, and he wasn't in the drawing room playing cards. Earlier, before the first dance, Edgerton and Henrietta had been eyeing each other and talking through the first dance. He couldn't remember seeing either of them since. He had not seen Miss Grey either.

He approached Mrs. Atherton. "A splendid ball, Mrs. Atherton."

"Why, thank you, Mr. Langdon." She squinted at him. "It is too bad about Mrs. Tromburg."

"Pardon me?"

"You hadn't heard? Mrs. Tromburg's headache forced her to take to her room. She said not to expect her to come back down tonight. It is a shame, since I was only trying to cheer her up and distract her by giving this ball for her." She clucked her tongue.

"That is a shame."

"And poor Mr. Edgerton also was feeling unwell. But he told me that if he is feeling better, he will certainly come down later for dinner."

Nicholas nodded politely.

"I see you have been enjoying dancing with the young ladies. You dance so well and are a favorite, as I have often observed."

Nicholas thanked her and managed to extricate himself rather quickly. Was Edgerton somewhere harassing Miss Grey? He went upstairs and knocked on Edgerton's door. There was no answer. Was he with Henrietta? But he didn't dare knock on her door.

He wanted to make sure Miss Grey was safe. He walked up another flight of stairs to her floor. All was quiet. Her door was shut. It would be improper to knock. She might think him no better than Edgerton. So he went back down to rejoin the dance.

After dancing twice more, Nicholas stood against the wall, thinking about Miss Grey. If only she had come to the ball. But he would see her in the morning. Surely he could wait.

"You look preoccupied." Sir John Lemmick, an old friend of Nicholas's father, came to stand beside him, holding a glass of brandy. "I'm used to seeing you dancing."

"Only taking a rest. You should ask Lady Lemmick for a dance. I see her standing all alone over there."

"Oh, I—"

"Father, please come and help me." Sir Lemmick's daughter rushed toward them, taking great gulps of air.

"What is it, Maria? Is the house on fire?"

"No." She swallowed hard. "I went up to see if I could help Henrietta. She went upstairs with a headache. But I can't get her to answer the door, and it's locked. Please come and help me get it open." She had turned her pleading look on Nicholas as well.

"Shall we have the butler open her door?"

Sir Lemmick and his daughter followed Nicholas as he made his way through the crowd. He found the butler in the dining room, instructing the footmen. They explained the situation, and the butler led their procession up to Henrietta's room. Only now more people had joined them. This could easily turn into an ugly scandal, depending on what they found in Mrs. Tromburg's room.

Nicholas hung back, wishing he hadn't come with them. Before they reached her door, Sir Lemmick turned around and said, "Ladies and gentlemen, I assure you, my daughter and I will take care of Mrs. Tromburg, whatever her needs may be. I pray you, go back to the ball and enjoy yourselves. We shall all be down soon."

The people slowly dispersed and went back down the stairs, and Nicholas was happy to disperse with them, just as the butler found the right key and started to open the door.

"She isn't here," he heard Miss Lemmick say.

"Langdon, where are you?" Sir Lemmick was squinting down the stairs, looking for him.

Nicholas stifled a groan. He wouldn't escape so easily. "I am here."

"Come, man. Help us look for her."

Nicholas came back up the stairs and reluctantly stepped inside the room as Sir Lemmick and his daughter looked bewildered. He waited as they searched everywhere, even in her wardrobe.

"She simply isn't here," Miss Lemmick said, her eyes wide. "What shall we do? Where could she be?"

"Darling," Sir Lemmick said, "Mrs. Tromburg is a grown woman. She . . . she can be responsible for herself. She does not need us following her around."

"But Father! She could be sick, unable to walk. Perhaps she wandered into the garden and could not make it back to the house."

Sir Lemmick and Nicholas exchanged glances.

"If she were sick," Nicholas said, "she would be in her room. Therefore, she does not wish to be found."

"Are you so suspicious? Father?"

Indecision and dread were all over Sir Lemmick's face. "Darling, please. Listen to reason. Mr. Langdon is right."

"Father, Mrs. Tromburg is my particular friend. You must look for her. You must help her."

"Very well. Mr. Langdon and I will search the garden and the stable and ask the servants if they've seen her. Meanwhile, go back to the dance, my dear, or go to your room, but please don't say anything to anyone. And we shall inform you as soon as we find her."

Miss Lemmick nodded, her mouth slightly open, her expression forlorn as she headed down the hall.

Sir Lemmick gave Nicholas an apologetic look. "Forgive me, Langdon. She strong-armed me. When you have a daughter, you'll understand."

Nicholas tried to put on his good-natured face and nodded. He and Sir Lemmick hurried down the back stairs and searched outside. It was dark, and they called out, "Anyone here? Hallooo! Anyone?"

Soon Sir Lemmick said, "Let's try the stable yard and ask the groomsmen."

He and Nicholas made their way to the stable area, which was crowded with extra horses and carriages, but the extra drivers and stable boys and groomsmen were nowhere to be seen. Finally, they located a few drivers standing outside the kitchen door just as Smith, Nicholas's valet, came toward them.

"Smith, have you seen Mrs. Tromburg?"

"Sir," he said quietly to Nicholas, and Sir Lemmick leaned in to listen, "one of the groomsmen saw Mrs. Tromburg get in Mr. Edgerton's carriage. A few minutes later, Mr. Edgerton left the house and got in the carriage with her and drove away. That was about an hour ago."

Nicholas wanted to ignore the information, to go back inside and forget it.

"Perhaps he was mistaken. Perhaps it wasn't Mrs. Tromburg," Sir Lemmick offered.

"Sir, a servant also saw Mrs. Tromburg leave from the back door a few minutes before Mr. Edgerton."

He wanted to shake Henrietta. How could she be so indiscreet, so stupid? Her reputation would be forever wrecked.

"Should we go after them and try to save Mrs. Tromburg's reputation? For my daughter's sake?" Sir Lemmick's expression was pained.

"Mrs. Tromburg is a grown woman, a widow, and she knows her own mind. I refuse to chase after her. If she wants to destroy her reputation, that's her decision."

"Just so. Quite right." Sir Lemmick shook his head and stared at the ground for a moment. "We shan't breathe a word. Only, what shall I say to my daughter? This is a fine, embarrassing way . . ." Sir Lemmick's words ended in an unintelligible mumble.

"Tell her the truth."

"What did you say?"

"Tell her the truth: that Mrs. Tromburg sneaked away with Mr. Edgerton. Let it be a lesson to your daughter in how *not* to behave." Nicholas stalked toward the house, the cool night air fanning his face. He went inside, thoroughly disgusted with Henrietta. She was a fool to ruin her reputation with Edgerton.

Nicholas rejoined the party as if nothing had happened, but forcing himself to be cheerful seemed impossible . . . until he thought of Julia, waiting for him in the garden in the morning.

He went through the motions of dancing with girls who smiled and prattled, went through the eating of dinner and the conversing with dinner partners, but as soon as he was able, he left the party. He found Smith talking with another valet, and they both trudged up to his room, which, with only one candle between them, was quite dark.

"Shall I light more candles for you, sir?"

"No, thank you, Smith. I only want to find my bed. But I must be up before eight in the morning." He yawned as Smith helped him off with his boots. "If I miss my nine o'clock meeting, I shall never forgive myself."

He lay down on the bed, groaning, and forcefully expelled the thought of Henrietta and Edgerton from his mind. Sleep soon fell over him like a warm blanket.

CHAPTER THIRTY-SEVEN

"Sir, wake up."

"Is it eight already?" Nicholas sat up and rubbed his face. He had to wash and—

"Sir, you must see this." Smith thrust a letter in front of his eyes.

He took it, his eyes immediately drawn to the signature, *Julia Grey*. He read its contents by the candle Smith held beside him and the light coming through the window. The further he read, the more his heart pounded.

"Sweet saints in heaven." Nicholas sprang out of bed and ran to the window, flinging aside the drapes. The sun shone dimly through the clouds. "Dear Lord, what time is it?"

"Eight o'clock, sir."

"No!" Nicholas grabbed a shirt and started dressing. "Go down and have a horse saddled and ready for me. And ask which direction the carriage went that was carrying Miss Grey."

"Yes, sir."

He had planned to dress carefully this morning, but now he had no thought for anything except speed. He had to catch up to Miss Grey.

***

Julia clutched her parents' Bible to her chest as the carriage took her farther and farther away from Donnerly Hall and Mr. Langdon. Hadn't he read her letter last night after the ball? Did he not want to speak to her before she left? Perhaps he had not awakened in time. Julia had delayed as long as she could, but the carriage driver seemed eager to get her on her way. No doubt the man wanted to get back to sleep off the drink he'd imbibed at the servants' own impromptu party the night before.

Eventually she had been forced to get in and let him drive her away. Did Mr. Langdon not care? Had her letter repulsed him with its effusion of sentiment?

Surprisingly, she didn't regret having given him the longer, more honest and direct letter. She was glad he knew how she felt about him . . . how much she loved him.

She marveled at what she had done. The old Julia would have been lightheaded and faint at the thought of writing such a letter, of flouting society's rules and laying bare her heart. And though he may reject her love, she still did not regret what she had told him. He was a respectable man who would not take advantage of her, and she saw nothing wrong with being so straightforward, even if society strictly forbade such declarations from a woman.

To take her mind off Mr. Langdon, her aching heart, and her nervousness at the new position and school she was traveling to, Julia opened her Bible and began to read. After a few chapters, she leaned back against the seat. Since she had been so alone in the Athertons' home, without a friend to talk to, she had formed a habit of pouring out her heart in prayer.

"I don't know what is ahead for me, but I pray you will make me strong enough to bear it." She missed Phoebe so much. "I still love my cousin and hope she will forgive me someday," Julia whispered into the empty interior of the coach. "I still want her to be happy."

And she wanted Mr. Langdon to be happy too. "Even if he doesn't love me, even if he's supposed to marry someone else, I still want you, God, to make him happy."

The next moment, Julia heard fast hoofbeats that did not belong to the horses pulling her carriage. They were coming closer and seemed to be coming from behind, finally drawing alongside the carriage. A male voice shouted something, and her carriage began to slow. Then it stopped.

She looked out the window. No one was there. She reached toward the door latch. Just as she leaned her weight against the handle, the door swung open. Julia fell forward.

Hands caught her upper arms before she could fall very far, and she stared into the warm brown eyes of Nicholas Langdon.

"As I told you before," he said, his chest rising and falling, "I must speak with you." His jaw and chin were shaded by a day's growth of beard, which, if possible, made him even more handsome.

The look on his face was so serious, she was suddenly terrified he was about to tell her he was marrying Mrs. Tromburg. He still held her arms so that they stood facing each other in the middle of the dusty road, closer than propriety allowed. Her heart seemed to stick in her throat.

Out of the corner of her eye, she noticed the carriage driver staring down at them from his seat.

"When you told me you were going to become a governess," Mr. Langdon said, his eyes intently focused on her, "I planned to come and find you just as soon as the War Office released me. I knew they would want me to report everything that had happened, and after I was able to help them apprehend your uncle, Edgerton, and the men they were sending to kill General Wellington, I would be free to come to you. But testifying took longer than I thought, your uncle fled the country, and they wanted to give me a promotion. There were endless meetings and talk of giving me a position at the War Office. Finally, the Prince Regent asked to meet with me."

"He did?"

"He did. And he wants to meet with you too, Julia."

"With me? Why?"

"I believe he wants to commend you for your work in thwarting the plan to kill General Wellington. But that is not why I came to Donnerly Hall. I have something else to talk to you about."

"Oh." They both leaned forward until their foreheads were almost touching.

"Thank you for your letter, Julia. You cannot know how happy it made me." He pressed his lips to her forehead and then drew back slightly to look into her eyes again. "I love you, Julia Grey. You have no equal in character, grace, and beauty, and I am asking you to marry me. And if you will accept my proposal of marriage, I promise to do my utmost to make you happy."

Her whole world was in the depths of his eyes. Was she dreaming? She could feel his hands holding her, see his thick black lashes and eyebrows and the black stubble on his chin and jawline, even the golden undertones in his brown eyes.

"Are you sure you want to marry a governess?"

"You will not be a governess anymore." He leaned down, so close it was surely very improper, so close she could feel his breath on her cheek. Then he closed his eyes and touched his lips to hers.

Julia caught her breath at his boldness and at the brief but heart-pounding kiss.

She whispered, "The coachman is watching us."

He did not pull away. His lips were still achingly close as he said, "You did not answer. Will you marry me?"

"Yes."

His eyes focused on her lips, and he sighed. Taking her hand in his, he turned to the driver. "Pray, be so good as to drive us back to Donnerly Hall."

He handed Julia in while he went to tie his horse to the back of the carriage.

The Bible she had just been reading lay on the seat next to her. "Thank you, God. He loves me," she whispered. She clasped her hands to her chest and tried to say a more coherent prayer, but it was impossible.

He suddenly opened the door and sprang into the carriage beside her. He picked up her hand and squeezed it, turning his body on the narrow seat to face her.

"Is it improper for me to kiss you here in the carriage," he said, a teasing glint in his eyes, "where the coachman cannot see us?"

Of course it was improper. But she wanted more than anything for him to kiss her again.

"I suppose," she said, her heart fluttering, unable to stop herself from staring at his lips, "it is not so improper, since we are engaged to be married."

He gathered her in his arms. Gazing deeply into her eyes, he caressed her cheek with his thumb, sending tingling sensations all the way into her fingertips. Then he tilted her head back and kissed her lips.

The kiss was so wonderful, she was afraid it would suddenly end, that she would wake up and he would disappear, just a dream or a figment of her imagination. A few minutes ago, she was an unloved, orphaned governess who was on her way to become a teacher at a girls' school. Now she was kissing Nicholas Langdon, the most wonderful man in the world.

He pulled away and her heart lurched. He smiled, a kind of sleepy look on his face.

"Thank you for your letter." He drew a circle on her cheek with his thumb and then traced her eyebrow, kissing her temple. "I knew I wanted to marry you for weeks, but that letter . . . I did not see it until this morning when Smith woke me and showed it to me. When did you leave it?"

She wasn't sure she could speak, with the way his thumb and finger kept caressing her cheek and jawline and chin, stealing her breath. She swallowed and said, "Last night."

"It was so late and so dark when I got back to my room, Smith and I somehow missed seeing it." He kissed her again. "I'm sorry I was not there at dawn when you left. You must have thought I didn't care."

"Yes."

"Darling. Sweet. Julia." He punctuated each word with a kiss. "I would have married you even though I didn't have a fortune to offer you. But thank God, now I do."

What did he mean by that? But she didn't want to ask him to explain, not wanting him to stop kissing her to do so.

He kissed her a bit longer and then drew back a little. "Are you not curious about my fortune?"

She blinked, trying to clear the fog his kisses had created over her thoughts. "You have a fortune?"

"The Prince Regent, it seems, is very grateful for your help and mine in thwarting the plot against England's general and military leader. He has requested Parliament and the House of Commons to reward me with the sum of thirty thousand pounds."

"Did you say thirty thousand pounds?" Her heart leapt in her chest.

"And he has said he hopes to reward you with the same amount. But I did not want to tell you until you promised to marry me. If you knew you had a fortune of your own, you might refuse me."

Was he making a joke?

"I should think my letter would have made it clear whom I love." She sat up a little straighter, pulling away from him a bit.

"Indeed it did. Forgive me." He drew her close again. "I should not tease you, but I tend to tease when I am deliriously happy."

Julia slid her arms around him and laid her head on his shoulder. "I forgive you," she whispered, unable to suppress a deliriously happy smile of her own.

"We shall go back and tell everyone," he said, holding her tight, "starting with Mr. and Mrs. Atherton, that we are getting married. I shall put all your things in my carriage, and we shall set off for Glyncove Abbey immediately. I shall have the banns read as soon as possible," he continued, "and we shall marry at Glyncove Church in four weeks."

"Oh dear." Julia's heart sank.

"What is it?"

"What about Phoebe? She must hate me. What will she say when she hears we are to be married?"

"I do not think you have to worry about that."

"How can you say that? Don't you know how in love with you she is?"

"Not anymore. She is engaged to be married, I just learned, before I came to Donnerly Hall to find you."

"To be married? To whom?"

"To Daniel Dinklage."

"Oh." Julia tried to imagine the two of them together. After all that Phoebe had said about him not being handsome enough for Julia. "How strange."

"It seems that Phoebe made an impression on Mr. Dinklage when they met in Bath several weeks ago. Once they were both back in London, Mr. Dinklage visited Phoebe during her distress over her father's flight from England and the accusations of his traitorous spying. Very few people did visit her, I would imagine. Dinklage's mother died a few months ago, and he was consequently free to marry whomever he wished."

"Oh. That is . . . good." Phoebe would have someone to take care of her, and perhaps she had come to love him. Stranger matches were made every day. "Truthfully, I am very glad to hear that. It is very good news, is it not?" And if Phoebe was contented in her marriage, perhaps she would be able to forgive Julia . . . someday.

"It is good news. And I have been given a release from my commission in the army and will be taking a position at the War Office."

"So you will be able to stay in London?" Her heart soared. He would not be sent back to the Peninsula to fight in the war!

"Yes. And you and I shall oversee a new project I have proposed to Wilson. We shall begin some money-making industries for the women in the East Side . . ."

Julia listened and nodded to all that he had to say, thinking how handsome he was, how warm and beautiful his eyes were, how perfect his lips looked, how good his kisses felt . . . How frivolous she was to be thinking such thoughts when he was talking of the children and their needs.

"I think that is wonderful," Julia said. "You and Mr. Wilson will do many great things in the East Side, I have no doubt."

He pressed his palm against her cheek, leaned forward, and covered her mouth with his.

Julia caressed his stubbly jaw with her fingertips. She was enveloped in a cloak of safety and warmth, as she stopped thinking and focused her attention on kissing him back.

***

At Donnerly Hall, Nicholas and Smith quickly collected his things. They transferred Julia's trunks from the Athertons' carriage to Nicholas's own, without seeing anyone except the servants. The rest of the house was still asleep after the late-night ball, so Nicholas quickly scribbled a note for his hostess, Mrs. Atherton, and left it with the butler, explaining that he and Julia were to be married and were off to Glyncove Abbey in Lincolnshire to stay with his family until the wedding.

When he and Julia entered the carriage again, he carried his portfolio.

"What do you have there, Mr. Langdon?" Julia asked. The lopsided smile tugging at the corner of her mouth was so adorable, he longed to kiss her again.

He cleared his throat. "I took your music, the songs that you composed, from your pianoforte at the Wilhern town house when I went to fetch your things."

She shook her head. "I am surprised you would think of those, as I did not think to ask you to take them."

"I did think of them. Arrogant sort that I am, I believed you would eventually accept my marriage proposal, and I took them to surprise you. The surprise is, I got them published."

She stared openmouthed. "You published my compositions?"

"On the contrary. That well-known publisher of music, Robert Birchall, published your music." He opened the portfolio to show her.

She ran her hand over the printed sheet music. "I can hardly believe it." A tear raced down her cheek. He reached out and wiped it away.

"Did I do wrong in having them published without your permission?"

"No, it's just so surprising. But I love it. I love you."

She threw her arms around him, causing him to drop the portfolio on the floor of the carriage so he could hold her properly.

"You are a published composer now," he said against her hair. "Published anonymously, but if you wish it, I shall tell the world you composed them."

"That is not necessary." She pulled away. He handed her his hand-kerchief, and she wiped her eyes. "It is enough to see them in print. I wonder if anyone will actually want to play them."

"I have it on good authority that they shall be favorably mentioned in *Ackermann's Repository*."

"*Ackermann's*? Can it be true? My own music in *Ackermann's*? Thank you, Nicholas. May I call you Nicholas? Just when we are alone?"

"My name has never sounded so sweet."

"It is the best gift, by far, that anyone has ever given me." She leaned against him, laying her head on his shoulder and squeezing his arm, and then lifted her head to kiss him.

He reveled in the feel of her beside him, in his proper Julia being bold enough to hug and kiss him.

Never had he so happily anticipated a long ride in a carriage.

EPILOGUE

For Julia, the next few weeks were a whirlwind of parties and introductions to various members of Nicholas Langdon's family—and furtive kisses with her future husband when no one was looking.

Nicholas procured a special license so that they could be married at the Glyncove parish instead of Julia's home parish in Warwickshire. He also sent his steward and a footman to Wilhern Manor, and they were able to retrieve the remainder of Julia's belongings.

But before they could marry, the Prince Regent summoned Julia and Nicholas to London. The prince made a very pretty speech praising both of them for their courage and tenacity in thwarting the assassination of General Wellington, England's famous war hero. The House of Commons approved the Prince Regent's proposal of a reward of thirty thousand pounds for Nicholas Langdon and thirty thousand pounds for Julia Grey.

Julia wrote—and rewrote several times—a letter to Phoebe telling her how pleased she was that Phoebe was married to a good man like Mr. Dinklage, and asking her to forgive her for her role in everything that had happened with her father, explaining that she had felt she had no choice. She did not receive a reply.

Though it pained Julia that her precious friend and cousin with whom she had spent most of her life could be estranged from her, she would hold out hope for better things in the future. One day they might be reconciled and could at least be friends again.

And on the day she became Mrs. Nicholas Langdon, the only thoughts in her heart were joyful ones.

ACKNOWLEDGMENTS

First of all, I want to thank my agent, Natasha Kern. She gave me the idea I needed for this story and resurrected my dream of writing and publishing a Regency romance. Natasha suggested I write a story about a hero who had gone to war and been injured, as there must have been many such men in Regency England, and make him a spy for England against their enemy, France. I am very grateful for her insights of every type—business, creative, and even personal. Thank you, Natasha.

I have to thank Nancy Mayer and all the knowledgeable authors and researchers and history lovers at The Beau Monde chapter of Romance Writers of America. Their knowledge of Regency England is astonishing, and I am forever grateful for their willingness to share that knowledge with their fellow authors. That being said, if there are historical inaccuracies, they are entirely my fault.

I want to thank my editor Faith Black Ross, my copy editor Michelle Hope Anderson, and publisher Amy Hosford for all their support and expertise. A novel is such a collaborative effort, and I am grateful for everyone who has helped or made suggestions, including Natasha Kern, Carol Moncado, Linore Burkard, Grace Dickerson, Faith Dickerson, and Debbie Lynne Costello.

I also want to express heartfelt thanks to all my readers who have posted positive reviews on Amazon, Goodreads, other review sites, and their blogs for my books through the years, not to mention the kind e-mails and messages on Facebook and Twitter. They are appreciated more than you know! May God bless you. I love my readers.

ABOUT THE AUTHOR

Photo © 2012 Jodie Westfall

Historical romance author Melanie Dickerson earned her bachelor's degree from the University of Alabama and has taught special education in Georgia and Tennessee. She has also taught English in Germany and Ukraine. Dickerson won the 2012 Carol Award in young adult fiction and the 2010 National Readers' Choice Award for best first book. Her novels *The Healer's Apprentice* and *The Merchant's Daughter* were both Christy Award finalists.

She lives with her husband and two daughters near Huntsville, Alabama. For more information, visit www.MelanieDickerson.com.